Caught ON Camera

CHELSEA CURTO

To those who worry about where they're going:
Look how far you've come.

(And to the girlies who love the moment in a romance novel when the
*guy says **fuck it**. This one is for you.)*

CONTENT WARNINGS

This story has a lot of laugh out loud moments, but I wanted to touch on a couple elements within these pages that might be triggering to some readers:

-on page panic attack
-mention of divorce and infertility (in passing, not descriptive)
-explicit language
-explicit sexual themes including multiple descriptive intimate moments between two characters and words that might be considered degrading (three times, briefly mentioned)

As always, my DMs are always open on Instagram (@authorchelseacurto) if you have any other questions or concerns about possible content warnings.

Take care of yourselves, friends.

CHARACTER CATCH UP

While Caught on Camera is technically a stand alone novel, it does mention characters from the first book in the series, Camera Chemistry. I wanted to give a quick catch up in case you haven't read book one so you don't feel lost.

In that novella, Aiden (a single dad to Maven) and Maggie meet a strangers photo shoot and have a one night stand. They end up falling for each other and live happily ever after.

Lacey is Maggie's best friend, and Shawn is Aiden's best friend, and the two have no interaction in Camera Chemistry.

As always, my DMs are always open on Instagram (@authorchelseacurto) if you have any other questions.

ONE

LACEY

TEN YEARS in the medical field, and I'm still not used to getting shit on me.

"I'm so sorry." Archie Greenburg's mother looks at me, horror-stricken. Her eyes dart to my cheek, then my forehead, and I let out a tiny huff. "He's had no problems with diarrhea. Especially not the explosive kind," she says.

"Really? Interesting." I grab a paper towel and wipe the fecal matter off my skin, counting down the seconds until I can shower and disinfect every inch of my body. I offer her a strained but understanding smile. Infant bowel movements are, unfortunately, part of a pediatrician's resume. "Don't worry about it. It happens all the time."

"All the time?" she repeats, and I don't think I've made her feel better.

"Yeah. It's no big deal." I stand and wash my hands in the small sink to the left of the examination table. I lather my arms up to my elbows and scrub until my skin turns red. "The good news is Archie is doing great. He's in the ninety-nine percentiles in height and weight. No developmental delays, and, as of today, he's up to date on all of his immunizations. You've got a healthy baby, Linna. We'll see him soon for his nine-month checkup."

"Are you sure?" She collects Archie in her arms and holds him close. I watch as she fixes the blanket around his torso and gives him a kiss on his nose. "We've been worried about him. He screams so much, and I don't think we've slept through the night since he's been born."

I glance at the young woman over my shoulder. I notice the bags under her eyes and her pale, sunken cheeks. There's dried spit up on her neck, and her hair sits in a tangled knot on top of her head. My smile eases into one of respect, of awe and admiration for tackling the difficult role of motherhood.

"Linna," I say gently. "You're not doing anything wrong. Infants approximate a sleep schedule similar to adults anywhere from three months old to a year. He's not behind; he's just taking his time. When I see you again, I'm sure Archie will be a totally different baby."

"Thank you, Dr. Daniels." She breathes out a sigh of relief and stands. "There's a reason you're the best pediatrician in the D.C. area. Why people put their names on the waitlist for your practice months before their baby is born. You're so good at what you do. Thank you for taking care of us. Thank you for looking at me like I'm a human and not someone who's trying their best but coming up short."

"Hang on." I rip off a paper towel and dry my hands. I lift my chin toward the colorful sign tacked on the wall. "What's number three?"

Linna dips her head and recites the line I make all the parents I work with say when they're in the building. "No self-deprecating. I'm doing an amazing job as a parent."

"And you are. But don't forget to take some time for yourself too, Linna. Your health is just as important as Archie's."

"You're right." She nods and buckles her baby in his stroller. "We'll see you in three months?"

"Shay and Lindsey will get an appointment on the books for you," I say.

"I'm sorry again about the..." she gestures to my face, and I laugh.

"Shit happens. Means he's doing just fine."

I usher her out of the room and wave off her second apology. I pull off my coat and walk down the hall to my office, slipping inside the private bathroom and locking the door.

Before I have a chance to hop in the shower and douse myself in blazing hot water, my phone rings in my back pocket. I answer and put it on speakerphone.

"Hey, Mags," I say, and I unlace my sneakers. "What's up?"

"Two questions for you," my best friend says, sounding out of breath. She must be heading out of the hospital next door where she works as a neurosurgeon, huffing and puffing as she climbs up the steep incline of the parking garage. "Are you coming to dinner tonight?"

"Yeah. I wouldn't miss our weekly tradition." I shimmy my scrubs down my legs and kick away the dirty cotton. I pull off my top and bra, dropping the clothes in the sink with two scoops of laundry detergent. "What's the second question?"

"Are you coming to Shawn's game on Sunday?" she asks. "Maven is bringing some friends for her birthday, so instead of sitting in the front row like normal, we're doing a suite. It's going to be a surprise."

I grin. "You're giving me a chance to embarrass my niece while eating unlimited food in a heated room? I'm in."

"Okay, good. We can talk about it more tonight. Aiden is all sentimental about his only daughter turning eighteen. He teared up last night when he asked Shawn if he could put us in a suite, Lace."

3

"That's because I'm not convinced Aiden is real, Mags. No male is that kind-hearted and genuinely nice. Are we sure he's not a serial killer?" I ask.

"You'd think after a year and a half of dating, I'd know if he was a serial killer."

"Not true. Look at Ted Bundy. That dude fooled people for *years*." I turn on the shower and put my hair in a bun. "Aiden could be fooling you, too."

"Can we not compare the love of my life—who is absolutely wonderful, by the way—to someone who used meat cleavers on people? And where the heck are you? Is that a shower?"

"A patient had explosive diarrhea, and I'm trying to clean up before my next patient," I say. "They really should disclose the ratio of the days you get shit on versus the days you don't in medical school."

"If they did that, there wouldn't be any pediatricians. Thanks for the reminder about why I'm glad I operate on people's brains." Maggie laughs. "We'll see you tonight. Love you."

"Love you too, Mags. Text me if you need me to bring anything."

I step in the shower and groan at the heat on my skin. My muscles relax under the steady stream of water and I sigh, grateful for the brief moment of self-care after six hours of being on my feet. I grab a bar of soap and lather my limbs, cleaning every crevice of my body while trying not to fall asleep standing up.

Ten minutes later with a room full of steam and pruney fingers, I wrap a towel around myself.

"Shit," I curse, realizing I didn't bring any clean clothes in with me. I open the door back to my office and shiver at the change in temperature. It's colder out here, and goosebumps pebble my arms.

"There you are," someone says, and I scream.

"What the hell, Shawn?" I ask, and I hold my towel tightly in place as I glare across the room.

Shawn Holmes, the youngest head coach in NFL history, current figurehead of the D.C. Titans—the hottest team in the league—and one of my best friends, grins at me from the couch beside my desk.

He's wearing an outfit that tells me he's either coming from or going to the stadium. Gray joggers. High top sneakers. A long-sleeved T-shirt with the D.C. Titans logo across his chest and a backwards hat.

He'd live in those clothes, if he could.

"Hey, Lace," he says.

"What are you doing here?"

"I was in the neighborhood. I brought you coffee." He lifts the cup in his hands, and I spot the logo of my favorite local cafe. My mouth practically waters at the sight of caffeine. "Please tell me you were in the shower alone."

I roll my eyes. "Of course I was in the shower alone. It's the middle of the day, and I'm working."

"Doesn't mean you have to be alone," he says, and his grin turns sly and mischievous.

"Gross. I don't need to know what you do in *your* office, and I'm never sitting in that chair that overlooks the football field ever again. Which is a shame, because it's so damn comfortable."

"Don't worry, Lace. I don't kiss and tell."

My cheeks heat, and I fumble with the stack of clothes I keep in a duffle bag under my desk. I grab two shirts before finding a pair of pants. "Give me two minutes. Let me change," I say, hurrying back to the bathroom and closing the door.

"Take all the time in the world," he calls out. "You're worth the wait."

"Do you use that line on every girl?"

5

"You know there aren't any girls."

I pull on my clothes and take down my hair, shaking the dark brown waves free. "Remind me why there aren't any girls?" I ask, and Shawn groans.

"I'm being a Good Samaritan and bringing you coffee. This isn't supposed to turn into an interrogation about my love life," he says.

"Non-existent love life," I say. I open the door and lean against the frame. His eyes soften when he sees me, and he sits up on the couch. "What's your ulterior motive with the drink?"

"Can't a guy bring his friend some sustenance, needing nothing in return?" He holds out the cup to me and I walk toward him, gratefully accepting the beverage. "Got a minute to take a breather?"

"Literally a minute. Thank you." I sit next to him on the couch and drop my head back against the leather. "Today's been so hectic. I had a nurse call out sick, then someone had to leave early because of a puking emergency at their kid's school. This pick-me-up is going to get me through the rest of the day."

"Do you need any help? I'm free this afternoon," he says.

"Are you qualified to administer shots to children? Immunizations, *not* alcohol. Can you also help a hospital that's suffering from a lack of funding? Because we're hurting as of late."

Shawn chuckles, a deep, rumbly sound that makes my insides squirm. "I can type on a computer, believe it or not. If you need another body behind the front desk, I'm your guy."

"That's okay. The girls are handling the chaos, but thank you for the offer. You might turn this place into a circus if the moms get a sight of you," I say. "The dads, too. One of People's Sexiest Men of the Year in our midst and all."

I glance over at him, and he's watching me. I've tried to

ignore it, tried to not think about it, but there's no point in denying the obvious truth: Shawn Holmes is hot as hell.

Tattooed arms, dark hair, light eyes that border on gray. Six-foot-six, with muscles in places I didn't know people could be strong. He's all-around handsome, but his smile is his most devastating characteristic. Wide and bright, it stops you in your tracks. It's genuine and a little shy, like he can't believe he's lucky enough to live a life like this.

I only know Shawn—a household name every football fan across America adores—because of Maggie's boyfriend, Aiden. They're best friends, and when she started dating Aiden after a one-night stand and a photo shoot that went viral, I met the very famous and very attractive Shawn Holmes.

I was expecting someone arrogant. Cocky. A self-centered guy who likes to dominate a room and conversations.

He's not, though. He's kind. Level-headed, thoughtful and patient. He's good with kids and stops to sign autographs for people who ask, not ever complaining about how long it takes. He loves his job, but he also works hard, not letting opportunities be handed to him on a silver platter. Shawn wants to earn the things he's given, and I respect the hell out of him for it.

We've gotten close over the last twenty-one months, honorary aunt and designated godfather to Aiden's daughter, Maven, and the single ones in our little group. He sends me funny videos he finds, and I'll text him when he's on the road, staying up late to hear about his games and consoling him with a pathetically stupid joke when his team doesn't play well.

If I fall asleep before him—which happens almost every night—I'll wake up to a photo of a city skyline at night—Manhattan, Boston, Oakland—the words *good night* written on the glass of the floor to ceiling windows.

"You need to stop with the sexiest man thing," he says, and he leans over to flick my ear. "It was a headshot photo of me on

7

the second-to-last page in the magazine. I wasn't on the cover, and I'm pretty sure they spelled my name wrong."

"What did they call you? Shawn Helms? You're not on the cover *yet*," I say. "When you win the Super Bowl next year, you might be."

"You sure I can't help with anything?" Shawn asks.

"No. I only have four patients this afternoon. I should be able to power through."

"You know where I'll be if that changes."

I turn my head and smile at him. "I do. Thanks, pal."

"You're welcome." He ruffles my hair then squeezes my knee. "See you tonight."

I bring the piping hot cup of coffee to my mouth, and I grin.

I don't care about his money or his name. He might be a god in the football world, but he's also the guy who remembers exactly how I take my coffee.

I like this side of him best.

TWO
SHAWN

"WANT A DRINK?" Aiden asks. He pulls down the hand mixer from above the oven and glances at me over his shoulder. "Beer? Whiskey?"

"I'll grab a beer," I say and head for the fridge, all too familiar with helping myself to whatever is inside. "Want one?"

"No, thanks. I have an early shift tomorrow. I'm getting too old; the hangovers hit harder than they used to."

"True, but that's not stopping me." I pop off the top of a bottle and sit on a barstool at the marble island. "Where's Mags?"

"Dropping Maven off at Katie's. The kiddo is celebrating her birthday with her mom the next two days, then I have her over the weekend," Aiden says.

"You and Katie should teach a class on co-parenting." I take a sip of my drink. "Years post-divorce, and you two have never had a fight. Plus, your new girl doesn't have any animosity toward your ex-wife. It's remarkable, really."

"Because Katie and I work better as friends." He shrugs and clicks off the stove, extinguishing the gas burners. "She's also attracted to women, and I love Maggie more than anything in the world."

"Any thoughts of proposing?" I ask.

"I've been thinking about it more and more lately. Maven's okay with it. She adores Maggie."

"But you're hesitant?"

"God, no. You know I still think she's out of my league. We just aren't sure marriage is the right path for us. We're both divorced. I'm close to my late forties, for Christ's sake. I think we're enjoying doing *this* right now. Loving each other without all the legal shit. Maybe that will change one day down the road, but for right now, it works," he says.

"You have to do what's best for you," I say. "There's not a one-size-fits-all happily ever after."

A phantom ache sprouts behind my ribs as I offer my support, and I rub my hand across my chest. The pain pops up from time to time when the people close to me talk about their significant others and the loves of their lives. About how happy and lucky they are, enduring heartache and sadness until a pivotal moment in history happened: the day they met The One.

It's jealousy, I think, not of the person but of their situation. Of having someone to come home to every night. Someone to share their day with, the good, the bad, and the mediocre moments in between.

The ache has turned more painful the older I get, more poignant and harder to ignore.

It's a stubborn reminder the years are moving faster and time seems to be flying by. Like a clock is ticking, counting down the seconds until I reach a point where it just makes more sense to be alone forever instead of dealing with the headache of dating.

"You okay?" Aiden asks.

"I'm good." I smile and jump off the stool. He gives me a look that tells me he knows I'm lying, but he doesn't press me for more details. "Let me help you."

"I've got it. You have a big game this weekend. Just relax."

"A big game where I'm standing on the sidelines. It's probably the least physically demanding job of anyone on the field."

"Still. The Titans are undefeated this season for a reason, Shawn. Give your brain a break."

"Fine." I sit back down and drink my beer. "If you insist."

"You'll be here for Thanksgiving, right?" Aiden asks, and I nod.

"I will. We have a home game that night, so I won't need to head to the field until about four. Are you cooking?"

"The works. Turkey. Mashed potatoes and stuffing. Maggie wants cranberry sauce, so we'll have that, too. What about Christmas? Are you going home?"

"Yeah. My sisters and their families are flying in, and it's going to be a big thing like usual. I'm going to drive to Philly and stay for a couple of days. I'm also giving the guys some time off between our game before Christmas and the game on New Year's Day. They deserve it."

"I can't believe Katelin and Amanda have kids. It feels like yesterday they were in middle school and we teased them because we were the high school freshmen," he says. "We thought we were so cool."

I chuckle at the memory of us in our early teenage years, friends from childhood to now. I've known him for forty years, and my family is his family. He doesn't visit my parents' house as frequently as he used to, too busy balancing shared custody of his daughter, a loving relationship, and a heavy workload at the local hospital where he's a pediatric oncologist, but there's always a place for him at the table if he wants it.

"I know. It's wild. Doesn't stop Mom from hounding me about more grandkids, though." I sigh and run my hand through my hair, the strands still wet from my post-practice shower. "I think she's expecting us to give her an entire football team of offspring."

"You haven't met the right girl yet," he says. "It'll happen soon. Plus, you know there are other options out there. Like adoption."

"Yeah," I say. "Maybe."

The front door to his apartment flies open, and Lacey comes tumbling inside like a bat out of hell. There's snow stuck to her dark hair, and her cheeks are bright pink. Her puffy jacket makes her look like a marshmallow, and her smile is bright, a beam that instantly warms the room.

"Hey," she says. "Am I late?"

I match her smile with one of my own. "Right on time," I say. "Do you want a beer?"

"Please." Lacey shucks off her jacket and hangs it on the rack by the door. She kicks off her black leather boots and walks toward me with fuzzy purple socks on her feet.

I gesture for her to take my seat and I move around the counter, grabbing a chilled bottle of beer and setting it in front of her. "How was the rest of your afternoon?"

"Tolerable. Thanks." She lifts the drink in my direction and takes a sip. "Hey, Aiden."

"Lace," he says, and he abandons the pot of boiling potatoes to kiss her cheek. "I heard you got shit on today."

"You got shit on and you didn't tell me?" I prop my elbow on the counter and grin. "What happened?"

"It was an accident, but it caught me off guard. I had poop under my fingernails." Her eyes flick to mine, and there's a sparkle behind the dark green. "That's why I was in the shower when you stopped by."

"Incredible," I say, and she swats at my shoulder. "Definitely makes your day interesting, huh?"

"It makes it something," Lacey answers. "Part of the job."

"I have a lot of respect for you all. I can't handle when someone pukes after a workout," I say. "I get queasy and sweaty. My hands turn clammy and I have to cover my ears."

"Maybe you shouldn't have such strenuous workouts," she argues, and I bark out a laugh.

"Touché, Daniels."

Our eyes meet, and we stare at each other for a beat. Lacey tips her head to the side. My lips curl up in a challenge, wondering who will be the first to break today. We play this game sometimes, when there's a moment of silence in the conversation or our friends are being nauseatingly sweet with each other and we're trying not to gag.

I lift my eyebrows and she sticks out her tongue, surprising me enough for a laugh to burst free from my chest. It's loud and it's sharp, and red flares to life on her cheeks with the sound.

"Where's Maggie?" Lacey asks. She curls her hand around her beer bottle and brings it to her mouth. I watch her take a sip before looking away.

"She'll be up any second," Aiden says. He grabs a long-stemmed glass from the cabinet and pours a generous serving of red wine in anticipation of his other half's arrival.

On cue, the door to the apartment opens and Maggie walks inside. Her arms are weighed down by a dozen shopping bags, and she leaves snow-covered footprints on the floor.

"Traffic is *horrible*," she says. "I thought I would get ahead of the holiday rush and do some Christmas shopping after dropping Maven off, but everyone's lost their damn minds with this early season snowstorm. I'm sorry it took me so long to get here. You all should have started without me."

"Hey, sweetheart," Aiden says. He takes the bags from her left arm and sets them on the floor, exchanging them with a glass of wine. He pulls her into a kiss, his fingers tugging at the belt loops of her jeans and a smile pressing against her mouth.

"Yuck," Lacey calls out. "Get a room, you two."

"Not in front of the children," I say, and I cover her eyes.

Lacey tilts her head back and laughs, and it's such a bright sound. It might be below freezing outside, but her laugh is warm. Inviting. Sunshine in human form, and one of my favorite noises.

She doesn't care that it's loud, or that a snort likes to slip through when she's cackling at something really, *really* funny. It's expressive. Bold and vivacious, just like her. A giant *fuck you* to anyone who's ever told her she needs to tone it down, because Lacey laughs like she does everything else in life: without a care in the goddamn world.

I like that about her.

"To be fair, it's no worse than that singer you were canoodling three months ago," Lacey says, and I roll my eyes.

"I wasn't canoodling anyone. Our agents thought it would be a good idea for some publicity since she had an album coming out and the football season was starting," I say.

Lacey folds her hands over mine, and she moves my palms away from her face. "Still. Watching you stick your tongue down someone's throat is on the list of things I really don't enjoy seeing."

"Jealous, Daniels?" I joke, and it's her turn to roll her eyes. "Who are you canoodling these days?"

"I'm bringing a date to your game next week, believe it or not," she says smugly.

She sits up on the barstool and crosses her arms over her chest. My smile slips at the edges. Burns out around the corners of my mouth, and I glance at her.

"What?" Maggie shrieks. She sprints across the room and nudges me to the side. "A *date*? When were you going to tell me?"

"Okay, calm down. I'm not marrying the guy. We matched on an app that I decided to re-download three nights ago when I was drinking wine in the bathtub," Lacey says. She takes another slow sip of her beer, and her tongue darts out to lick away a drop of alcohol she leaves behind. Some of her bravado wavers, and she waits for a long pause before speaking again. "He's nice."

"Nice?" I scoff.

She narrows her eyes, and a challenge flares in her gaze. "Yeah," she says. "Nice. Is that a problem?"

"No. I just think you should be aiming higher than nice," I say. "Mr. Rogers was nice. Do you really want the guy you're sleeping with to be like Mr. Rogers?"

She hums and sets down her drink. Runs her hand through her hair and twirls the ends around her fingers. "I'm weird about meeting people for the first time, so I mentioned the game next week when we're back down by the field in our usual spot. He said it sounded fun. It gives us a buffer in case we don't have anything to talk about."

I squint and try to tell if she's lying. As far as I know, Lacey doesn't date. Her job at the pediatrician's office in downtown D.C. takes up most of her time. She barely gives herself room to breathe, working from seven to six then spending the other free hours with her friends.

Her life is a constant go, go, go, and in the months that I've known her, she's never talked about a guy outside a passing mention of a one-night stand or quick hookup.

"You're bringing a guy to my game?" I ask, and something hot flares behind my eyes. My hand flexes at my side and my muscles clench tight, like I just finished a grueling workout under the summer sun.

"Yeah," Lacey says. "Not for Maven's birthday party. The one after. Is that okay?"

"Of course it's okay," I say. "Why wouldn't it be?"

"I don't know. They're your seats. I don't want you to think I'm taking advantage of you or something. Using our friendship to impress other people."

"I don't think that."

"Okay, cool." Lacey flashes me a smile, and the moment of tension is gone.

I'm not sure why I care she's bringing someone, but every home game, Lacey is there in the front row with an ear-splitting grin. Whenever the Titans are down, whenever we're lining up to kick a game-winning field goal and I'm too nervous to watch, whenever we score a touchdown to take the lead and the rest of the team is celebrating, I find her in the crowd. She's not hard to spot; it's like she's a magnet and I'm metal.

I've never been distracted on the field before, but Lacey never fails to catch my eye.

If something *is* going to distract me, I'm glad it's her.

She always laughs like a maniac and waves her arms in the air, looking like she belongs at a rave rather than the sidelines of a packed football stadium. Then she turns around and shows off the name stitched on the back of the jersey I used to wear when I played in the league.

Holmes.

Maggie pulls her off the stool and puts her through an interrogation about the guy she's been talking to. Lacey says he's in finance, and I want to roll my eyes.

Fucking snoozefest.

"You good?" Aiden asks, his eyebrows pinched and a spatula in his hand.

"Why wouldn't I be good?"

"You got a little testy when Lacey said she was going on a date," he says cautiously, and I can tell he's treading lightly to make sure he doesn't ask the wrong thing.

"Testy?" I laugh so hard, my shoulders shake. "I don't care if she brings a date, Aiden. I guess I'm bummed because the games are our thing. You all hang out on the field beforehand. Half the team tries to flirt with Lacey, but she shoots them down. I stop by before halftime to say hi, and after, we go to the diner near the stadium for milkshakes. It'll be an adjustment to add someone new to the mix, but I'll survive. If Lacey likes him, I'm sure he's a great guy."

Aiden bobs his head in a slow nod before dipping his chin and biting back an obvious smile. "Okay. If you're sure you're good."

I clamp a hand on his shoulder. "Never better."

THREE
LACEY

MAVEN BLINKS BACK tears as she gapes at the suite.

It looks like an explosion of pink decorations, with eight dozen balloons and streamers. There are buffet tables with steaming food. An extra-large sheet cake covered in buttercream frosting sits on a table in the middle of the room, and each leather stadium seat has a jersey draped over the back.

"This is so cool." She grabs a bite-sized burger and inhales the food faster than I can blink. "Uncle Shawn did all of this?"

"Yeah." Maggie drapes her arm around Maven's shoulder. "He came up here earlier. He wanted to make sure your birthday was perfect. Lacey picked up the cake from your favorite bakery, and your dad asked for the buffet to have all of your favorite game day foods."

"You only turn eighteen once. Go big or go home," I say, and Maven wipes her eyes.

"Thank you so much. All of you." She reaches out and squeezes her dad's hand, and the three of us wrap her in a bone-crushing hug she doesn't try to pull free from. "This is the best birthday ever."

After a minute, her friends tug her away from the embarrassing display of affection and move on to gush over the amenities of the suite.

It's Shawn's personal box, the one he donates to the team for charity invitations or season ticket holder upgrades. I've never been up here before, only sitting in the seats he has for us down by the field.

I don't think he likes to flaunt his wealth, preferring to let others enjoy it instead.

It looks like an apartment. Despite the large space and how many people are together inside the four walls, it still feels cozy. Warm and welcoming, with blankets stacked on the velvet couch and the heat set at sixty-eight.

Glass windows overlook the field, and they're so clean, you'd think we were standing on the turf. Televisions hang on either side of the room, and they all broadcast the pregame coverage on a national network. I see Shawn's face flash across the screen, the picture of him with his fist raised in the air and sports drink dumped on his shirt from a game last month.

I imagine him up here earlier in the day, inflating balloons and leaving party hats on the counter, and I giggle.

"What?" Maggie asks. She hands me a drink, a fruity concoction with a pineapple hanging off the rim of the glass and a little umbrella speared through the ice.

"I'm picturing Shawn lugging a trash bag of decorations up here, and it's the funniest thing in the world," I say.

"He's a good guy, isn't he?"

"One of the best."

Every detail is thought out, meticulously executed to make sure Maven has the best day ever. I pull out my phone and type out a quick message to Shawn, knowing he only has a matter of minutes before he'll be running out of the tunnel and onto the field.

ME

We just got to the suite. It looks incredible. What time did you get here to set up? I could've helped.

SHAWN

Around seven. The security guards were confused why I had pink party hats. Can't wait for that article to come out. I can see the ESPN headline now.

ME

You're the father to a secret love child, or you're having an affair with someone who has kids.

SHAWN

No good deed goes unpunished. Anybody need anything?

ME

Not a thing. Good luck today. We'll be cheering loud.

SHAWN

See you after, Lace Face.

ME

Not if I see you first, Shawn Yawn.

SHAWN

Stupidest nickname ever.

ME

You started it.

SHAWN

I'm forty-six. No one should be calling me Shawn Yawn.

> Sorry, pal. You did it to yourself. Can you go do
> your job, please? I see your guys running onto
> the field.

I grin as the crowd roars to life, a growing crescendo of noise when they start to cheer. I feel the excitement and energy from seventy thousand fans pulse in my blood. The exhilaration turns tangible as my heartbeat matches the stomp of their feet and the clap of their hands.

I've never been a sports girl, and the only thing I know about football is the D.C. Titans are *good*. They have the best record in the league and they're heading into this weekend undefeated, the only team without a loss.

A lot of it is Shawn's doing.

They hired him four years ago, back when the Titans only won two games all season. You couldn't give your tickets away for free, and premium seats sold for a fraction of the cost. The stadium was empty, and the fans that stuck around to watch the train wreck unfold did nothing but boo and toss garbage on the field.

The locker room was toxic and negative. Management was poisonous, and there were multiple harassment claims. A player even faked an injury just so he could sit out the rest of the season instead of getting beat by six touchdowns every week. The future of the team was bleak, and rumors swirled about a sale of the club for dirt cheap to a business tycoon who would've taken the Titans out of the city and moved them to San Diego where the weather is pleasant three hundred and sixty-five days a year.

Then Shawn came in and wiped the slate clean. He started from the lowest of lows an organization could be, and slowly earned the players' trust. He didn't just give them work to do and sit on his ass; he worked his ass off, too.

Lining up next to his guys on the fifty-yard line for sprints. Staying late and dripping sweat in the grueling summer months when they practiced lateral passes and trick plays at training camp. Throwing on a beanie and a pair of gloves as he ran two-point conversion drills with his quarterback in the freezing cold, a rookie he drafted in the sixth round out of Howard University. He could see the potential in the kid who, three years later, would win the NFL's MVP award, the youngest to ever do it.

That's just how Shawn is, though.

He commits and gives his all, all the time.

It's how he approaches his friendships. How he treats the responsibilities of being Maven's godfather. How he acts with his family and the volunteer activities he participates in not because he has to, but because he *wants* to.

He exemplifies the purest form of servant leadership I've ever seen.

It's not for show, a smile for the camera that turns into a frown when the flash goes off. It's not for money—he's the first coach to take a salary cut so the rest of his staff can have league-leading assistant coach pay. It's not because he thinks he has to check a box. He hires based on ability, not gender, and that's why he has eight women as assistant coaches. His players respect them because *he* respects them.

He's a friend who remembers details; birthdays. Favorite foods. Allergies. He knows I love to collect magnets when I travel somewhere. After being out of town for an away game, he always comes back with a gift for me: the silliest memento for my fridge he can find.

A hunk of cheese when he was in Wisconsin. An apple from New York. A beaver after a Texas circuit, hitting Houston and Dallas in the same month. It's supposed to be the mascot of some gas station chain, but I don't understand the joke no matter how many times he tries to explain it to me. The bright red double-decker bus from London when they played abroad last season.

There's nothing but good bones in his body and a good soul in his chest. I'm lucky to have him in my life.

Maggie nudges my side, and I blink. The fluorescent stadium lights dim for the national anthem and player introductions.

"Aiden's crying," she whispers.

"He cries at the dog videos you send him," I whisper back. I look over at her boyfriend wiping his eyes, and I smile. "He's the gold standard for dads. Men in general, really."

Maggie and I met in medical school after a seating chart mix-up with our last names. We embraced the faux pas and became fast friends who stood in each other's corners not just in biochemistry and anatomy, but outside the lecture halls, too. We lean on each other in moments of darkness and pain. Laugh our asses off at all of our horrible mistakes—like the time she told me to get bangs, and the time I told her to wear a white dress to our annual hospital holiday gala. She ended the night with a red wine stain on her crotch.

She's dealt with a lot in her personal life, experiencing a divorce and finding out she's infertile all before turning thirty-one. Maggie is resilient, though, a woman who fights like hell for what she wants. She's brighter these days and never not smiling. Aiden plays a big part in that.

They are star-crossed lovers and soulmates who both got a second shot at love, meeting at a Valentine's Day photo shoot and having a sizzling one-night stand.

Neither could get the other out of their head after their rendezvous, and they discovered they worked in the same hospital, separated by a quick elevator ride without even knowing it. The rest is history, a happily ever after for a couple who deserves nothing but good things in life.

Aiden treats Maggie right. He loves her loudly and softly, in front of everyone and when no one is watching. I always catch him looking at her, this dopey smile of adoration on his face, like he can't *believe* she's his.

I want to make jokes about how over-the-top their love is, but the older I get, the closer to mid-thirty and beyond I am, the more I want that, too. Someone who finds me in a crowd and looks at me like I'm the only one in the world.

I've never had a love like that before. The selfless, all-encompassing type you're not sure is real because you're so sickeningly happy, you're waiting to wake up from a dream. Swept off your feet with butterflies in your chest. Joy and elation and *togetherness*.

Maybe I'll find it one day.

"Let's go Titans," Maggie bellows, and I shove those lonely thoughts away.

"I see Uncle Shawn," Maven says. She presses her face against the window, and her friends crowd around her.

"That's your uncle?" one girl asks. "Wow."

"Technically he's my godfather, but uncle sounds better," Maven explains.

"He's *hot*," another adds.

"How many tattoos does he have?"

"Ew, stop," Maven says. "He's so old."

Aiden rubs his hand over his face. "Christ," he grumbles. "I'm not ready for her to date."

"Sorry, honey." Maggie slides her arm around his waist and rests her head on his shoulder. "It's going to happen one day soon. Maybe it already is."

He glances at her, and there is terror in his eyes. "What do you know? We're a team here, Maggie Houston. Don't keep secrets from me."

"Nothing, I swear," she laughs. "I promise I'll tell you if she mentions a boy."

"Or a girl," I say, and Maggie nods in agreement.

"Or a girl," she repeats.

I watch Shawn stand on the sideline and adjust his headset over his ear. He shields his eyes under the brim of his hat and turns his head, scanning the stadium. When he spots our box, he waves and smiles from ear to ear.

Maggie and Aiden are distracted, arguing over curfew and first dates. The teenage girls move on to the buffet table, grabbing plates and silverware and gabbing about the elasticity of football pants. I'm the only one paying attention to him, and I step toward the window and wave back, matching his megawatt smile.

Shawn spins his finger and I roll my eyes, turning to show him his name on the back of the jersey I'm wearing. It's one of his from when he was a tight end in the league. He tossed it in my face at the start of last season when I said I didn't have anything to wear to his game. When I tried to return it, he told me to keep it.

So I did.

I don't even care that it's not a Titans jersey.

I cut the nylon down the center and opened it up to keep cool in the warmer months when we're standing outside for four, five hours at a time. With the temperature hovering around forty degrees today, I added a turtleneck and leather pants. I hold my hair off my neck so he can read the letters I bedazzled with glitter and sparkles.

When I turn back around, he gives me a thumbs up. I laugh and shake my head, our routine perfected after going to so many home games over the last two seasons.

"Time for kickoff," Maggie says. "Want to grab some food?"

"I'll eat after the first quarter," I say. "I'm always nervous until someone scores."

"Look at you knowing your sports terminology." She pinches my cheek. "Did you stay up late studying what a punt return is?"

"I read an article or two. When I bring that guy next week—his name is Matthew, by the way—I want to make sure I don't sound like a total idiot."

"Lace, you could never sound like a total idiot. I'm pretty sure you could explain how paint dries and make it interesting," Maggie says.

"Well, thanks, but it's not that big of a deal. He likes sports, so I figured I'd at least try, you know?"

"Just as long as you're not trying to be something you're not for someone else. Shawn doesn't care that you don't know anything about sports."

"I'm not dating Shawn," I say. "Come on. They're about to kick off. You know I like the little cheer everyone does."

Maggie takes my hand. We settle into the leather seats and prop up our feet. The Titans win the coin toss and elect to defer. I lean forward and try to gauge Shawn's level of nerves. He never admits he's worried, always the pinnacle of calm, cool and collected, but there are telltale signs if you know where to look.

Hands in his pockets or arms crossed tightly over his chest, palms tucked under his shoulders. Pacing back and forth over the turf, his attention on the ground rather than the field. Moving his sunglasses to the top of his hat and squinting into the sun.

When the huddle breaks and the defense takes the field, he's still looking at me, and I don't see an ounce of strain on his face.

FOUR

SHAWN

I TAKE a deep breath and sit down at the media table. I adjust the microphones and smile at the horde of reporters who are here for the postgame news conference. The press room is always busy these days, packed from end to end with a sea of faces, iPhones and tape recorders, but it's almost overflowing this evening.

It's the effect of being undefeated in a tough division, a Cinderella story four years in the making. I remember the days when there were only a handful of journalists who stuck around after the games, six rickety chairs set up in a small cluster to make it look busier than it was.

There's a different energy when you're winning, a hot streak you hope to push to the next game, then the next. There's a buzz, a whisper of electricity, the slow build of something very big, very important on the horizon.

"Nice win, Coach."

"Shawn, do you have any comments about Darius Wallace's injury?"

"One at a time, yeah?" I ask the crowd, twisting off the cap of a water bottle and chugging half its contents. I nod at Marcus

Monroe, a beat writer I've known since college. He's the only one in the room who stuck around when we were in the dredges of hell, and I always let him ask his questions first. "Go ahead."

"Darius' injury," he starts, and I wait for him to continue. "Have you talked to him? We saw him in the medical tent, then he went to the locker room at the start of the fourth quarter."

"Yeah, I sat with him for a few minutes after the game. He's in good spirits. We'll get an MRI done, but right now it doesn't look like an ACL tear. When I know a timeline, I'll share that with you," I say. Marcus gives me a salute, and I point to a woman sitting in the front row. A notebook balances on her skirt, and there's a tape recorder in her hand. "Tell me your name?"

She blushes. "Sammie," she says. "Sammie Stone from The D.C. Sentinel's digital division."

"Thanks, Sammie. What do you have for me?"

"You allowed Chase Jones to throw for three touchdowns, and the Raptors' offense rushed for a hundred and fifty yards. Any adjustments as you get ready for a Thanksgiving showdown against the Minnesota Tornadoes in two weeks?"

"The Raptors played well today," I say, giving credit where credit is due. "Their offense looked sharp, and their QB has a strong arm. I remember two plays off the top of my head where we should've had a sack, but we were slow off the line of scrimmage. We'll run some drills this week, but I think it comes down to the guys being tired. They've been playing hard for three months, and what we're doing is clearly working. I'm not worried." I move my attention to the back row where it's standing room only. I smile at the intern from The Athletic, a kid I met last week who's going to school for journalism. "Kendall," I say. "I know you have something to ask."

"Thanks, Coach." He turns through his pages of notes. "Sorry, I had it here."

"No rush. Are you staying in town for Thanksgiving?" I ask.

"Yeah. My parents are local. Hang on, it's in my other note-book. I'm so sorry." He digs in his bag, frantic, and I laugh.

"Kendall. Seriously. Take your time. I could tell a joke, but I'm not funny. At least, that's what my goddaughter tells me. But she's eighteen. Teenagers aren't allowed to think *anyone* is funny, right? It's part of their creed."

A laugh rolls through the crowd and I lean back in my chair, pushing my sleeves up my arms. It's boiling in here, the heat set on high and the maximum occupancy a suggestion, not enforced. A bead of sweat trails down my cheek and I bat it away with the back of my hand before taking another sip of water.

"Found it," Kendall exclaims, and I smile.

"Good man. The floor is yours."

"The Titans are 10-0 halfway through November. Five years ago, this same team on an eight-game losing streak. What do you attribute to the success?" Kendall asks.

"Man, you could've just asked me how we got our shit together." I rock forward and rest my elbows on the table. "I attribute our success to hard work. That's it. I have fifty-three guys in the locker room who bust their ass every single day, and sixteen men on the practice squad waiting to take their spot. They go all in at practice, on game day, in their personal lives with their diet and sleep schedules. I think it's the knowledge of being close to something. Of knowing if you work just a little harder, put in a little more effort, it can be yours. It's going to hurt either way, but it hurts a whole lot less when you have a victory to ease the ache. These guys want to win. I know they're capable. They know they're capable, and it's not an overnight thing. It's tweaking and fixing and learning and adjusting. Sometimes everything lines up, and magic happens. Right now, everything we touch is magic."

The room grows quiet. Half the journalists jot down my

response in their notebooks, pens on paper and handwritten in short form and abbreviations to go back and review later. The others bend over their laptops and their fingers fly over the keyboards faster than I can think.

My phone buzzes in my pocket, and I pull it out under the table. I unlock the screen, and the background of our team photo from the start of the season is replaced with Lacey's name.

LACE FACE

Can you stop charming the fine people of the media and come out here so we can get some milkshakes?

Please?

Attachment: 1 Image

I huff out a chuckle at the photo of Lacey laying on the concrete floor out in the tunnel, her right arm flung over her head in an obvious state of duress. Her hair looks like a halo around her head, and she's flicking off the camera with her left hand.

ME

God, please don't die. I'd have no one to ridicule for ordering a chocolate and orange shake. Life would be sad.

LACE FACE

Too late. I'm withering away. See you on the other side.

A full-on laugh tumbles out of me, and the room turns silent. I look up, and everyone is staring at me. My cheeks flame under their attention, and I tuck my phone away.

"It's time for me to run," I say, pushing back in my chair and standing up. "Thanks for coming out to the game today. Get home safe, and we'll see you all next week."

There are a few last-minute questions shouted at me, but I tune them out. When I walk out the door, coach mode goes off. It's a separation—a *needed* separation—of my professional and personal lives.

No one tells you what the transition is like from player to assistant coach to head coach in a matter of six years. It's a different world on this side of the field, with microphones and cameras and strategic planning. My first season on the sideline with a headset instead of a helmet, I ran myself into the ground.

I was constantly awake until four in the morning, delirious and drunk on whiskey as I sorted through plays and lineups. I slept around, trying to find an outlet for my stress and the pressure of this new gig, and I thought being in the bed of a model was the answer. I stopped visiting my family, stopped seeing Aiden and Maven, and I only emerged from the dark cloud I lived in on Sundays, Mondays, and Thursdays.

Fifteen pounds, three months without sleep, and a phone call from my mother yelling at me that she was scared about my health—both physical and mental—later, I decided to go to therapy to get some help on how to balance the new role I had taken on.

I've learned ways to prioritize the different parts of my life. I set a hard stop to football talk and shut off my work phone. I don't read articles about the team unless I'm in my office and on the clock. I give the guys two full days off a week, an unheard of freedom in our grueling sport.

People forget their mental and physical health matters, too.

I take my job seriously. I respect that I've been given a gift to do *this* as a career, but that's all this is. A career. One that could end any day. Watching guys throw a football back and forth isn't above the people I care about, and if my friends want to see me, then I'm finished for the day. Everything related to work can wait until tomorrow.

I smile at the athletic trainers as I walk down the hall lined with posters and players' pictures. I stop to shake hands with the photographer from the Associated Press and ask him to email me any photos he might have snapped of Maven and her friends in the suite, so I can share them with Maggie and Aiden. I'm in such a good fucking mood, like I'm on top of the world. Winning helps that elation, but the other stuff does, too.

Like my goddaughter sprinting to me and throwing her arms around my neck, whispering *thank you* in my ear. Signing jerseys for all the girls at her birthday party and posing for a photo where they put bunny ears behind my head. Kissing Maggie's cheek and shaking Aiden's hand. Laughing as Lacey pretends to fall over when I walk by, acting like she's worshiping me.

"Our savior," she says. "We're not worthy."

"Get up, you weirdo," I say. I offer her my hand and she takes it, standing back on two feet. "Did you have a good time in the box?"

"It was incredible. The service was fantastic, and everyone was attentive. People called me Ms. Daniels, and I panicked because that's *my mom*." Lacey chuckles. "Do I look like I'm in my sixties having a midlife crisis?"

I look her up and down, and I appreciate the tight leather pants that hug the muscles on her long legs. The jersey hanging off her shoulders and the jewelry clasped around her neck—a silver heart sits in the hollow of her throat. The earrings dangling from her ears and her pink cheeks, half from the cold and half from screaming at the top of her lungs. I swear sometimes I can hear her yelling from the stands over the roar of the crowd.

"No." I tap her nose. "You're too hot to be having a midlife crisis."

"High praise from Playboy's Player of the Year."

"Fucking hell, Lace. Did you do an internet dive of all my accolades?"

"Of course I did. You can't be friends with the league's youngest head coach in history and *not* know about their amateur modeling career. Who cares about your Rookie of the Year award when you were Mr. December in a calendar back when you were in college? The bow was a nice touch," she says.

"I'm never talking to you again." I walk away, ignoring her laughter and quick footsteps to chase after me. She jumps on my back and my hands hold under her thighs, carrying her toward the garage and my parked car. I look over my shoulder at Maggie and Aiden. "Did you drive or take the Metro?"

"Drive," Maggie calls out, and she waves at us. "We'll meet you there."

I set Lacey on the ground when we get to my Range Rover, and I open the door to help her safely inside.

"I could've ridden with them," she says. "I know you like to turn your brain off after games."

I slide into the driver's side and glance over at her. "How do you know that?" I ask, peeling out of the parking lot and passing the throes of people still exiting the stadium.

"I saw you do it once. You put on your headphones, close your eyes, and listen to classical music." She pulls her knees to her chest, and her white high-top sneakers rest on the leather seat. "Is it superstitious?"

"No." I flick on my blinker and change lanes, heading for the diner. I shift in my seat and grip the steering wheel. "I'm surprised you didn't figure it out during your research."

"I was giving you a hard time." Lacey reaches out and rests her hand on my arm. Her palm is warm against my skin, and I can feel the blood returning to my limbs after hours outside. "I'm sorry if I made you uncomfortable."

"You didn't. There was an article published a couple of years ago by—" I take a deep breath. "I dated someone at the tail end of my playing career, and it was serious. Serious enough where she lived with me and came to all my games. I guess I wasn't moving fast enough for her, and when I didn't propose to her on our one-year anniversary, she dumped me and aired all my dirty laundry to a tabloid for a hefty chunk of change."

Lacey gasps. Her hand tightens on my arm, and the press of her fingers is grounding. They keep me calm and relaxed as I tell a story I've tried to forget. I'm not sure what compels me to share this with her. I don't know why the urge to give her every little detail sits on the tip of my tongue, just that I *want* to. I want her to know this side of me.

"I'm so sorry that happened to you," she says. "Showing intimate parts of the person you dated to the masses is downright mean."

"Yeah. She always wanted to be in the spotlight, and by releasing some of our text messages and private things about me, she really catapulted her way to stardom." I laugh, and it's rough and humorless. "Anyway. The article talks about the panic attacks I sometimes have. Decompressing after games helps get rid of that tension, and for some reason, I gravitate toward classical music as the antidote that calms me down. My grandmother used to play Pachelbel's Canon all the time on this shitty little stereo she had in the kitchen of her condo, and I started to associate it with being safe."

Lacey is quiet, but her touch on my arm is unwavering. When she finally talks, her words are soft. "I'm so sorry that happened to you, Shawn. What a terrible thing to experience. I can't imagine trusting someone with such sensitive and vulnerable information, only to have it thrown in your face. I know it might not mean much, but to me, the panic attacks make you a superhero."

I frown and look over at her. "What do you mean?"

"You have the ability to fight off these thoughts of yours, which isn't easy. You don't let the negativity win. And if it does win sometimes, that's okay. That doesn't make you less. It makes you *more*. You're an incredible human learning to juggle the balance between your mental health and being on the field, and I respect you for it. Thank you for sharing part of yourself with me."

"Thank you for listening," I say. I clear my throat and fold my left hand over hers. "Okay, enough of this heavy shit. We have milkshakes to devour."

"I've been waiting for this all day," Lacey says, and she squeals excitedly. "Want to split a plate of loaded fries?"

"Of course I do. But only if we get extra cheese sauce."

"Deal."

We pull into the parking lot of the diner a few minutes later. There's no sign, no flashing neon lights to announce you've arrived. It's hidden, three left turns off the main road and tucked between a laundromat that's open twenty-four hours a day and a group fitness studio. Blink and you miss it, which is why I love it so much.

I'm not a football coach with an eighty-million-dollar contract here, but an average guy with his friends, eating greasy food and dunking French fries in my vanilla milkshake. There are no cameras, no interviews, no reporters. I can relax. Take a deep breath and just *be*, a luxury I so rarely get to enjoy.

Lacey unbuckles her seatbelt. She jumps out of the car and closes the door behind her. I watch as she puts a beanie with a little pom pom on her head and runs her palms up and down her arms, trying to stay warm. She laughs, and her breath cuts into the chilly night air as a puff of white dances from her lips.

Her eyes find mine through the dashboard smudged with handprints and covered in a thin layer of dust. I think there's a drawing of a dick near the rearview mirror, a gift from one of my players who was trying to be funny.

When she smiles, it's slow and indulgent. It starts soft, at the edges of her mouth and in the wrinkle of her nose, before tugging upward and splitting her face into a full-fledged grin. She motions for me to get out of the car and follow her inside.

I can't explain it, but the invitation to join her makes me feel higher than our win did.

FIVE
LACEY

"WHAT THE HELL am I supposed to wear?" I ask Maggie. I toss a dress onto my bed, then a sweater and a stack of scarves. "It's literally freezing outside. There's snow in the forecast, and I'm going on a date. This is hopeless."

"Okay, it's not hopeless," Maggie says, and she rifles through a row of hangers with a determined look on her face. "What about—no, that's not practical. Neither is that. Okay. This." She pulls down a navy-blue cashmere sweater and hands it to me. "With leggings, your big puffy jacket, and a beanie."

"I'm going to look like a blueberry."

"At least you'll be a cute blueberry who is warm." She pats my head affectionately and tugs me to my feet. "We have to leave in twenty minutes. Is Matthew meeting us there?"

"Yeah." I grab a pair of fleece-lined leggings and high socks. "I don't want him to know where I live in case he turns out to be a psychopath."

"Sweetie, you need to stop watching those true crime shows. One day you're not going to want to go outside anymore, and I'll be sad. Who will I eat lunch with?"

"Your adoring boyfriend. What do we think? Sports bra or sexy bra?"

"Sports bra. You don't want to give it all away on the first date."

I fling a pair of underwear at her head, and the purple thong whizzes past her ear. "You literally slept with Aiden four hours after meeting him."

"I'm not sure we even made it that long." Maggie bites her bottom lip and grins. Color splashes on her cheeks. "I think it was only two and a half hours."

"Rub it in, why don't you? I'm going with sexy. Even if he is a dud, we can go back to his place after and have a little fun," I say.

"There's my sex-positive girl," she says, walking out of the closet and knocking her knuckles against the door. "Get changed."

I pull off my sweatpants and T-shirt, changing them out with my winter weather outfit. I braid my hair in two long pigtails and throw a beanie on my head, remembering to grab my mittens and clear fanny pack.

I'm excited to meet Matthew in person and get to know him better. We've spent the last two weeks talking, and he seems like a good guy. He lives a couple blocks away and has a golden retriever, Daisy, he walks up to the National Mall when the weather is nice. He told me he's not sure what he's looking for, but he enjoys talking to me.

A cheesy line, but it's not fair to judge him; I'm not sure what I'm looking for either.

Something serious, maybe? Someone to have fun with without any labels? I'm standing on a tightrope, awkwardly teetering between the desire to commit to someone, *just* someone, and enjoying what life can be like as a single woman.

I have a good job and a good set of friends. I know what I like and I have my fun. I also know I'm young and I don't need to decide anything about the future right now, but the nights I spend in my apartment alone have shifted from empowering self-fulfillment to loneliness. There's an ache in my chest when I imagine the thousands of people out there happy, living with their person and content as a clam. I'm not sure how to combat that longing of missing out on something important that everyone else around me seems to have.

I guess by putting myself out there and going on dates to football games with men I meet online.

"Ready," I call out. I grab the lucky pair of white sneakers I wear on game days and hustle down the hall. "I just need to find my jacket. Where's Aiden?"

"He got tied up at the hospital and is meeting us there." Maggie grins and tugs on my hair. "You look hot, Lace."

"Like a hot blueberry." I tie my shoes and grab my keys. "I feel like today is going to be a good day."

"Do you think the Titans are going to win?"

"No. I mean, yes, I do. I can't explain it, but it feels like something big is going to happen."

"Sounds like someone is excited about their date. Maybe Matthew is going to be the love of your life," she says.

I don't have the heart to tell her I don't think it has to do with Matthew at all.

"LOOK." Maggie points at the pixelated screen across the field from us. "It's kiss cam time. Oh, I love when they do this. It's so cute to see so many people who love each other."

"What if the camera people get it wrong?" I ask. "What if the couple they show are brother and sister? Second cousins? What if someone is getting dumped at the game? Things could get weird."

She laughs and turns to Aiden, no doubt asking him to do something that will get them on the big screen. Maybe he'll hold up his shirt and flash the stadium. Do a stupid dance where everyone points and laughs. There's nothing Maggie could ask for that he wouldn't give her.

I glance over at Matthew, my date, who's standing next to me. His hands are shoved in the pockets of his jeans and his eyes are narrowed on the railing in front of us. He looks miserable.

"Hey," I say. I nudge his shoulder with mine in an act of single people solidarity. "Are you having a good time?"

"Yeah," he answers, but it doesn't sound convincing. "It's just colder than I thought it was going to be."

"The winter games can be brutal. Do you want my jacket? That drink warmed me up."

The mulled wine we grabbed in between the first and second quarter at the bar in the lounge downstairs soaked into my bloodstream and gradually heated me from the inside out. It's a liquid protectant to the frigid bite of cold in the air, and it feels like I've stepped into a furnace. Transported myself to someplace tropical, with a mountain of blankets resting on my chest.

"Nah." He rocks back on his feet and exhales. I see his breath, and he shivers. "I'm fine."

"Okay." I shrug and look up at the jumbotron, smiling as the camera pans to an older couple with matching tracksuits underneath their down coats. They wave, their hands clasped together and wrinkles on their skin. "Look how cute they are."

"Kiss cams are so fucking stupid," Matthew declares. "Half the PDA is probably fake. Orchestrated by a P.R. team to give someone good press. And almost all of these relationships will end in a breakup."

I've never met someone with so much disdain for in-game entertainment before, and I frown.

"They're just average people, Matthew. I like it. It's fun to see so many generations and so many kinds of love. Look." I gesture to the screen. "Those kids are probably on a first date, too. Oh. And there's a dad with his daughter."

I smile at the man holding up his little girl *Lion King* style, joy clear on her face as he peppers her rosy cheeks with kisses. I'm about to mention the group of fraternity guys who are shown next, the men who lift their beer as a protest to love and chug back their drinks, when my own face appears.

I squint, and I wonder if I'm staring in a very large, very confusing mirror. I lift my hand and the me on the screen—the one that's two stories high and large enough to see from Dulles Airport nearly thirty miles away—lifts their hand as well.

"Lacey." Maggie shakes my shoulders. "That's you."

"Oh," I say, and I wave. "Cool."

There's an awkward pause where I glance at Matthew. He looks at me like he just ate a lemon, and, if I blinked, I would've missed the way he inches not closer, but *away* from me, as if begging for distance between us.

Hurt barrels into me. I know this man isn't my soulmate. I'm never going to see him again after today, but a kiss is harmless. It doesn't mean anything, a quick peck to appease the guy behind the camera who's in apparent control of our destiny.

"Fucking weird," Matthew grumbles again, unaffected by the growing sound of boos around us. "Conformist pawns."

I want the ground to swallow me whole.

I shake my head and try to convey to the cameraman there's clearly not going to be any kissing happening in section 101, row A, but he doesn't get the hint. The lens lingers on us and magnifies us for seventy thousand people to see.

To see and make fun of.

Sad violin music starts, and I'm close to catapulting myself onto the field with an imaginary medical event just to get away from here. If I clutch my chest and hold my breath, they'll be forced to put me on a stretcher, right? Maybe I can slip someone a fifty-dollar bill to push me to the ground.

"Oh my god," I whisper, and I grab Maggie's hand. "What is going on?"

"I don't know," she whispers back. "Do you want me to kiss you? Hell, Aiden could. We can share him."

"You're a good friend," I say, and my voice wobbles and cracks around the edges the longer I stare at my pathetic face. "This is embarrassing. It's like those dreams you have where you show up to school with no clothes on and everyone makes fun of you."

"They're not making fun of you, Lace. They're making fun of Matthew."

I look at him again, with his set jaw and the wrinkles on his forehead. He's firm in his anti-kiss cam stance, and I have to hand it to him: I've never seen someone so hellbent to rebel against a stadium game.

It feels like hours pass before the camera finally leaves us alone, but I'm sure it's only a matter of seconds. It flashes through the crowd and finds another couple to show. This pair makes up for the enthusiasm we were lacking.

They use their tongues and hands, a generous display of public affection that turns so raunchy so quickly, whoever is in charge of the entertainment pulls the cord on the camera entirely, and a blank screen winks back at us.

"Thank god," I mumble. I turn to face my date and I put my hands on my hips. "Uh, that was awkward."

"I told you I think they're dumb. Why would I kiss you in front of all these people?" he says. "Just because everyone else did?"

"I don't know, Matthew, because it's a joke? Because clearly the more you antagonize the person running this game, the more they're going to poke fun at you? Because that was *morti-fying*? You could've kissed my cheek. Or my hand. Outright rejecting me on national television hurts."

"I'm not rejecting you," Matthew argues. He sighs and steps toward me. His hands cup my cheeks and his palms are ice cold on my skin. When he smiles, hope bubbles inside me. Maybe we can salvage this, a first date that's not a total disaster. "I just don't like to be told what to do. Especially by someone getting paid minimum wage to hold a camera. What a stupid fucking job. Imagine doing that for a living."

"Oh." I nod, as if that's a perfectly logical explanation for humiliating me. A *fuck you* to the working class from the finance bro. "Okay."

A fresh wave of boos work their way through the stadium. I pry his hands off my face and glance at the field, expecting to find a Titans player hurt, but the timeout is still going. The team is huddled in a tight circle with their heads bowed and their arms draped around each other's shoulders.

Instead, I see us projected on the screen again, my mouth popped open and Matthew holding up his middle fingers. His hands are so red, I'm afraid he might be starting to get frostbite.

"Just kiss her, bro," someone calls out.

"You suck," a kid eight rows back yells.

"She deserves better," a woman two sections over hollers.

"Dump his ass!" a girl shrieks, and there's a round of applause at her drunken battle cry.

"Excuse me," I say. "I need to use the restroom."

I weave through the row of people, ignoring their apologies and the embarrassment of the last five minutes. I run up the stairs and out onto the stadium concourse. I fly past the snack stand that makes delicious cinnamon sugar pretzels. I dodge a beer cart and a tower of cotton candy. I don't stop running until I lock myself in a bathroom stall and bury my face in my hands.

SIX

SHAWN

"HEY." I snap my fingers and try to get the guys in the huddle to pay attention to the play I'm drawing up. They turned their backs on me thirty seconds ago, and it feels like I'm talking to a brick wall. "Why is no one listening to me?"

C.J. Miles, star running back and former Heisman trophy winner, laughs. He switches his helmet from his left hand to his right and pops his hip out to the side. "This guy still won't kiss her. Why won't he kiss her? I would. She's so hot."

"Dude's an idiot," Peter Bellamy chimes in, and there's a rousing murmur of agreement.

"I don't give a shit about who's not getting kissed or who's hot," I say.

"Are you sure about that, Coach? It's—"

"I don't care who it is. We're down by a field goal with four minutes to go until halftime. We haven't trailed in a game all season, and we're lucky to only be down three. Can we remember why we're here, please? It's not to watch an episode of *The Bachelor*. It's to win a Super Bowl, right?"

"Yes, Coach," eleven men say, and I nod.

"Good."

I draw out the next series of plays I hope we can execute well enough to get us into field goal range before we head to the locker room for halftime. Twelve minutes away from the crowd to regroup will do us some good.

We're playing like shit today, with sluggish legs and soft tackles. An interception, a missed extra point, and more penalties than we've had all season haven't given us a great half. Nothing is going our way, and if we don't fix our mistakes after the break, we'll be walking out of the stadium with our first loss of the year.

I cap the red marker and stand. A chant starts to run through the stadium, and it vaguely sounds like *asshole, asshole*. I've never heard it so animated in here during a timeout; I can barely think.

"What the hell is going on now?" I ask, having to yell over the crowd.

"It's the kiss cam," Kristen, one of my assistant coaches, says.

She gestures to the jumbotron that should be showing our guys hustling back to the line of scrimmage. I don't see jerseys but *Lacey*, her face as red as fire and her hands trembling at her sides. The guy next to her shakes his head and crosses his arms over his chest, refusing to look her way.

"What the fuck?" I grumble. I push a water cooler out of the way, and it topples to the ground. Yellow sports drink soaks into the grass, and plastic water bottles roll to the left and right.

"This is the eighth time they've shown them," Dallas Lansfield, my kicker, says. He claps his hands together and practically skips in place. "Fuck, I kind of hope she punches him."

"I hope she kicks him in the balls," Odell Sinclair says from the stationary bike he's riding to keep his hamstrings warm. He pedals in place and wipes his face with a towel. "Dude deserves it. Lacey is hot as hell. Have you seen her ass? I want to bend her over and—"

"Odell," I snap. "Shut the hell up. One more word out of your mouth, and I'm benching you for the rest of the game. Aaron." I point to another assistant coach who springs to life. "Come here."

He fumbles with his headset and pulls the microphone off his ear. "Yes, Coach?"

"Tell whoever's in charge of that shit to knock it off. No more kiss cam. If they give you pushback, you say it's a direct order from me. Got it?" I bark out.

"Got it," he says, hurrying away and leaving his clipboard behind.

I put my hands on my hips. Anger burns in my chest and works its way up to my shoulders and neck. Annoyance and irritation prick my vision, and I don't remember the last time I was this pissed off. I squeeze my eyes shut and try to block out the image of Lacey's mortification broadcast for all to see. For all to *laugh* at, making a mockery out of something she was so excited about.

She sent me a text this morning thanking me again for the extra ticket. She followed it up with a long voice memo, an emphatic and passionate but sleep-fogged rant that told me she wouldn't hesitate to have security escort her date out of UPS Field if he even *dared* to cheer for the other team.

Titans forever, she said through a yawn. I listened to it four times while I sipped my coffee, smiling at the way she trailed off halfway through, clearly dozing back to sleep for a minute or two. I think she was snoring at one point.

I kept it for prosperity.

And blackmail.

"Coach."

An elbow nudges my ribs, and I snap my eyes open, lost in the last few minutes.

"What?" I say.

"It's fourth and one. What do you want to do? Go for it or

kick?" Kristen asks. She's staring at me, and I rub my jaw, uneasy under her unyielding gaze.

How the hell did I miss the last three plays?

"Kick," I say roughly. "With how poorly we're executing today, I don't want to give them a shot with the ball with any time on the clock. Dallas, let's go."

He jogs past me and buckles his helmet as the offense runs off the field.

"Are you okay?" Kristen asks, and I shoot her a sharp glance.

"I'm fine. Why wouldn't I be?"

"I don't know. Your shoulders are up at your ears and you look tense."

"Nervous," I say, and she hums.

I don't think she believes me.

I don't think I believe myself.

Chicago calls a timeout like I expect them to. Dallas uses the two minutes to stay loose, swinging his leg back and forth and staring down the goalposts. He mumbles something under his breath and raises his arm to check the direction and speed of the wind. Satisfied, he picks up the ball and tosses it between his hands. He looks over and gives me a thumbs up, nothing but confidence on his face.

I wish I could say the same.

I feel like I'm going to throw up. My heart is stuck somewhere between my stomach and my throat, and I don't know why I'm so worked up over a kick.

A whistle blows, and the guys line up. Our center, Bryce Bigby, snaps the ball perfectly to our holder, Justin Rodgers. Dallas pulls his leg back and punts the shit out of the kick. I watch the ball soar through the goalposts with yards to spare as time expires.

"Thank fuck," I say, and I tap Dallas on the helmet as the team runs off the field. "Nice kick, kid."

"Thanks, Coach." He grins at me, a clump of grass stuck to his face mask and his eye black smudged on his left cheek. "And thanks for trusting me."

"You know I have your back. Always."

We shake hands and the team disappears to the locker room, more enthusiasm in their voices than they had ten minutes ago. My assistant coaches follow them and I'm left alone, anxiously waiting for the interview I have to do before I can head off the field, too.

A reporter approaches me, and I smile. "Shawn?" she asks and I beckon her over.

"Remind me of your name," I say. "I'm better with faces."

"Courtney," she says, and I snap my fingers.

"Courtney, right. I'm sorry. I try to make it a point to get to know everyone, but there seems to be too many people these days." I nod toward the camera in front of her. "Are we on?"

"In ten seconds," she says, and I nod again.

"I'm sure the guys upstairs are roasting us right now," I say, and she suppresses a laugh.

"You said it, not me." The light on the camera turns red. "Coach, Dallas knocked down that field goal to tie the game heading into halftime. What are you going to work on in the second half?" she asks and extends the microphone she's holding my way.

"Well, Courtney, we need to be more aggressive. We were slow off the line of scrimmage—again. It's the same thing that plagued us last week. We had guys who were open and dropped the ball, and that interception really hurt us. That's why there are two halves, though. We're going to clean it up and come back better after the break."

"This is the first time all season you found yourself in a deficit. How do you think the team reacted to being down three?" Courtney asks.

"Being down three is a heck of a lot easier to come back from than being down fourteen or twenty-one. It's a sixty-minute game. They outplayed us the first thirty minutes, and that's why they were able to take that lead late in the second quarter," I say. "We'll bounce back."

"What do you—" she laughs. "Hang on. I can barely hear myself. What is that?"

I hear it too, the noise loud enough to ring in my ears. I whip my head toward the stands and my eyes zero in on Lacey. Her face is buried in her hands and she shakes her head from side to side. That goddamn camera is on her again, and my eyes narrow.

"For fuck's sake," I say. Courtney's mouth pops open at the vulgarity, and she nearly drops the microphone. "Excuse me."

I jog toward the stands and the row of seats my friends sit in every game. The distance isn't far, barely fifteen yards, but it feels like miles.

"Shawn," Maggie says as I approach them, and I hear her desperation for me to do something. *Anything.* I'm going to find the cord to that camera and snap it in half.

Lacey looks up. She stares at me with red-rimmed eyes and tears on her face. I've never wanted to take away someone's hurt before, but when I see the pain etched into her frown and the way her shoulders curl in, I want to burn the world to the fucking ground.

"What the hell is going on?" I ask.

"I don't know," Lacey says. Her voice is thick with emotion, and my heart lurches further up my throat with the sound. "He won't... he hasn't... It's fine. I'm okay."

I turn my attention to the guy next to her and his hoodie and jeans. The stupid hat he's wearing that covers his blonde hair. I could bench press him if I wanted to. Easily. The twerp can't weigh more than a hundred fifty pounds soaking wet.

"What's your deal?" I yell, and he scowls.

"None of your fucking business," he snaps. "Your stadium fucking sucks."

"It's not nice to make a lady wait," I say.

I jump onto the concrete blocks that separate the stands from the field. I pull Lacey toward me by her pigtails and settle my hand against the side of her neck. Her heart races under my palm, and I run my thumb down the column of her throat. Teardrops catch on her eyelashes, and her nose is as pink as a peony in spring.

Lacey grabs a fistful of my shirt and clutches the cotton like it's her lifeline. Maybe it's to keep me from falling headfirst to the turf. Maybe it's to pull me closer. Maybe it's to steady herself, because if she's feeling anything like I am, it's dangerously close to levitating high above the crowd.

I bring my mouth to hers, slow enough so she can stop me if she wants, and her breathing hitches.

When she doesn't pull away, I smile big and wide. She gives me a shy grin in return and I press my lips against hers, kissing my best friend in front of seventy thousand people without a damn in the world, just as snowflakes start to fall from the sky.

SEVEN
LACEY

SHAWN IS WARM, and he smells like sweat and grass.

He's still smiling; I can feel the edges of his beam soft against the corners of my mouth. His hand moves from just under my jaw to my sternum and his fingers spread wide across the neckline of my sweater, like he's desperately searching for bare skin to touch.

He makes a frustrated sound from the back of his throat when he comes up short and finds none, as if what we're doing isn't good enough and he wants *more*.

I think it's the best kiss I've ever had.

My hands move from his chest to his hair, and his frustration burns out. It fades to delight, to splendor when he tips my chin up with the hook of his thumb and his tongue brushes against my lips. It's questioning, hesitant. An ask, not a demand. An invitation if I want it, and I melt into him as his kisses turn hungrier, reminiscent of a man starved.

I might burst into a million pieces. I might turn to stardust and ascend to the clouds or somewhere beyond because every press of his fingers, every exhale and little huff of appreciation when I touch the stubble on his cheeks, every inch he pulls me closer drives my want, my *need*, higher and higher.

Heat caresses the back of my neck. It licks up the line of my spine and across the soft skin of my stomach hidden by clothes like a wildfire. Shawn is slow, purposeful, and a laugh slips out of me when his teeth sink into my bottom lip in a way that should hurt, but feels nothing but magnificent. The sound reverberates down my body when he tugs me closer, his arm looping around my waist and his hand heavy against my hip.

I can't think. I can't speak. I've never had someone take their time when they kiss me, exploring, relishing, *indulging* in me like I'm a prize they won and want to show off to the world.

He tastes like peppermint, as if he chugged a sugary seasonal drink before he waltzed over here and stole my breath away. Or marshmallows, maybe, my favorite topping in a warm mug of hot cocoa on a cold winter's night.

It's savory and sweet on the tip of my tongue, with a touch of spice. A hint of what else could be hiding behind the press of his mouth, wicked deliciousness that only comes out after dark when he has you alone in his room and spread out on his bed.

Is this how he kisses everyone? I think from the deep recesses of my brain. The small part of me that's still functioning, that still has my feet on the ground. *Or just me?*

Shawn drops his forehead to mine, and I blink my eyes open. My vision is hazy, foggy and lust-filled, but I can see him as clear as day. Tiny snowflakes hang on the ends of his eyelashes. Another lands on his nose and lingers there before melting away.

His cheeks are flushed. It's cold outside, but he's as hot as the sun. His thumb traces up my jaw and across my mouth. He pulls at my bottom lip like he's claiming it for himself. As if that kiss didn't just tattoo his name across every inch of my body.

"Lacey girl," he says, and his voice is low. Rough, and it

sounds like my name has been pulled from the trenches of his chest. An exaltation he wants to bellow to anyone who will listen.

My head is slow to catch up with my body. My limbs are heavy and my brain is working a few steps behind. How could it not be after he sent me to outer space?

Our gazes meet, and there's fire behind his eyes. A blaze burns in the flecks of gold in his irises. The longer he stares, the longer his attention doesn't waver, the more I think I'd like the flames to engulf me. Make me one of theirs and never let me go.

He takes a deep breath, and his chest heaves with the guttural inhale. My mouth opens to say something, *anything*, but words don't come out. What little train of thought I have left vanishes when the flash of a camera goes off in my face, and a thousand white spots pop up in my vision.

"Shawn, any comment on your relationship with this woman?" someone asks, and I reel back.

My eyes widen, and my hand trembles as it covers my mouth. I look to my right and see a photographer. Their camera is in their hands and their finger hovers over the shutter button, ready to snap another picture.

Reality rushes into me, a wave that knocks me off balance.

Football game.

Kiss cam.

National television.

My best friend kissing me in front of thousands of people.

Shit.

"Delete it," Shawn says, and there's not a lick of kindness behind the command as he holds out his hand.

The photographer cradles the Nikon to his chest. The lens is so long, it could probably spot every pore on my face. Capture the horror in my eyes and the fear wedging its way between my shoulder blades like a visitor overstaying their welcome.

"You can't do that." He lifts his chin defiantly in a challenge. There's a badge hanging from his neck, and I see his name in big, bold letters. **DARYL KENNEDY, ESPN.** "It's private property."

"This stadium is also private property. Delete it and hand over the disk, or I'll make sure you never step foot in here again," Shawn says, and I can *feel* his threat between my breasts. At the base of my spine, a fierceness I've never heard from him before coming from his mouth.

"Asshole," the photographer grumbles. He pops out the disk and drops it in Shawn's hands.

"Thanks," Shawn says, and he shoves the disk in his pocket to keep it safe. He turns his attention back to me and tucks a piece of hair that's snuck free from my braids behind my ear. "Are you okay?"

"Me?" The word squeaks, and I clear my throat. "I'm—I'm fine. Why... why wouldn't I be? Are you okay?"

"I'm okay, but I have to get back to the field," he says without any urgency.

He's still holding my hip with one hand, and his fingers are dangerously close to the small space of bare skin under the hem of my sweater. I'm still clutching his hair, and the dark brown waves are soft against my palm. Neither of us let go.

"Okay," I answer.

"We'll talk later?"

"Of course. Milkshakes, right?"

"Milkshakes," Shawn repeats. "Right. Just like always."

His mouth closes then opens. There's something else he's not saying, but silence hangs in the air between us. Aiden is the one to break it.

"Shawn," he says, a gentle coaxing. "The guys are out of the locker room. The second half is about to start."

Shawn's hand falls from my side, and he scoots back. His

fingers curl around the metal railing and his eyes turn less soft as he looks over his shoulder.

"I'll see you all in the tunnel after," he says gruffly. His gaze flicks back to my face, and there's that dazzling smile again. My heart flutters in my chest, a hundred butterflies waiting to take flight when he runs his knuckles down my cheek and adds, "see ya, Lacey girl," so softly I know it was only meant for me.

"Bye, Shawn," I whisper.

I'm not sure if he can hear me over the surrounding noises; the round of applause, the whistles that pierce the late afternoon sky, the loud music pulsing through the speakers and an announcement from the public address system, but I hope he can. I want him to know we're still *us*.

He slides off the concrete blocks and jumps to the field, waving off assistance from two nearby security guards and someone from the medical staff. He runs toward his team as he talks into his headset and adjusts the bill of his hat, leaving footprints behind in the fresh dusting of snow. Accepting a jacket from someone on the sidelines, he shrugs the coat up over his shoulders and buries his hands in his pockets.

Those same hands touched me, *caressed* me, like I was something precious. Something to be adored. No man has ever treated me so delicately.

I grip the back of my chair and collapse into my seat. It's quieter down here, and I can block out the noise and the people trying to get my attention.

"Lacey," Maggie says. She drops into the plastic chair beside me. Her knees knock against mine, and she takes my hands in hers. They're softer than Shawn's, but not nearly as warm or nice to touch. "Are you okay?"

"I'm good." I lift my chin and give her a smile I hope is convincing. I nod toward the field and gesture vaguely at someone in a jersey doing something sports related. It's better than stewing in my thoughts. "I hope the Titans can keep their momentum in the second half."

Maggie snaps her fingers in front of my face and frowns. "One kiss with Shawn and suddenly you're a football expert?"

I laugh and rest my head on her shoulder. "I'm fine, Mags. Really. That was clearly a friend helping out another—*shit*. Where's Matthew?" I ask.

"He left," Aiden says, and he's trying not to smile. "He had some nice comments on the way out about the middle class and how people who work in hospitality suck. It was weird. The crowd gave him a nice farewell, too. I've never seen so many people flick off a single person in my life. Well, that's not true. I saw a Red Sox game in Boston once, and—"

"Honey," Maggie says. "Now is not the time."

"Sorry." Aiden gives her a sheepish grin and takes the seat on my other side.

"What a disaster," I say. "Is it wrong that I feel bad for Matthew? This is my fault. I should've just—I don't know. Hid under my seat or not let the antagonizing get to me. Oh, my god. I was pushing him to do something he didn't want to do."

"Your fault?" Maggie asks. She shakes her head and hugs me tight. "That was not your fault, sweetie. If this was about a personal boundary he didn't want to cross, he would've expressed that to you *or* he wouldn't have made a spectacle about the whole thing. This was an exertion of his power and trying to be better than everyone else. If he doesn't want to kiss the woman he's on the date with, even in a platonic, friendly and fun way, then he's not the one for you. You're someone who always looks for the fun in life, Lace."

"I didn't like that kind of attention," I admit. "I felt trapped. Like it was an invasion of privacy, almost."

"Let's sue the camera guy," Aiden declares, and I pat his arm in appreciation. "Fuck him and fuck him for not getting the hint the first seven times."

"Seven?" Maggie asks. "I think it was more like nine."

"Let's just forget it happened, okay? It's no big deal. Matthew is gone, the camera is gone, and the Titans are playing in a close game. We have other things to worry about," I say.

"Are you sure you're alright?" Maggie asks, and I nod.

"I've never been better, Mags, but I could use another drink. I'm freezing my ass off."

EIGHT
LACEY

I WAKE up to my phone vibrating under my pillow.

I grab the alarm clock sitting on my bedside table and toss it on the mattress when I see it's only five thirty in the morning. I didn't plan to be up for another two hours.

The vibrating starts a second time and I fumble with my phone, sitting up when I see my mom's name on the screen.

"Mom? What's wrong?" I ask, still half-asleep.

"Why didn't you tell me you were dating Shawn Holmes?"

"What are you talking about? I'm not dating Shawn. Where would you get that idea?"

"The news," she says. "The internet. Every person in the world except my daughter, who used to tell me everything."

Dread ices my blood. I pull the phone away from my ear and my fingers fly across the screen to search my name on the internet. What once used to show my LinkedIn profile as the top hit, followed by a handful of articles I've written for various children's pediatric magazines, is now replaced with a photo of Shawn's mouth on mine at UPS Field and dozens of headlines from gossip websites.

Kiss cam gone wrong—or right?

Was this kiss cam kiss staged or real? Body language experts weigh in.

Who is Lacey Daniels, Shawn Holmes' new leading lady?

Single no more! Everyone's favorite NFL coach is finally off the market.

Caught on camera! A scorching display of public affection at a sporting event—and we are here for it.

"Fuck," I say. "*Fuck.*"

"Lacey," my mother admonishes. "Language."

"Sorry." I press the pads of my fingers to the space between my eyebrows as pressure pulses across my forehead. "We're not... it's not like that, Mom. Shawn and I are friends. *Just* friends."

"That sure doesn't look like *just friends* to me," she says with a laugh. "I need more friends like yours."

"Oh, my god. This is all a misunderstanding. It was just a stupid thing that happened at his game."

"Well, someone better tell the media that," my mom says. "They talked about you on *Good Morning America*. You were the pop culture moment of the day."

"Pop culture—you've got to be shitting me." I grab a pillow and put it over my face, screaming into the silk cover until I'm hoarse. "I have to go, Mom. I have to fix this."

"Are you sure you don't like him, Lace? The pictures of you two were very cute. And kissing in the snow? It's like those Hallmark movies I love so much."

"Of course I like him. He's one of my favorite people in the world. I just don't like him like *that*," I say.

My mom hums. "Okay. Call me later. I love you."

"Love you too," I say.

I end the call and pull up my Instagram, nearly dropping my

phone when I see I have three hundred thousand new followers. A full inbox. Comments and likes on photos from ten years ago, back when I wore skinny jeans and had a temporary tattoo of a butterfly on my left shoulder.

My profile has always been public, easily searchable by anyone who has my first and last name. There's nothing incriminating on it, no glorification of illegal activities that would get me in trouble with the state medical board or have my patients' parents not trust me.

I love my job, and I've worked hard to earn the accolades I've achieved over the course of my career. I would never act like an idiot then post it on social media.

But this sudden influx of attention means people I don't know are finding these snapshots of my life. People who have never met me are flocking to cherished personal moments. Commenting on images of loved ones—on *Maven*—and criticizing her appearance.

"Goddammit," I curse, and a knock on my apartment door has me flying out of bed.

I'm close to being sick. Acid churns in my stomach and bile sits in my throat. I stand on my tiptoes and peer through the peephole, breathing out a sigh of relief when I see Maggie's anxious face on the other side. I turn the knob and fling the door open, and she wraps me in a hug.

"Are you okay?" she whispers in my ear, her hand stroking my hair and her arms around my shoulders.

"I don't know what's going on, Mags."

It's my apartment, but she's the one to guide me to the couch. The one who sits me down and kisses the top of my head. She disappears for a minute or ten, returning to the living room with two mugs in her hands.

"Talk," she says, and she thrusts a cup of tea in my direction.

"I went to sleep last night thinking whatever happened at the game was behind us. Shawn and I made a couple of jokes at the diner. He ruffled my hair and told me I use too much teeth when I kiss. I elbowed him in the stomach and said his tongue is too slippery. It was *fine*. This morning, I wake up to this massive shit storm and headlines saying I'm dating the NFL's most eligible bachelor. How did we get *here*?" I ask.

"A video of the kiss got posted online," she says slowly. She brings the chipped mug to her lips and takes a sip. "On TikTok. It has fifteen million views."

I almost spill my tea. It sloshes dangerously close to the rim of the cup and a few rogue drops fall onto my fingers as I gape at her. "Fifteen million?" I repeat. There's no way I heard her correctly. "How is that possible?"

"Social media." She shrugs and sets her saucer and teacup down next to the photo of us at medical school graduation over ten years ago. We're both in our black robes and doctoral tams, smiling proudly on a warm spring day. "It can be a blessing and a curse."

"Right now, I'd say it's a curse."

"Why, exactly?" she asks. "Everyone thinks you're dating the hot football coach. Is that really that bad?"

"I don't want to date the hot football coach," I argue. "I don't want to date anyone, and certainly not my friend who's seen me puke in a toilet after a tequila shot too many."

"We are *never* doing tequila shots again," Maggie says firmly. "But what if..." she trails off and grabs the blanket off the arm of the couch. She drapes it over our legs and runs her palms across the fleece. Her fingers work the fringe on the ends into tiny little braids. "What if you used it as leverage?"

"Leverage?" I bring the cup of tea to my mouth. I take a sip and hum my approval at the teaspoon of honey and splash of milk she added. "What do you mean?"

"Hear me out," she says. "We have the annual hospital holiday gala next month."

"What does that have to do with Shawn?"

"Nothing—*yet*. But it could. He's one of the biggest names in sports. A previous Super Bowl winner. A current NFL coach with a hot winning streak. He's young, he's good looking, he's wealthy. Plus, he's a *nice guy*. You know Director Hannaford has a pattern of promoting people who bring in the best silent auction prizes to the gala. With a boyfriend like Shawn who could offer a coaching lesson or two for someone's kid who's trying to get on the varsity football team, well, the donations would triple. The hospital and all its affiliates—including your office—need funding. Badly. This could be an answer to that problem," she says.

"So, I'm extorting him for his athletic talent and pretty face," I say flatly. "How is that fair?"

Maggie laughs. "You're not extorting him, Lace. It's for the kids. And he would know your intentions ahead of time. You can keep up the dating through the gala, then pretend you broke up. Hannaford wouldn't care by that point. It'll be a new year, and all he sees are dollar signs."

I weigh her words and consider them carefully, because what she's saying makes sense. A *lot* of sense, and I hate that she lays it out so logically.

It's no secret the hospital director looks forward to this time of year; he makes his rounds and asks what items the staff will be donating. The fancier the item, the more impressed he is.

More donations and more funding mean better medical equipment for our patients who desperately deserve it. It also means higher wages and more staff, so everyone can stop working such long hours. The overtime is nice, but five twelve-hour days in a row is *brutal*.

The position of chief physician at the pediatric office has

been open for months, waiting for a replacement. Hannaford mentioned it once a few months ago in passing, but I never thought anything of it. Never considered throwing my name in the ring or dropping off my resume in his mailbox—especially because he referred to me as Nancy, and I didn't have the guts to correct him.

Auctioning off a couple hours with Shawn—complete with a private tour of UPS Field—could go for a quarter of a million dollars, easily, and that's chump change to a lot of the folks that come to the gala. It's far more profitable than the fruit basket and bottle of wine I was planning to bring.

"He would do that as a friend, though," I argue. "I don't have to tell the world he's my boyfriend to get him to do something nice; he's always visiting the kids in pediatric oncology. I'm surprised he's never offered to donate any of his athletic services before. He and Aiden have been friends for a lifetime."

"Shawn doesn't like the spotlight," Maggie explains. "He comes to the hospital in a hoodie and a hat so people in the hall can't recognize him. When he donates, he donates anonymously —and he's donated *a lot*, Lace."

My hands are sweating. I set the teacup down and rub my palms over my T-shirt before twisting the cotton into a knot in my fist. Unease settles in my stomach, a rock with a heavy weight sinking further and further to the ground.

"That would make him uncomfortable," I say, and my voice sounds like a thousand splinters sticking up on a piece of wood. "I'd never want to make him uncomfortable."

"Maybe he could benefit from this arrangement," Maggie says. "Maybe he could find a way to use you, too."

I cringe. "Can't we just use each other as friends? Or not use each other at all?"

"You could, but the *girlfriend* of a star NFL coach sounds a lot better than a *friend*. Plus, it's the holidays." She sighs wistfully and glances out the large window to her left. The glass is nearly frosted over, but you can see the city covered in a blanket of white, six inches of snow coming down overnight. "This time of year is magical. It's romantic. Holding hands while you ice skate and try not to fall over. Sitting in front of a fireplace, curled up with a blanket and a good book. Doesn't that sound nice? Who does it hurt if you two pretend for a little while?"

"I have to talk to Shawn first," I say. "This is a *big* ask of him."

"How is he handling all of this?"

"No clue. I woke up to a phone call from my mother, saw the frenzy that the damn kiss created, and opened the door for you."

Maggie scoots closer to me. She puts her head on my shoulder and sighs. "How are *you* handling all of this?"

"I don't know. I didn't realize there would be repercussions because of what he—*we*—did. It was bigger than a spur-of-the-moment thing—they're talking about it on *Good Morning America*. I just don't want anyone to get hurt," I say. My eyes start to sting, and I blink away tears. "He's my best friend, Mags, and I'd never want to jeopardize our friendship."

"Was it a good kiss?" she asks.

My smile pulls at the left side of my mouth, then the right. I rub my thumb over the spot Shawn kissed yesterday. I can still feel him there, a phantom touch that followed me home after we slurped down milkshakes and devoured a plate of cheese fries—just like always.

What's different is the lingering buzz on my lips, the memory of his teeth sinking into my skin and the sound he made when I pulled on the ends of his hair, right above his ears.

I was messing with him when we were joking around; his tongue isn't too slippery. Everything about the moment was perfect, down to the snowflakes that stuck to his cheeks. I wanted to kiss those off, too.

"Yeah," I admit. "It was good."

Maggie giggles and squeals. "I knew it would be. Nothing about it looked nice."

"It wasn't." My smile dips into one that's secret. Something I'm not ready to share with anyone else yet. "He said I deserved better than nice. And I do."

NINE

SHAWN

THE INTERCOM in my living room buzzes—again—at half past seven on Monday night.

"I don't want to talk to the press, Arthur," I tell my doorman for the tenth time today. I lean against the wall and scrub my hand over my face. "The answer is still no comment. And if they want more than that, they can go through my publicist. Haley is in charge. I'm not saying another word."

"It's not the press, sir," Arthur says. He pauses, and I hear a muffled conversation followed by a laugh. "It's Ms. Daniels."

Lacey.

"Send her up," I say, and my heart drops to my feet.

I pace in front of the door, and I'm practically vibrating with nerves. With anticipation. With fear. With... with a whole slew of other emotions I'm not sure how to process, because I'm delirious, I'm hungry, and I'm in desperate need of a shower. And a good night of sleep after spending last night tossing and turning.

Today has been a fucking mess. I fielded calls from my publicist and family all morning. I ignored the stream of messages the players sent to me, three hundred emails piling up in my inbox before noon.

They're nothing substantial. Stupid GIFs and memes of a wedding chapel. A dozen hearts and links to engagement rings. A screenshot of an order placed for an industrial-sized box of condoms with the caption, *wrap it up, Coach.*

I turned my phone off for good around three, wedging it between my mattress and bed frame and refusing to check it again. I shoved my laptop in there, too. I might keep them there forever.

They've been distracting, hours of mindless scrolling on gossip sites that think they have all the facts. Glimmers of our lives thrust into the public eye. It's scary how many strangers care about two people they've never met.

I've wanted to talk to Lacey all day. To reach out and ask how she's doing, but I haven't had a second to breathe. When I stepped outside to grab lunch with Aiden, bundled up in our hoodies and jackets in what I thought was a decent enough disguise, I was bombarded with microphones and a reporter from TM-fucking-Z asking if I wanted to talk about my "whirlwind romance."

We went right back in and ordered takeout, but I couldn't eat the sushi we had delivered.

It's been hours of stewing, hours of thinking—*knowing*—I did something wrong.

In the moment, though, I wasn't thinking. I saw Lacey hurting, and I did something about it. A quick fix and temporary Band-Aid that comes with colossal consequences but...

I wouldn't take it back.

That was the best kiss of my fucking life.

I've gone twenty-one months without having any sort of attraction to Lacey besides acknowledging the well-known fact she's a gorgeous woman with a wicked smart brain, a kind heart, and a sharp sense of humor that has me clutching my sides with laughter almost every time she talks.

I never wanted to fuck her or touch her, but there's a physical component now.

I know what her mouth feels like against mine. I know how soft she is and how sweet she tastes. I know that when you bite her lower lip, she arches her back and lets out a little moan. I know too many things about Lacey Daniels, and I didn't get a lick of sleep because of them.

I'm not sure I'll ever sleep again.

She barely has time to finish knocking before I'm opening the door and she's *there*. I've never been so glad to see someone in my life.

"Hey," I say.

"Hi," she answers. She smiles, and it reaches every corner of her face. The little wrinkles around her eyes and across the bridge of her nose. Her rosy cheeks. The confident roll of her shoulders and the flip of her hair. "Can I come inside?"

"Of course." I step back and gesture her in. We always hang out at Maggie and Aiden's, but Lacey strolls into my apartment like she's been here a thousand times. She surveys the foyer then heads for the living room, and I'm hot on her heels. "Can I get you a drink? Some water? Wine?"

She looks at me over her shoulder. Her hips sway from side to side as she crosses the floor and takes a seat on the couch. She kicks off her boots, leans back, and tucks her legs up under her. "I'll take a whiskey," she says.

"We're diving in, huh?" I ask.

"It's been a day."

"I'll drink to that." I head for the liquor cabinet situated under a framed photo of my team at the Super Bowl in 2010. I pull out two highball glasses and unstop the decanter of amber liquid. "How do you take it? On the rocks?"

"Neat," she says, and I glance up at her, impressed. "And I'll take three fingers."

"My kind of woman," I say.

I pour two matching glasses and take the seat beside her on the couch. I hand her one of the drinks and she knocks it against mine.

"Cheers," she says, and she downs half the contents in a single gulp.

"How are you doing?" I ask, too afraid to drink my alcohol.

"Did something bad happen?" Her eyes meet mine, and I see a twinkle in the green. "I'm okay. Today's been a lot. I'm off on Mondays, thank god, and it's given me time to do some damage control. I haven't quite convinced my mother we're not together, but I'm close."

"Same." I swirl the liquid around and bring the glass to my lips. I take a small sip and relish in the bite of harshness on my tongue. "I gave the guys today off. Half because I'm mentally exhausted, and half because I didn't want them to give me shit. You should see some of the things they've sent me. I don't know how they don't have second-hand embarrassment from the crap they've said."

"Ah. So that explains the Just Married flower arch down in your lobby. There are roses everywhere. I crushed about a hundred petals on my walk to the elevator," Lacey says, and my mouth pops open. I'm going to *kill* them. "Just kidding. I would've kicked it down."

I laugh. "You and me both."

"Fuck the patriarchy."

"Hear, hear."

"I'm not showing up under the most selfless pretenses, though," she admits. She finishes the rest of her drink and sets the glass down on the table to her left. She props her elbow up on the arm of the couch and cradles her cheek in her hand. "I want to talk to you about something."

"What's up?"

"The kiss. Or, more aptly, the aftermath of the kiss."

The blood drains from my face. I knew this was coming, a conversation that needed to be had about the mistake we made. Her words echo in my ears and I turn my glass around in my hands, staring at the grooved edges instead of her.

"I'm sorry, Lace. It was stupid, I know. I shouldn't have—"

She interrupts me by lifting her hand, and I stop talking. "I'm not mad. It's in the past, and we can't change the past. Besides..." she dips her chin, and her assuredness drops. Wavers around the edges and turns bashful and shy. "It was a good kiss."

I blow out a breath and throw back the rest of my drink. I might need four more. Fuck, maybe I need the whole decanter.

"It was a very good kiss," I agree, and my voice catches in my throat.

"I have a favor to ask. The hospital has our annual holiday gala in December. It's a big fundraising event with a silent auction and an open bar. They rent out one of the Smithsonian's," she starts.

"Which one?" I ask.

The question catches her off guard. Derails the speech she has planned. Her fingers trace the outline of one of the square decorative pillows propped under her thigh, and she smiles. "The Museum of American History."

"My favorite. I love the Sesame Street stuff. I was a big fan as a kid."

"Really? I can't picture you doing anything except catching a football and yelling into a headset."

"Picture it. I was in front of my television every Thursday to watch the new episodes with a bowl of Cheerios. I needed a place to turn my mind off and just be a kid, you know? People were talking about the high school team I'd play on when I was ten. Where I was going to go to college when I turned thirteen. The NFL before I even took an algebra class. I didn't have a lot of chances to grow up like the rest of the kids my age. When I saw Big Bird and Elmo, it reminded me I was *allowed* to have those childish moments. I was allowed to still be figuring everything out."

"It was your safe space," she says softly. She adjusts her position on the couch and turns her body to face me. Her knee presses against my thigh, and I hate that I want to reach out and touch her. "Just like classical music."

"I never thought of it that way, but you're right. My thoughts are constantly in overdrive. I like places that... that calm me. That bring me back to earth. That let me know it's okay to make mistakes because I'm human, just like everyone else, and I'm going to mess up."

We lapse into silence, but it's the comfortable kind. The quiet between two friends who are contemplating, considering and pausing for reflection. I so rarely get these moments, a career in a fast-moving sport where it's nearly impossible to blink without missing something important. But against the leather of my couch and with her by my side, I'm content.

"It feels wrong to ask for my favor now," Lacey says. "It's selfish."

"You? Selfish? Impossible."

"You haven't heard what I'm going to say."

"Doesn't change my opinion. You facilitated a program where children without insurance can get general pediatric care and immunizations, Lace. There's not a selfish bone in your body."

She huffs. We're sitting so close, I can feel her exhale on my skin and down the line of my neck. It slips underneath my T-shirt and lodges behind my ribs.

I *really* want to touch her, and I don't know why.

"The holiday gala at the hospital," she says. "Tickets just to get in cost two thousand dollars a chair, and that doesn't include any of the bids on items people donate. My boss decides who his favorite employees are by what they bring to the silent auction. The more valuable the item, the more you get on his good side. It's all about the money to him. There's this job opening I'd be perfect for, but he hasn't filled it yet."

"Your boss sounds like a dick. Want me to buy the hospital and fire him? Replace him with someone who actually cares about his employees?" I ask.

Lacey laughs. "Yeah. Okay. Like you have that kind of money."

I tilt my head to the side and stare at her. "I do have that kind of money."

"Thanks for the offer, but a hospital close to going into debt doesn't sound like the best investment." Her chuckle is feeble, and she shakes her head. "I was wondering if you—if we—could play into this charade of us being in a relationship. And maybe you could donate some one-on-one coaching sessions for the auction? Just a couple of hours. It would help the hospital, and only be until the new year."

"You want us to date?" I ask, and I blink at her.

"Pretend to date," she clarifies. "Not for real. Just until the gala."

I stand and head back to the liquor cabinet. I grab the decanter of whiskey and pour myself another glass—fuller this time, and the liquid nearly spills over the rim. It's going to give me the courage I need to propose *my* idea, the one that just came to me while I stared at her and talked about my childhood.

"I'd be open to that, if you'll do something for me in return."

"Anything."

"You come home with me for Christmas. You meet my family

so they can get off my back about my love life. And, to sell that, you'll have to come around the stadium more. Attend a couple of team functions. That kind of thing."

"Wow." She blows out a breath and runs her hand through her hair, twirling the ends around her fingers. "I was not expecting that."

"Both my sisters come home for the holidays. They have big families with kids and partners. I'm happy showing up by myself, but I stick out like a sore thumb at the dinner table. With this news coming out that we're allegedly dating and I'm settling down... it got my mom's hopes up. I know it's a lot to ask. You can say no; I won't be mad. I guess I'm thinking if we're on this train we might as well ride it."

Lacey is silent. She looks over her shoulder at the floor-to-ceiling bookshelves on the far side of the room. Her eyes move to the Christmas tree in the corner, the real one Maven forced me to buy even though it's not Thanksgiving yet. She lands on the photos hung on the walls, the happy memories of childhood and my career displayed in three dozen four-by-six glass frames.

"Okay," she says. "But I have a couple of conditions."

"Let's hear them."

"First and most important: this doesn't change our friendship. If at any point either of us feel weird or uncomfortable, we take a step back. I don't want to compromise the almost two years we've spent getting to know each other as friends just for a holiday gala or family dinner."

"Agreed," I say. "What else?"

"We tell Aiden and Maggie it's fake when we see them on Thanksgiving. I don't want to lie to them."

"Or Maven," I add.

"No physical affection unless it's necessary," she continues. "Physical complicates things, and we're going to have a lot on our plate. We don't need complicated."

"I'll get on board with the physical affection boundary, but if we're going to do this, we're going to be exclusive. We're not dating other people, real or fake. No one touches you but me."

Her throat bobs, but she nods in agreement. "Fair. That could be messy."

"Especially with this media circus on us," I say.

"We need to set an end date," she says. "A hard stop where we know this arrangement will be over, so there isn't any confusion."

"New Year's," I suggest. "It's after the holidays. We'll both get what we want out of this, then go our separate ways."

"Separate ways as fake romantic partners," Lacey says. "Our friendship is non-negotiable."

"Would you miss me, Daniels?" I joke.

She turns her head, and our gazes meet. There's apprehension behind her eyes, the courage she fostered when she waltzed in here in a slow demise. Her chin dips, and her eyelashes flutter closed, then open.

"Yes," she says, so soft I almost miss it. "I would."

The three words lodge themselves in my chest. Nestle right against my heart in a spot I want to protect and keep safe. It's an ache, almost. A bruise that won't go away.

"You're never going to get rid of me, Lace," I say. "We're friends for the long haul."

Lacey lets out a breath, and her smile is tentative, hesitant. I find myself wondering how I could make her grin again. "Good." She checks the silver watch clasped around her wrist and stands. "I should get going."

I rise to my feet. "I'll see you at Thanksgiving, right?"

"Right. I'm bringing pumpkin pie."

"God." I groan in anticipation of the homemade dessert she bakes for the holiday. She brought one last year, and I licked the crumbs clean off my plate. The dollop of whipped cream, too. "I'm going to gain ten pounds."

"Wouldn't kill you." She holds out her hand and wiggles her fingers. "Pleasure doing business with you, Holmes."

"And you," I say.

Her palm is dwarfed by my massive hand, and we shake our arms up and down until a laugh bursts out of her and she pulls away, untangling our limbs and walking backward to the door.

"We'll talk more soon?" she asks.

"I'll text you tomorrow," I promise.

"Looking forward to it."

"If there are any reporters still lingering around, Arthur will keep you inside until you can grab a car home."

"Where's the fun in that?" Lacey asks. "I'm going to tell them we had raunchy sex and give them all the salacious details. Food was involved. Balloon animals, too."

"Balloon animals? What the hell would you do with balloon animals?" I ask.

Her smirk is infectious, lightning to my system. "I don't know, Shawn. You're a smart guy. Be creative," she says, and I hear her cackling all the way down the hall.

TEN

LACEY

I WALK into pandemonium on Thanksgiving.

Chester, Maggie and Aiden's tabby cat from the rescue shelter in town, darts between my legs. Maven scoots past me on the skateboard she got for Christmas last year and waves hello. I spy Maggie in the kitchen, clutching a wine glass in her hand like her life depends on it. Her cheeks are pale and her eyes are wide. She mouths something to me, but I can't understand what she's trying to say.

Her parents and Aiden's parents are meeting for the first time today to celebrate Thanksgiving with their children. The older couples crowd around a charcuterie board decorated with jam and crackers and artisanal cheeses, and it seems like everything is going well.

I shut the door to the apartment with the heel of my boot. I revel in the laughter, in the conversation and warmth welcoming me as I walk inside. I might not be home with my family for the holiday, but this is as good as it gets.

"Hey." Shawn slides up next to me. He bends down and kisses my cheek, his hand on my hip and his cologne tickling my nose. I smell a mix of spice and sweet, and I smile at the familiar scent.

"Hi. Happy Thanksgiving." I stand on my toes and kiss his cheek in return. "Am I late?"

"No. Maggie and Aiden did two airport runs this morning at the crack of dawn." He takes a step back and eyes my leather skirt and the tights on my legs. "You look nice."

"Thanks. So do you," I say, and I admire his plaid shirt unbuttoned over a plain white tee. His jeans fit him impeccably well, and the sneakers on his feet look freshly cleaned. "It's good to see you in something other than your joggers."

"I probably should have worn something with more give in the waist. The button on my pants is going to pop open before we finish cutting the turkey." Shawn smiles. "Let me take those pies from you."

"So you can eat them?" I elbow his stomach as I head toward the kitchen, meeting nothing but muscle and firm lines of a toned body. He was probably at the gym before heading over here this morning, sweating with the sunrise. "I don't think so, buddy."

"Just a taste," he says.

"You can wait, just like everyone else."

"You don't play fair."

"I play fair. You're the one who's lacking self-control."

His hand rests heavy on my elbow and his fingers press into my skin, burning their way through the sleeve of my shirt. His grip tightens on my arm, and he stops me from moving forward. With a tug and a spin, I'm facing him, and I nearly drop the two pies as my back connects with the foyer wall.

"I have plenty of self-control, Lacey," he says, and there's a roughness in his voice that wasn't there before. "But you should know I can be very persuasive when needed."

His touch moves to the inside of my wrist. He rubs a small

circle over my pulse point with his thumb, and I wonder if he can feel my heart hammering in my blood. I can.

Shawn blinks, and for the first time since I've known him, I notice the freckles across the bridge of his nose. A dusting of dots that look like constellations in the night sky. I see the hint of gray in his eyes, the hue as light as a wisp of smoke. Heat radiates from him, a furnace that engulfs me and draws me closer.

A rebuttal sits in my throat, but I swallow it down. I'm not sure what I want to say, because with Shawn staring at me, words are hard to come by.

"Thank god you're here." Maggie breaks the spell between us. Shawn takes a step back and my arm falls to my side. He runs a hand through his hair, and I remember to breathe. Color takes over his cheeks, and he clears his throat. "Are you two okay?"

"Fine," we say in unison.

"Shawn was trying to weasel his way into getting a slice of pie, but it didn't work. Guess he's not as persuasive as he thought he was," I say, and I wink in his direction. The pink on his cheeks deepens to crimson red, and I count his blush as a win.

"There will be plenty of time for pie later. I'm in crisis mode. Marjorie, Aiden's mom, and my mom are planning a lunch for next week. They live seven hundred miles from each other," Maggie says.

"And that's bad, why?" I ask.

"What if my mom tells her about the time I snuck into the turtle exhibit at the aquarium? Or when I laughed so hard at a stand-up comedy show, I peed my pants? God, or that I failed my driver's test the first time I took it because I can't parallel park to save my life? I like Marjorie thinking I'm a delightful woman. I need you as backup."

"To be fair, I think it's a rite of passage to fail the parallel parking portion of the driver's test. A test of resilience, if you will," I say. "And of course Marjorie will think you're a delightful woman. Just don't tell her you and Aiden fucked on the counter where she's currently eating crackers, and you'll be all set."

"Jesus," Maggie mumbles. She loops her arm through mine and pulls me toward the kitchen. "Maybe I should leave you over here."

"Careful with the pies, Mags," Shawn says. "Don't let Lacey drop them."

"You and these damn pies," I answer. "I'm going to smash one in your face if you're not careful, and they're not even that good. They have way too much nutmeg."

"Smash away, Lace. If I want something, I tend to get it. And I want those damn pies."

"Yeah?" I run my finger across the whipped cream on top of the smaller dessert, and I hold out my hand. "Prove it."

He narrows his eyes. "Are you sure about that?"

"Of course I am." I wiggle my fingers. "C'mon, *honey*. Where's that self-control?"

I'm taunting him. Riling him up for a reason I don't know, but it's fun to watch his eyebrows lift in surprise. To watch his lips twist into a smile that makes other girls weak in the knees. For me, it just makes me smile, too.

"If you insist, *sweetheart*," he says lowly, and *oh*, I kind of like it when he calls me that.

His fingers fold around my wrist and his tongue sneaks out of his mouth, running up the length of my finger. His lips close over the tip, over the purple nail polish I painted on last night, and he sucks the topping right off.

I did not think this through.

It wasn't meant to be erotic and sexy, foreplay to an activity we'll never partake in because we're *friends*, but that's what it feels like this is.

His eyes pin me with a heated gaze. His tongue licks over my knuckles and he hums, a satisfied rumble from the back of his throat. The sound vibrates against my skin, and my breathing hitches.

I haven't been with a man in months, too busy with work and wanting to spend my evenings in the bathtub with a glass of wine and a trashy reality show instead of making idle conversation with someone who doesn't know what an erogenous zone is. If this is what I've been missing, though, I need to get back in the game. Nothing has felt this *good* in a long time.

I almost moan when Shawn's teeth drag up my finger and leave little bite marks on my skin. He can tell, the asshole, because he smirks.

"Delicious," he says. It's barely more than a rasp, and I feel the three syllables down to my toes. I wonder how they would feel against my neck and the hollow of my throat. Between my legs. A kiss on the underside of my breast and the rest of my naked body. "I told you I can be persuasive."

"Maybe. But you're still not getting any pie," I say when I find my voice, dragging Maggie with me as I escape Shawn's clutches.

"What was *that*?" Maggie asks. "Is there something you need to tell me?"

"Yes," I say, and her eyes light up. "But not in the way you're thinking."

"Are you sure about that?"

"Positive."

"AIDEN, THE TURKEY WAS PHENOMENAL," I say. I lean back in my chair and stretch my arms over my head. "Much better than last year."

"Last year it was bone dry," he says from across the crowded table, shaking his head. "That's what I get for being distracted by football."

Shawn wipes his mouth with his napkin and sets the cloth on his empty plate. "I thought we could wrap up today by each share something we're thankful for this year. I do it with my guys in the locker room, and it's a nice reminder of what the day is about."

"That's a great idea, Uncle Shawn. I'll go first," Maven says, and she bounces in her seat. "I'm thankful for my friends and my family. Oh! And having strong enough legs to run cross-country and track. And to play soccer."

"You have your mother to thank for those legs, Mae. I just have tree trunks," Aiden says. He nods at Katie, his ex-wife, who smiles and rests her head on her partner's shoulder. "I'm thankful for a good co-parenting relationship which allows us to spend holidays with our magnificent daughter. I'm the luckiest dad in the world."

"Ugh, gross." Maven sticks out her tongue. "You're being uncool, Dad."

"I'm thankful for both sets of our parents being healthy enough to travel to see us," Maggie says. "I've always wanted a big Thanksgiving. Thank you all for making my dream come true."

We go around the table, and everyone shares what makes today special to them. Pets and food and the crossword puzzle in the Sunday newspaper. An upcoming trip to Aspen and long walks on the beach at the tail-end of summer. When it's my turn to share, I cross my legs under the table and smooth my hands over my skirt.

"I'm thankful for the opportunity to slow down," I say. "My life is busy with work and patients and people needing me. And, as much as I love my job, I'm grateful to take a deep breath and spend a few hours with people I care about. Maggie and Aiden, thank you for opening up your home to us and giving us a place to be today. It means a lot."

Maggie reaches over and takes my hand in hers. She sniffs and blinks away tears. Her shoulders shake with quiet laughter. "Damn you for making me emotional," she says.

"I'm sorry." I nudge her. "What are best friends for?"

Shawn scoots back in his chair and stands. Our attention settles on him, and he smiles. "I'm thankful for each and every one of you at this table. I know what I signed up for when I took the head coaching job with the Titans; being away from my family for long stretches of time. Games on holidays. A chaotic schedule that makes it difficult to keep people around. We're not blood, but you all are my family, too. I'm such a lucky bastard that I have you all in my corner."

"To found family," I say. I lift my glass, and everyone follows suit. "And to the people who surprise us."

Shawn's eyes wrinkle in the corner and he grins at me, a display of joy I scoop up and hold close to my heart.

ELEVEN
SHAWN

"WILL you stop rinsing the dishes? You're going to be late," Aiden says.

"I have a few minutes," I argue. "I don't need to be at the stadium until five. It's only three. You're a doctor. You can do math."

"I can, and I also know you shouldn't be spending your last minutes of quiet bent over a sink with soap up your arms. How does your back not hurt, old man?"

"Asshole." I laugh and fling a handful of suds at him. "I do yoga in the morning. It's how I stay so limber."

"Must be nice. I have to sit down to tie my shoes." Aiden dries the sauce pan he used for the gravy and sets it to the side. "How are you feeling about the game today?"

"Good. The weather is nice. The guys had a productive session with Dr. Slater, our team psychologist, yesterday. They talked about burnout and maintaining intensity when it feels like no one can touch us. Lunch was fucking superb, and I'm in a decent mood. Things are going well."

"That speech you gave at the table tugged at my heart-strings." He clasps my shoulder. "I know you miss being home this time of year, but I'm glad we get to spend the day together."

"Me, too. Thanks for having us."

His eyes flick over to the living room where Maggie, Maven and Lacey sit with mugs of hot chocolate and a third slice of pie. Both sets of their parents left for their hotels, wanting to grab a nap after the meal. Katie and her partner dipped out, too, on a shopping mission to hopefully beat the crowds at midnight.

"How are you doing after the kiss cam shit show? You and Lacey seem to be okay."

"We're fine, but we wanted to talk to you all about something," I say. I turn off the faucet and dry my hands with the dishrag hanging under the sink.

"Is this a good something or a bad something?" Aiden asks.

"It's... something. And probably not what you're thinking."

"You don't know what I'm thinking."

"I don't, but I see that smirk on your face, and you need to cut it out," I say.

"Am I wrong for wanting my friends to get together? You make each other laugh. You have fun with her. It looks like there is chemistry," Aiden says. "Is there not?"

"No. Not... not like that. Nothing like that. It's platonic. I enjoy being around her," I explain. "How can you not? She's *Lacey*."

He hums and drapes a towel over his shoulder. "Okay," he says.

"Okay?" I narrow my eyes. "What do you mean, okay?"

"I mean, okay. If you say you don't have any feelings for her, then I believe you."

"It's weird you're not putting up a fight."

"It's weird you think I would try. Come on. Grab your dessert plate and tell us what you want to tell us," Aiden says.

I cut a heaping slice of pie and cover it with whipped cream and an extra dash of cinnamon I find in the spice cabinet. Lacey's baking is top-notch, and the stomachache I'm going to have on the field later will be worth it.

We walk to the living room and Aiden takes the spot on the couch next to Maggie. He presses a kiss to her forehead and she looks up at him, color splashed on her cheeks and love in her eyes.

Lacey's gaze meets mine, and she sticks out her tongue. I huff out a laugh and sit in the chair by the electric fireplace I love so much, the leather warm under my legs and a blanket behind my back.

"We have something to share with you all," Lacey says. She sets her empty plate aside and scoots to the edge of the couch. She crosses her legs and folds her hands on top of her knees. "Shawn and I are going to be seeing each other as romantic partners through the holidays. We wanted to give you all a heads up because there might be photos of us looking cozy and intimate, and we don't want to give anyone close to us the wrong idea about something that isn't true."

"You two are *dating?*" Maven asks. She claps her hands together and squeals. "Oh, my god. This makes me so happy."

"Sorry to burst your bubble, kid," I say. "It's fake. We don't like each other like that."

"Why not?" Maven's smile falls into a frown. "You two are always laughing with each other. I see you look at her when you think no one is watching. Plus, Lacey is so fun and so pretty. You can't do much better than her."

"Wow." Lacey grins and gives Maven a fist bump. "I didn't even pay her to say so many nice things about me."

"Best aunt ever." Maven's attention flicks to me. "What do you have to say for yourself, Uncle Shawn?"

The tips of my ears burn pink under her scrutinizing gaze.

Teenagers are fucking *ruthless*, and it feels like I'm walking into an interrogation.

"While I agree with your sentiments, Mae, Lacey and I enjoy spending time together as friends. We're both very busy people, and relationships are a lot of work. Work I'm not sure we have the energy for right now."

Lacey nods in agreement. "Shawn is one of my favorite people in the world, but our love lives aren't the priority. With this plan, there won't be any pressure on us to act a certain way or spend a certain number of hours together. It's all for show."

"My mom desperately wants me to bring someone home for the holidays," I say. "It's a whole family affair. My sisters come, and they bring their partners and kids. I'm sick of people looking at me like I'm a pathetic pile of sh—crap just because I'm alone at the dinner table on Christmas."

"And I'm going to have Shawn accompany me to the holiday gala at the hospital like you suggested, Mags," Lacey adds. "He's also going to donate a couple of coaching sessions for the silent auction. Plus, it might help my chances of getting the chief physician position at the office."

"We can both get what we want out of this," I say, ping-ponging off of her. "Think of it as a business transaction. An exchange of goods and services. My agent is going to release a statement this afternoon before the game confirming I'm in a relationship with someone and we're asking for privacy. Lacey's going to be in the box this evening so the press can get some photos, and that will be that."

"Privacy?" Aiden laughs. He drapes his arm around Maggie's shoulder and pulls her close to his chest. "Shawn, you couldn't walk outside your apartment building without getting run over by photographers and reporters the day after the kiss cam. The masses found Lacey's social media accounts within hours. They ran a whole segment on ESPN about your dating life and how your personal relationship might affect the Titans' chances of making the Super Bowl. A reach, if you ask me, but you're naïve if you think you two are going to have any privacy."

"I think it's too late to not use it to our advantage," Lacey says, and she pulls on the hem of her short skirt. I see frills at the top of her thigh-high stockings and I avert my eyes, my hand running over my jaw. "We kissed in front of thousands of people. The video circulated, and if we're going to be the subject of conversation without even being present for the discussion, we're going to find some good in this. Shawn coming to the gala will do tremendous things for our list of sponsors. Going home with him for Christmas means less family strain, and everyone is happy. Actions have consequences. What we did is out in the world now, whether we like it or not, and I'm not letting anyone but us control the narrative."

Lacey is firm and final, her decision about how we move forward made. My feet drop to the floor and I stare at her. I wish there was a way to hide her away, to keep her out of the spotlight and not thrust her into this world of interviews and invasive questions.

The media—and the public—are in a phase where they want to know everything about athletes and who they are dating. I can blame the starting quarterback for the Cincinnati Renegades for that. He started seeing a music superstar in September, and the internet lost its damn mind over the images of him helping her out of a car.

Since then, a gossip reporter has been staked out at every professional sports stadium, trying to get the dirt on who the men in the leagues might be bringing to bed every night. It comes with the territory; the better your team is, the more atten-tion is placed on you. And with attention comes interest in knowing every detail about your life.

I should have left Lacey out of it.

"How is this going to work?" Aiden asks. "Are you all going to be affectionate with each other? What are the rules? What do you need from us?"

"We need you to not start shit," I say, and I narrow my eyes in their direction. "No meddling. I know what you're both thinking, and the answer is no. We do what we have to in front of the cameras. In here, with you all, it's exactly the same as it's always been."

Maven looks around the room. "What are they thinking?"

"Adult things," I say. "I'll tell you in five years."

"I am an adult," she answers, and she rolls her eyes as she flops back against the couch cushions. "Still think you two should just date."

"Thanks for the comments from the peanut gallery." I cut off a bite of pie and shove the forkful of food into my mouth. "This is going to work out just fine."

"Yeah," Lacey agrees. "No drama. No feelings. No one gets hurt. We're adults, and we're going to come out of this as friends. It's no big deal, really."

"Okay," Maggie says. "If you think this is going to work, we support you. It's a good idea, and if it makes everyone happy, that's even better. Just—" she glances at Aiden, and he gives her a nod. "We love both of you. Can we talk about the other side of this for a minute? I know I might have suggested it, Lace, but I'm worried about what happens if something goes wrong. What if someone gets hurt?"

I look over at Lacey, and she chews on her bottom lip. I know we talked about our friendship coming first, but there's always the possibility of something derailing our plan. She's probably thinking the same things as me.

What if this tears our friendship apart?

What if I lose her in the process?

What if I fuck up the good things I have going for me?

Friends who love me. Nieces and a goddaughter who look up to me. A team I've worked so hard to bring back from the brink of extinction. A family who gives me shit about being single, but deep down, really just wants me to be happy.

"That's not going to happen," Lacey says. She stands from the couch and walks toward me. She perches on the arm of the chair I'm sitting in, and I'm kind of tempted to pull her into my lap. "Shawn and I both know how fortunate we are to have you all in our lives. We'd never do anything to jeopardize that. This is going to be fun." She looks down at me and smiles. "I don't know about you, but I could use a little fun in my life. Maybe you can whisk me off to Saint-Tropez on your yacht. Oh, or you could take me skiing in the Alps."

I match her smile with one of my own. "Sorry to disappoint you, but I don't own a yacht."

She rolls her eyes. "No yacht? Is it too late to end this relationship?"

I laugh and hold up my plate. "I guess I'll buy a yacht if it'll make you happy. I need to keep you around for your baking."

"Asshole." She laughs and shoves my shoulder. "Glad to know I'm appreciated."

"See?" I grin at my friends. "We're going to be just fine."

TWELVE
LACEY

"THANKS FOR PUTTING me in the box tonight," I say as Shawn opens the door to his Range Rover. "It's freezing outside."

"What? Standing in the cold doesn't sound appealing?" he asks. He offers me his hand so I can climb inside the car, and I take it. "Could've fooled me."

"Frostbite on my toes is not on the list of things I enjoy, believe it or not." I wiggle against the leather interior, grateful for his fancy car with its fancy heated seats he can start from upstairs. "Who are you playing today?"

"The Tornadoes. They have the second-best record in the league behind us. If we want to go to the Super Bowl, they're going to be our toughest competition in the post season." Shawn starts the ignition and adjusts his mirrors. "I told Dallas his sister can sit in the box with you tonight. She's in town with her daughter visiting for Thanksgiving, and I didn't think they'd have a lot of fun down in the bleachers. Don't worry—she's chill. I've met her once or twice, and she's down to earth."

"That was nice of you. There's plenty of room to share. It's going to be weird being at a game without Maggie and Aiden."

"Maggie fell asleep mid-bite on the couch. I don't think she'd enjoy watching football tonight." He chuckles and pulls onto the road. "Snow's really coming down, huh?"

"The news said it's a record for the most amount of snowfall this early in the year. I like it." I glance out the window and smile at the houses decorated with Christmas lights and big blow-up reindeer. "It makes it really feel like the holidays."

"We leave for California on Thursday. Not a lick of snow out there," he says.

"Do you ever get messed up with time zones? It must be confusing being in a different place every week."

"It's not too bad. Three hours is manageable. When we were in London last year for two weeks, I was fucked up. I couldn't sleep for days. The jet lag hit my ass hard." He glances over at me and grins. "That's what happens when you get old."

"Okay, Father Christmas. Should we talk about the logistics of tonight?"

"So forward of you. Buy me dinner first, Daniels."

I flick his ear. "Be serious for a minute."

"Fine." He turns off the radio and silence fills the car. "We enter the stadium through the player's tunnel off the garage. There is usually a reporter or two lingering around, but I'm not sure how many will be there tonight. More, probably. Maybe some cameras, too. To the left is the hallway the press can't access, so we're safe in there. Security will take you up to the box, and no one is allowed in without credentials. You don't have to worry about being bothered. After the game, I talk to the guys in the locker room, then I have a league-mandated press conference that lasts about twenty minutes. Then we'll be good to leave."

"League-mandated?" I ask. "It's required of you? I had no idea."

"Yeah. The commissioner is trying to foster this relationship between the coaches and the media. I respect the freedom of speech and why he's doing it, but I also think we need to put some boundaries in place. When we were on a losing streak my first year, some dickbag journalist thought he was being funny when he called my playing career a joke. He said he couldn't believe a team would hire someone without any experience as the head coach—especially someone who had a panic attack on the field back in college. As if that diminishes all my other capabilities. He said some nasty things about one of my sisters, too, and I almost climbed over the table and punched him. I've matured a lot since then, believe it or not."

"Fuck that guy," I say fiercely. "Using personal shit in an interview should be off-limits."

"Should be, but it isn't. It makes no sense to me; these people want to hound us with their questions, but the second an athlete speaks out about any of the political or social issues happening in our world, we're told to shut up and just play." Shawn sighs. "It is what it is. Anyway, tonight shouldn't be too bad. Someone might try to stop us when we're walking in, but other than that, we should be okay."

"Are we going to—" I swallow and adjust the beanie on my head. I don't know how to bring up this subject without it sounding weird. "Touch? Hold hands? I don't want to be caught off guard."

"Oh." His eyes flick over to me, then back to the road. "I didn't think about that, to be honest."

"We could," I say. "Hold hands. That's safe, right? You've held my hand before—remember the time after we went out for Maggie's birthday? I couldn't walk straight after those strawberry daiquiris."

"You almost walked into the road." His grip tightens around the steering wheel, and he nods. "Okay. Hand holding is allowed in front of the cameras."

"Where should I wait while you're doing the press conference? Do you think they're going to ask about me?"

"They're definitely going to ask about you. I was planning to just reiterate what I said before about wanting privacy, but if you want me to say something else, I will. It's not like they don't know your name."

"What do you think would get them off your back? Ignoring it or giving them the answers they want?"

"Answers, probably. I've found the more honest and open I am with them, the less they care and the less digging they do. They're like vultures when it comes to secrets; the elusive rumors always intrigue them more than the confirmed suspicions. When I was in high school and waiting to announce my college decision, they swarmed me after every game. I kept putting it off and putting it off. After I announced, it was quiet as hell. Like a breath of fresh air."

"I want you to answer however you feel comfortable. Whatever feels right in the moment. Like you said, they know my name. They already know things about me, and they're just waiting for you to say it, too. I trust you, Shawn."

I reach over and fold my hand over his arm. He's still in his clothes from Thanksgiving lunch, and there's a duffle bag in the backseat full of his game day attire. I like that he sets aside his professional life when he's not at work. It doesn't bleed into his friendships or dominate conversations. If you talked with him on the street and he didn't say his name, you'd never know who he was.

There are two sides to Shawn Holmes, and I like that I get to see both of them.

We've never arrived at the stadium together before. I usually ride with Maggie and Aiden or take the Metro when the weather is nice. Shawn always shows up three or four hours before kickoff to run through plays with his squad and write out last-minute lineup changes. He's pushing his time today, though, after eating a second piece of pumpkin pie and sipping a hot coffee. I had to practically drag him out of the chair in the corner of Maggie and Aiden's living room. He rubbed his eyes when we stepped outside into the cold winter air to wake up.

"That means an awful lot, Lace Face," he says softly. "I know I can't stop every nasty article that might be printed about you or tell you to block every asshole comment on your photos on social media. But I promise to protect you from what I can control. When you're with me, you're going to be safe, alright?"

"Alright." I nod, and I feel his words in the center of my chest.

They inflate like a balloon and fill the space behind my ribs and next to my heart. He's such a good guy, and I believe him with my whole soul.

We cruise down the highway, and the traffic is light for a late holiday afternoon. Shawn parks the car in his designated spot, and I give him shit for having **HEAD COACH** written on a sign like he's all big and fancy.

I guess to these people, he is.

I only see the guy who has a speck of whipped cream on his cheek.

I lick my thumb and lean over the center console. I wipe away the remnants from dessert, and he smiles.

"Flirting with me, Daniels?" he asks with the lift of his eyebrow.

"In your dreams, Holmes," I say, and I tug on his ear. "It's time to get out of the car, isn't it?"

"Mhm. You could stay in here the whole game, if you want. I can have someone wheel out a television for you."

"You have a lot of power, don't you?"

Shawn laughs. "Hardly. It took two weeks for me to get a new water bottle because it had to go through the proper channels before being approved. I don't get special treatment."

"NFL head coaches: they're just like us." I open my door and jump out of the car. I adjust my skirt and do a spin. "Do I look okay? Like I can pull off being the girlfriend of the league's most eligible bachelor and everyone's favorite golden boy?"

"I am *not* the league's golden boy," he says.

"Yes, my friend, you are. The people love you."

He climbs out of the car and walks toward me. He looks me up and down, and he smiles big and wide. "You look great. Minus the hole in your shirt, of course. Was that intentional?"

"What?" My hands reach for the hem of my sweater, and I search for the snag. "Where?"

He flicks my nose and laughs again. "Made you look."

"Asshole. I don't want to look like an idiot in the photos that are inevitably going to wind up on some gossip site."

"You could never look like an idiot." He holds out his hand in invitation. "Ready for the shit storm to begin?"

"Yeah." I take a deep breath and thread my fingers through his. His palm is warm, and I feel steady when he gives my hand a squeeze. Like I can conquer all of my fears. "Let's do this."

THIRTEEN

LACEY

I STAND in the crowded hallway and wait for Shawn after the game. Some of the players' families pass me, and they smile and wave as they head out to the garage. I wring my hands together, and hope I don't look ridiculously out of place.

"Hey." I glance to my right and see January, Dallas' sister, standing by the bathroom. She holds her daughter's hand and walks over to me. "Are you okay?"

We sat together in the box and had a great time. Shawn was right; she is down to earth. She's hysterical, an aspiring standup comedian who's a single mother busting her ass to give her kid a wonderful life. She also made my first game without Maggie and Aiden so *fun*, and all the fears I had about being here alone melted away.

"Yeah, I'm fine." I sigh and rub my forehead. "I'm still learning how everything works. I'm used to sitting in the stands and waiting for Shawn out in the tunnel with my friends. No one used to know my name. I could buy peanuts without someone pointing at me. It's different now. There are reporters and cameras and people who want to talk to me. And it's silly.

I'm... I'm nobody. Nobody important. Sorry. I'm being so dramatic."

"You're not dramatic at all." January scoops up her daughter, Lilah, and holds her in her arms. "It can be overwhelming. I'm the sibling of a player, not even a significant other, and people are fucking weird around me. They ask me to get jerseys signed without bothering to learn my name. They ask questions about Dallas' personal life as if I know how many people he's slept with. One girl showed me the voodoo doll she has of him, and asked if I wanted her to make me one, too. I can't even imagine what this must be like for you. Having your face put on the internet and posted on social media like you aren't a real human with real feelings is bizarre. Couldn't you have picked someone a little less well known?"

"I'll remember that for next time." I grin and rub the back of my neck, trying to get rid of the ball of tension that sits there. "It's a lot. And I realize how much of a privilege it is to say that. I'm sure millions of girls out there wish they were dating someone in the league—especially someone as kind and special as Shawn. It's just going to take some getting used to."

"It is," January agrees, and she squeezes my shoulder. "You aren't alone."

"Maybe I'll be more comfortable by the postseason," I joke, knowing fully well Shawn and I won't be faking a relationship when February comes around.

That ship will have sailed and we'll have gone our separate ways, both getting what we want out of this quick holiday fling.

I wonder if he'll still want me to come to the Titans' games. I wonder if he'll be dating someone new, and I wonder if he'll fly her out to the Super Bowl if the team makes it that far. There's a twist in my gut when I picture him with his arm around a leggy blonde at the press conference after the big win.

"Lacey? Are you okay?" January asks, and I smile.

"I'm fine. It's been a long day with Thanksgiving, then the game." I lean forward and pinch Lilah's cheeks. "I'm going to miss my new buddy. How long are you in town for?"

"Only until Sunday. I go back to work on Monday, and as much as I'd like to stay, having a toddler isn't cheap." She laughs and kisses Lilah's head. "If you ever find yourself in Georgia, my door is always open. It's a small door, with toys on the floor and a crib shoved in the corner of my bedroom, but it's open."

"Hey." I give her a gentle nudge. "A home isn't measured by the size of the structure. It's measured by what's inside. And I can tell your home has a lot of love."

"It does." January looks down at her daughter and smiles. "I wouldn't change a thing."

"There are my favorite girls." Dallas walks out of the locker room in his suit and tie with outstretched arms. Lilah squeals and wiggles, trying to get closer to her uncle. He takes her from January's hold and spins her around. "Lilah Bug. I missed you while I was playing."

"Hey, Dal," January says.

"Hey, sis." He kisses her cheek then turns to me and grins. "My third favorite girl. I shouldn't let Coach hear me say that, though. He might give me extra laps."

"Shawn can share," I joke. "Great game tonight. You all played well."

"12-0, baby," Dallas calls out, and Lilah screams with delight. "We're going to the championship."

"We've got some more games to win before that happens," a deep, rumbly voice says, and I turn around to find Shawn watching us with a smile on his face. "And I did hear you, Lansfield. You should plan to show up to practice early on Saturday."

"Dammit," the kicker groans.

"Dammit," Lilah repeats, and we all burst out laughing.

"Such a bad influence, Uncle Dallas," January tuts, and she

takes her daughter back. "It was great to meet you, Lacey. You have my number, right?"

"I do. If you're ever back in town, let me know. I'd love to get dinner," I say.

"Me too." She peers over my shoulder and looks at Shawn. "You've got a good one here."

His eyes meet mine, and his gaze is soft. "I do, don't I? Come here, sweetheart," he says, and, *gosh*, I like how nice that word sounds coming from him. I want to wrap it up in a bow and keep it for myself.

I bite my bottom lip and shuffle toward him. He slides his arm around my waist and pulls me close. He drums his fingers against my hip, and I shiver at the contact. I didn't wear his jersey tonight, opting to keep on my clothes from lunch instead. There's a small sliver of space between the start of my skirt and the hem of my shirt, and his pinky grazes across my skin.

It's maddening, and I kind of want to tug him into the supply closet to our right and see how his fingers feel on other parts of my body. Especially when he does it a second time, a slow drag that has my back arching and my toes curling.

I think the bastard is doing it on purpose, and I hate him for it.

"Happy Thanksgiving," I blurt out, and Shawn chuckles into the top of my head. "Get home safe."

The Lansfields leave, and I turn to swat Shawn's arm. He grins at me and cocks his head to the side.

"Something wrong, Daniels?"

"No," I huff, and I put my hands on my hips. "I'm fine."

"You look a little worked up."

"No thanks to you," I mumble, and his attention bounces to the hollow of my throat. "Do you want to go to the diner? You're probably exhausted, aren't you?"

"We can't break tradition," he says, and his voice is hoarse.

He coughs and lets go of me, taking a step back. "A milkshake is exactly what I need right now."

"What are we waiting for? Let's go," I say, and we head to his car.

"Did you have fun tonight?"

"It was a blast. January is so sweet. Lilah is cute, too."

"Do you want kids?" Shawn asks, then stops in his tracks. "Shit. I'm sorry. That was an incredibly personal question."

"I do want kids, but not my own." He gives me a curious look, and I smile. "I want to adopt. There are so many children out there who need a loving home, and I think I could provide that for them. I'm an only child, and I've dreamed of having these big Christmases with holiday cards and matching pajamas. Like, eight of us around the kitchen table and wrapping paper everywhere." I pause and my smile turns sheepish. "That was an overshare, wasn't it?"

"No," he says quickly. He stops us by the door out to the garage and puts his hand on my shoulder. "It wasn't an overshare. I want to know these things about you. I *should* know these things about you."

"Because we're pretending to be in a relationship, right?" I ask, and he shakes his head.

"Because you're my friend, and I care about you. I want to know all about your dreams, Lacey."

"You do?" I swallow, and heat invades my cheeks. "My dreams are boring."

"I highly doubt that. There's not a boring bone in your body," Shawn says. He touches my cheek, and I let out a breath. "Will you share your dreams with me?"

"Will you share yours with me?" I ask. "This goes both ways."

"I'll tell you anything you want to know."

"Anything?"

"Anything." He nods and hooks his thumb around my chin. "Ask away, Lacey girl."

When he calls me that, I want to melt into a puddle.

When he calls me that, it's hard to remember this arrangement of ours has an end date.

"Do you want kids? Do you want to get married?"

The questions race out of me. I don't know why I'm curious, but something in my chest tells me I need to find out. Since I've known him, Shawn's never dated anyone seriously. I've heard him mention a few one-night stands, but nothing that's lasted for longer than twenty-four hours.

He's not a player or someone who gets around a lot. He also doesn't talk about his conquests like they're a prize to show off. There's a hesitancy, I think. A reluctancy to go *all in* on someone with feelings and emotions. He'll enjoy the physical release a couple of beautiful women can give him, then he goes back to being suspiciously single, a puzzle I haven't quite figured out.

"I do," he says, and his voice hitches lower. Quieter, like he's revealing a secret side of himself no one else has ever seen. "I want both, but I'm picky."

"Picky how?" I ask, and I don't know when I got so close to him. I don't know when I grabbed a fistful of his shirt or why my heart starts to rumble in my chest. I don't remember his fingers curling around the back of my neck.

I just know that I like it.

"I'll tell you one day soon," he murmurs. His thumb brushes over my bottom lip. "Preferably when you're not standing in front of me wearing a short skirt and boots that make your legs look nice and long."

"What's wrong with my skirt?" I whisper. "I like my outfit."

"It's distracting," he says. He smiles, and it's a wicked, handsome thing. "And we have a date with milkshakes and a plate of fries."

"Right." I nod, and it feels like I've been doused in cold water. "Milkshakes," I say.

Shawn's hand falls away from my face, and he nods toward the door. "You first."

"What? Why? Please don't tell me you're going to try and scare me."

"Maybe I want to look at your ass when you walk away, Daniels."

I burst out laughing and shake my head. "Wow. At least you're honest, right?"

"What are friends for?" he asks, and I poke him in the ribs.

Friends, I tell myself.

That's all that we are.

Except this feels *a lot* like flirting.

A game we're playing, to see who can crack first.

I give him a sly grin and spin around, swaying my hips from side to side as I walk to the garage. I look at him over my shoulder and his eyes are heated. He's staring at my ass without any shame.

Point, me.

FOURTEEN
LACEY

ADDY, one of the nurses on duty, pops her head into my office.

"Lacey? There's someone here to see you," she says.

I frown and check my calendar. My afternoon is light, and I have thirty minutes until my next appointment. I even had time to sit down and eat lunch at my desk today, a small miracle for an office that's suffering from a staffing shortage during the holiday season.

"There is? Who?" I ask.

She breaks into a grin. "I think it's better if you come out here and see for yourself," she says.

I pull on my white coat and push the sleeves halfway up my arms. I move down the hall, anxiously wondering who could be waiting for me. Maybe it's Director Hannaford popping in to see what I'm bringing as my silent auction item. When I turn the corner into the waiting room, I stop in my tracks.

Shawn is near the reception desk talking with a group of kids. He's down on their level and nodding along to whatever they're saying. When he tilts his head back and laughs at something funny, my insides turn to mush.

"He's been here for ten minutes and hasn't looked bored

once. Not even when Benny Tyler sneezed on him," she says, and she gives me a knowing grin. "You're so lucky."

Shawn glances our way from across the room. He smiles when he spots me and stands up, towering over the boys and girls vying for his attention. I walk toward him, and I feel like I'm missing the hint to a riddle.

"What are you doing here?" I ask.

"Hi, baby," he says, and he winks. "I brought you a coffee and a muffin. Do you have a minute?"

"Do I—what? Yes. Uh, yeah." I pat his shoulder awkwardly, and it probably looks like I'm trying to dust off a piece of lint instead of showing him affection. "Thanks... babe."

Shawn rolls his lips together, and I can tell he's trying not to burst out laughing. "Can we go to your office?"

"Sure. Yeah." I look at the girls behind the reception desk. "I'll let you know when I'm ready for my two o'clock."

"I have some things to talk over with Ms. Lacey," Shawn tells the group of kids. "I'll see you all again soon, okay? Everyone has the invitation to the Titans' mini-camp I gave them? Good. It's almost time for the holidays. You all are going to be on your best behavior for your moms and dads and guardians, right?"

"Yes," the group says, and they hang on to his every word.

I can barely get them to look at me when I'm handing them a lollipop.

"That's what I thought." He ruffles their hair and steps toward me. He rests his hand on my lower back and holds the hallway door open. "Lead the way, Lacey girl," he murmurs low in my ear, and my feet forget how to move for a minute.

It takes a gentle nudge from Shawn for me to step forward, and I swear the asshole chuckles under his breath. We weave past nurses and patients and parents who stare at the giant man walking behind me as if they've seen a ghost.

He looks wildly out of place here, with his backwards hat

and the tattoos down to his hands, but he doesn't *act* out of place. He acts like this is exactly where he belongs.

He says hello. He stops to give a little girl a high five. A mother pulls a dirty napkin from her purse and he signs it with a flourish, not batting an eye at the ketchup stain his signature covers. When we make it to my office, it feels like I'm floating on air.

"*Baby?*" I ask as I shut the door behind us. "That's a new one."

"What?" He tilts his head to the side and grins. "Not a fan of pet names?"

"I don't have a lot of experience with them, I guess." I shrug and sit on the couch, patting the spot next to me. "It'll take some getting used to."

"How do you feel about sweet cheeks? Probably a no, right?" Shawn asks, and he sits down beside me. "Muffin?"

"Please stop." I giggle. "Both horrific."

"Fine. If you say so." He hands over a paper bag and the cup of coffee. "Here you go, bumblebee."

I swat at his arm and pull out a muffin. "Careful, Shawn. I might rely on you to make sure I'm caffeinated and fed." I grin and take a bite of the pastry. "Why are you really here?"

"It's been a few days, and you've survived your first game as a WAG. I wanted to check on you and make sure everything is okay," he says.

"WAG?" I wrinkle my eyebrows and brush some crumbs away from my mouth. "What does that mean?"

"Wife and girlfriend. Sports world slang."

"Does that imply athletes have wives *and* girlfriends?"

"Some do, but those are the shady assholes."

"And you're the good guy who's never cheated on his girl-friend, right?"

"No, I haven't. I never understood the point of cheating. Why be with someone if you don't want to be with *just* them?" Shawn asks.

"Ah. There's a modern-day Romeo. A Casanova."

He waves off my teasing and leans back, his long arms stretching over the back of the couch. "Seriously. Everything's good?"

"We were with each other until midnight on Thanksgiving. I texted you on Friday and Saturday. We watched football with Maggie and Aiden on Sunday. Why are you stopping by today?"

Shawn shrugs. "Guess I just wanted an excuse to see you, daffodil."

I roll my eyes, but I smile. "You don't need an excuse to see me, but I'll take it. Everything is fine. I'm glad you confirmed our relationship to the press. My social media comments have turned quiet the last couple of days. No complaints from me."

"I'm glad. Making sure you're okay is my number one priority, but I'll admit I'm also here under somewhat false pretenses. I'm taking a page out of your book. Cornering you like you cornered me at my place and suggested we pretend to date."

"I did not *corner* you." I set down the drink and food on the small glass table in front of us. I wipe my hands on my scrubs. "What's going on?"

"Nothing bad," he says. "It's my mom. I've been dodging calls from her since all of this," he gestures between us, "started. We have a weekly family video call scheduled for tonight, and I was hoping you could be there, too, to make it a little easier?"

His voice hitches at the end, and he doesn't have his usual confidence. He seems hesitant and unsure. Nervous, almost, like he's afraid to hear my answer. His broad shoulders curl in and his smile wavers. His eyes flick to mine then look away, suddenly interested in the stack of medical books I have on the floor against the far wall, and his leg bounces up and down.

I reach out and put my hand on his arm. I run my thumb up

his forearm and over the intricate artwork on his body. I wonder if the tattoos span across his chest. Over the curve of his shoulder and onto his back, too. I wonder what kind of designs he has over his heart, and I wonder if I'll ever get to see them.

The tattoo on his hand might be my favorite. It covers the whole back of his palm, and it's unfairly hot.

"Of course I'll be there," I say gently. "What time were you thinking?"

"Seven? I can make dinner or we could order in. I'd invite Maggie and Aiden, too, but it's their date night," Shawn says. "Are you okay with it being just the two of us?"

"Totally fine. We've hung out alone together before. It's not like I'm going to jump your bones just because you put a plate of meatloaf in front of me," I say, and Shawn laughs.

"Is that your way of telling me you want meatloaf for dinner?" he asks, and I shrug, nonchalant, as my lips curl into a smile.

"I wouldn't hate it. Wouldn't hate mashed potatoes, either."

"Deal. We can eat then tackle the Holmes clan," he says. He adjusts his hat and sighs. "There's going to be an interrogation."

"I'm good with parents," I say, and I motion toward the door. "It's kind of my job. Want me to bring wine? Dessert? For the record, this isn't a date."

His smile matches mine. "It's not, huh?"

"No." I shake my head and swipe the coffee off the table. "Definitely not. It's a required event we're obligated to take part in. Just like you joining me at the hospital gala."

"Right. And the team's holiday party you're going to come to," Shawn adds.

"Exactly. All of those things are *not* dates. They're pieces of our plan we *have* to do to get through the holiday season happy and with a promotion."

"And with a happy family," he says, and I nod.

"Bingo."

Shawn checks his watch. "I need to head to the stadium for a team meeting. Arthur will let you up when you get to my place."

"What's it like to have a doorman?"

"About the same as not having a doorman." He knocks his knee against mine and points at the muffin. "Finish your food, rose petal."

"Thank you, by the way. That was nice of you to bring me caffeine and a snack, and I really appreciate it." I stand up. I offer him my hand and make a spectacle of pretending to pull him off the couch. "Please don't break too many hearts on your way out. This is a pediatrician's office, not the emergency room."

"If you insist." He grins and heads toward the door. "See ya, Lace Face."

"Bye, Shawn Yawn. I'll let you know when I'm on my way."

"Sounds good. Miss you already, angel butt."

"Oh, my god. I'm going to hurl a stapler at you if you don't stop," I say.

He laughs and blows me a kiss on his way out, a gesture that makes my belly swoop low and a smile split across my lips.

FIFTEEN

LACEY

I KNOCK on the door to Shawn's apartment, and my heart hammers in my chest. I think about turning around and walking away, but suddenly he's *there*, in front of me, and I can't remember my name.

He looks good. *Really* good. His hair is damp, like he just got out of the shower, and his skin is tinged pink. A dark pair of jeans sits low on his hips, and his white shirt stretches across his broad chest. I can see his whole sleeve of tattoos, and he's barefoot. I smile at the nail polish on his toes.

"Going for a new look?" I ask.

Shawn leans against the door frame with a lazy grace. "Maven was trying out polish colors. I was the guinea pig."

"I like the pink."

"Really? I'm partial to the purple."

I laugh and hand over a bottle of wine. "Here. For you. For us, I guess."

"Thanks, Lace. Come in." He gestures me inside, and I step into his apartment.

I've been here once or twice—like the night I came over and proposed this whole scheme to him—but I didn't have a chance to really look around. It's an open concept layout, with high ceilings and gigantic windows. Sleek and modern, I see touches of personality throughout the space. In the pictures on the wall. The throw blankets on the couch. A plush rug in the living room. It's inviting and welcoming, and I relax as I walk into the kitchen.

There are pots on the stove. Something is cooking in the oven, and a delicious aroma wafts through the air. Placemats are set up on the island with two barstools, and wine glasses sit on the marble counter.

This man is *not* your typical bachelor.

"How can I help?" I ask.

"You can pour yourself a drink and take a seat," Shawn says. He maneuvers around me and taps my hip as he passes. A spark runs through my body with the press of his fingers. "How was the rest of your work day?"

"Good. Uneventful. The kids were disappointed to get a shot from me after you gave them free admission to the weekend camp in January. Thank you for that," I say. I slide onto a stool, and my legs swing back and forth. "That was very kind of you."

"Don't mention it. I try to hand out as many vouchers as I can to kids in the community. The revenue and finance departments might hate me, but I don't care." Shawn bends over the stove and stirs the pot. "Need a wine opener?"

"Yes, please."

"Top drawer on your right."

I lean over and rifle through a collection of scissors and other odds and ends. "Not hiding anything shady in here, are you?"

"Like I'd put all my weird shit out in plain sight," he laughs. "That's what my bedroom is for."

"Don't tempt me. I'll go snoop."

"Snoop away. What's mine is yours, frog legs."

I throw the wine cork at him and pour myself a glass. "Would you like some?"

"Sure. Thanks."

"To the best fake boyfriend I've ever had," I say, and Shawn grins.

"To the most beautiful fake girlfriend in the world," he answers, and I blush.

"Stop. You pretended to date that musician. She's gorgeous."

"So? I said what I said. Most beautiful." He knocks his drink against mine, and we take a sip in tandem. "Wow. That's good."

"It's from the liquor store up the road. I got it for twenty bucks."

"Impressive." He takes another sip and moves back to the stove. "Doing anything fun this weekend?"

"Maggie and I are going to try to get together. You leave for California soon, don't you?"

"Thursday. We kickoff around one in the afternoon west coast time on Sunday, then we'll fly back home that night. We're playing the worst team in the league, but I don't want to let our guard down."

"You'll be fine," I say. "Do you like road games?"

"Seeing different cities is fun, but I enjoy being home. It's not even like I have something waiting for me here like some of the other guys." He pulls a pan out of the oven and sets it on a hot pad. He turns to face me and leans against the counter. "It's just nice to sleep in my own bed. To be in my own space."

"I understand. Well, I don't *really* understand, but I know what you mean. Whenever I have a medical conference or I'm out of town, it's fun for a day or two. Then I'm counting down the minutes until I can be back where I feel safe and secure." I smile. "And, hey. You do have things waiting for you here. You have Maggie and Aiden and Maven. And you have me. We're friends. *Best* friends," I add. "You're not alone. You know that, right?"

"Yeah," he says. Our gazes meet, and we stare at each other. "I do know that."

"Good. Do you want to continue this heart-to-heart, or can we eat first?"

"Food. We don't have much time before the familial discussion begins. Maybe we can show up drunk," he suggests. "That would be a hoot."

———

HALF AN HOUR LATER, I'm full.

We pile our dirty dishes in the sink, and Shawn waves me off when I try to offer to wash them. He pulls me to the couch in his living room and hands me a blanket.

"Am I—do I—should we touch each other?" I blurt out. "Keep our hands to ourselves?"

"If you wanted an excuse to touch me, Daniels, you could've just asked," he says, and I roll my eyes. "Sit close to me. Like you love me so much, you're going to be sick."

I pinch his cheek. "Like this?" I scoot across the velvet until our thighs press against each other. Until I can feel the heat from his body and smell the wine on his lips.

He stares down at me. His gaze bounces to my mouth before he looks away and reaches for the laptop on his coffee table. "Perfect," he murmurs, and the praise notches into a spot at the base of my spine.

"What's your mom's name?"

"Kelly. My dad is Michael. My sisters are Katelin and Amanda." He clicks a few keys on the keyboard and sits back. "Tap my foot if it gets overwhelming."

"Why would it get over—"

"There they are," a woman says. Her face pops up on the screen next to an older man with gray hair, and she waves. "Hi, sweetie."

"Hi, Mom," Shawn says. His arm falls around my shoulders as two other boxes appear on the computer and younger women join the call. The pair look so much like Shawn, I have to do a double take. "This is Lacey."

"Hi, Mr. and Mrs. Holmes." I wave back. "Nice to meet you."

"She's beautiful. Isn't she beautiful, Michael?" Shawn's mom asks, and I blush. "Please, call me Kelly. I'm so glad you could join us tonight."

"We just finished up dinner," Shawn says. "Wanted to run through the Christmas plans with you all while we're all here."

"I'm so glad you're coming up," one of his sisters—Katelin, maybe?—says. "The girls are going to be so excited to see their uncle."

"We're going to drive up on the 22nd," he says. His fingers drum against my shoulder, and I nestle a little closer into his embrace. "We'll have to head out early on the 26th—I gave the guys Christmas off, but we're going to get in two practices before we head back on the road."

"Any time with you is better than no time with you," Kelly says. She turns her attention to me and smiles. "Lacey. Tell us about yourself."

"Oh." I sit up straight, not prepared for this. "I'm a pediatrician. My best friend is dating Aiden. That's how Shawn and I met." I glance up at him, and he's smiling down at me. His beam is encouraging, and it helps shake my nerves. "We started spending more time together, and we kind of fell for each other."

"I read the article you did for the *Journal of Pediatrics*. You're really smart, Lacey," the other sister says, and my cheeks turn even more red.

"You did? Wow, thank you." I fiddle with the ends of the blanket and twist my hands together. "I'm sure it was pretty boring."

"No way. Your opinions on bacterial pneumonia were fascinating," she says, and I want to bury my face in Shawn's chest.

I spent weeks researching the article, and I put in long hours at the library while also working full shifts. I've been recognized by colleagues for my contributions, but hearing it from a stranger holds extra importance to me. Someone looked it up because they *wanted* to, not because they *had* to, and that consideration makes me want to burst with pride.

"She's the smartest person I know," Shawn says. He rests his free hand on my thigh. I'm not sure if you can see the touch through the camera, but I don't even care. I like how his palm feels, warm and heavy on my skin.

"Thank you for letting me join you all for the holidays. It means a lot," I say. "I know traditions can be important to families."

"The only tradition we have is making cookies on Christmas Eve," sister one says.

"And a snowball fight on Christmas morning," sister two says.

"Don't forget Mom's famous egg frittata for breakfast," Shawn adds, and he's grinning from ear to ear. "Best food I'll eat all year."

"So come hungry and with an arm ready for throwing snowballs?" I ask. "Got it."

"She's going to fit right in," sister two says, and everyone nods in agreement.

"How's it been after the viral video?" Kelly asks. "You two are taking care of yourselves, right?"

"It's been fine," Shawn says, and his fingers trace up my leg. I'm not sure he realizes he's doing it, but I don't stop him. "The circus has died down temporarily. I have someone keeping an eye on Lacey, just in case a toolbag from the internet decides to act like an idiot."

My head whips to my left and I stare at him. "You *what?*" I ask, not sure I heard him correctly. "You have someone following me?"

"They aren't following you," he says. "They're making sure you're safe."

"That sounds a lot like following to me." I glare at him. "When were you going to tell me I had a stalker?"

"Hey." Shawn touches my cheek and tips my chin back. "If you want me to get rid of them, I will."

"That would be nice," I say. "Are they peeping in my windows, too?"

He glances at the screen and gives his family a sheepish smile. "We better go. I'll call you next week, Mom, to make sure everything is finalized."

"Sounds good. Love you, honey. It was great to meet you, Lacey," Kelly says, and I plaster on a smile.

"It was nice to meet you all too," I say, and I wave goodbye. "See you soon."

Shawn closes the laptop, and he sighs. "I'm sorry I didn't tell you."

I stand up and pace around his living room. "Why is someone keeping an eye on me? Are you expecting something bad to happen?"

"No." He stands up and tugs me toward him. "I care about you, okay? A whole fucking lot. And I know I'm not the most popular guy in the world, but I get letters from fans every week. Weird shit, like notes from women that say they want me to be their baby's daddy."

"I know I give you shit about your fraternity boy calendar

shoot, but you know I'm not great with football. How famous are you in the sports world?"

"I won five Super Bowls. I have the league record for most touchdowns in a season. I'm fairly famous," he admits. "I can't really control it, and now that you're associated with me, it's my responsibility to keep you safe. I am *going* to keep you safe, Lacey. I'm sorry for not telling you. That was shitty of me."

I suck in a breath. My eyes prick with tears, and I dip my chin. "You care about me?" I ask. My voice wobbles, and I sniff. "A whole fucking lot?"

"Yeah, Lacey girl," he says softly, and he tucks a piece of hair behind my ear. His thumb traces down my jaw, and my skin feels hot under his touch. "I do. Is that okay with you?"

"Yes." I nod. "That's okay with me. I care about you, too."

"Good. I promise this guy isn't looking in your windows or going through your underwear drawer. He just makes sure you get to and from work safely. He goes home at seven on the dot, and he'll stop the minute I ask him to. Some of the players on the team have security for their other halves, too."

Before I know what I'm doing, my hands are holding his shirt and I'm tugging him toward me. "I've never had someone take care of me before. Not really," I say. "Not like this."

"It's an honor to be the first," Shawn says.

"I'm sorry for getting worked up and jumping down your throat."

"And I'm sorry for not telling you."

I look up at him. He's watching me intently, and he smiles when our eyes meet. It's a different smile from what I've seen from him before. This one is secretive, almost. Soft. Special, too. It makes my heart skip a beat and my throat go dry.

"Will you let me know when you get to California?" I ask.

His touch dances down my throat and his hand settles around the back of my neck. "Worried about me, Lacey girl?"

"Yes," I whisper, and I don't miss the way he doesn't use my last name like our usual sparring matches. "I am."

Shawn hums, and I feel hot everywhere. I think lava courses through my blood at the sound. "I'll miss you," he says. "Life's more fun with a fake girlfriend by my side."

"I'll miss you too," I say back. "But only because you can cook your ass off."

He laughs and frees me from his hold. He heads back toward the kitchen, and I watch him go. "Speaking of, want dessert?" he asks over his shoulder. "I have ice cream in the freezer."

"Sure." I touch my neck where his hand rested, and I take a deep breath. "Sounds perfect."

Perfect, I think. *Just like him.*

Oh, *shit.*

SIXTEEN

SHAWN

"CURFEW IS MIDNIGHT," I say to the guys, and I stare at them from the front of the bus. "You are all grown men. I don't want another call from the front desk complaining about people sliding ice cubes down the hallway and pretending like they're bowling. Got it?"

"Yes, Coach," the team says, and I smile.

"Good. Have fun today. Nothing illegal. Nothing that will knock you off your ass. Wear your sunscreen and drink your water. It's warmer outside than it is at home, and I don't want anyone to be dehydrated at practice tomorrow. I'll see you all at ten in the morning. Last person on the field has to run five laps."

Dallas stands and holds out his arm. The other guys mimic him, a makeshift huddle forming in the aisle of the rented motor coach.

"Titans on three," he bellows. "One. Two. Three."

"Titans," they all yell, and they follow it up with a roar.

Some pound on the windows. A few others jump up and down and stomp their feet. A swell of pride rolls through me as I watch their enthusiasm.

There was a time when guys were ashamed to say they

played for the Titans. They refused to wear their jerseys and got into heated arguments in the locker room. There's a different culture in place now. It's one of respect. Of unity. Of love for each other and knowing the guy next to them on the line of scrimmage is willing to go the extra inch with them.

I don't give a shit about Super Bowls or how much money I make. At the end of the day, when my coaching career is over, I hope they don't talk about how many games I've won and lost.

I hope they talk about how I helped these men fall in love with the sport that changed their lives. I hope they talk about how I was part of something bigger than me.

"What are you doing today, Shawn?" Jackson Swift, my head assistant coach and defensive coordinator, asks. He leans against the seat and rests his elbows on the vintage fabric. "Got any plans?"

"Not really. Might go to the pool and enjoy the fresh air." I grab my bag and turn my phone off airplane mode, something I forgot to do when we touched down at LAX ninety minutes ago. "What are you all getting into?"

"We were thinking about going to Disneyland. Want to join?"

"Thanks for the offer, but I have to pass. My goddaughter would kill me if she found out I went to a theme park without her. Let me know if you're back in time for a nightcap, and we can meet up."

"Sounds good." He reaches out his hand, and I shake it. "I'll send you a text."

The team files off the bus one by one. They clasp my shoulder and shake my hand. Ruffle my hair and call me *Dad*. I'm giving them all shit—I know they'll be in bed by ten, tired after a long day of travel and soaking up the west coast sunshine. I slide my sunglasses onto my face and step off the stairs. I'm greeted by palm trees, warm air, and a breeze laced with sunscreen.

My phone buzzes in my hand, and I look down to see a stream of text messages come in. Three from Aiden. One from Maggie. Four from Maven asking what she should get her dad for Christmas. I fire off a quick response that, no, a walker isn't a funny gag gift, and she should respect her elders. She sends back an emoji with its tongue out, and I chuckle. Lacey's name pops up next, and I smile as I open our thread of messages.

> **LACE FACE**
>
> Have a good flight!
>
> I forgot you have a team plane and don't have to fly commercial like us plebeians. What's it like not having to deal with TSA and the general public who don't know you can't bring a liter of soda through airport security?
>
> Another instance of NFL coaches: they're just like us.
>
> I should start a series.

I burst out laughing. Instead of answering her with eighteen different messages like she sent me, I decide to call her instead.

"It's Malibu Shawn," she says when she picks up on the second ring. "How's the weather on the west coast?"

"I think I'm already getting a sunburn." I look up at the sky and squint. "There's not a cloud to be seen. Just a lot of blue."

"Rub it in, why don't you? It's twenty-seven degrees here. Twenty-seven."

"Bright side: you haven't been shit on yet today, have you?" I ask.

"No. Small victories, I suppose," she says.

"There's that positive attitude."

"What are you doing with your day off?"

"It's more like an afternoon off. I might sit by the pool," I say.

"Why don't you go to Disneyland? Seems like a fun thing to do."

"Some of the other coaches are. I would, but I promised Maven I'd bring her out here next year and do the park with her."

"Can you stop doing things that solidify you as the cool adult?" Lacey asks, and I hear her shit-eating grin through the phone. "You're making me look bad. All I can offer her are lollipops and stickers from the office."

"Some would say those are the finer things in life." I grab my suitcase from the pile of bags and slip the bus driver a fifty-dollar bill. "How's D.C.?"

"Not bad. Maggie and I are going out for a wine night tonight," she says, and the excitement in her voice makes me smile. If there's one thing I know about Lacey, it's that she loves to spend time with her friends.

"Sounds fun. Is anyone harassing you?"

"Nope. The most activity there's been around here is a mom of a patient asking if I could get you to sign a hat for her husband for Christmas. No one is sending me creepy fan mail or following me down the sidewalk. Guess I'm not that interesting."

"You're plenty interesting, and I can definitely sign a hat for her. No problem." I pull open the heavy glass door to the hotel lobby and nod at a family behind me to go ahead. The dad does a double take as he passes, and I hold back a laugh. "Maybe I'll sign a batch of them so you can keep them in your office."

"Oh, really? Wow. That would be awesome. Thank you." She pauses and clears her throat. "I better get going. I have a couple more appointments today, and I haven't had lunch yet."

I check my watch and do the time zone math in my head. My smile slips into a frown. "Lunch? It's almost three in the afternoon."

"I know. There was a mix-up on the calendar, and I got double booked. We worked it out, but I've been busy all morning. I might power through until dinner. The place where we're going has a delicious burger," she says.

My fingers curl around the door handle, and my spine stiffens. It might be close to seventy degrees outside, but a cool feeling of irritation works its way up my back. "Please eat something before you go out drinking, Lacey."

"I'm fine," she says, and if she were in front of me right now, she'd definitely be waving me off. "I'll text you later."

"Send me your location when you leave tonight?" I blurt out, then I slap my forehead with the heel of my palm. "Just in case."

"Worried about me, Holmes?" she teases, and I swallow down the lump in my throat.

"I'm your boyfriend, Lacey," I say lowly.

"Fake boyfriend," she whispers so softly, I have to press my phone against my ear to hear her.

"Doesn't matter. Fake. Real. I don't give a shit. I take care of what's mine, and right now, you are mine."

I'm met with silence. Neither of us say anything else, and I wonder if I went too far. It's the truth, though; I do worry about her. People are out of their minds these days, and being associated with a professional athlete comes with certain risks. I'm going to do my damnedest to protect her from whatever lunacy comes from being with me.

She is mine—not in the literal sense. I don't own her. She can do what she wants, and she knows that. That woman is as independent and fierce as they come.

But as long as she's going to be attached to me, I'm going to look out for her well-being. I'm going to make sure she's fed and she's safe and she's happy. I'm going to buy her what she wants and spoil the shit out of her.

When this ends in a month, I'll still look after her, just from further away.

She's not getting rid of me that easily. I'm never letting Lacey Daniels out of my sight again.

"Okay," she finally says. "Okay, I'll send you my location."

"Good. Thank you. I hope you have fun with Maggie."

"Thanks, Shawn Yawn. Have fun in Cali. Catch some waves, bro," she says, and I laugh. We're right back to our normal selves.

"See ya, Lace Face."

I hang up and head into the lobby. The team crowds the space, grabbing their room keys and bottles of water. Bystanders pull out their phones and snap pictures. A couple whisper and point. Another flicks off the guys, and Dallas answers him with an enthusiastic wave and an offer to sign the man's shirt.

Glad to see our media training is paying off.

I spot Darcy, the team's assistant, lounging in the corner on the sofa. Prim and proper with perfectly curled hair and painted red nails, she's unbothered by the chaos. She's used to the routine of checking us in and out of hotels after four years in her role.

There was an away game last season when porn got charged to someone's room. She had to use the team credit card to pay off the balance for three videos titled Diving in her Folds, and mortification rolled off of her as she signed the receipt.

I've never laughed so hard in my life.

"Hey, Coach," she says, smiling up at me. "What's up?"

"Can you do me a favor?"

"Is it the jerseys? I have them out with dry cleaning already."

"No." I shake my head and rub the back of my neck. "It's a personal favor."

"Oh." Her eyes widen and she sits up straight. "What's up?"

"Can you have some food delivered to Lacey's office in D.C.?

She hasn't eaten yet, and I know she's not going to get something on her own."

Darcy's face softens, and she pulls out her phone. Her thumbs fly across the screen, and I see an app open with a dozen culinary options. "Of course. What does she like?"

"Sushi, I think?"

"You don't sound too sure."

"Yeah." I nod and remember the time we went to an all-you-can-eat restaurant. Lacey devoured ten plates of spicy tuna rolls like it was a walk in the park. She leaned back in the booth with a sleepy grin on her face after she tapped out. "Sushi for sure. Use my credit card."

"You got it. I'll get it ordered and sent to her within the half hour."

"Thanks, Darcy. I appreciate you."

"Don't mention it. Hey." She stops me from leaving with a touch to my wrist. "I wanted to say I'm happy for you. I know how hard you work, and I'm glad you found someone who helps you slow down. Lacey's great, too. I was wondering when this would happen, and I'm so glad it did."

"Wondering?" My eyebrows wrinkle, and I stare at her. "What do you mean?"

"She's always there for you, and she doesn't seem to care who you are. That's not a bad thing," she adds quickly, backpedaling like she's going to get in trouble. "I just mean it's clear she's not with you because of your fame or money. She really likes you, and that's refreshing."

"Oh." My skin is prickly, and I nod. "Right. Yeah. She's—she's great. We're happy."

"I can tell. I haven't seen you smile this much in years." Darcy stretches out her leg and taps my sneaker with hers. "Go get checked in. I made sure you were on a separate floor from the guys. I'll send you a text when the food gets delivered."

"You're a lifesaver."

Thirty minutes later, after I unpack my suitcase and open my computer to answer some emails, my phone pings on the desk. I open it and find a picture of a bag of takeout with a single red heart.

LACE FACE

Thank you.

Don't tell anyone else, but you're my favorite.

ME

The feeling is mutual, Daniels.

We'll keep it our little secret.

I dip my chin and grin from ear to ear.
Darcy is right.
I really haven't smiled this much in years.

SEVENTEEN

SHAWN

THE FINAL WHISTLE SOUNDS, and I check the scoreboard.

We lost.

We didn't just lose—we lost to a team that hasn't won a single game all season.

I rip off my headset and throw it at the concrete wall behind me. I flex my fingers and shake out my hands. My eyes close, and I rub my chest as I take a deep breath, hold it for a count of five, then exhale. I haven't felt like this in years. The slow and gentle claws of anxiety and panic latch onto my back and crawl up to my shoulders.

Breathe, I tell myself. *You're fine.*

I inhale again, and when I exhale, I feel better. I'm more stable and aware of my surroundings.

The roar of the crowd doesn't help me think—it hasn't helped me think all game. The half-full stadium of fans has been incessant, screaming at the top of their lungs and slapping the seats to distract us.

And *fuck,* did they distract us.

We had a chance to tie with ten seconds on the clock, but Jett, our quarterback, didn't notice the Grizzlies defense shifting.

He got sacked—hard—by a four-hundred-pound defensive tackle who drove him into the ground like he was a dog's chew toy as time expired.

And that was that.

We kissed our undefeated season goodbye.

I hear a whistle. I blink, and I see Dallas taking off from the sidelines. He runs straight for the player who took down his teammate and throws a punch at him. The benches start to clear, and I stare, flabbergasted, as mayhem unfolds. The refs blow their whistles again and try to regain order.

It's useless. I sprint onto the field and pull my players off the opposing team. I nudge them toward the tunnel and shake my head when they try to defend their actions.

I have to pick up Dallas around his middle to get him off the defensive tackle. He's never so much as hurt a fly, and now his fists are running rampant, trying to punch anyone wearing a white jersey.

"Hey," I snap. "Knock it the fuck off."

"That was an illegal hit," he exclaims. He thrashes in my arms and tries to break free. He's barely a hundred and sixty pounds with all his equipment on, a weight I can easily lift with one leg, and it's funny he thinks he's going to get very far. "He grabbed Jett's facemask and probably gave him a concussion."

"And you think trying to hit someone three times the size of you is going to fix it?" I deposit him on his feet and motion toward the locker room. "Get out of here."

"But Coach—"

"But Coach nothing. You're supposed to be my captain, man, and you're out here acting like an idiot. Get it under control," I say.

Dallas hangs his head. He nods and pulls off his jersey. "I'm sorry," he mumbles, and he sounds so much like the shy and introverted twenty-two-year-old we drafted four years ago, my heart hurts a little bit.

The walk through the tunnel with my assistants is quiet. My phone buzzes in my pocket, but I ignore it. A headache blooms across my forehead and down my neck, and I try to rub the ache away. When I get to the locker room, I find fifty-three men with towels over their heads and disappointment on their faces.

"Hey," I say, and they all look up. "Before I get started, I want to say that what happened out there at the end of the game was unacceptable. I don't care if we get beat by fifty; storming the field and going after their players like that isn't who we are. I get you're mad. I get you're fired up. I get that losing sucks, but trying to be a marauder?" I scan the room and level Dallas with a look. "That shit isn't going to fly here."

"Yes, Coach," Dallas says.

"I should suspend you for instigating a fight," I say. "If I don't, the league might."

"I understand," he mumbles. "It won't happen again."

I know it won't. His record is pristine, and the anger was a clear spur-of-the-moment thing, caught in a heated battle to protect his teammate. I won't tell him this, but I'm proud as hell he had the guts to do that.

"Now for the game itself." I slide my hands into my pockets and rock back on my heels. "It wasn't our best performance. We got sloppy in the fourth quarter, and the mistakes we made were lazy. Jett." I glance at our quarterback. He has an ice pack on his head and a purple bruise on his shoulder. "Did you see the defense shifting before the snap?"

"No." He shakes his head, and he looks a little dazed. "It was too loud. I only noticed when I went to throw. That's my fault."

"I'm going to take the blame," I say, and I turn back to Dallas. "I should've listened to you back in the second quarter. We should've kicked and held them off on defense for the last thirty seconds leading into halftime. It wouldn't have given them a chance to run back a touchdown and take a lead we couldn't recover from. I trust you, and not listening to you was shitty."

My kicker perks up. "You're in charge, not me," he says.

"Yeah, but you—*all* of you—have the right to stand up to me when you think we should do something different. This is a team sport, and we're not going to win by only listening to my play calls. It's a collective effort. Going forward, I'll be better at getting your opinions. And I want you all to hold me account-able, okay?"

The team nods, and a murmur of positive agreement spreads through the locker room.

"Good. Now let's talk about the loss. It sucks, doesn't it? It hurts like hell. It makes you think we're not good, and every-thing we've worked on this season has been for nothing. It makes you question the lunges we do, the miles we run, and the drills we practice over and over and over again. But do me a favor. Look up. Look around this room. What do you see? Fifty-two other guys who are feeling the same way you are. You're not carrying this burden of disappointment alone. Yeah, we can be pissed about this for a couple of hours, but tomorrow is a new day. And you know what tomorrow means? Forward. A chance to try again. We got the first loss out of the way—better now than in the postseason, right? We're going to remember this feel-ing, and we're going to carry it with us for the rest of the year. We're not going to hang on to this specific loss—that doesn't do us any good. We can't change the past. What we are going to do is acknowledge that we don't want to be here again. So, we're going to forget that there's a tick mark in our loss column, and we're going to come back stronger next week. All of us," I say. "Me included."

The guys lift their heads and their shoulders relax. Dallas grins at me, and his eyes twinkle.

"Being the best shouldn't be comfortable," he says. He stands up and looks around the room. "Comfortable means we're not doing it right. I don't know about y'all, but I don't want to be comfortable. I want a Super Bowl ring. If that takes losing two or three games to figure out how to get one, then so be it. The people who are successful are the ones who can embrace change. We'll dust ourselves off, get back home, go back to the drawing board, and start fresh on Tuesday. Hands in, boys. Want to do the honors, Coach?"

I nod, and a huddle forms around me. "Titans on three," I say. "One, two, three."

"Titans," they all bellow with renewed energy, and I can't help but smile.

"We'll bounce back. Go shower. Bus for the airport leaves in an hour," I say.

"Shawn, the media is ready for you," Darcy says, and I sigh.

"Let's get this shit show over with," I mumble.

I follow her down the hallway to the visitor's press room. Unsurprisingly, it's packed to the brim and overflowing with reporters and cameras. I check my phone as we walk in, and I see Lacey's name on my screen. I slide open the message and read it.

LACE FACE

Sorry about the game, pal.

ME

You watched?

LACE FACE

I'm the girlfriend of a football coach now. Of course I watched.

130

> What did the headset you threw do to you? It looked like you had a personal vendetta against it.

I huff out a laugh and bite my bottom lip. My fingers fly across the keyboard and I take a seat at the table.

ME

> A lot of things.

> Going into media. I'll text you in a few.

I pocket my phone and glance out at the crowd of people. "Before we get started, I want to acknowledge what happened after the loss. My guys know they shouldn't have gone onto the field like that, and we're handling it." I pause for a breath. "What else do you all have for me?"

A guy in the front row raises his hand. I don't recognize him, and I gesture for him to go ahead.

"Levi Smith, L.A. Confidential," he starts. "Shawn, your first loss of the season comes after you've confirmed your first public relationship in years. Do you think there's any correlation between your coaching performance and your personal life?"

I blink, and my mouth droops into a thin line. "Are you implying that because I'm dating someone, the team lost?" I ask. "I want to make sure I'm understanding you correctly."

"Yes and no. What I mean is, now you have outside influences that might distract you from doing your job. Do you think the decision to run the ball instead of kick in the second quarter might have been because you were busy thinking about something else?" Levi asks. "Or, more particularly, someone else besides your players? Is it safe to assume football isn't your number one priority anymore?"

I smooth my palms over my thighs. I dig my fingers into

my quad muscles, and I let out a breath. "I'm going to be honest with you, Levi. That's the stupidest fucking question I've ever heard," I say, and his eyes widen. The fine I'm going to get for the profanity will be worth it. "My personal life has no impact on my ability to coach a football team. The woman I'm seeing wasn't at the game today. She wasn't sending me messages when I was on the sidelines. You know why we lost? Because I made a bad call. A couple of bad calls. It happens. That's *sports*. It's part of being a coach. I love football more than anything else in my life, and I love my team just as much. I would never do anything to jeopardize their season, and to imply I'm becoming bad at my job just because I have a significant other is illogical. So far-fetched, I'm not even sure what possessed you to ask such an asinine question. Do not drag her into this, because she has no fault in what happened on the field. If you mention her again, you won't like my next response. Now I'll take another question, but if anyone else wants to talk down on the person I care about, we're going to have a problem."

The rest of the reporters heed my warning.

They ask what we're looking forward to adjusting for next week, and who I think played the best game from start to finish today. How crowd noise played a factor down the stretch, and when someone asks where Dallas, a southern boy from deep in the heart of Georgia, learned to punch, I burst out laughing.

"I'm going to cut it off here," I say. "I have a plane to catch. I'll see some of you next week back in D.C. Get home safe."

I slip out of the media room. I didn't realize how tense I was until I let out a breath and my shoulders begin to relax in the hallway.

"Bus is ready to go," Darcy says.

"Thanks. I'll meet you out there in a second," I say.

She nods and waves, disappearing around a corner. I pull my

phone back out and my finger hovers over Lacey's name. I call her before I can think twice.

"Hey," she answers.

"If you read an article about me going off on a reporter, just know that I was doing it to defend your honor," I say.

"Really?" There's a smile behind her question, and I lean against the wall. "Tell me more."

"This guy tried to get a rise out of me. He insinuated that because I'm dating someone, I don't care about football anymore. It felt like he blamed the loss on my personal life, as if the two go hand in hand." I snort and shake my head. "I gave him a piece of my mind."

"I would've liked to see that." She laughs, and the sound warms me through the phone. "Thank you for sticking up for me. Are you doing okay?"

"Yeah. It's been a long day, and I'm ready to be home."

Lacey is quiet for a minute, and I pull the phone away from my ear to make sure the call didn't drop. "You can stop by my place when you land, if you want. I have beer. Or I can make you some tea if you don't feel like being alone," she says softly. "But, after the afternoon you've had, you might want to be alone."

I don't want to be alone. I want to see her, because I feel like Lacey could be the bright spot on this absolutely shitty day. My empty apartment doesn't sound nearly as appealing as a warm drink with her where I can shut off my brain and not talk about anything related to football.

I can just... be.

I like that about her.

She lets me be myself.

"I'd love to come over," I say. "It would be nice to see you. I'd like that a lot."

"Yeah?"

"Yeah."

"Okay. I'll see you soon."

"It's going to be late," I say. "Is that alright?"

"I'm off tomorrow. Just let me know when you're on your way," she says.

"Will do. See you soon, Lace Face."

"Bye, Shawn Yawn."

We hang up, and I've never been so excited to get on a plane and head home.

EIGHTEEN
LACEY

MY PHONE VIBRATES in my hand and jolts me awake.

I sit up on the couch and rub my eyes. I kick off the pile of fuzzy blankets I'm buried under and stretch my arms over my head. My phone buzzes again, and Shawn's name pops up on the screen.

"Hey," I say when I answer. My voice is scratchy, and I clear my throat. "Hey. Hi. Are you here?"

"I'm out front. I woke you up, didn't I?" he asks.

"What? No. I've been awake." I stand up and yawn. "I'll buzz you in."

"You're a terrible liar, Daniels." He chuckles, and I smile as I press the intercom and hear the click of the lobby door locking in place behind him.

"I'm on the tenth floor. Elevators should be right in front of you."

"I can't believe I haven't been to your apartment before. How is that possible?"

"Because we always go to Maggie and Aiden's. Neutral ground. Plus, you know they have the best snacks."

"I like the sculpture in the lobby," Shawn says. "Very abstract."

"What do you think it is? I say it's a woman holding a fruit basket. Maggie says it's a dog."

"Wildly different interpretations, and you're both wrong. It's a rock formation." The elevator dings in the background. "Kind of looks like Stonehenge."

"What? You're out of your mind. It does *not* look like Stonehenge. That's the best description you can come up with?"

"I'll try again another day," Shawn says. "After I've had a full night of sleep."

"You must be exhausted," I say, and I feel guilty for inviting him over.

It was selfish of me to want to check on him after he traveled across the country, but something in his voice made me want to see him.

"Less so now," he answers, and the elevator doors open. "What number are you?"

"Twelve. Go right, then left."

I can hear the thud of his shoes through the phone. The swish of his coat and his quiet breathing. I count to ten, then there's a knock on the door. I open it and find Shawn smiling, his phone still in his hand and a beanie covered in snow on his head.

"Hey," he says, and there's an echo in my ear.

"Hey," I answer. "Come in."

We end the call, and he steps into my apartment. I close the door behind him and shift nervously on my feet. I wonder what my home looks like through his eyes.

It's much smaller than his place, and I didn't have time to clean up before he got here. There's half-folded laundry on the chair in the living room. Four blankets are on the couch, wrinkled and crumpled in a ball. My dinner plate is still on the kitchen table, and there are drops of tomato sauce on the counter.

I'm suddenly self-conscious. Like I should've put more of an effort in before he got here. Maybe I shouldn't have invited him over at all because *middle of the night rendezvous* aren't part of our normal friendship M.O., but *fuck*, I wanted to see him. Especially after the Titans lost.

I feel exposed. It might be because it's the middle of the night. It might be because the lights are dim and the sky is dark. Whatever the reason, it's like he can see every part of me. The *real* parts I lock away during the day.

I'm not embarrassed or ashamed. I've worked hard to become the woman I am. I've made mistakes. I've learned lessons and worked on myself. It's a new milestone for me to let someone see *this* side of me, though—the side that doesn't have everything together, but is trying her damn best.

"Sorry it's messy," I blurt out. "Mondays are usually my day for chores."

"I like messy. It's perfect," Shawn says from over his shoulder, and I think my heart swells three sizes in my chest.

He walks around my apartment, nodding his head and admiring the pictures on the wall. He stops when he gets to one of me at the beach three summers ago. My jean shorts are unbuttoned. I have a bucket hat on my head, and my cheeks are as red as a tomato.

"You look happy," he says. His fingertips dance over the glass frame, and he traces the outline of my legs. The waves crashing behind me and the sun hanging in the sky. It's intimate, and it almost feels like he's tracing me. "Your smile is my favorite smile."

"What?" I walk over and stand next to him. I tilt my head to the side and study my scrunched nose. My closed eyes. My arms out at my sides like I'm a bird trying to take flight. "That's not a smile. I look silly."

"That's a Lacey smile." He looks down at me, and our gazes meet. His eyes are soft, and his mouth hooks up in the left corner. It's slow and careful and something that stretches wider the longer he stares at me. "It's unique and special. Just like you."

A blush flares to life on my cheeks. "If I knew you were going to dole out so many compliments, I would've invited you over sooner. You sure know how to boost a girl's ego."

"It's not boosting if it's the truth," he says, and his shoulder nudges mine. "I like this picture a lot. Can you send me a copy?"

I stare at him, my mouth hitched open and my brain about to explode. "You want a copy? Why?"

"I have photos in my wallet of the people I care about. Maggie and Aiden. Maven. My family. I don't have one of you. This one would be perfect."

"Oh." I tuck a piece of hair behind my ear and my head bounces up and down in a chaotic nod. "Yeah. I'll send you a copy. I'll give you an accordion full of photos, if you want."

"What about a photo of us?" he suggests. "I haven't posted you on my social media yet."

"Why would you want a picture of me on your social media when you're going to have to delete it in a few weeks?"

Shawn shrugs. "My publicist said it would probably be good PR. Might make your hospital director believe you when you tell him you're bringing me to your gala."

"Right. Of course. That makes sense. Do you—should we take one right now?" I ask, and my voice catches in the back of my throat.

He turns to face me, and the softness in his eyes is replaced with heat. There's a fire behind the gray, the start of a blaze that threatens to burn me alive. "If we take one right now, people will know I'm over here when it's late. After hours. When we should be sleeping."

"It would make sense that a couple would see each other late at night," I say, and I'm not sure I'm talking above a whisper. "When else would we..." I trail off, and I snap my mouth closed.

His smile turns wicked. He bends down and crowds my space. "Finish that sentence, Lacey girl," he murmurs in my ear, and I shake my head.

"I don't want to. I shouldn't."

"Why not?"

"Because it could get me in trouble," I say.

"Were you going to say when else would we fuck?" he asks. He plays with the ends of my hair and twirls a strand around his finger. "That's the best part of a relationship, right? Getting to fuck whenever you want."

I think we're playing a game again, but this time, I'm going to be the one to crack. I've stopped breathing. I'm going to spontaneously combust, and my time of death is going to be just after two in the morning. It's the only outcome of this, all because my best friend is looking at me and saying *fuck* in a way that makes me want to squeeze my thighs together.

Preferably with his head between them.

"I haven't... it's been..." I swallow and fan my face. My body has never felt so hot or so close to turning into a dangerous inferno. "Give me your phone."

Shawn hands over the device without being told twice. I pull up his camera and frown when I see his head cut out of the frame. He laughs, rich and deep, and drags me to the couch.

"Sitting is better," he says as we fall onto the cushions.

"Maybe if you weren't a giant, then we would fit better," I laugh.

"We fit just fine. Come here." Shawn picks me up and sets

me in his lap. He leans me back against his chest and takes the phone from my hands. "My arms are longer."

I'm too distracted by solid muscles and firm lines to grin. I'm caught off guard by his hand cupping my neck and his cheek pressing against mine. It's intimate—far more intimate than we've ever been—but it also feels *right*.

"You going to smile for me, Lacey girl?" he asks, and this man has to know what he's doing, right?

He has to know he's taunting me in a way that makes me want to straddle his thighs and kiss him senseless. To pull him into my bedroom and find out what he looks like under the light of the moon. I've never, *never*, had thoughts like this about Shawn before, but now I can't stop.

His hands under my shirt.

His breath warm on my naked body.

His laugh in my ear when I come, a gentle encouragement as he gets me there.

Damn him. Damn him for being seductive without even trying. Damn him for making my imagination run wild. A vision of a tattooed arm around my naked waist flits through my brain, and I have no clue what to do.

"Smile," I repeat. "I can smile."

My lips split into a grin. My hair is unbrushed and my eyes are heavy, woken up from a deep slumber a few minutes before, but I look *happy*. My cheeks have color. You can see my teeth and the little wrinkles around my mouth. Shawn's smile matches mine and he snaps away, photo after photo of us saved on his phone.

"There we go," he breathes out, and a sensation in my chest twists and turns. "Perfect."

I'm not sure anyone has called me perfect before, but when Shawn says it, I believe him.

His hand falls away from my neck. I scoot off his lap and

onto the plush cushions. "Would you like some tea?" I ask. "Water? Something stronger?"

He looks up from his phone. His gaze bounces to my legs, then back to my face, and his throat bobs as he swallows. "Tea would be great. Thanks."

I all but run into the kitchen and turn the kettle on. I fumble with the mugs on the top shelf in the cabinet and nearly bring the whole shelf down on me. I wait for the water to get hot and peek around the corner to make sure Shawn hasn't gone anywhere.

He's still there on my couch, phone in his hand and a small smile on his lips.

Gosh, he's beautiful. I think I could stare at him for hours.

"Milk? Sugar? Honey?" I call out, and my voice is half an octave too high. I clear my throat and shake my head, rattled by the last five minutes.

"However you take it," he answers.

I pour the piping hot water into the mugs. I add the tea bags, a splash of milk and a touch of honey to each before returning to the living room.

"I made chamomile, so you aren't still awake in three hours," I say. "I hope that's okay."

"Sounds good to me," he says. He takes the mug and sighs contently as his fingers wrap around the warm porcelain. "Thank you. This might be the highlight of my day."

"My tea isn't *that* good, so I guess your day was that bad?" I ask, and I take a sip of my drink. "We don't have to talk about it if you don't want to."

"No, I—" Shawn stops talking. He sits up and looks around. "What's that noise?"

"Oh." I set down my mug and grab a blanket to fold. "I put on some classical music before you came over. You said it helps you decompress, and I thought it might be nice after the loss.

I'm sure your head's been going a mile a minute since the game ended."

He blinks at me. "You put on music for me? The music that I like?"

"Yeah," I say, and I'm painfully aware I might have severely overstepped a boundary he shared with me in a moment of regret.

"Lacey," he says, and his voice is ragged and strained. "This is —thank you. I've been looking forward to seeing you all night, and this... this is..." He swallows and scrubs a hand over his face. "I'm really happy right now."

"You are? You don't look really happy. You look kind of constipated."

A laugh bursts out of him, and he shoves his drink onto the table next to the couch. He holds out his arms. "Can I hug you?" he asks, and I've never nodded so adamantly in my life.

I move toward him, and his palms settle on my hips. I rest my chin in the crook of his neck, and my hands grab a fistful of his shirt. "Talk to me," I whisper, because I'm desperate to make sure he doesn't carry these burdens alone. "You don't have to be perfectly put together around me, Shawn. You can let it out. You're allowed to be a little broken. I won't think any less of you."

"Today was horrible. The loss sucks, yeah. But the guys acted like they've never played a game of football before in their lives. Dallas was swinging at people. My quarterback thinks he messed up when it's my fault we ran the ball instead of kicked. I had to listen to a reporter try and blame the loss on my relationship with you. And to top it all off, I read some of the comments on social media after the game, and they're all shitty. Saying we should dismantle the team. That I'm overpaid. That you're a distraction and women have no place in sports." He exhales, and the sigh tickles my forehead. "It's a lot."

"What can I do to help?" I ask. "Right now, what can I do?"

"Nothing. Being here with you is enough." He runs his fingers through my hair, and I let out a sigh. "It's nice to have something to look forward to when I get home. This is exactly where I want to be. Exactly what I need."

"The guys will bounce back," I say softly. I trace the outline of one of his tattoos—a bouquet of pretty purple flowers, right below his bicep—and drag my nails down his skin. "Fuck that reporter, and fuck the people on social media. So what if the game didn't go how you thought it would? Big deal. Everyone made it on the plane healthy. Everyone made it home in one piece, and the good news is you can start again tomorrow. You can adjust. That's why the Titans hired you—because you know how to problem solve. You know how to fix things. I don't know much about football, but I know your heart and your drive. I know you're going to lead those guys to their best season yet."

"Maybe I should hire you as our sports psychologist. I believe every word you just said."

"Good." I poke his chest, and his muscles flex under my touch. "It's the truth."

"I brought you something." He reaches into his pocket and jostles my shoulders. He pulls out a magnet, and I grin. "It's a California burrito."

"What is a California burrito?" I ask. I take the gift from him and run my fingers over the grooved edges. "It looks massive."

"It has fries in it instead of beans and rice," Shawn says. "It's a San Diego staple, and a total artery clogger. L.A. has them too, but they're not nearly as good."

"Fuck my health. I want one now."

"We'll go and get one. I know a place in the city that does a decent replica. I'll take you."

"I'd like that," I whisper.

We settle into quiet. A symphony of violins and cellos works its way through the living room, and I don't dare speak again.

Not when Shawn's breathing levels out and his hold on me loosens ever so slightly. I think he fell asleep, exhausted from the day and six hours of travel, until he sighs in my ear.

"Thank you," he whispers. "Thank you for being my friend. Thank you for... for being a safe place for me. Thank you for letting me be here. I wouldn't want to be anywhere else."

It's vulnerable and earnest, such a juxtaposition from the coach who threw a headset at the wall after the game and nearly told a reporter to fuck off. *This* is who the real Shawn Holmes is —a man with the kindest soul and the gentlest heart.

He pulls me close—closer to him, so we're almost fused as one. I smile and close my eyes.

Our relationship might be fake, but I wouldn't want to be anywhere else either.

Here with him is magic.

NINETEEN

SHAWN

"WHAT ARE YOU DOING TONIGHT?" I ask Lacey. I prop my phone between my shoulder and ear and uncap a dry erase marker with my teeth. "Are you busy?"

"No plans," she says. I hear a sink turn on, and the rip of a paper towel. She must be in her office. "Why? Did you have something in mind?"

"I rented out an ice rink so the team can decompress after the loss the other day. They're all bringing their families, too. Maggie, Aiden and Maven are coming. I wanted to invite you."

"You rented out a *rink?*" she asks. "How rich are you?"

"I didn't just rent out the rink. I rented out a whole farm." I chuckle. "But to answer your question, I'm rich."

"Like, how many millions?"

"Turning into a gold digger, Daniels?"

"No," she huffs, and I swear she's rolling her eyes. "It's something your fake girlfriend would know, right?"

"You've never looked up how much I make?" I ask, genuinely curious.

All the information about my contracts—both when I was a player and now as a coach—are online and out in the world for anyone to find. I always assume more people know my net worth than my middle name; it's a common occurrence for athletes to talk in contract numbers rather than personal information.

"No. Why would I?" she says. "If you wanted to tell me, you would. I don't really care how much you make, but since you're out here renting out entire farms, I think I underestimated you. Are we talking about Louis Vuitton or Kate Spade level of money?"

"Sweetheart, I could buy you all the Louis Vuitton you want and have plenty of money left over."

"Oh, Christ," she mumbles, and she blows out a breath. "Is it uncomfortable for you to tell me?"

"Not at all. Does it make you uncomfortable to hear it?"

"No. You know I don't care about that, right?"

I grin and draw a couple of exes and ohs on the whiteboard. "Right. Well, when I played, I was on a ten year, ninety-eight-million-dollar contract," I say.

"What the *fuck*?" she exclaims. "Are you shitting me? That is... that is a ridiculous amount of money."

"The NFL is the most profitable league in the country. They bring in thirteen billion dollars a year, and they pay their players well."

"Thirteen billion? Hang on, I need to sit down. You're blowing my mind here, Shawn."

"Want me to tell you about the coaching contract?"

Lacey sighs like hearing these numbers is a chore, and it makes me grin even wider. She truly does not give a shit about how much I'm worth, and I love that about her. "You might as well."

"Eight years, eighty million," I say. "It's on the low end, but it's my first contract as a head coach." I shrug even though she can't see me. "We'll see what I get when it's time to talk about extensions."

"Holy mother of God. You could buy an island."

"I could, but I donate a lot of it instead. Seems better for the environment. Besides, what would I do with a thousand acres all to myself? You wouldn't be there, and I'd miss your pumpkin pies."

A laugh tumbles out of her, and I heave a sigh of relief.

I hate having conversations about money, especially with people I care about. I'm lucky to be surrounded by family and friends who don't give a shit about my paychecks. They've never asked me to pay off their mortgage or to buy them a car, but it's a slippery slope. Money can be messy, and the last thing I want is for Lacey to think I'm different because of how many zeroes I have in my bank account.

I know her heart, though.

It wouldn't matter if I had ten dollars or ten million dollars to my name. She'd still give me shit, and that makes her one of the good ones. Someone I always want in my corner.

"Okay, so renting a farm is like chump change for you," she says. "Got it."

"It's a small place outside the city. A local business. I'm supporting the economy," I explain. "I promise I'm not show-boating."

"Ah, I see. The Good Samaritan strikes again. Really, though. That's thoughtful of you, Shawn. What a great way to kick off the holiday season," she says.

"I know firsthand how hard it can be to be away from people you love during this time of year. Sometimes I feel guilty for taking away from the players' free time, and I want to remind them I know they're human."

"They know what they signed up for," Lacey says, and her voice is soft and soothing. A balm to an ache in my chest I didn't know was there. "But it sounds like it's going to be a great time.

I'm sure they could use a little fun before the last games heading into the new year."

"Yeah. Everyone tends to get more stressed out the later into December we get. I don't know. I just want them to have clear minds and a few hours where they don't have to be the tough guys they're known to be on the field," I say. I stare at my white board and erase the play I just drew out. "Anyway. What do you think?"

"I'll be there. I haven't been ice skating since last Christmas, so I'm going to be a little rusty. It's nothing a couple of falls and a warm cup of hot chocolate can't fix, though," she says. "Am I supposed to dress up? Should I wear a reindeer costume or make myself look like a Christmas tree? Oh. I can be that guy from *Die Hard*. Talk about holiday spirit."

"Please don't tell me you think *Die Hard* is a Christmas movie."

"Shawn, it literally takes place on Christmas Eve. How is it *not* a Christmas movie?"

"Because the day it happens has no relevance to the plot. In fact—" I shake my head. "No. We're not arguing about this. I'm about to head into a meeting, and I don't want to be all fired up."

She laughs again, and *fuck*, I love that sound. Even through the phone it makes me smile.

"Fine," she says. "We'll argue more about it tonight."

"Looking forward to it, Daniels."

"You're such a nerd. See you later, Shawn Yawn."

"Bye, Lace Face."

MY CHEEKS HURT from smiling so much.

The entire team—every player, every coach, and all of their family members—have descended on Mulberry Farms. They're spread out from the gingerbread hut to the hot chocolate buffet, surveying the row of glass jars full of marshmallows, candy canes, and nutmeg to add to their drinks.

Some carry trees out to their cars, tying the Douglas firs down with twine and bungee cords. Others decorate sugar cookies, and a food fight breaks out when Dallas swipes a thumb full of frosting across Maven's cheek. I'm sitting on a little wooden bench on the outside of the skating rink, happily watching the madness unfold.

"Hey." Lacey plops down next to me and nudges my shoulder. "There you are."

"Are you having fun?" I ask, bending over to lace up my left skate.

"So much fun. I think I ate too many cookies, though. My stomach is killing me." She works her fingers through her hair, braiding the long strands and tying them off with a hair tie. "Want to hit the ice?"

"I'm not very good," I admit. "I might need your help."

"I don't think I'm going to be the best teacher," she says, "but I'll do my best." She stands up and wiggles her hand. I smile and take it, laughing as she tries to pull me to my feet but almost topples backward in the process. "You're not light."

"I'm over two hundred pounds," I say. I rise to my feet and keep our hands locked together. "Have you been deadlifting?"

"Deadlifting my wine glass to my mouth," she answers, and I laugh again.

We shuffle toward the rink, and Lacey checks both ways before dragging us onto the ice. Her free hand grips my forearm, and we wobble on our feet.

"Easy," she says. She moves in front of me and skates backward, her eyes on mine. "Pretend like you're gliding."

"Believe it or not, they don't teach us how to glide on the football field," I say. "It's more about tackling and leveling a guy onto his ass." I lean my shoulders forward and try to make myself smaller. "How am I doing?"

"I'm not sure you'll be competing in the Olympics anytime soon, but it's not the worst beginner skating I've ever seen," she says. She holds both of my hands, and she swings our arms back and forth. "Relax. I'm not going to let you fall."

"Says the girl who claimed she was rusty."

"It's like riding a bike." She lets go to do a spin then faces me with a grin on her lips and a few pieces of hair in her face. "See? No injuries here."

I reach for her palms again, and she intertwines our fingers. I like when she touches me. She's warm and soft, and her thumb runs over the knuckles of my left hand. We settle into a rhythm, with her pulling me around the oval and me only flailing mildly. Her laugh makes me smile, and when I come close to face-planting on the ice, she grabs under my arms and keeps me stable.

"My guardian angel," I say after we've done six laps.

Her cheeks are pink. A small bead of sweat rolls down her neck and catches in the hollow of her throat. It's obnoxiously sexy and I purposely *don't* look at it, averting my gaze and focusing on my jeans instead.

"You're doing great," she says. "I'm going to grab some water and take a break. Do you want something to drink?"

"I'm good for now. Thanks, buttercup."

She rolls her eyes and flicks my ear. "Try again. And don't go too far away. I don't want to find you on your back in the middle of the rink going into cardiac arrest."

"How old do you think I am?"

"Old enough to not think *Die Hard* is a Christmas movie," she answers, and she darts away.

I tip my head back and laugh. I hold onto the boards as my

team skates by, and I duck when someone throws a clump of ice at my head.

"You're having fun," Aiden says. He drapes his arms over the side of the rink and grins, staying on solid ground. "Is there a reason you're pretending to not know how to skate when I distinctly remember you winning the junior hockey league MVP when we were eight?"

My ears turn red, and I dip my chin. "Because I like watching Lacey pretend to know what she's talking about."

"Ah." Aiden hums and leans forward on his elbows. "Right. Because otherwise she wouldn't hold your hand. Got it."

I throw up my middle fingers. "Because it's *fun*."

"And if she started to fall?"

"I'd catch her," I answer automatically. I look up to meet his gaze, and I see he's smirking. "What?"

"Nothing. It's just interesting."

"Oh, here we go. What's interesting?"

"There's no press around. Your family isn't here, and neither is our boss. You don't have a reason to pretend like you two are dating, and yet you can't stop looking at her. It's okay to like her, Shawn."

"I don't—we're having fun. As *friends*," I add, and his smirk doesn't go away. "We don't like each other."

"Are you sure about that?"

"Of course I'm sure. Yeah, we've been spending more time together, but hanging out doesn't mean we're falling in love. She's... it's nice to be around someone so down to earth, you know? Someone who calls me out on my shit and isn't afraid to go toe-to-toe with me. It's refreshing, honestly. Did you know she doesn't know how much money I make? I blew her mind with that one." I run my hand through my damp hair. Sweat clings to the strands from a half an hour of exertion. "Can't you let us be?"

"I'm sorry. I don't mean to meddle or make a mountain out of a molehill." He holds up his hands in apology, and I nod my forgiveness. "It's good to see you happy. That's all."

"I'm always happy," I answer, and Aiden levels me with a knowing look.

"Not like this, you aren't," he says, and he clasps my shoulder. "You lost your first game of the season, but you haven't stopped smiling. When you played in the league, you moped around for a week before you let that shit go."

"I've grown up. I have to show the team that it doesn't bother me, otherwise the guys will hold on to the loss, too. We won't be able to move forward."

"Right. Yeah. And it has nothing to do with the five-foot-six brunette who's waving at you from across the way?"

My gaze travels to the other side of the farm. Lacey is leaning against the wooden bar with Maggie, a smile on her face and a hand on her hip. She *is* waving, and I glance over my shoulder to make sure she's waving at *me*. I lift my hand and wave back, and a grin creeps onto my lips.

Now she's holding up a chalice, a drink that looks suspiciously different from the water she said she was going to get. She pretends to chug it, and I laugh.

"No," I say. "Not *just* because of her. Because of other things, too."

"Got it. Well, the good news is you shouldn't have a hard time selling your relationship to your parents or Director Hannaford," Aiden says. "I just hope you two remember this is fake. I don't want either of you getting hurt."

"Of course we remember it's fake. There's only twenty-five days to go until we can give up this ruse," I say, and I kick the blade on my skate into the ice. "The next few weeks are going to fly by."

TWENTY

LACEY

"SHAWN HAS A NICE ASS, don't you think?" I ask Maggie. I lean against the bar and take a sip of my water. "Objectively speaking."

Maggie lifts her eyebrows. "Objectively speaking? What does that mean?"

"Just, you know, if you weren't dating Aiden, you'd think Shawn has a nice ass, right?"

"Sure, I'd think that. But when did *you* start thinking that?"

I glance across the farm to the rink where Maven and Shawn are doing laps around the ice. He looks steadier on his feet now, and more confident in his movements. I bite back a smile as I watch them.

"It might be a recent development," I admit, and Maggie drags me to a small corner underneath a piece of mistletoe.

"Spill," she says, and I kiss her cheek before plopping onto a bench.

"I don't know what's going on. It feels like we're flirting with each other, which is something we've never done. It's almost like there's this unspoken game we're both playing, and we're trying to see who's going to crack first."

"Game?" Maggie stares at me, confused. "What kind of game?"

"I don't know. Sometimes I think he's about to kiss me. Other times I kind of want to climb him like a tree and—" I take a breath. "Whatever it is, it's because we're spending time together, and I haven't been laid in a *very* long time."

"Okay, that's a possibility." She nods and swirls her drink around in her glass. "But what if you're attracted to *him*, Lace?"

I snort. "No way. Shawn and I have been friends for a while, and I've never had an attraction toward him before. If I did, that crush would've already come up, right?"

"Maybe. I don't know. I think you can develop feelings for someone over time, too. Like, maybe because you're spending so much time together, you're getting butterflies when he's around. But don't listen to me. I'm not a relationship expert. I'm dating someone I slept with after knowing him for a couple hours and could tell he was the one after spending one night together."

"What's it like to be God's favorite?" I ask. I sigh and put my chin in my hand. "I wish I knew what Shawn was thinking. Is he trying to get me riled up because he thinks it's funny? Is he doing it because that's how he feels, too, and he wants to test the waters?"

"Here's an idea: you could *ask* him how he feels," she suggests. "Healthy communication goes a long way."

"Alright, let's pump the brakes. What if I ask him and I'm reading everything wrong? I might ruin our friendship."

"What if you ask him and you *aren't* reading everything wrong?" she counters. "Then you could be in a relationship with your best friend."

"Too risky," I say. "Maybe we could do a friends-with-benefits thing. We could fuck once and get it out of our systems."

Maggie chokes on her drink, and I pat her on the back. "You want to sleep with Shawn?" she asks.

"Have you *seen* him? His hands are massive, and you know what they say about guys with big hands. And, fuck, those tattoos."

"I'm all for sexual exploration and doing what makes you happy. If that's sleeping with Shawn, then I'll cheer you on. Just be careful, Lace. It's hard to separate emotions from the physical component sometimes. I mean, hell. Aiden and I were supposed to have a one-night stand without any strings attached. Now look at us; we're buying bowls at Williams Sonoma on the weekends."

"Yeah, but you two are relationship people. Shawn and I aren't. We're both single, and we've been single for a while. I don't know what to do, Mags. It drives me crazy when he touches me. I'm using my vibrator every night and I *still* think about what his head would look like between my legs," I say.

I should tell her he had food sent to my office on the day I was too busy to pop out and grab something for myself.

I should tell her he stopped by my apartment after the Titans' loss. I fell asleep on the couch and woke up in my bed the next morning, and I think he carried me there. I found a piece of scrap paper with *good night* written in his handwriting on my kitchen counter when I made a cup of coffee, and I grinned for five minutes.

I'm not sure I didn't dream the whole encounter.

Spending time with him has been nice. He's thoughtful and considerate, and if I *were* looking to date someone, he's exactly the kind of guy it would be. But we're from different worlds; I end the day covered in boogers with cotton balls in my pockets and dark circles under my eyes. Shawn lives in a penthouse apartment and makes *millions of dollars* a year. He said he was picky, and that probably means he's looking for a woman who wears Prada and Chanel out to Sunday brunch. Someone who can talk to reporters and not make an ass of themselves.

We work so well as friends. We've always worked as friends, and we've never crossed that line. I can't help but be curious about what it would be like to tumble into bed with him, though.

Not when he calls me *his* and manages to find the two inches of bare skin under my outfits and touches me there.

He's attractive and single. We're doing things *real* couples do, just without the physical payoff.

And I kind of want the physical payoff.

I'm a firm believer that men and women can be sexually attracted to each other without letting it turn messy with feelings and love declarations. I'm someone who knows what I want, and I want to have some fun with Shawn.

If we already agreed we'd walk out of our fake relationship as friends, why can't we say the same for after we see each other naked?

"You're thinking hard," Maggie says, and I bite back a smile.

"Sorry. I'm distracted. What are you getting Aiden for Christmas?"

"Oh." She blushes and takes a long sip of her drink. "I'm giving him boudoir photos of me. I thought it would be a nice callback to how we met, except with even fewer clothes."

"I love that." I wrap my arm around her and rest my head on her shoulder. "I'm so happy you're happy, Mags. You deserve it."

"It's not the life I thought I'd have, but I think that's what makes it even more special. The best things are unexpected, and finding Aiden and Maven was certainly unexpected. I'm so grateful for my little family," she says, and she wipes her eyes. "Sorry. You know the holidays make me emotional and sentimental."

"I know. You don't have to apologize to me. I love you for your tears. God knows you have enough for the both of us," I say, and she laughs.

"I do, don't I?" She pokes my side and lifts her chin. "Someone's coming this way."

I glance up and see Shawn walking toward us. He smiles as he approaches, his hands tucked in his pockets and his hat backwards on his head.

Why does he have to be so goddamn attractive?

"Ladies," he says. "Why do I feel like you two are causing trouble over here?"

"Us? Trouble? Never," I say. "Did you give up on ice skating?"

"It's a lot more fun when you're there." He grins and tips his head toward the bar. "Want a drink?"

Maggie squeezes my thigh. "I'm going to check on Aiden," she says, and I know she's leaving us alone on purpose. "Have fun."

"Did I say something wrong?" Shawn asks, taking the empty seat beside me.

"No. We were catching up on some things. Problem solving, if you will," I say.

"Did you solve all the problems you had?"

I look into his eyes, and under the light of the moon and the fairy lights hanging from the rafters of the open-air pavilion, they look grayer than normal. Like something I could get lost in if I didn't glance away.

"Yeah. I think we did."

"Anything I can help with?" he asks, and I shake my head.

Not unless you want to fuck me in a gingerbread house at a Christmas tree farm.

"Nope," I say, and I can tell my voice is strained. "All good."

"You're such a shitty liar," Shawn says, and his thigh presses into mine. "Remind me to never ask you to cover for me if I need help hiding a body or something."

"Yes, because the man who tips really well is definitely going to find himself involved with a murder cover up," I joke. "Hey.

Are we doing Christmas presents? Should I get something for your parents and sisters?"

"We give each person a gift, and then my nieces have a shit ton of things to open on Christmas morning. Don't feel obligated to bring anything, though."

"You spoil the shit out of those girls, don't you?" I ask, and Shawn gives me a bashful smile.

"Guilty. They're still at the age where they like toys like Play-Doh and Barbie dolls. I've known Maven since she was born, and it's been weird to watch her go from playing with Legos to buying makeup and getting her driver's license. I never feel old until I look at the people around me and see how much they've grown up."

"Then you feel ancient?"

Shawn wraps his arm around me and tickles my side. I squeal and swat at his shoulder, trying to push him away. He's too big, a solid mass I don't stand a chance of moving. One of my hands ends up on his thigh and the other ends up on his stomach, just above the waistband of his jeans.

My laughter dies in my throat.

Shawn is such a *man*, with firm lines and taut muscles.

I've never been with someone who has such a physical presence before. Who could pick me up, toss me over his shoulder and not break a sweat. He's carved from the finest marble, the muse for every great Renaissance artist's depiction of the perfect male form.

God, I want to be under him. On top of him. Stretched out in his bed with the sheets around us as he took his time with me and learned my body in the most intimate ways.

"Lacey girl," he whispers.

I love when he calls me that.

His fingers trace my jaw and fan out across my sternum. It's the same spot he touched when he kissed me at the game, a frenzied search for bare skin that left me feeling dizzy and lightheaded.

I feel the same way now.

I lift my chin, and it's an invitation for him to kiss me if he wanted to. A door to open to make this something *more* than a pretend relationship. Shawn's eyes bounce to my mouth, and I think he's considering it. His lips part, and he sucks in a sharp breath. He leans in closer, and his nose brushes against mine.

How is he this warm? It's thirty degrees outside, and he's keeping me from shivering. I can feel the heat from his hand over the fabric of my sweater, and I want to feel that heat everywhere.

Fuck. Okay. Are we doing this?

"Smile!"

We jump apart like we've been caught doing something illegal.

I guess we were doing something wrong; kissing my best friend is *not allowed* to happen.

Darcy, the team's assistant, is beaming at us. She holds up her phone and taps the screen.

"Darcy," Shawn says, and I've never heard him so irritated before. Her name sounds like venom, and maybe he's not as nice as I thought he was. "What do you need?"

"I'm taking some photos for the team's social media accounts," she explains. "People love to see the guys doing everyday things like learning how to ice skate. Can you two get together?"

"Sure," I say brightly. I wiggle across the small bench until my shoulder presses against Shawn's. "How's that?"

"You look like you two don't know each other. Can you at least pretend like you enjoy each other's company?" she laughs and angles her phone down. "You can't be out of the honeymoon phase already."

Shawn puts his arm around my waist. I rest my hand on the center of his chest, and I can feel his heart racing under the tips of my fingers. I sneak a look at him, and his cheeks are pink. It's almost like he's winded and trying to take in as much oxygen as he can.

"Smile, Lacey girl," he murmurs, and it sends a shiver down my spine. "You can pretend you like me for a minute, right?"

"It'll take a lot of energy, but I'll survive," I say out of the corner of my mouth as Darcy snaps away. "Why do you call me Lacey girl? It's the only pet name you've ever used twice."

"Because I can tell you don't hate it. And because you're my girl."

I'm going to burst into flames. Incendiary tension sparks and cackles between us, and I'm close to pulling away. I *need* to pull away. His orbit is too strong, too powerful to break free from, but if I don't, I'm going to do something stupid.

Like kiss him. Ask him to stay awhile. Knock down the walls I've put up to ward off men who are intimidated by my success, causing me to constantly diminish my accomplishments to seem more likable and dateable. Take him home with me and strip off his clothes so I can trace every inch of his toned physique. Bite his tattoos and taste the smooth skin of his neck.

His *girl*.

Hell.

I'm in a *heap* of trouble.

"Oh," I say, and I've lost all train of thought. "I don't hate it. I—I like it. I like it a lot."

"I know you do. You're so easy to read, Lacey." Shawn glances at Darcy. "Did you get what you need?"

"Yeah." She slips her phone in her pocket. "Thank you. The fans are going to adore these. They'll be the first photos of you two on our accounts. I know you released a statement, but words come and go. Pictures are forever."

Darcy waves and disappears, heading for the candy cane trail.

"Want to hit the rink again?" Shawn asks, and I nod.

"Sure." I stand up and toss my empty water bottle in the garbage can. "Do you still need my help?"

His eyes meet mine, and he holds out his hand. "Please," he says, and I like how that word sounds coming from him.

I wonder what else I could do to get him to say it again. I wonder how I could get him on his knees and make him *beg*.

I thread our fingers together and lead him toward the ice. A bolt of awareness hits me when he squeezes my hand tight.

I don't think letting go of Shawn in a few weeks is going to be as easy as I thought it was.

TWENTY-ONE

SHAWN

WE'RE FINALLY BACK in the groove after the loss in Los Angeles last week.

I think the night at the farm helped. Everyone is in a better mood. Our offense is sharp, and Jett completes every pass. Our defense doesn't miss a beat, and they sack the Knights' quarterback eight times.

The whistle sounds, and I grin as our players run off the field. It feels like we're unstoppable as we head into halftime with a twenty-eight-point lead.

"Nice work, everyone," I say as the guys jog toward the tunnel. "Let's come back stronger in the second half."

They lift their hands toward the crowd in appreciation of their support, and the hometown fans give them a warm round of applause. Dallas stops beside me and he slings his arm around my shoulder.

"What are you doing?" I ask.

"I'm admiring the view," he says with a grin.

"Why are you being weird? You're always the first one in the locker room so you can eat your bag of Skittles."

"Maybe I found something I like more than Skittles."

"I don't care what you do with your personal time," I say. "Just wrap it up, and don't be a dick to her."

"Ah, Coach." He pats my chest and points toward the crowd. "You might care what I do with my personal time."

"What are you—" I stop talking when I spot Lacey standing in the front row of seats, just like she always does. Except today she's not wearing my jersey. She's wearing *Dallas'*. "What the fuck?"

"She asked Darcy for one of my jerseys. I even signed it for her. Don't tell me there's already trouble in paradise?" Dallas asks, and I hear the smirk in his voice. "Can't keep your lady satisfied, old man?"

"Get in the locker room," I say through clenched teeth. "Before I bench you for the second half. Or the rest of the goddamn season."

Dallas laughs and pulls away from me. "You got it, Coach. You don't need to worry, though. It's all fun and games. What's life if you can't laugh with the person you love, right? See ya back there."

He disappears, and I rub my jaw. Lacey is turned to the side and talking to Maggie. She uses her hands to gesture animatedly about something, and I watch her for a minute. I notice the way she tips her head back and laughs. The long stretch of her neck, barely visible under her white turtleneck.

And that fucking *jersey*.

I want to rip it from her body. Tear it to shreds and leave it in a dozen pieces at her feet. I want to pull it off her with my teeth and make sure it's *my* last name stretched across her back.

Fuck.

I pinch the bridge of my nose and take a deep breath. Jealousy clouds my vision, and I flex my fingers in irritation.

Why do I care so much?

The guys have known Lacey for a while. At the farm the

other night, they kept stealing her away to skate with them. To buy her an eggnog and to decorate cookies. They all love her, and it's obvious why.

She treats them like they're humans, not like they're athletic gods she puts on a pedestal. She asks about their families, about where they went to college and what they're doing for the holidays without an ulterior motive. When they talk, she genuinely listens and actively participates in the conversation.

She's smart as hell, and while I know she supports the team, I like that it's not her entire personality. I like that she has a kick-ass job and doesn't spend all her time trying to be the players' favorite person. She exists and they exist, and it's the best of both worlds.

So why the *fuck* am I pissed she's wearing a jersey that's not mine?

I pull off my headset and jog toward the stands, waving to my friends as I approach them.

"Shawn," Maggie yells from above me. "Great game so far."

"Think the guys could score a couple more touchdowns?" Aiden asks. "Jett's on my fantasy team, and I could use a bigger buffer."

"I'll get right on that," I say, and I drag my eyes to Lacey. "Can you come down to the tunnel?"

"Sure." She fiddles with her necklace and swallows. "Is everything okay?"

"Everything is just fine." I grin and hitch my thumb over my shoulder. "I'll give security the okay. Meet me by the supply closet in three minutes."

I shove my hands in my pockets and stride across the turf toward the tunnel. It's going to take her longer to get there, but it'll give me a minute to clear my head. To take a deep breath and think this through.

I *need* to think this through.

I nod toward the security guard waiting near the locker room, and I pace back and forth over the concrete floor.

Lacey wore that jersey to get a rise out of me. I know her; she's playing a game. I don't know what the end result is going to be, but she's trying to push my buttons, and I hate that it's working.

"Hey." Lacey runs up and clutches her side. "Are you okay? Is it a panic attack? What can I do to help?"

That jealousy goes away. The roar in my chest settles, and I blink at her.

"No. It's not that." I pull her into a supply closet and close the door behind us. I turn on the small overhead light and stare at her. "Why are you wearing Dallas' jersey when you're supposed to be dating me?"

"Oh." She laughs, but it's feeble. Strangled and nervous, I think. "Um. I don't have a Titans jersey. I thought I should get one."

I hum and take a step closer to her. Her back connects with the shelving unit behind her, and the boxes on the shelves rattle. She watches me, but I don't back down.

"Interesting. And this was a sudden change of heart?" I ask. "A spur-of-the-moment decision?"

"Yes," she whispers. "I'm just trying to be a supportive fan."

"So it wasn't to piss me off? To see how I'd react?" I put my hands on either side of her head and cage her in. "A way to get me to remind you that you're mine?"

"Am I yours?" she asks. She reaches out and grabs my shirt, her gaze meeting mine. "I'm not sure that I am."

My eyes bounces to her mouth. *Fuck*, I want those lips around my cock. I want to kiss her. I want to hear what kind of sounds she makes. I want to drop to my knees and bury my head and tongue between her legs. I need to walk away from her because I'm six seconds from acting on these lowered inhibitions, and that would get me in serious trouble.

I'm not allowed to want her, but I do anyway.

"Lacey," I croak. My right hand curls into a fist, and it takes every ounce of self-control to pull away from her.

"Do it," she whispers, and she lifts her chin in a dare. "I know you want to. I want you to, too."

She's taunting me, showing off something I can't have when all I want is just a taste. The smallest bite, then I'll be satisfied. I'll be good. I won't ask for anything else.

I grab her by the belt loops of her jeans. I tug her into my chest and cradle her cheek with my hand. I tilt her head back so I can look at her, and she's smiling at me.

"You make it impossible to stay away," I say.

"So don't," she says, and the challenge hangs heavy in the air between us.

"Fuck it," I ground out, then I bend down and crash my mouth against hers.

It's even better than the first time.

Lacey's lips are soft, like little clouds I could curl up and fall asleep on. They're warm, too, the cold from outside reaching every inch of her except for her mouth. My hand drops to her neck and I hold her there, my thumb at the hollow of her throat, so she can't escape.

She moans, and I swallow the sound down. Hearing her want this, want *me*, makes me greedy. Selfish. Out of my mind with lust and need. I want her so fucking bad. I convey that through the press of my lips to her cheek. To just below her ear and the space underneath her turtleneck I find when I pull her collar down, on a desperate quest for more of her. My tongue runs up her throat and she makes a noise that's so sexy, I want to get her to make it again.

"Shawn," she whispers, and my name is a plea. She arches

her back and wraps her arms around my neck, in no hurry to break our contact.

I scoop her up under her thighs and walk us backward until I find a solid wall. Her legs settle around my waist and her heels press into my lower back, a fire kindling at the base of my spine.

I'm hard as hell, and I don't try to hide it from her. She must be able to tell because she rolls her hips and grinds into me in a way that makes me see stars. I lose myself in her for the quickest of seconds, thrusting up into her, over her jeans, like I could *really* make her mine.

Fuck, I was so wrong.

I'm nowhere close to being satisfied.

I need to be inside her. On top of her. Underneath her and at her mercy, so her pretty pink fingernails can leave little claw marks on my shoulders and bare chest.

My mouth finds hers again, and she kisses me so hard, I think I leave my body. Her hand trails down my chest and she reaches between us. She cups my length over my joggers, and I almost drop her.

"Lacey," I groan.

I get caught up in the moment, and I pull that stupid fucking jersey over her head. I toss it behind me, and I don't care if I never see it again. My palm sneaks up under her shirt, and I run my thumb along the underside of her breast.

"Please," she says. "Touch me, Shawn."

I can't tell her no, can I?

I pull down the fabric of her fancy bra and I pinch her nipple between my thumb and pointer finger. "Hold your shirt up," I say, and I don't recognize my own voice.

I've never been this turned on before. Close to giving myself a few quick jerks in my pants just so I can finish at the sight of her in front of me.

She fumbles with her clothes and pulls the bottom of her

shirt up under her chin. I can only see one side of her, but it's fucking divine. She's the perfect size, big enough to fit in my hand, and *god damn*, I want to come on her chest. On her face. Inside her tight pussy. I want to push her tits together and fuck my cock with them.

I lower my chin and swirl my tongue around her nipple, biting just hard enough for Lacey to hiss and grab the ends of my hair.

"Fuck, Shawn," she says, low and soft in my ear.

"Look at you," I say. I trace the bite marks I left on her fair skin. I twist her nipple until it's swollen and pointed, and I grin. "So pretty."

Her fingers dance across the outline of my cock, and I lurch forward. *God*, what I wouldn't give to have her hand around me. To smear the lipstick on her fuckable mouth and make her eyes fill with tears while she choked on my dick. I want to fill her up until she can't walk, until she can't speak, until all she can do is thank me for making her feel good.

"Where the hell is he?" someone shouts from the other side of the door to the supply closet, and I freeze. "Halftime is over in two minutes."

"He was just here," another voice says.

"Shit," I say. I pull Lacey's bra back in place and make sure her shirt covers her stomach. I set her down on the ground and adjust my pants. "We need to go. I need to go."

"Okay." She nods and touches her mouth. "The game."

"The game."

"Should we—" she swallows, and her eyes drag down my body. She licks her lips when she sees the hard on I'm sporting, and color invades my cheeks at the satisfied twinkle in her eye. "Leave together?"

"You first." I squeeze my eyes shut and try to think of

anything other than Lacey naked or what it would feel like to bury myself inside her. "I need a minute."

"Right. Yeah. Okay. Um. Alright. I'll see you back out there," she says softly, and I nod.

"Sounds good."

"Shawn?"

I open my eyes when she says my name. She wrings her hands together and fixes her hair. I think she's avoiding eye contact, because she's looking at everything *but* me now.

"Yeah?" I ask.

"We're—we're okay, right?"

"Of course we're okay, Lacey girl." I kiss her forehead and squeeze her shoulder. "Just don't even think about putting Dallas' jersey back on. Next time, I'll cut it off you."

Lacey laughs and bobs her head. "Okay. Only your jersey from now on," she says.

"Atta girl." I tap her hip. "I'll see you after the game."

"Good luck in the second half, angel," she says. "No. I hate that, too."

"You'll find something you like." I wink and roll my shoulders back. "Cheer loud for us, Lace Face."

"Always, Shawn Yawn." She gives me one more look, then turns and heads for the door. She slips out into the tunnel, and I let out a breath.

I want to tell her to come back, but I know I can't. This is a slippery slope we've stumbled down, and it's all my fault.

I shouldn't have kissed her again.

I shouldn't have let her see how easily she affects me, but it's too late now.

I got a taste, but now I want the whole fucking thing.

TWENTY-TWO

LACEY

I PACE in front of Shawn's apartment for five minutes before I finally have the courage to knock.

I sent him a text asking if we could talk, and he invited me over for a drink.

It's dangerous to be here so late in the evening, but the dark sky on the way over gave me the motivation I needed to actually stand here and wait for him to open the door. If it was noon or three in the afternoon, I wouldn't have dared.

He's going to tell me I'm out of my mind. That this is a *bad idea* and something we definitely *can't do*.

But if he's still thinking about that kiss in the supply closet like I am, I think he can be persuaded.

Shawn opens the door a second later, and he smiles when he sees me. "Lace," he says. "Come in."

"Thanks," I say.

I step past him, and as I glide inside, I'm painfully aware of how short my skirt is. The velvet material barely hits the top of my thighs, and, paired with the knee-high boots I have on, I might as well not be wearing any clothes at all. I unzip my jacket and glance at him over my shoulder.

"Let me take that for you," he says with a hoarse voice, and his eyes dart away from my ass.

He looks like he got caught doing something bad, and I bite the inside of my cheek to keep from grinning as I hand him my coat.

"Appreciate it." I stroll into his living room and marvel at the floor-to-ceiling windows. "How was your day?"

"Long. I have a busy week. The holiday party is Wednesday night, then we leave for Cleveland on Friday." He leans against the wall and crosses his arms over his chest. "Want to tell me why you're here?"

"Can I have a drink?" I ask. I perch on the edge of the sofa and smile at him. I catch his gaze moving down the length of my legs before he nods and heads for the liquor cabinet.

"Whiskey again?"

"Let's make it bourbon this time. Neat."

"Sure. You still want three fingers?" he asks, and there's a low tug in my belly with his question.

I smooth my hands over my skirt and get out the imaginary wrinkles. "Yes, please. I can handle it. Thanks."

"I'm sure you can."

Shawn makes our drinks and walks toward me. He hands me a glass and we knock them together. I take a sip and indulge in the sharp sweetness on my tongue. I wonder if it would taste better if he was the one tipping my neck back and pouring the mahogany liquid down my throat. Not stopping until my mouth was full and the liquor trailed down my neck, a mess he'd gladly lick up.

"Delicious," I say, and I'm stalling for time.

"I know you didn't come here just for a drink. Not when a beautiful woman like you could go to any bar in town and drink for free," he says. He sits next to me and drapes one arm over the cushions of the couch, and the other holds his glass. "Are you okay?"

"I'm fine." I take another sip of my drink and set it down on the table next to me. "I have a proposition for you."

"Another proposition?" he asks. He lifts his eyebrow and sits forward. His T-shirt stretches across his chest, and I look away from his distracting biceps. "I can't wait to hear more."

"Maybe proposition isn't the right word. Amendment is more accurate. I want to make an amendment to our current arrangement," I say.

"Well go on, then," Shawn says, and his voice is a caress against my cheek. "Tell me what you're thinking."

Suddenly, I'm not sure this is a good idea after all. I've lost my bravado because he's looking at me, and I'm thrown back to when he took me in his mouth and made me want to jump from the highest cliff into a pool of glittering wonder below.

Three minutes with him, and I nearly tipped over the edge, frustration and longing and tension rising to the surface like an old friend.

Friend.

Shawn is my *friend*.

A friend who was hard when he was kissing me.

I can do this.

"I want you to fuck me," I blurt out, and Shawn nearly drops his glass. His eyes widen and his mouth opens like he's about to interrupt me, but don't let him. "A one-time thing, to get this attraction to each other out of our systems. I know you were affected by our seven minutes in heaven. I was too. If we just do it once, it'll scratch that itch. We can go back to *not* kissing each other and pretend like it never happened."

He stares at me, then he does the one thing I was not prepared for: he *laughs*.

Shawn throws his head back and his shoulders shake. He

clutches his chest and tries to catch his breath. I frown as his deep and rumbly laughter rings in my ears.

"What's so funny?" I ask.

He sets down his drink. "You want us to fuck?"

"That's what I said, isn't it?"

"Yeah, but I'm trying to understand why."

"Because I'm not the only one who liked that kiss, Shawn. I thought about it all night last night when I got home from the game. I replayed it when I used my vibrator this morning," I say, and he lets out a strangled sound.

Good. I want him to suffer. My toy wasn't nearly as good as his fingers would be, and I've been daydreaming about how deep he'd be able to get all afternoon.

"I'll admit the kiss was good," he says, and his laughter stops. "Better than good. You're hot as shit, Lacey. And, in the spirit of transparency, I thought about you when I jerked off in the shower last night," he adds, and the tips of his ears turn red. "But hooking up with each other could complicate things. Didn't we agree to *not* be physical? Fucking goes against that plan."

"We did, but that was before we realized the chemistry between us. You've seen my boob, Shawn. What's a little more?" I ask, and I hate how desperate I sound.

Shawn rubs his hands together. His eyes bounce away from my face and his attention catches on the low-cut sweater I tugged on before I left my apartment. It's cruel to tease him like this, I know. But I'm a woman with needs, and he's the only one who I want to fulfill them.

"Just once?" he asks slowly, like he's trying to process what I've asked and is seriously considering going along with the idea.

"Just once. We have one good night, and then tomorrow it's like nothing happened," I say.

"You want me to finger you and then pretend like it never happened?"

173

I swallow and play with the zipper on my boot. "Yes."

"You want to say my name when you come and then pretend like it never happened?"

"Mhm. That's exactly right."

"You want me to taste your pussy then sit down next to you at Maggie and Aiden's house for dinner and pretend like it never happened?" Shawn asks, and I nod.

"Yup. We're adults. We've both had one-night stands before. What makes this any different?"

"Because we're best friends who constantly orbit in each other's vicinity," he says. "We're going to see each other on holidays for the next forty years. What if it's awkward?"

"You saw my boob, Shawn," I say again. "I touched your dick. But here we are, having a conversation like it's no big deal."

He runs his hand through his hair and leans forward. "If we do this, we don't tell anyone," he says. "Not Maggie. Not Aiden. No one. It's just between us."

"Fine," I agree.

"One time. That's it."

"That's what I said."

"We stop if anything feels weird," he says.

"Define weird," I ask, and he levels me with a look.

"Like when I tell you to sit on my face and you start to giggle," Shawn answers. "That means it feels weird."

Oh.

I squeeze my thighs together.

I *do* want to sit on his face. There's nothing weird about *that*.

"Okay," I say, and my voice is barely above a whisper. "That's fair."

He throws back the rest of his drink and wipes his mouth. "We're going to do this my way."

"And what way is that? A quick fuck, then you send me home?" I ask.

Shawn shakes his head. He moves across the couch and lifts me into his lap. His fingers graze up my thigh, and I think I'm going to die. I can feel him hard beneath me, and his cock presses into the curve of my ass.

"No, Lacey girl," he whispers in my ear. He brushes my hair to the side and drags his teeth down my neck. I let out a shallow breath and close my eyes. "If we're going to do this, we're going to do it right. I'm going to take my time. I'm going to savor you. I'm going to have you every way I want, and *fuck*, do I want you." He folds his palm around my leg, and he spreads my thighs apart with a gentle shove. "Open up. Let me see how bad you want me to slide my fingers inside your pretty cunt."

Oh, *hell*.

My knees open, and I relax against him. I feel my heart race in my chest, and I've never been so turned on in my life.

This man knows what he's doing. He's someone who knows how to please and what gets a woman off. There's not a selfish bone in his body, and that's going to spill over into the bedroom, too.

I just know it.

"Shawn," I say, and I tremble against him.

"Last chance to back out, Lacey," he says. He kisses my ear, and his fingers tap against the inside of my thigh. "Because once you tell me yes, I'm going to make sure no man is ever good enough for you again."

"Yes. Yes. *Yes*, Shawn," I say. I think I might shout it. I might scream it a hundred different ways because he hums at my enthusiasm.

"You thought you could come over here in this outfit of yours and get me to do what you want, didn't you?" Shawn pulls the left side of my sweater down, and cold air bites against my bare skin. "Would you have gotten on your knees for me, Lacey?"

"Not before you got on yours first."

He chuckles and works the strap of my bra down. My nipples are already hard, and my back arches as his touch moves across my body.

"Fuck," he whispers, and he tugs on the other side of my sweater. He unhooks my bra, and my breasts spill free. "Your tits are incredible. I want to suck on them. I want to come on them, too. Would you let me do that?"

"You can do whatever you want to me," I say, and I mean it. "Anything. Everything."

TWENTY-THREE

SHAWN

I DON'T KNOW what I was expecting to happen when Lacey asked to come over, but it wasn't her in my lap, her legs spread wide and my fingers inches away from sliding inside her.

Fuck.

I can smell her. I can see how wet her underwear is. The little scrap of lace is drenched, and I want to pull it off and shove it in her mouth so she can taste herself. So she can keep quiet while I fuck her into the mattress and leave a handprint on her ass. A mark that reminds her who was there when she tries to sit down at work tomorrow.

I want to ruin her, but I can't ruin my best friend.

She's too good.

But if I only get her once, I'm going to make sure she won't forget me anytime soon. I'm going to claim her, so every time someone else is inside her, she'll be thinking of *me*.

I lift her off my lap so she's standing. She wobbles on her feet and turns to look at me.

"Take off all your clothes," I say, and I lean back against the couch, palming myself through my sweatpants. "I want to watch."

Lacey nods and yanks her sweater over her head. Her tits bounce as her arms come back to her sides, and I have an alarming infatuation with her chest. I've never been a boob guy, but hers are spectacular.

She unzips her boots and steps out of the sinful leather shoes. She plays with the buttons on her skirt and walks toward me with a sexy sway of her hips. Her hands rest on either side of my thighs, and she's so close, I could kiss her.

"Do you want me to go slow?" She unbuttons the first button on her short skirt, and my cock twitches under my hand. "Or do you like to go fast?"

"Slow," I say, and I'm losing all mental capabilities. I thought I was a smart man, but when she unfastens the second button and I can see the top of her thong, I can't remember my name. "Fuck, you're so hot."

"You sure know how to make a girl feel special," she murmurs.

The last button comes undone, and with it, so does my sanity. Lacey turns around and bends at the waist, shimmying the skirt halfway down her ass. She runs her palms over her ass cheeks, and I lean forward. I take her underwear in my teeth, and when I snap the elastic against her skin, she lets out a whine.

"Off. I told you I wanted to see your pretty cunt," I say.

Her skirt falls to her feet and she steps out of it. I'm breathing so hard, you'd think I was running a marathon. Mile twenty, when your legs start to ache and your lungs begin to burn. Looking at her like *this* is suspiciously close to what I imagine heaven is going to be like.

Lacey pulls off her underwear, and I grab them before they can fall to the floor. I put them in my pocket and stare at her, not wanting to miss a single thing. She drops her head back as her hands trail down her neck and her soft curves. Her fingers twist her nipples, and she moans.

"If you don't touch me," she says, "I'm going to do it myself."

"Like you'll get any argument from me," I say. I shove my hand down my sweatpants and give my cock a tug. I can't *not* touch myself while I watch her. She's a goddess.

My eyes roam down her body and I appreciate the figure I've only ever seen with clothes on; her nice tits. Her flat stomach. The thighs I want to suffocate me when I put my head between her legs. Her bare pussy and the glistening arousal I can see from here.

"I thought about you," she whispers. Her fingers tease across her stomach and up the inside of her thigh, and I'm close to panting like a dog. "This morning. I pretended it was you fucking me, not my toy."

Jesus Christ.

I've never been with a woman so confident. Someone who tells you *exactly* what they want with no shame. It's the biggest turn on, and I've never been so glad for a late-night text message in my life.

"Was it good?" I ask. My voice is thick with lust, and I stroke myself again. "Did you like playing with yourself and thinking it was me?"

"I know you'd be better." Her smile is wicked and her eyes flicker with mischief. "You'd take such good care of me."

"Of course I would." I grab her and spin her so she falls into my lap. Her legs spread wide, and I give her pussy a light slap. "I told you I take care of what's mine, Lacey, and you're mine."

I trace my fingers along her entrance. Her moan is soft and long, and I suck on her neck, trying to find all the spots she loves to be touched the most. I hope I leave a mark.

Lacey rolls her hips, and I know what she's asking for. She's practically grinding against me.

"Shawn." Her hands rest on my thighs, and her nails dig into my muscles. "I'm naked and in your lap. What do I have to do to get you to finger me? Beg?"

I laugh and kiss her forehead. I wrap my arm around her waist and circle her clit. "I thought I was supposed to get on my knees first," I say in her ear, and she smiles.

"One of us better soon, or I'm leaving."

"I'm going to take my time, remember?" I slip my finger inside her, and she groans. "*Fuck*, Lacey. You're so tight."

"So much better than a toy," she pants, and I grin.

"Let's get you ready for my cock. You want that, don't you?"

"More than I want anything else."

"Needy slut, aren't you?" I whisper, and my free hand wraps around her throat.

"Only for you," she says, and I almost blow a load in my pants.

God help me when I fuck her.

I slide my finger out of her and bring it to her mouth. I trace her lips until they're coated in her arousal and I lean forward to kiss her. My tongue runs along the seam of her mouth, tasting her, and she's better than the finest desserts in the world.

I switch our positions again, and I move Lacey to the couch. I drop to my knees in front of her and my gaze bounces all over her body. Her skin is flushed pink and her hair is a mess. Her chest rises and falls and she's watching me with hunger in her eyes.

"Hold yourself open," I say roughly, and she grabs her legs under her knees faster than I can blink. Her thighs widen, and I fucking love seeing her up close. "There you go. Just like that. You're such a good girl for me."

I *see* her melt at the praise. She blushes an even deeper shade of red, and her ass wiggles on the cushions. Her lips pull up in a smile, and she's waiting to hear what else she's doing right.

"So good," I whisper against her mouth. I kiss her softly, distracting her as I slide two fingers inside her. She arches forward, and I sit up on my knees so I can get two knuckles deep. "But you also want to be a little bad, don't you, Lacey girl? You can be both with me."

"Yes," she whispers. Her eyes are full of tears, but she tips her chin up so I can kiss her again. "I want to be both for you, Shawn."

"That makes me so happy, Lacey. God, your pussy likes my fingers, doesn't it? You're fucking dripping on my hand. I'm going to add a third finger, okay?"

"Okay." Her legs shake, and she blows out a breath. "I want a third."

"That's my girl." I kiss her knee and slowly work my ring finger inside her. She cries out, and I grin. "Such a good slut taking all the fingers I'm giving you. Look at you; you're so fucking wide and wet for me."

"Shawn," she moans, and my name has never sounded so nice. I want to hear it on repeat, in the middle of the night, when I'm remembering the stretch of her pussy and how she clenches around me. "Please. I need to come."

My thumb finds her clit, and I circle her until she's shaking. Until there are tears on her cheeks and her knuckles turn white. She's close, and I smile when I hear the hitch in her breathing.

"That's what does it for you, isn't it? Three fingers buried inside you while you dream about my cock? God, I can't wait to fuck you so hard, you won't be able to walk straight tomorrow," I whisper in her ear, and I feel her orgasm race through her. "There you go. That's perfect. You're so pretty when you come, Lacey girl."

Lacey lets out a sob. Her hands fall from her legs and her

thighs quiver as she rests them on the couch. There's a wet spot on the cushion and her knees are still open, still inviting me in. I lean forward and lick her pussy, my tongue lapping up all that she'll give me.

"I-I can't. Shawn," she whispers, and she claws at my shoulders. "I can't do another one."

"Yes, you can. You can give me one more, can't you?" I slap her clit, and she shudders out a ragged breath. "How many times did you come this morning with that toy of yours?"

"Twice," she pants, struggling to speak.

"Which means you can give me three." I part her with my fingers and I tease her clit with my tongue. Her legs squeeze tight around my head, and I hope to god this is how I go. "One more, Lacey. I promise it'll feel good. You can—*fuck,* that's it. There you go." I slide my fingers back inside her, and she tightens around me. "Good girl. So fucking good for me."

"Please don't stop," Lacey whimpers. "I need it."

"A toy isn't going to cut it anymore, is it? You're going to be dreaming about me when you play with yourself from now on, wishing you had my fingers to fuck. My tongue to lick up your mess."

"You, Shawn. I need you."

She needs *me.*

I have to squeeze my eyes shut so I don't combust. I can't finish before I fuck her, but every time she clenches around me, it's getting harder and harder to control that urge to not just let go.

I bite the soft skin of her thigh. "God *damn* Lacey, the way you tighten around my fingers drives me crazy. I can't wait until I can come inside you. I'm going to send you home with it dripping down your leg. A reminder of why you came over here tonight. That's it. There's my second one. That's for me, isn't it?"

Her next orgasm comes quicker than the first. Her entire

body shakes, and as she calms down, her muscles relax. She stops sniffing, and she lets out a slow breath. I kiss both her legs and set them on the floor. I rub her knee and sit back on my heels, staring at her.

"Hi," she says, and she pushes up on her elbows. "That was..."

"What you came here for?" I ask, and her lips curl up into a smile.

"Better than I could have ever imagined." Her eyes flick to the front of my pants, and she reaches for me. "Come here."

I move toward her, and she kisses me. She snakes her hand down my body and pulls on the waistband of my joggers. "Ask to take them off," I say, and her cheeks turn as red as fire.

"Can I take them off, Shawn?" she asks, following directions. I lift an eyebrow, and she squirms. "Please?"

I like hearing her say that. It makes me feel on top of the world. I scoop her up in my arms and head for my bedroom. "Only because you asked so nicely, sweetheart."

TWENTY-FOUR

LACEY

THE LAST FIFTEEN minutes were an out-of-body experience.

I know I'm here in Shawn's apartment, but I don't think I'm actually *here*.

I'm still soaring above the clouds, higher than the stars, and I never want to come down.

Sex always feels good, but he scrambled my brain with those orgasms; it's never felt *this good* before.

The way he talked to me and praised me lit a fuse inside of me, and now he's carrying me down the hall. Kissing me softly and slowly. Savoring me like he said he would, and this is the most beautiful I've ever felt. The most adored and wanted.

It's intimate and soft, a different side to the man who whispered filth in my ears a few minutes ago.

Shawn kicks a door open and walks inside a room. He turns on a lamp, and I look around. It's clean in here, just like the rest of his apartment. A king bed sits in the middle with a dozen pillows and a comforter that looks like a cloud. I can see the city behind the headboard, and I smile at the twinkling lights.

He sets me down on the mattress and takes a step back. I'm completely naked while he still has all of his clothes on, and there's a moment of self-consciousness. A second where I feel like this is entirely one-sided and he doesn't want me like I want him. I cover my chest with my hands and Shawn shakes his head.

"Don't do that," he says, and he pulls his shirt over his head. "Don't hide, Lacey girl. Not from me."

The endearment lodges itself between my breasts. Behind my ribs, dangerously close to my heart, because I'm *his* girl.

At least for the next few weeks.

I stare at him as he undresses, and *god*, Shawn is a devastating man. The tattoos that go down his left arm span across his chest, too, right over his pectoral muscle. There's an array of colors and shapes and designs, and I want to learn what each one means.

His body doesn't seem real but something an artist created. Sharp lines. Powerful muscles. Tan skin. A dusting of dark hair that trails down his stomach.

I stop breathing when he pulls off his sweatpants and lets them fall to the floor. He's not wearing any underwear, and seeing him naked makes my mouth go dry. His cock hangs thick and heavy between his legs and I watch his fingers fold around his length as he gives himself a tug.

I don't know where to look; it's hard to focus on one spot when there's so much I want to see. My eyes drag back to Shawn's, and he's watching me with heat behind his gaze.

"I'll never hide from you," I say. I hold out my hand and he takes it. He kisses the tip of each one of my fingers, and he rests my palm over his heart. "You're the only person I want to be myself around."

His eyes soften as he climbs onto the bed. He moves across the mattress and holds himself above me on his hands and knees. I sit up and kiss him, my nails massaging his scalp and the spot where his shoulder meets his neck.

"You're the only person I want to be myself around, too," he says, and there's a shift in the air.

This is more tender than out in the living room. Soft. Romantic, almost, if a one-night stand could be considered such a thing.

Maybe it's silly to think that, but it's nearly impossible not to as he traces my jaw and cups my chin in his hand. As he stares at me and eases me onto my back. There's such care and consideration to his actions, and I feel like I'm the only girl in the world.

"I got tested six months ago," I whisper, wanting to have this conversation before we turn mindless. "I haven't been with anyone since."

He nods and pulls down my bottom lip with his thumb. Smears my lipstick a little in the corner and drags it down my cheek to make me look thoroughly wrecked. "Same. Negative on all tests."

"I'm also on birth control."

"What are you saying? No condom?"

"I want to feel you." I take a deep breath and try to steady myself. "But I'm sure you... you might have... I'd never do anything to put you in an uncomfortable position or trap you or anything."

"I would never think that," he says fiercely. "I trust you completely."

"Okay." I nod and wrap my hand around his cock. I stroke him up and down, and his eyes flutter closed. I think he's trying not to lose too much control too early. "Then it'll just be us."

"Going to fuck you raw," he says through a strangled exhale. "Really make you mine."

For the night, I want to say, but I keep that thought to myself.

"How do you want me?" I ask. I run my thumb over the head of his cock, and I rub the pre-cum I find there down his length. He lurches forward and nearly falls on top of me, but catches himself at the last second. "What makes you feel the best? You made me feel so good, Shawn. I want to make you feel good, too."

"Anything with you is going to feel like heaven." He taps my knee and lifts his chin. "Move up to the headboard."

I slide across the sheets and lean back against the stack of pillows. I open my legs and rest my hand on my stomach, impatiently waiting for him to join me. Shawn stares for a minute before he shakes his head, like he's trying to rid himself of thoughts he shouldn't be having. He positions himself between my thighs and tips his mouth to mine.

"Do you want me?" I ask him, and in the dead of night there's no one around to hear his answer. No one to see the way he kisses me and pulls me close. Up here, it's just us, nothing but the light of the moon, the stars in the sky, and our naked bodies as we reach for each other.

"You know the answer to that," he says into my neck like it's a secret. His tongue runs up my throat and he bites my earlobe. When he sucks on my skin, I let out a sharp breath. "I've never wanted someone as much as I want you."

Shawn pushes inside of me. Gentle at first, as I arch into the pillows and get used to his small thrusts. Harder when my hands grip the sheets on either side of my body because I'm afraid I'm going to fall. There's a gradual build up and then he's moving faster, harder, lifting on his knees and getting deeper as he tries to find the best position.

He fucks like he kisses; possessively. With every part of himself. Teeth on my neck. A hand taking my arms and pinning them above my head. Words of encouragement whispered in my ear and a soft laugh when I arch my back and ask for more.

"Harder," I say through a gasp, because as mind-numbing as this is, I still want more.

I lift my leg so he can drive deeper into me, and he lets out a string of expletives at the new angle. His muscles flex and his eyes squeeze shut, concentration painted beautifully across his face.

"Lacey. I can't—" He swallows, and I watch the bob of his throat. The shade of crimson on his cheeks and how hard he is between my legs. In and out, the rhythm makes me dizzy with lust. He's still inside of me, but I already want more. "If I go any harder, I'm going to come. I'm not going to last for you."

"So come," I say.

My hands escape from his hold and move up his chest. They settle around his neck and I pull him toward me. I kiss his throat. Lick at his collarbone and sink my teeth into his shoulder. He makes a sound from deep in his chest, a rumbly noise of pleasure I love instantaneously.

Shawn opens his eyes. He looks down at me and thrusts so hard, the headboard slams against the window. I'm afraid the glass might crack.

"I said I'm getting three from you." He reaches between us and his thumb finds my clit. He rubs in a circle, and there are spots in my vision. "I don't come until you do."

"Such a gentleman," I get out. He pinches me hard, and flashes of color sparkle behind my eyelids. "Can we switch positions?"

"What do you want to try?" he asks. His thrusts slow, and he looks distressed. On the verge of ecstasy, but not close enough.

"Can you fuck me from behind?" I look away and bite my lip. "It's my favorite position."

Shawn squeezes my cheeks and turns my head so I have no choice but to look up at him. "What did I say about hiding from me?"

"To not." My hand curls around his bicep, and I hold on to him for support. "I'm sorry."

"You never have to apologize," he says, and he slides out of me. My cheeks heat when I see his cock is almost dripping, and I know most of it is from me. "Get on your hands and knees for me, Lacey. Let me watch your ass bounce while you take me from behind."

I crawl down the bed until I have enough space to get into position, and I look at him over my shoulder. Shawn is touching himself, and his hand gives his cock a couple of pulls.

"You don't need permission," I say, and the wind gets knocked out of me when he rests his palm against my backside.

"It's a shame we said only once. I've been wanting to take your ass since the minute you walked into my apartment tonight," he says. He kisses the top of my spine and pushes down on my shoulders until my chest rests against the bed. "I bet you'd like that."

My eyes roll to the back of my head, and I nod. "Yes. I like—I like that, too."

"I knew you would. We'd have to work up to that, and we don't have enough time. Guess I'll have to dream about it," Shawn says, and he slides two fingers back inside me. "You're still wet for me, aren't you? You've been so patient."

"I've been good, right?" I ask, and I'm desperate to hear his answer. "I can still have a third?"

"Oh, Lacey girl, you've been so good, and I want you to come around my cock this time. Once you do, I'm going to fill you up with my cum because I know that's what you want." He leans forward and lines himself up with my entrance. "I'll tell you a secret: once is never going to be enough. I'm going to think about you every goddamn night until the day I die."

Shawn slams into me, and my eyes fill with tears. I grip the sheets and moan with delight as he gives me every inch of himself. It's chaotic. It's messy. It's the best I've ever had because it's *him* and it's perfect.

He touches me everywhere. I can feel myself teetering toward that precipice of pleasure, a ledge I so badly want to jump from. The orgasm races down my spine to my belly. It takes my breath away and I moan so loudly, I'm surprised the walls don't shake.

"Lacey," Shawn says, and all his control seeps away.

He thrusts into me, one hand on my chest and the other around my neck. I think I'm grounding him now, the one to keep him stable and afloat as he lurches forward and pulses inside me.

We stay like that for a minute; him folded on top of me and my ass lifted in the air. When he pulls out, his release trails down my leg. His fingers dance up my thigh and through the mess he left behind. I bury my face in the sheets, and hot mortification and lust roll into me as I lower myself onto his finger and take every drop he can give me, aching for more.

"Good girl," he murmurs. "Not wasting anything, are you?"

Shawn kisses my shoulder. He collects me off the mattress and pulls me into his lap. I dip my chin and bury my face in his chest as he brushes the hair out of my eyes.

"Um." I clear my throat. "I should go."

"Stay with me for a minute. Let me hold you. Can I do that?"

I nod and take a deep breath. I pull away and look up at him. He's watching me as he rubs soothing circles on my back. "That was good," I whisper.

The best I've ever had.

"Are you okay? I didn't—"

"No." I shake my head. "You didn't. It was perfect. Exactly what I needed."

"Is the itch scratched?" Shawn asks.

"Yeah. Yeah, I think it is. Thank you for your service."

He chuckles and brushes his nose against mine. "You're not going to disappear on me, right?"

"Never. You're stuck with me, buddy."

"Good." His eyes bounce to my mouth and they linger there before darting away. "Let me call you a car."

"I can take an Uber. Shouldn't take long."

"You'll let me know when you get home?"

"Yeah." I untangle myself from him and I slide across the mattress, planting my feet on the floor. I look back at Shawn, and he's lounging on his elbow, staring at me. "What?"

He shakes his head and pulls on my wrist. I tumble back to him, and he surprises me when he kisses me. I sigh against his mouth and the warm, soft lips I won't get to taste again. I'm tempted to climb on top of him. To straddle his lap and ride him until morning. He's half-hard under me, and his hand closes around my neck again like my favorite piece of jewelry.

I'm never going to look at that tattoo the same way again.

"We can't," he says when I guide him to my entrance, desperate to feel him again. "We said one time."

"It's still the same time," I answer, and I was a fool to think just once with him would be enough. "You kissed me first."

"You came to my apartment looking like a goddess and begged me to fuck you."

"I didn't *beg*."

"You sure about that, sweetheart?"

I sigh and rest my forehead against his. He blinks up at me, and there are stars in his eyes and a smile on his lips. "I'm going to go," I say, but I don't make any effort to leave.

"Okay," Shawn says, and his hand stays on my hip, keeping me in place.

"In a minute."

"Just a minute."

"Soon."

He chuckles and kisses me again. "You can stay as long as you want, Lacey girl. I'm not going to kick you out. But if you stay, I'm going to have you again, and I know that goes against what you want."

What if I want him?

"Thank you for tonight," I say. "I'll see you soon for the holiday party."

"Looking forward to it. I'll get us a car and pick you up at seven. Your clothes are in the living room, by the way."

"Right." I bob my head and climb off of him. I kiss him one more time and move away from the bed. "I'll let you know when I'm home."

"Thank you. I'm keeping your underwear, by the way," Shawn says, and I bark out a laugh. "For prosperity."

"Fine." I scoop his shirt off the ground and pull it over my head. I'm swimming in the cotton and it reaches past my knees, but I don't care. "Then I'm taking your shirt."

"Fine."

"Good."

"Glad we settled that."

"Bye, Shawn Yawn."

"See ya, Lace Face," he calls out.

I leave his bedroom and grab my scattered clothes off the floor. I sneak out of his apartment and shut the door quietly behind me. I lean against the wall in the hallway and close my eyes. My phone buzzes in my hand and I open the text message.

It's from Shawn, the words *good night* written on the window directly above the rumpled sheets where we just laid. My heart twists in my chest, and I think I've made a terrible mistake.

TWENTY-FIVE

LACEY

"PEARLS OR NO NECKLACE?" I ask Maggie. I step out of my bathroom and hold up the piece of jewelry. "What do you think?"

"I think you look *hot*. Holy shit, Lacey," Maggie says. She gapes at me from my kitchen sink and sets down her drink. "Where did you get that dress? I've never seen it before."

"I ordered it online." I adjust the thin strap on my shoulder and check my reflection. "Does I look alright? It's not too tight?"

"You look better than alright. My god, woman. I love Aiden with my whole heart, but your hips are sexy. Do a spin, please, so I can admire your ass," my best friend says, and I laugh.

I twirl around and show off the form-fitting gown. It's a deep shade of blue, like the summer sky at dusk, and hugs every curve of my body before flaring out at the bottom. I felt beautiful the moment I stepped into it, and I need all the confidence I can muster going into tonight.

It's been forty-eight hours since I slept with Shawn, and the memory of his mouth on my lips is still there. It hasn't faded away yet, and I wonder if it ever will. I wonder if it will be an invisible mark I carry with me until the end of time.

"Lacey? Are you okay?" Maggie asks, and I blink out of the trance I've fallen into, a memory of his head between my legs and how beautiful his tattoos look under the light of the moon.

"Yeah. Sorry. There's a lot on my mind with work and the chief physician position," I say.

It stings to lie to my friend, but I cannot, under any circumstances, tell her what happened in Shawn's apartment. It's our secret, something I'll remember when he rests his palm on the small of my back later tonight. When he hands me a drink and brushes his lips across my cheek like the doting boyfriend he is.

Fake boyfriend.

"No necklace," she says. "A necklace will take away from the neckline, which is my favorite part of the dress."

"No necklace it is." I set the pearls on the kitchen counter and put in my earrings. "I wish you and Aiden could come tonight."

"I'm sure it would be fun, but we've both been busy at work, too. We're taking the week of Christmas off to visit his family with Maven, so I feel like I'm just trying to hang on until then." Maggie sits on one of my barstools and swings her legs back and forth. "How's it been dating Shawn?"

"Pretending to date Shawn," I say, and I clasp a small silver bracelet around my left wrist. "Good. Nothing's different from how we are as friends. He's still kind and thoughtful, and he still brings me magnets. I wish I knew why he was single; he's the perfect guy. Has Aiden said anything?"

"Not really." She shrugs and brushes a pile of crumbs into the sink. "I don't think there's a story or anything. Maybe Shawn has never felt comfortable around a woman before. I'm sure it's hard to trust someone as an athlete. You wonder if people like *you*, or the fame that comes with being associated with you."

"Oh." I smooth my hands over my dress and remember how

Shawn told me he was picky. I wonder if that's what he meant. "I never thought about it like that. That's kind of sad, isn't it?"

"Of course it's sad. Shawn protects his heart, and he's very selective about who he lets in. Hopefully, by dating you, he sees that there are good people out there who like him for him."

"Pretending to date me," I say again, and Maggie narrows her eyes. "What? I don't want anyone to be confused when this ends in a couple of weeks." My phone buzzes on the counter, and Shawn's name pops up on the screen. I answer his call and smile. "Hey."

"Hey. Sorry I'm a few minutes late. It's snowing again, so traffic is a nightmare. I'm out front, though. Make sure you bring a coat," he says.

"Will do. Do you want anything from my place?"

"I'm all set. The limo has drinks. It also has snacks, too, in case you get hungry."

"*Limo*?" I ask. "Why are you picking me up in a limo? I thought by getting us a car, you meant ordering an Uber."

"The team sent me one, and it's the only night of the year I let myself act like I'm wealthy. Plus, we can listen to Christmas music with surround sound."

"Now you're speaking my language. I'll be down in just a few minutes."

I hang up and grab my black clutch. I shove my phone and lipstick inside and glance up to find Maggie watching me.

"What?" I ask, and I run my fingers through my hair. I curled it earlier, and the soft waves fall to just below my shoulders. "Do I have a stain on my dress?"

"You're smiling," she says.

"Why wouldn't I be smiling? I'm in a good mood."

"Because Shawn is downstairs?"

"Because I'm going to a fun holiday party with delicious food, a cotton candy machine, and gingerbread cookies made by the best bakery in the city," I say. "And, yes, Shawn will be there too, but I'm not smiling because of *him*. Having my friend there is a bonus."

"Right." Maggie nods. "Of course."

"Stop." I point my finger at her, and she grins. "You're not allowed to go home and tell Aiden anything."

"Is there something to tell?"

"Not a damn thing." I huff and slide my long coat over my shoulders, tying it tight around my waist. "Will you lock up when you leave?"

"I will. Have fun tonight, Lace. You deserve to smile more," Maggie says. "If Shawn is the one that makes you happy, that's fine by me."

"I'm ignoring you," I say, and her laughter follows me to the elevator.

I head down to the ground floor and shiver when I walk outside. I look up the street, and I spot the black stretch limo parked a half block up. Tucking my hands under my arms, I start my trek down the snow-covered sidewalk.

"Hey." I hear Shawn's voice and watch as he jumps out of the car. He jogs toward me in his tuxedo and leather shoes, carefully navigating the wet and sloshy terrain. "Need some help?"

"I did not think this through." I smile as he offers his hand, and I gladly take it. "Thank you."

He maneuvers me past a snowbank and into the plowed streets of downtown. My heel gets stuck in a clump of salt, and I wobble on my feet. Before I can topple over and ruin my dress, Shawn lifts me in his arms and carries me bridal-style to the limo.

"I should've had the driver pull up closer to your door," he says. "I'm sorry about that."

"That's okay. This is very helpful."

"I like to be helpful."

I pat his chest and fix his bowtie. "I know you do."

When we reach the car, he opens the door and sets me carefully inside. I slide across the seat and bask in the warm leather and dim lighting. You'd never know it was hovering around thirty-one degrees outside while you were in here.

"Want some champagne?" Shawn asks as he sits beside me. He leans forward and pulls out a bottle from a bucket of ice. "It came with the limo."

"I mean, I feel like we kind of have to, right? It's too bad we don't have some caviar too." I smile as he pours me a drink. "What should we toast to?"

"How about the best fake relationship ever?" He lifts his glass toward me, and I knock it against mine. "The easiest partnership I've ever been a part of."

I take a sip of the drink and the bubbles pop on my tongue. "That's the fanciest shit I've ever had. You probably drink this every night, don't you? I can see you walking around your apartment, chugging straight from the bottle."

"Fuck you." Shawn laughs and elbows my side. I scoot closer to him as the driver heads down the road. "You've been in my apartment with me. Have you seen any bottles of champagne lying around?"

"Just because I didn't see them doesn't mean they aren't there," I tease, and Shawn takes a deep pull from his drink. A drop of alcohol hangs on the corner of his mouth, and I want to lick it away. "Maybe you save it for after hours."

"You've been in my apartment after hours, too," he says, and his voice is an octave lower than before. Silky smooth, like the bourbon he gave me *that night*. "We can pretend like it never happened, Lacey, but you can't expect me to forget about it completely. You haven't, have you?"

I stare at him with wide eyes, and my hand trembles as I take another sip of the champagne.

I could lie.

I *should* lie, because being honest goes against the rule of *forgetting it ever happened*.

Maybe it's the expensive drink in my hand making my tongue loose or the intimate atmosphere of the limo, but I want to be honest.

I've tried *really fucking hard* to forget about him and how *good* his hands felt on my body, but I can't. I *can't*, and I hate him for it.

I hate myself more for getting us into this mess in the first place.

"No," I whisper. I tip the glass back and swallow the rest of the champagne. "I haven't."

I wonder if we could be friends who kiss.

Friends who hook up now and then without the big and messy and complex feelings that come with being in a relationship.

Friends with benefits and all the fun stuff like sex.

It would be easy, and we wouldn't have to worry about there being an end date because we already *have* an end date in place.

With the way Shawn's looking at me right now, I want to crawl into his lap. I want to take off my coat and let him touch me. If we weren't headed to an event where he has to give a speech and we have to smile for the cameras, I'd ask the driver to pull over so I could have my way with the six-foot-six man next to me.

"We said one time." Shawn glances away and fiddles with his shiny watch. I've never seen him wear it before, and the silver looks freshly polished. "We have to stick to that."

"I know. I can control myself."

I think.

My eyes flick to the tattoo on the back of his hand, and the confidence I have in myself wavers.

"Good," he says, and he pours himself another drink. "Because I'm not sure I can."

"You're going to have to try, buddy. We can't make this more complicated."

"You stained my couch," he says, and I turn to glare at him. "It was worth the cleaning bill."

"Oh my god." I bury my face in my hands. "We really can never talk about this again."

"Okay." Shawn laughs. "Want to talk about tonight instead?"

"*Please*," I say, because if we don't, I'm going to ask him what he did with the pair of underwear he kept. "I'm excited."

"Everyone is excited you're coming. It's low key, but we did invite a few members of the media. There will be cameras and reporters. You're definitely going to get stopped, but it shouldn't be anything invasive tonight."

"Am I allowed to say we're spending Christmas with your family?" I ask. "Or is that an overshare?"

"No, that would be nice. My mom called yesterday and grilled me about you. Where you went to school. Where you did your residency. What some of your hobbies are. Luckily, I knew all the answers, but there's this small part of me that thinks she knows we're lying."

"Then we'll do a good job of selling how in love we are tonight," I say. "And at the hospital gala. And then at Christmas. There won't be any doubt in her mind."

"Did you ever hear from that guy you were at the game with?" Shawn asks, and a muscle in his jaw twitches with the question. "Did he apologize for leaving and treating you like you were worthless?"

I blush, and hot flashes of that kiss in front of the entire stadium run through my mind. "No. He did an interview with Barstool, though. Talked about how I led him on when I was already dating you. I didn't read too much into it."

"Want me to buy the company and kill the story?" he asks, and for half a second, I think he might do just that. "I could hire a hitman, too, if you want to go that route instead."

"No," I laugh. "It's fine. Let's have a good night together. He's a distant memory at this point."

"What was his name? Chad?"

"Matthew."

"Oh, even better. It all makes sense now." Shawn nudges my knee with mine. "Fuck him. I'm sorry for bringing him up. How was work today? Has it been busy with the holidays?"

"Everyone tends to get sick when the weather changes, so we've seen an uptick in patients. We're posting an opening for an additional pediatrician, though, thank god. Maybe that will mean I can stop running around and eat three meals a day."

"I think I'm going to have to have lunch delivered to your office every day from now on. I'm going to sit on the couch and watch you eat. You can't be skipping meals, Lacey girl. You have to take care of yourself."

I blow out a breath and wring my hands together. "Sometimes I'm busy taking care of other people, and it's hard to put myself first," I admit, and it's scary to be so honest with him.

"Maybe we can work on that, yeah?" Shawn asks. He touches my cheek, and I nestle into the warmth of his palm. "If your day is busy, let me know. I can easily order you something. I'm going to take care of you, remember?"

"Okay. I can do that," I whisper.

"Thank you. I know you're fiercely independent, which is a trait I love about you. You can fight your own demons and slay your own dragons, but I'm here, too. I just want to make sure you're fed and maybe hold your hand every now and then along the way when the going gets tough, okay?"

I nod, and my eyes sting with tears. "Okay," I say again, and there's a heavy pressure in my chest.

I don't know why his help makes me want to cry, but it does.

I think it's because accepting help isn't easy for me, and Shawn is so nice. He's not overbearing or controlling, and knowing he's picked *me* to be the one to take care of makes me feel adored in a way I've never been before.

He doesn't think I'm weak or incapable of doing things on my own. He's offering a hand to make sure I don't go under the water for too long, and it's the kindest thing anyone's ever done for me.

The car rolls to a stop in front of a hotel with a white facade, and I wipe my eyes. I look out the window and gasp. Christmas trees adorned with lights and decorations line the walkway to the door. Stanchions are set up on the sidewalk, and a small crowd of people wait outside. Some have cameras while others look like fans, bundled up in coats and wearing Titans hats on their heads.

"It's beautiful," I say.

"Goddammit Dallas," Shawn mumbles, and he adjusts his tie. "He was doing a live stream on some app earlier and told his two million followers where the party would be. I'm surprised it isn't more of a clusterfuck out here. I swear I need to confiscate his phone from him."

"Guess we better get inside before that happens," I say. I turn to face him, and I giggle. "Hang on. You have a piece of hair that's sticking straight up. You can't go out there looking like that."

"What?" Shawn pats the top of his head, and my giggle turns into a laugh. "Where?"

"Not there." I take his hand in mine and brush it over the small strands by his ears. "Here. That's better."

"Thanks," he says, and his gaze meets mine. His fingers wrap around my wrist and his eyes bounce over my face. "Your hair, for the record, looks perfect. *You* look perfect."

"Oh." I exhale softly, and the blush on my face deepens. "Thank you."

The limo door opens, and the driver holds out his hand. "Mr. Holmes, we're here," he says.

It's for the best we're getting out of this car, because Shawn is looking at me like he did two nights ago at his apartment; with longing on his face and hunger in his eyes.

We know how *that* ended.

"Ready?" he asks me.

I nod and climb out of the limo, gratefully accepting the driver's assistance as my foot lands on the street. Before I can blink, Shawn is around from the other side of the car, and he takes over helping me make my way to the sidewalk.

"Thank you," I whisper, his hand in mine and his arm around my waist.

Fake, my brain screams. *This is all an act.*

Then why does it feel so real when he kisses the top of my head and leads me past a group of photographers, ignoring the flashes of their cameras because he's too busy looking at me?

TWENTY-SIX

SHAWN

"SHAWN!"

"Coach Holmes, over here."

"Oh my god, he looks *so hot*. And so does she. Talk about the ultimate power couple."

I keep my arm around Lacey and lead her up the sidewalk toward the hotel. The mob of fans has grown, and I want her close by my side. I doubt anyone is going to do something stupid at a Christmas party on a Wednesday night, but I'm not taking any chances.

I stop us in front of a small group of reporters, and I smile at them. "Thanks for coming out tonight," I say. "We only have a minute before we need to head inside. There's talk of a nacho bar, and I'm a sucker for anything with queso on it."

Lacey's shoulders shake, and I glance down to find her laughing. She tries to cover it up with a cough, but it's obvious she has something to say.

"Sorry," she whispers. "Forget the champagne in your apartment. I'm picturing you walking around with a bag of Taco Bell at midnight."

"I fucking love Taco Bell," I whisper back. "The BellGrande nachos are my favorite."

"Another installment in my NFL coaches: they're just like us series."

"Ms. Daniels," a reporter says, and Lacey whips her head to the right. "This is your first official outing with Coach Holmes. What are you looking forward to tonight?"

"Um." Lacey's posture straightens, and she lifts her chin. "I'm excited to spend time with the team and learn about the toy drive they're doing for the holidays. There's a list of drop-off locations on the Titans' website where people can donate gifts for children in need this holiday season. I encourage everyone to check out the information, and to contribute if they can. Besides that, the guys are so fun. Any evening with them is a good time."

"A kiss on national television is quite the way to announce your relationship. How have the last couple of weeks been?" someone else asks, and Lacey relaxes against me.

"Go big or go home, right? They've been great. Shawn's absolutely wonderful. I'm sure you all see that, but he's truly one of the good guys. We're going to his parents' house for Christmas, and I can't wait to meet his family."

"Shawn, any comment on the allegations that the San Diego Suns have been stealing signs from other teams in the league?" Marcus Monroe asks, and I frown.

"I haven't heard any details about the allegations yet, so I don't want to speculate, but there's no room for cheating in sports. Play fair, or don't play at all," I say.

"What's it like dating a woman who's not used to being in the spotlight? Has that been an adjustment?"

"I like that Lacey is outside of the sports world, because I can go home and be myself with her. I can shut off the work talk and have a normal life. I'm not sure how many of you all know this, but she's a pediatrician, and she's incredible at what she does. I've popped in to visit her at work, and to see her in action and interacting with the kids shows she's so passionate about her career. If you're looking for another cause to donate to this holiday season, the hospital that's the parent company of her office could use your help with funding. I'll put a link up on my social media later tonight," I say. I glance over my shoulder and see the team starting to congregate in the lobby of the hotel. "If you'll excuse us, Lacey and I are excited to spend the evening with the best guys in the league."

A couple of other people try to ask us questions, but I lead Lacey inside. She pulls me into a small alcove tucked away from the hustle and bustle before we get very far.

"You didn't have to say all those nice things about me," she says. "Tonight is about your team."

"What are you talking about? Of course I did. You're here with me, and I want to brag about you. I'd say the same things if you weren't here with me."

"Thank you for mentioning the hospital. We need any kind of help we can get."

"Hopefully you'll get some traffic after tonight," I say, and I nod toward her long peacoat. "Want me to take that for you? I can run it to coat check."

"Sure." Lacey sets her purse down on the windowsill and unties the knot at her waist. She shrugs off the outer layer and hands it to me. "Thanks."

I stare at her, and my mouth goes dry.

Fuck, she looks beautiful.

The floor-length dress she's wearing hugs her curves through her waist and hips, then fans out around her feet. I can see the hint of black heels and red toes, and I think I'm going to go into cardiac arrest.

I'm used to seeing Lacey in game day clothes. Casual things she wears when we're at Maggie and Aiden's and drinking beer on the couch or her scrubs. There's been the occasional short sundress in the summer months when it's stifling outside, something flowy and light to keep the heat at bay, but nothing this fancy.

It's also the first time I've seen her since *that night*.

I've pictured her walking away from me while wearing my shirt for the past two days, but seeing her like this after fucking her into my mattress is an entirely new feeling.

Jesus fucking Christ.

I want her again.

Badly.

My eyes roam down her body, and I'm not being sly about checking her out. She knows it, too, because she rests her hand on her collarbone. Her fingers fan out over the top of her chest, and she smirks. She turns to the side so I can see the curve of her backside, and I have to bite my knuckles to keep from moaning.

Her fucking *ass*.

I didn't get to appreciate it as much as I wanted to when we were together, but now I want to drop to my knees and worship it. I want to put her foot on my shoulder and run my hands over her cheeks. Slip my fingers into her underwear to see how wet she is and make her come apart.

"You look—" I swallow and clear my throat. "You look hot, Lace. Like a lot of trouble."

"Yeah?" She reaches up and runs her nails down my neck. I'd like it if she ran them down my back, too. "Trouble can be good, you know."

"I know, and you're the best kind." I grab her hand and kiss the inside of her palm. "Thank god I haven't seen you in a dress like this before. I would've asked to hook up with you a lot earlier in our friendship and messed everything up."

Lacey laughs. "There's a waiting period before you can propose a one-time fuck with your friend. Gives you enough time to learn enough dirt on a person so you can blackmail them if they try to never talk to you again."

"See? Trouble." I tug her toward me, and her chest presses against mine. "Thank you for coming with me tonight."

"What are fake girlfriends for?" she asks. "We should probably get in there. I see someone with a microphone, and we don't want to slip in late. Don't you have a speech to give?"

"Yeah, I do. Lead the way, Daniels," I say, and I hand off her coat to a hotel staff member.

"You're going to look at my ass again, aren't you?"

"Of course I am. You can't show up in an outfit like that and expect me to *not* check out your ass. For the record, it looks just as good with clothes as without, and I'm kind of wondering what it would look like with my handprint on your skin."

"A high compliment." Lacey pats my cheek and heads for the grand ballroom where the party is taking place. She glances at me over her shoulder, and I have to drag my attention away from her hips. "Oh, one more thing. It would look fucking fantastic with your handprint on it, but I guess we'll never know, will we? Save me a dance, Holmes."

This woman is going to kill me.

THE PARTY TURNS rowdy after I give my speech.

Music blares from the speakers, and handles of vodka are passed around. Dallas is standing on a table, and my defensive line have taken control of the DJ booth.

I'm hiding out in the back of the room, a pain in my head and a tightness in my chest. I need a minute away from all the noise, but it's not much better over here.

I chug back the last sip of my beer and stand up, sliding out of the side entrance unnoticed and out into the hallway. There's a door to my left, and I push it open to a parking lot.

I find a spot on the curb and sit down, stretching my legs out in front of me. The snow soaks through my pants, but I don't care. It's quiet out here under the stars, and I can breathe a sigh of relief in the cool night air.

Behind me, I hear the click-clack of high heels. I turn my head to the side, ready to hide behind a bush, when I spot Lacey walking toward me. She's not wearing her jacket, and she rubs her hands up and down her arms.

"What are you doing out here?" she asks. She stops a few yards away from me and tilts her head to the side.

"I needed a minute. It was getting too loud in there for me. I felt…" I trail off and shake my head. *Weak*, is what I want to say, but I know my therapist doesn't like that word. "I felt overwhelmed."

"I understand." She points at the spot next to me, the dirty sidewalk covered in salt and sand to keep snow from sticking to the concrete. "Can I join you?"

"I don't want you to ruin your dress." I take off my tuxedo jacket and set it on the curb. "But I'd love if you joined me."

Lacey smiles and walks my way. She plops down beside me and scoots close. "The stars are pretty tonight," she says.

"Yeah. They are." I tip my head back to look at the sky. Snowflakes start to fall, and I shiver. "Are you having fun?"

"I was until I saw my date disappear." She rests her head on my shoulder and loops her hands around my arms. "I was worried about you. Are you okay?"

I hesitate. The last time I talked about this with someone, it ended up all over the internet. It made me close off, keeping personal details to myself instead of divulging them to everyone who asks. I don't owe anyone anything, but I know Lacey isn't like that.

She's asking because she genuinely cares, and she wants to make sure I'm alright. I'm not used to that feeling, and the tension in my chest loosens the longer she stays by my side.

"It felt like the beginning of a panic attack," I explain, and I offer her a shrug. "It's the second time it's happened this season, and I don't know what's been going on lately."

She hums and stares out at the parking lot. "I'm not a therapist, but I have an idea. Maybe it's because you have a lot on your plate. The Titans have the best win streak of your career as head coach. You kissed your friend in front of seventy thousand people and you told your parents you're bringing that same friend home for the holidays as your girlfriend, even though you aren't really dating." She pauses and chuckles softly. "What am I forgetting?"

"When you put it that way, it's a wonder I haven't fallen apart yet." I laugh with her and put my chin on the top of her head. "Thanks for putting it in perspective. It's good to see the big picture."

"Just think: you only have a couple more weeks until we can stage a break up. You can go back to focusing *just* on football. The Titans will make the Super Bowl. I'll get the promotion I want, and we'll all live happily ever after," Lacey says.

My smile dips into a frown. I know our agreement has an end date, a very obvious circle on the calendar that tells us when we're going to part ways, but I've liked having Lacey around.

I guess Lacey's *always* been around, but it's fun to have someone to bring to events and to talk to late at night. It might stay like this when we walk away from each other, but it might not. She'll have a boyfriend eventually, and I'll probably have a girlfriend somewhere down the road. You can't stay up and text your best friend until two in the morning when you have someone else sleeping beside you, can you?

"Why are you single?" I blurt out, and she pulls away to glance at me. "Sorry. I didn't mean to shout it at you. You're just... you've been great these last couple of weeks. Is there a reason you don't date?"

"It's not so much that I don't date, but more like I don't *like* to date." She pushes her shoe into a melted pile of snow and moves the heel from side to side. "I'm going to say something that's going to come across as incredibly narcissistic, and I don't mean for it to sound that way."

"Well, fuck, now you have to tell me," I say. I turn my body so our knees press against each other, and I watch her, anxiously waiting to hear more. "Go on."

"A lot of men are intimidated by my success and my career. And, I know I'm not a literal brain surgeon like Maggie, but even her ex-husband made comments from time to time about how *he* was supposed to be the breadwinner in the family, not her. I worked hard in school. I took out loans and paid them off. Now I'm making good money, and I shouldn't be embarrassed by that. Men I've met have asked if I'd quit my job when I was ready to settle down. If I'll stop working when I decide to have kids and start a family. That's kind of bullshit, isn't it?" Lacey asks, and there's passion in her voice. "I'm a woman who makes two hundred thousand dollars a year. I'm smart and I'm successful. I don't have time for boys who don't see my worth and expect me to change to fit *their* needs."

Lacey's always been so sure of herself, conviction in all her conversations and no self-doubt with her decisions in life. It's not that she's a bragger or someone who can't accept criticism; it's more that she's *proud* of herself, and she damn well should be.

"Good for you for recognizing your worth. The dudes that

say that stuff to you get off on belittling women. It's not a good look, and we're not all like that. I promise. You deserved to be valued, Lacey, because you're a fucking diamond."

"I know you're not all like that. Especially when I come here tonight with you and—" Lacey pauses and shakes her head. "Anyway. Why don't you date? What skeletons do you have in your closet? You're the nicest man I've ever met. You're kind and compassionate, and you know how to make a girl feel good."

"Ah." I rest my elbows on my legs and stare straight ahead. "Guess it's only fair. You showed me yours, now I have to show you mine."

"Tit for tat. You're safe to share your stories with me, Shawn."

I *am* safe with her. Lacey makes me want to be myself—I don't have to throw up a tough facade or pretend I'm someone I'm not. I can show the vulnerable parts of a man who's still working on himself and trying to break the stereotypes associated with being an athlete.

"I've been in the spotlight since I was ten years old," I say. "Interviews, highlight reels, media days, a massive contract when I turned twenty. Whenever I meet someone, the first thing they see is Shawn Holmes: the football player. The tight end who won the Super Bowl a couple times and was part of a dynasty franchise. No one ever asks how I'm doing or what I'm going through. It's always, *hey, what happened in that game last night?* Or, *should've caught that ball, Holmes,* and *maybe you should've gotten your college degree and done something important with your life.* Even women see how they could benefit from being with me; the monetary payoff. Brand deals. I've been careful about who I let get close because of that fear of not being loved for me, but being loved for what I bring to the table. I didn't think that was possible until I met you. You don't give a shit about how much money I make or if my team wins or loses. Yeah, you support me and want me to do well in my career, but it's different with you. You're one of the only people who sees me as a person, which has always been my dream. And that... that makes me feel like I'm the luckiest guy in the world," I whisper.

"You are a person, Shawn, and I *do* see you," Lacey says. She crawls into my lap and holds me in her arms. "You're not more than me because you have a Super Bowl ring and millions of dollars in your bank account, and you're not less than me because you didn't go to medical school and dropped out of college after your junior year. You have hopes and dreams and fears. And, sure, you're a popular guy with a famous last name people talk about on the news sometimes. But do you know how *I* know you? You're not the guy under the stadium lights or running back a touchdown. To me, you're Maven's godfather. You're the guy who bought her tampons when she was on her period and lets her paint your nails. You're the guy who treats my best friend like she's your sister and welcomed her with open arms when you realized how head over heels she is for *your* best friend. You're a loving son who cares about his family, and you're a man with a good heart and a good soul who desperately wants to do good in this world." She touches my cheeks, and her hands are ice cold. "Anyone who doesn't see what's beneath the jersey and headset is missing out. You are the most perfect person I've ever met, and I'm so lucky to have you in my corner."

I look at Lacey, and it hits me square in the chest.

She's my favorite person in the entire world.

I don't know what I'm thinking when I take her hands in mine. When I lift her chin and press my lips to hers, just that I *want to*.

I *have* to.

I need Lacey Daniels like I need oxygen.

She sighs against my mouth and kisses me back, and I'm warm all over.

"Does this count as breaking our rules?" I ask, and I dip my chin to trail a set of kisses down her neck.

"No, this doesn't count. We can be friends who kiss, right?" Her hands clutch my collar, and she drops her head back. "Platonic kissing buddies."

"In that case, you're the best buddy I've ever had," I murmur into her shoulder. She pulls on my hair, and I kiss the skin under the thin strap of her dress. "Fuck, I want you."

"Kissing only," she says, but she grinds against me. She lifts her dress and I can *feel* her. Hot and wet and trying to touch me everywhere.

"You sure make kissing fun."

"We should stop."

"Okay," I agree, and I bury my face in her cleavage. "We'll stop."

"In a minute."

"I've heard that before," I say, and my hands move over the swell of her ass. "We really should stop, though, because there are cameras everywhere, and the last thing we need is you on some gossip website without your dress on. I'm sorry. I shouldn't have started this."

"I'll share the blame. I climbed in your lap."

"Equally guilty parties." I stand up and set her on the ground. "Let's head back inside. Your fingers are turning blue."

"I'm okay." A snowflake hangs on the tip of her nose, and she doesn't look the least bit cold. "You still owe me a dance."

"We don't have any music," I say, and Lacey shrugs.

"That's okay. We can make our own music."

I take her hand in mine and pull her close. I wrap her in my arms to try to warm her up. She rests her head on my chest and we sway side to side.

"Really, though," I whisper in her ear. "I'm lucky to have you in my life, Lacey girl. Thank you for being my friend. Thank you for seeing me. You make me happy."

"You make me happy too, Shawn. I'm always going to see you, even when you have trouble seeing yourself. In your dark moments, I'll be there. Don't ever forget that."

We dance until the snow accumulates on the ground around us, and I've never been more at peace.

TWENTY-SEVEN
LACEY

I CLIMB into bed with a glass of red wine and my vibrator.

After a long day at work, I need some self-care.

I love what I do, but sometimes the hours get to me. Today was one of those afternoons, another shift where we were understaffed and had a waiting room full of kids who needed to be seen. I stayed late to finish up the last appointments, and I'm glad to be off my feet.

I settle back against my pillows and take a sip of my drink before setting it down on the bedside table. I grab my vibrator and smile as I hold the toy in my hand. I've been worked up since the Titans' Christmas party when I climbed into Shawn's lap. It was another mistake, and I seem to be on a kick of making poor decisions.

He's out of town this weekend for an away game though, so at the very least I can behave myself until he gets home Sunday night.

I click on the toy and move it slowly over the silk tank top I put on after my bubble bath. I drag it across my nipples and sigh. I like sex, but I've always loved foreplay so much more. It's intimate, a chance to get to know your partner and learn what they like.

So many people rush toward the end goal, but I like being teased. Being brought close to the edge yet not falling totally over. I like when someone takes their time with me. Touches me everywhere and *savors* me.

Like Shawn did.

No.

I'm not allowed to think about him.

I shake my head and clear my mind. Pleasure pricks my skin as I move the toy down my stomach. When I bring it to the front of my silk shorts on the lowest setting, I moan as I find the spot I like the most.

I'm pulled from the moment when my phone rings on the mattress beside me. I let out a frustrated sound and grab it off the bed, seeing Shawn's name on the screen.

"Shit." I click off the toy and set it next to my wine. "Hey," I answer, and I hope I don't sound out of breath. "How's Cleveland?"

"Boring," he says. "The best part of this town is a restaurant where you can build your own tacos. I had seven for lunch."

"You didn't make it to the Rock and Roll Hall of Fame? That's like a cultural landmark."

"Already been. I can only learn about the history of the Rolling Stones so many times."

"True." I laugh and prop myself up on an elbow. "The fourth or fifth time might make you a groupie."

"Exactly. I didn't wake you up, did I?"

"Isn't Cleveland in the same time zone as D.C.?"

"Yeah, it is, but if you've had a day like me, you'd feel like it was midnight, too."

"No. I just got in bed with a glass of wine. What happened? Is everything okay?"

"Dallas' leg is bothering him, so he might be out on Sunday. Jett has food poisoning, and he barfed his brains out on the flight over. I'll be shocked if he can play. One of my assistant coaches admitted to me they're in a relationship with a player on another NFL team, and my mother keeps trying to get me—us, I guess—to come down a day earlier when I can't," Shawn says. "It's just... when it rains, it pours."

"Shit." I sit up and cross my legs. "What does that mean for your assistant coach? Are players allowed to date coaches?"

"Nope. Definitely not allowed. It's antiquated, but those are the rules. We're trying to figure out how to handle it going forward, but she's scared, and that sucks. You have to pick between the person you love or your job? Everyone's a consenting adult. Who cares who's fucking who?" He sighs, and I swear I can feel his exhale through the phone. "Sorry. I don't mean to unload all of this on you."

"You're not unloading; you're telling me about your day. That's what friends do."

"Thanks, Lace. Enough about me. How was your day?" he asks.

"Fine, yeah. I had a long day at work, but nothing too terrible. I made some pasta for dinner, took a bubble bath, now I'm in bed with a glass of wine and—" I stop short of mentioning my toy. "And it's the perfect night."

"Sounds like it. Any fun plans this week?"

"This week is so busy. There's game night with Maggie and Aiden and the hospital gala."

"Then it's almost time for our trip."

"You're coming to game night, right? I know we lose every week, but I can't be the third wheel with the lovebird couple."

"I'll be there. Those two are really obsessed with each other, aren't they? And to think, we're the ones who kind of set them up."

"Imagine if you didn't volunteer Aiden for that photo shoot," I say.

"And imagine if you didn't encourage Maggie to flirt with him. He was over the moon when she gave him attention."

"It makes me happy. They're both good people, and I'm glad they found each other. We make fun of them, but I think they have what we're all searching for, right? True love and someone who would set the world on fire for us. That's special." I sigh, and I'm sure I sound like a kid reading a fairy tale. Caught up in the idea of a happily ever after I'm not sure I'll ever have. "This got really deep, didn't it?"

Shawn laughs. "Yeah, it did. I'm happy for them, too, though. Those two are going to last forever."

"Hang on. Let me grab my wine and we can toast to them." I reach over and lift my glass off the bedside table. As I do, I knock my vibrator to the floor and it turns on. "Dammit."

"What was that?"

"Nothing."

"It sounded like something. Are you okay?" he asks.

"I'm fine. All good over here."

"Are you sure? It was pretty loud."

"It's my vibrator," I blurt out. "It, uh, fell when I was getting my wine."

The other end of the phone is quiet. I down half my wine before shoving the glass aside. I think Shawn might have hung up, but then I hear his breathing hitch.

"Were you using it?" he asks, and his voice takes on a different tone.

It's lower now, and silky smooth. It matches what he sounded like *that night*, and I'm transported back to his penthouse apartment, his hand around my neck and his mouth everywhere.

"I was before you called," I whisper.

"Why'd you stop?"

"I couldn't exactly keep going when I was talking to you."

Shawn is quiet again before he says, "you could use it."

"W-what?"

"You could use it with me on the phone."

"I'm—that's..." I take a deep breath and close my eyes. "You want me to?"

"It wouldn't go against our agreement, would it?" he asks, and I flop back against my pillows. "I'm not the one doing it to you. You are."

I squirm on the sheets as I listen to his loophole, and I like the logic. "Okay. Do you want to watch?"

"*Fuck,*" he breathes out, and it's a strangled word. "I'd love to watch."

"Hang on."

I chug the rest of my drink and grab the toy. We've already seen each other naked; what's one more time? I FaceTime Shawn, and he answers right away.

"Hey."

The room is dark, but there's a lamp somewhere off camera that makes his skin look golden and soft. He's shirtless and his hair is wet; he must've just gotten out of the shower.

I've never had phone sex with someone before, but this is *Shawn.* I can trust him.

"Hi."

"You look pretty tonight," he says, and his eyes bounce across the screen.

"Thank you." I angle the camera so he can see my legs, and I bring the toy to my chest. "I wish you were here," I say, and I blush as the admission slips out of me.

"I wish I was too. Are you going to show me what we'd be doing if I was with you?" Shawn asks, and *hell*, that's hot as sin.

"We'd be doing *a lot* of things if you were with me."

He leans out of the frame for a second before popping back up. He flips his camera and I can see the front of his sweatpants. "I'm already hard."

"I want to watch you, too. Can I watch you come?" I ask.

"You can have whatever you want. We can get off together."

"What do you like best? Do you want to see me? Do you just want to see the toy?"

"I want you to do whatever you feel comfortable with, Lacey girl. I want to see you take care of your pussy the way you know I would if I was there. But we both know I'm better than a toy," he says.

"You are." I nod and prop the phone on the bedside table against the bottle of wine. I pull off my top and bottoms, not wasting any time, and I'm naked in front of him. Shawn flips his screen so I can see his face again, and he looks anguished. Like he'd climb through the screen to get to me if he could. "I like to tease myself."

"You like when the guy works for it. You love to be touched, don't you?" he asks as his hand disappears, and I know he's touching himself.

"Yes." I click on the toy and circle my nipples with it. I remember what he said the other night about something he wanted to try, and I push my breasts together and run the vibrator up and down in my cleavage. "This is what it would look like with your cock," I say.

"Fuck, that's hot. I'm bigger than that, but we'd make it work, wouldn't we? I fit in your tight pussy just fine."

I nod and bring the toy to my clit. I moan as I move it in a small circle, and the vibrations run through my body like live wires. "It feels so good, Shawn."

"Can you come a little closer to the camera? I want to see how wet you are," he rasps, and I crawl across the mattress.

"Is that better?" I ask, and he nods.

"Yeah, Lacey girl, that's perfect. You're so perfect. Look at you already wetting that toy. You're needy tonight, aren't you?"

"I've been thinking about this all day." I click up the speed, and my legs spread wider across the mattress. "I've been thinking about you, too."

"What about me? How you wish I was buried inside of you? You know we can't."

"That's why I want to," I say, and I feel the beginning of my climax within reach. "I want what I can't have."

"Can you lie on your back for me, pretty girl, and spread your legs nice and wide?" Shawn asks, and I blush. "Remember when you did that on my couch? I liked seeing you like that."

"I'll do anything for you." My back rests on the bed, and I scoot toward the phone. "Do you like what you see now?"

"I'm fucking obsessed with what I see. How do you like to get off? Do you use your fingers? Do you fuck yourself and get nice and deep?"

I slide two fingers inside of myself, and I arch off the bed. "It feels so good, Shawn. God, I wish you were here. You get much deeper than I can."

"I'd like to watch you like this when I'm right next to you. Your fingers and a toy. I could play with your tits. You could suck on my dick, too. Would you like that?"

"I'd love that. I want to taste you. I didn't get a chance to." I increase my rhythm, and I'm so close. "I need to come, Shawn."

"You can come, Lacey girl. You've been so good," he says, and his praise notches its way down my spine. "I've loved watching you. I want you to come first, then I will after, okay? Can you let me see how good you make yourself feel?"

The orgasm overtakes me. I feel it from my head to my toes, and I writhe on the bed as wave after wave of pleasure and ecstasy roll through me.

"There you go. You're such a good girl for letting me watch. Fuck, you're getting your sheets all wet, aren't you?" Shawn says.

Another round of nirvana zips through me with his words, and I hold the toy against my clit until my legs stop shaking. I toss the vibrator away and lay on my back, panting as a bead of sweat rolls down my cheek.

"Wow," I breathe out.

"You okay?" Shawn asks, and I sit up. I give him a lazy, satisfied smile, and he chuckles. "You're just fine."

"It's your turn," I say. I grab my phone off the table and lay on my side. "Unless you already—"

"No." He shakes his head. "I didn't. I was waiting for you."

He flips his camera, and I see his hard length. He got rid of his sweatpants, and he's stroking himself. I lean forward and frown.

"What are you holding?"

"Your underwear from the other night," he says, and I almost come again.

"That's hot," I whisper. "You brought them with you?"

"Yeah. Wanted to get off to you."

I watch as he wraps the lace around his cock and moves his hand up and down. "God, you're so big."

"I stretched you out the other night, didn't I? You took me so well, though, Lacey girl. Every fucking inch."

I'm entranced by his movements and the way he knows exactly what he likes. Quick jerks of his wrist that have his hips lifting off the bed. "Are you thinking about me, Shawn? Are you thinking about how good it felt to come inside me?"

"Fuck," he grunts. "Yeah, I am. I'm not going to last much longer."

"You know I don't care about that." I push my breasts together, and he makes a sound from the back of his throat. "I just care that you fill me up."

"Lacey," he says, and it's like a warning. As if he's got me by the hair and is about to finish down my throat. "You're incredible."

"Look how good *you* are, Shawn. Such a good boy for me. Do you want to come?"

"Please," he begs, and I smile.

"Let me watch. Pretend I'm on top of you. Don't waste a drop," I say.

Shawn groans, low and long. His release covers his hand and my underwear. His hips lift one more time before he stills and his heavy breathing subsides.

"I think the only word I have left in my vocabulary is fuck," he says, and he flips the camera so I can see his face again. "But, *fuck*."

"That was fun." I bring my legs to my chest and rest my chin on my knees. "I like being your friend."

He laughs. "You're the best friend I've ever had. Sexiest, too."

"What? You don't get off with your friends on the phone all the time?"

"I've certainly never done that with Aiden. There's a first time for everything."

"'Tis the season of good tidings and cheer. Phone sex too, I guess."

"You're funny." Shawn opens his eyes, and he sits up. My underwear is still wrapped around him, and I've never seen something so sexy in my life. "I should go clean up. I made a mess."

"Me, too. Thanks for helping me decompress," I say, and he gives me a salute.

"Right back at ya, Daniels. I don't even remember what my problems are anymore."

"Funny how that works. Have a good rest of your night. I

hope tomorrow is a better day. And we'll be cheering for you on Sunday."

"Thanks. I'll see you at Maggie and Aiden's."

We stare at each other, and I realize I don't want to hang up with him. I want to keep talking and ask about their practice tomorrow. I want to find out if the Christmas tree in his apartment is real or fake.

I think I might just want... *him.*

"Are you okay?" Shawn asks, and I smile.

"I'm fine. I'll talk to you tomorrow."

"Right. Yeah. Tomorrow." He looks like he wants to add something else, but he doesn't. "Bye, Lace Face."

"See ya, Shawn Yawn."

I click off my phone and throw it face down on the bed like it burned me. I stare at it and shake my head.

Nope.

There's no way I'm falling for my best friend.

If anything, it's just a silly crush. Post-orgasm affection toward the guy giving me attention. There aren't any *actual* feelings involved.

But why the *hell* is there an ache in my chest when I think about him walking away from me when the new year strikes?

TWENTY-EIGHT
LACEY

"PLEASE DON'T TELL me we're playing charades again tonight," I say to Maggie. I pour a glass of wine and slide it her way. "If I have to act out racquetball or tennis one more time, I'm going to scream."

"No charades, I promise." Maggie laughs and takes a sip of her drink. "It's a game Aiden found online."

"A game he found online? Lovely. What could go wrong?" I lean over and turn up the Christmas music playing from my phone. Bing Crosby croons about a white Christmas and I smile, secretly hoping a massive snowstorm blows through the Mid-Atlantic just in time for the holidays. "Are we still celebrating Christmas together on the 30th?"

"Yeah, we'll be back home by then. Aiden mentioned Shawn is leaving for an away game on New Year's Eve—that's the night you all are going to stop pretending you're dating, right?"

"Yeah." I grab the bottle of wine and pour myself a glass. Hearing about the approaching end date of our agreement makes my stomach twist with disappointment. "We're heading back from his parents' house on the 26th, and that will be that."

"I can't believe how fast the month is going. We have the gala in two days, and then it's basically Christmas. Everything is flying by." Maggie jumps off her barstool and heads for the oven. She slips an apron decorated with candy canes and snowflakes over her head and grabs two oven mitts. "Are you doing okay?"

"With what?"

"Your fake relationship with Shawn. I know you were panicking when the video first circulated. Everything's been alright since then?"

"Yeah." I nod and cross my legs. "I'm fine. The buzz has started to die down, and I don't get eight thousand comments on my social media photos when the Titans make a dumb play anymore. It's been a whirlwind, but a good whirlwind. I've liked getting to know the guys on the team, and I feel lighter these days."

She glances at me, and her face softens. "You're allowed to be sad about it, Lace. You and Shawn have been spending a lot of time together. It makes sense that you might get attached."

"I'm not getting attached," I say, and I can hear the aggression in my voice. Like I have to defend how I'm feeling toward Shawn when I'm not even sure *how* I'm feeling toward him.

We've been spending a lot of time together, and I've enjoyed every minute.

And, yeah, the physical component was a nice bonus, too—the man knows what he's doing in the bedroom. I'm still thinking about his head between my thighs and the desperate way he asked me to bring the camera closer so he could watch me come.

The kisses, too.

The kisses were phenomenal, and making out with him was better than all of my other bedroom experience with past partners.

But I've liked the quieter, less assuming things, too.

The morning texts and the late-night phone calls when he's

walking around his apartment and trying to get his mind to settle.

The magnet he brought me from Cleveland: it's the Rolling Stones logo and came with a note that said *don't be a groupie, Daniels.*

How his eyes always find mine and the way his smile pulls up in the corners when he catches me watching him.

I don't hide it anymore. He knows I'm looking at him because he's busy looking at me, too.

I just don't know what it all *means.*

Do I like *him*? Or is it just the attention I like, the first time I've let a man get close to me in years?

I never used to feel a swoop in my belly when Shawn touched my shoulder, but now I do.

I never used to lie in bed and stare at the ceiling, wondering what he was thinking about and hoping he missed me like I missed him. And I *do* miss him when he's not here; I miss his laugh and how his nose scrunches when he smiles. I miss his voice low in my ear and his hands in mine.

I especially miss his gentle heart, that one that sent food to my office yesterday and today. I teared up in the bathroom after the delivery driver dropped off a big paper bag, overwhelmed with the recognition that someone out there cares about me very much.

I'm still not used to being cared for, but I'm learning.

The door to Maggie and Aiden's apartment opens and Shawn comes barreling inside like I summoned him.

He looks *good*, with his mussed-up hair and pink cheeks. The white sweater he's wearing makes his skin look tan and soft, and his joggers hug his thighs in all the right places. I avert my gaze and take a long sip of my wine.

"Hey," he calls out. "Sorry I'm late. Our team meeting ran long."

"No worries," Maggie says. "Aiden is still in the shower. Want something to drink?"

"Sure." Shawn shrugs off his coat and hangs it on the hook by the door next to mine. "What are we having?"

"I brought a bottle of that wine we had when I was at your place," I say, and Maggie gives me a look. "What? We hang out without you all."

"Frequently?" she asks.

"A handful of times."

"We've had a couple of video chats, too," Shawn says as he walks toward the kitchen, and my cheeks flame scarlet red. He smirks and bends down to kiss my forehead. "Hey, Lace. How was your day?"

"It was good. Thank you for lunch, by the way. The sushi was delicious," I say, and I loop my arm around his waist to give him a hug. "Want to sit?"

"Nah, I'll stand. I've been sitting all day." He turns his attention to Maggie, who's busy staring at us. Her gaze bounces between my forehead and Shawn's waist. "Can I help with anything, Mags?"

"No," she says slowly. "The cookies are just about done."

"What did I miss?" Aiden asks, walking into the kitchen to join us.

"Lacey and Shawn hang out without us," Maggie says. She scoops the cookies off the sheet pan and onto a plate shaped like a Christmas tree. "And they video chat, too."

We also watch each other get off. His dick is fantastic, and he has a pair of my underwear somewhere in his apartment, I think, but I keep my mouth shut.

"Wow. I'm kind of jealous." Aiden rests his chin on Maggie's shoulder. "Do you do anything fun?"

I reach over and grab a sugar cookie, taking a big bite. "Nothing noteworthy."

Shawn hums. He leans toward me, and I swear his lips brush against my ear. "You're playing with fire, Lacey girl. Seems like someone didn't forget what she was supposed to forget. Did you think about me last night when you were using your toy?" he asks just low enough so no one else can hear, and heat races up my spine. "Because I thought about you."

"Flirting with me, Holmes?" I ask. I tip my chin up and stare him down. He grins, and I see the wrinkles on his nose that I love so much.

"In your dreams, Daniels," he says with a sparkle in his eye, and I desperately want to kiss him.

I want to grab him by his collar and press his mouth against mine. I want to slip my hands under his sweater and run my palms along the ridges of his body; the smooth planes and firm muscles I've started to fantasize about when I'm in bed and thinking about him.

I think he wants to kiss me, too. I see the same flare of heat behind his gaze as the night in the supply closet and when I was in his apartment.

This is a dangerous line I'm toeing, and I need to get off the high rope before someone gets hurt.

But why is it so hard to walk away?

"OKAY, the game is *how well do you know your partner?*" Aiden explains. "I found a bunch of questions online, and I figured they'd be good to ask you all before you head to Shawn's parents' for the holidays. It's a quiz to make sure you two can pass the test of appearing like you're really in love."

I groan and bite the head off a reindeer cookie. I've had six already, and my stomach is starting to protest. "Not fair. This is going to be entirely one-sided. What are you and Maggie going to do? Watch?"

"We'll play too," Aiden says. "It'll be fun. I promise it's nothing too lovey dovey."

"The first question you give us about something like wedding vows, I'm out," I warn.

"What? You don't want to show up on Christmas with an engagement ring and really blow everyone's minds?" Shawn jokes. He leans back against the couch, and his thigh presses against mine. "The reactions would be hysterical."

A sensation I've never experienced before squeezes tight around my heart and my lungs as I think about an engagement ring on my finger.

An engagement ring from *Shawn* on my finger.

I thought I'd hate it, but I don't.

It sounds kind of nice.

"We might as well go get married in Vegas," I joke back, and he chuckles.

"Not a wedding in a church kind of gal? This is something I should know in case someone asks about our future plans."

"No. I think I'd want something spontaneous. Small, with the people I love. Nothing fancy. No tuxedos or centerpieces. You know that's not me."

"It's not, and that's okay," he says, and I see his hand twitch at his side.

I think he wants to reach out and touch me.

"The game is working already," Aiden says, and he sounds positively giddy. "Okay. I'll ask each of you a question. You'll write your answer, then you'll both hold up your whiteboard with the responses. We'll see how well you do."

"Going to kick your ass, Daniels," Shawn murmurs in my ear. "I know you like the back of my hand."

"Oh, yeah?" I uncap my dry erase marker and lift my eyebrow. "Game on, Holmes."

"Shawn, what is Lacey's least favorite food?" Aiden asks, and we both scribble down our answers and hold up the whiteboards. "Okay. You both wrote mushrooms. Nice job."

"See?" Shawn says, and I roll my eyes.

"One question right does not mean you know me."

"Lacey, how does Shawn take his coffee?" Aiden asks, and I grin.

"Easiest thing ever," I whisper under my breath.

"You've never seen me drink coffee," Shawn whispers back.

"I have. You had some on Thanksgiving," I answer, and we flip over our whiteboards.

"With a splash of milk and a half spoonful of sugar. Well done, you two," Aiden says, and I stick out my tongue.

The game continues for twenty minutes, and Maggie and Aiden don't even bother jumping in. They're having too much fun seeing if Shawn and I get our answers right to join.

Neither of us misses a question; I correctly guess his favorite color (purple), how he eats his eggs in the morning (over easy), and what his biggest fear is (spiders, surprisingly).

He does the same, knocking questions about me out of the park; the first time I broke a bone (eleven, thanks to a scooter mishap), my biggest pet peeve (people who don't return their shopping carts at the grocery store, which Maggie vehemently agrees with) and the place I want to visit the most in the world (the Galapagos Islands, because I have a weird infatuation with tortoises).

"Okay, we're down to the last question. You two have passed with flying colors, but here comes a tough one," Aiden says. "Lacey will be first. What is she most looking for in a partner?"

My breath catches, and I dip my chin. There's no way Shawn

231

knows the answer to this; we might have talked about our pasts during his team party, but I wasn't specific about what I want.

We turn the whiteboards over, and I stare at what Shawn's written. There are two words, and they perfectly match my own.

An equal.

"Told you I know you like the back of my hand," Shawn says softly, and my skin heats. "You want—you *deserve* someone who isn't intimidated by your success. Someone who looks at you and sees all your wonderful accomplishments and lifts you up. Someone who isn't afraid. Someone who knows you're worth more than a million tons of gold. I hope you never settle for less than that, Lacey girl. Promise me you won't."

The air is still and silent. I stare at him, and I swear my heart crawls up my chest and sits in my throat. I nod, and my eyes never leave his as I say, "I promise."

"Good," he murmurs, and he drags his thumb down my jaw. "Anything less than that means you're out of their league. Hell, you're out of everyone's league."

Not *his* league, I think, a fuzzy thought that bubbles in my brain as I wipe my board clean. That's exactly how Shawn treats me, and I wonder if I'm lucky enough to be struck by lightning twice.

Doubtful.

Meeting him was fate; to expect someone just as wonderful is a pipe dream.

"Okay. Same question for Shawn," Aiden says, and I wonder if he can sense the shift in the room.

This answer is simple. He told me when we were sitting in the parking lot of the hotel the other night as snow fell from the sky, but I would've known even if he didn't share. Shawn wears his heart on his sleeve, a stitched little thing I can see from a mile away. He tries to hide it, but I know.

I feel it down in my soul.

We flip our boards, and I smile when I see we've written the same answer again.

To be seen.

"You know I see you, right?" I ask him, because I want him to be sure. I scoot across the couch until the scent of his cologne and shampoo tickles my nose. "Not just as the football coach. I see all of you, and gosh, I like what's there. I always have. When this ends, I'm still going to see you, Shawn. The real, full you is one of the most marvelous things I've ever gotten to experience, and I feel lucky that we met all those months ago."

He drops his board and pulls me into a hug. He's become so familiar to me, and my body relaxes against his. I don't care that Maggie and Aiden are watching and the jokes they'll probably crack after. Right now, I just want to be in his arms.

"Thank you," he whispers. "You really are my favorite person in the entire world. If they gave out plaques, you'd have a dozen of them."

"Just a dozen?" I ask, and I laugh into his chest. "I need to step it up."

"No. You're perfect exactly as you are."

Maggie clears her throat, and Shawn and I pull apart. I tuck a piece of hair behind my ear and bite back a smile.

"Great game, Aiden," Shawn says. "I don't think Lacey and I will have any problems convincing my parents this is real."

"No," Aiden says. He drapes his arm around Maggie's shoulder and smiles into the curve of her cheek. "I don't think you will."

I run my palms over my jeans, and I scoot a half inch further away from Shawn. I'm afraid I'm going to try to kiss him if I stay too close. "Thanks for doing that, Aiden. It was fun."

"Anyone want more cookies? More wine?" Maggie asks, and she stands up from the couch. "A battle plan for how we're going to survive the gala, because if I have to hear another joke about operating on someone's brain, I'm going to snap?"

The rest of the night is lighter with lots of laughter, but I can't stop thinking about what Shawn said.

I do deserve someone who knows my worth, and the more I look at him, the more I think the person who can treat me like that has been right in front of me all along.

TWENTY-NINE
LACEY

SHAWN KNOCKS on my door when I still have a towel wrapped around my body.

"Coming," I call out. I hurry across my living room and unlock the door. "Hi."

"Hi," Shawn says, and he grins. "I didn't know the dress code for tonight was towel casual."

"Who needs black tie when you can wear terry cloth instead?" I joke. "Come in. I just need to get dressed, clearly, then I'll be ready to go."

"Take your time. I can keep myself occupied for a few minutes. You'll let me snoop through your drawers, right?" he asks.

"Check out the one to the left of the stove. That's where I keep all the good stuff."

"Oh." Shawn sticks out his arm, and I notice the bouquet of hibiscus flowers he's holding. "These are for you."

"They're beautiful," I whisper, and I lean forward to smell the petals. "Where did you find flowers this late in the year? I thought everything died two months ago. Maybe it's just me. I can't even keep a cactus alive."

"I bought them from a greenhouse down in Florida. The guy who owns the place was happy to send me one in every color."

"Another local business where your photo is on their wall," I say. "My parents live down in Florida."

"Do they? I'm sorry you can't see them for the holidays. I'm stealing you away."

"You aren't stealing me away. I'm going willingly. My dad has some health issues, so this time of year raises his stress levels. We do a Christmas celebration in late January, and they leave up their decorations until Valentine's Day."

"Is your dad doing okay?" Shawn asks, and the sincerity in his question makes me smile.

"He's doing much better. I'm working with his insurance to cover some of his hospital stays and it's a little overwhelming. Healthcare in our country is obscenely expensive, but he's home, and that's all that matters."

"There really ought to be a law that says people who work in the medical field get free healthcare for their family," Shawn says. "Seems fair to me."

"Ah. If only. If you decide to run for president, that could be your platform. You'd have my vote."

"And it's the only one that counts."

"My mom is a little disappointed she doesn't get to meet the great Shawn Holmes, but she'll get over it." I laugh and lean against the wall. "She thinks you're cute."

"I am cute."

"I know you are."

His cheeks turn pink, and so do the tips of his ears. He scuffs his shoe against the hardwood floor and clears his throat. "Maybe I could meet them sometime. We could take a trip down. I like Florida, just not in the summer."

"You want to meet my parents?" I ask.

It's the first time he's ever mentioned an *us* after New Year's Eve.

A *we*.

The possibility of this situation we've found ourselves in continuing past our end date hangs in the air like a question mark instead of a period. A comma, perhaps.

Something open-ended rather than closed off and punctuated.

I know we'll still be friends on January 1st and beyond; we vowed that would never, ever change.

But wanting to meet my parents goes past what a *friend* would do, right?

Shawn shrugs. "You're meeting mine. Of course I want to meet yours."

"Right. Yeah. We could—we'll see if we can work anything out." I push off the wall and point to the bouquet. I need a distraction from thinking about the future with this man. "I've never seen a violet hibiscus before. It's gorgeous. Could you put them in water for me? The vases are in the hall closet."

"You got it. Go get ready. I'll be on flower duty," he says.

"Thanks." I squeeze his shoulder and head for my bedroom. "I was indecisive on a dress, but I finally found one I liked."

"What color did you go with?" he asks, and his voice echoes down the hall. "The pictures you sent me earlier almost had the whole rainbow. You were just missing orange."

"I decided on red," I say. I crack the door to my bedroom and drop my towel. "I thought it was festive."

I rummage through my dresser and find the green strapless lace bra I'm going to wear tonight. I clasp the hooks together and slide it up my chest. The underwear matches, and I look like one of the Christmas ornaments hanging on my tree.

"Flowers are done," Shawn calls out, and I grab my dress off the bed.

"Okay. Two more minutes and I'll be ready." I pull on the zipper at the back of the gown, but it doesn't budge. "Shit."

"Everything okay?"

"Yeah." I yank on the zipper again, and it doesn't wiggle an inch. "Okay, I lied. The zipper on my dress is stuck. I'm afraid I'm going to rip it if I pull any harder."

"Want me to try?" he asks, and his voice is closer than before.

"Please. If I can't get this up, I'm not sure what else I can wear."

"I think one of the other eight dresses you have would be just fine." He knocks on my bedroom door. "Can I come in?"

"I'm, uh, not wearing any clothes. Well, that's not true. I'm wearing underwear."

There's a pause before Shawn speaks again. "I can close my eyes. Or you can hand it to me and I'll fix it out here."

"It's nothing you haven't seen before."

"Doesn't mean I automatically get to see it again."

"Right." I swallow and take a deep breath. "It's okay. You can come in."

Shawn pushes the door open, and my room feels smaller than it did three minutes ago. The walls seem like they're caving in, and heat rushes up my body.

"Where's the fashion emergency?" he asks, and his eyes stay locked on mine.

I gesture vaguely to the bed—the same bed he saw me get off on—and he nods. He lifts the dress off the mattress and studies the zipper.

"Do you think you can fix it?"

"Yeah." He uses his teeth to work the zipper down, and I wonder how it would feel if he used his teeth to take off my underwear. "There you go."

"Wow. That sure was easy."

"I grew up with two sisters, remember? I could work in fashion if football doesn't pan out."

"Thank you," I say, and our fingers brush as I take the gown from him. A jolt of electricity zips up my arm, and I shuffle backward. "I appreciate you."

"Don't mention it. I'm happy to help." Shawn runs his hand through his hair, then he hitches his thumb over his shoulder. "I should, um, let you get dressed."

"Could you help me zip it up?" I ask. "In case there are any more snags?"

"Yeah." He nods, and his eyes darken. They look almost like dark shadows now, a dangerous shade that's going to get me in trouble. "Of course."

We both know what I'm doing, and we both know how this ends. I'm playing with fire, but I think I want to burn.

I step into my dress and bring it up and over my hips. I slip the thick straps onto my shoulders, and the satin feels cool on my blazing skin. Shawn watches me, his attention hanging on to my every movement.

I've never felt more powerful.

I turn around so my back is almost flush against his chest. His fingers dance across my shoulders and down my spine. He presses his lips to the base of my neck, and I shiver from the heat of his mouth.

"Thank you for helping me," I whisper.

"It's my pleasure."

"I'm thanking you for a lot of things tonight."

"They're things I want to do," he answers, and his words are sin on my bare skin. "Things I like to do." He tugs on the zipper of the gown and drags it up my spine. It's torturous, almost, how slow he goes. "Going to take care of you, remember?"

"Yeah." I nod and rest my head in the crook of his neck. "I remember."

"You look like a goddess," he says in my ear, and his teeth nip at my shoulder. "You make me want to lose control."

"You can, if you want." I close my eyes and arch my back. "I'd let you."

"It would make this more than one time between us."

"Yeah, but we've kissed since then. We can be friends who kiss." I take his hand in mine and trail his touch down my neck. I settle his palm at the top of my chest, and his fingers fan out across my breast. He makes a strangled sound from the back of his throat, and my lips curl into a smile. "Friends who fuck." I roll my hips and feel him hard behind me, his length pressing into my backside. "Friends who take care of each other. Forget the goddamn rules."

"Lacey," he murmurs, and my name is silky smooth. His hand moves down my body and he takes his time, like he's waiting for me to stop him, but I'm not going to. "Is this what you want?"

"Maybe we can keep having fun until we end our agreement. Be physical. Touch each other and make out. We both want to," I say. I roll my hips again, and Shawn's breath catches on an exhale. "We do what we want until New Year's, then we can go our separate ways. Quit cold turkey."

"Okay." He nods into my shoulder, and I wrap my arm around his neck to pull him closer. "I'd like that. I've tried to stay away from you, Lacey girl, but it's damn near impossible."

"What do you want, Shawn?" I ask, and I kiss the spot on his throat I know he likes.

"Am I not making it obvious enough? I want you," he answers, and my world stops spinning. "Badly."

"You have me," I say, and he bunches my dress at my waist.

His large palm holds the fistful of satin, and I inhale sharply. His other hand snakes around my body and traces the lines of my underwear. When he snaps the elastic against my skin, I'm transported to mind-numbing bliss.

His foot wedges between mine, and he pushes my legs apart. I relax against him and he kisses me soft and slow. There's tongue and teeth and passion in the way he nips at my bottom lip. I feel him pour every ounce of himself into the press of his mouth, and I meet him just as eagerly, ravenous—*starved*—for his affection.

It's like we're competing to see who can drive the other the most out of their minds, and I think he might be winning.

Shawn's fingers circle me over my underwear. His thumb presses against my clit, and a low, pleased hum escapes from his mouth.

"Already wet. I love you like this. I love having you like this."

"How?" I breathe out, and rationality is close to flying out the window. "Horny?"

"No." His touch is unhurried and lazy, not a care in the goddamn world about how long it takes to get me to where I want to be. "Mine."

He dips his fingers beneath my thong, and he groans in my ear when he finds the spot between my legs where I'm aching for him to touch.

"Shawn. Please," I beg, but he doesn't move any faster. My eyes flutter closed and I feel that gentle pull in my belly, the gradual rise of pleasure building up my spine.

"Do you like that?" he asks. His voice is thick with lust and need drips from his question. Two fingers slip inside me, and he holds me tight against his chest when I cry out and squirm against him.

"Yes," I pant, and it's ridiculously close to a plea. "I love when you touch me. You know exactly what to do."

"Because I know you." He kisses my neck and his mouth

sucks a hot line down my throat. He's going to leave a mark, and I'm going to show it off. "Best you've ever had, right?"

He's taunting me, teasing me, just the way I like. When I get close to falling over the edge, he pulls me back in a game of tug of war. I'm frustrated. I'm electric. I'm warm all over, and every inch of my body sparkles under his hand.

"No one can take care of me like you do," I say, and his grip on my waist tightens. I think he might rip my dress when he thrusts his hips forward and rubs his hard length against my ass. "No one treats me right like you do."

Shawn adds a third finger, and I see stars. My mind goes blank as he tips my chin back and kisses me hard, possessiveness behind every press of his mouth. "Such a good girl for me," he whispers against my lips, and the praise makes me melt. It makes me grind into his palm, desperate for *more*. "You're going to come on my hand, aren't you, Lacey girl? Then we'll sit next to our friends and they'll have no idea I stretched you out. They won't know I filled your pussy with my fingers to get you ready for my cock. You're going to be begging me for it, aren't you? Fucking dripping for it."

I cry out. Maybe I scream, I don't know. Whatever noise I make, I transcend from my body as my orgasm crashes into me like a tsunami, wave after wave of delight rolling through me. I writhe against him, riding the high as the circles on my clit turn into a gentle slap, making sure I get every second of pleasure I deserve.

"You're alright," Shawn's soft voice says. "I've got you."

I open my eyes and blink, trying to adjust to the room around me. I wobble on my feet, my legs heavy and aching. Shawn leads me over to the edge of my mattress and pulls me into his lap, holding me tight as my breathing returns to normal.

"Holy shit," I whisper. There are spots in my vision, and my skin feels tight on my body. "How are you—why do—*fuck,* you're good."

He laughs into my hair and drops a kiss on the top of my head. "Can't deny we have chemistry."

"We definitely do." I let out a content sigh and snuggle into his chest. "Do we have to go to the gala?"

"Might be kind of obvious if we're both missing," he says. He kisses my forehead and adjusts the strap of my dress on my shoulder. "You know Maggie will panic."

"She will." I sigh again and stretch my arms over my head. "I could sleep for hours, though. I finally found a way to unwind after a stressful day; it's your fingers."

"Happy to help." Shawn smiles and tucks a piece of hair behind my ear. I like that he can't stop touching me. "Should we get going?"

"Yeah. We can't show up too late. I want to surprise the shit out of Director Hannaford when I introduce you to him." I wiggle in his lap, and I feel that he's still hard. "Do you want me to help you take care of that before we leave?"

"I do, but we'll save it for next time," he says. "Since we're friends who fuck now."

"I guess we are," I say, and I give him a slow grin. "Let me freshen up, then we can head out."

"Okay." He taps my hip, and I stand up. "I'll wait for you in the living room."

I peek a glance at him as I walk to the bathroom, and he's watching me with soft eyes and the biggest grin. I give him a matching smile in return because I'm happy too, I realize. Shawn makes me happy.

When I'm with him, I feel like I can fly.

THIRTY

SHAWN

I HAVEN'T BEEN to the Museum of American History in years, but it's exactly how I remember.

It's dark inside, and dozens of Christmas trees adorned with white lights sit on the perimeter of all the rooms. Crystal snowflakes hang from the ceiling, and I spot mistletoe in every doorway. For a hospital with a staffing shortage, it seems a little over the top.

I guess that's why there are four hundred people in dresses and suits mingling around, waiting to spend money.

Lacey holds my hand as we weave through the crowd, stopping to say hello to a handful of coworkers along the way. Some people do a double take when we pass like their eyes are deceiving them, and I chuckle to myself.

I know I look different in a tuxedo than a hat and joggers. I'd probably look twice, too.

"Want a drink?" she asks as we make it to the part of the museum set up with large round tables. We're sitting with Maggie and Aiden, and I'm sure that's not a coincidence. "There's a bar over there."

"A drink sounds great. What're you going to have? Beer? Wine?"

"I'm thinking bourbon or whiskey," she says, and my mouth twists into a smile.

"A recent favorite?" I ask, and there's a twinkle in her eye.

"You could say that." She gives my arm a light tug, and we head for the long line of folks waiting for the bar. "They're going to serve dinner, then Hannaford is going to give a speech. After that, the silent auction will be open for an hour and a half while everyone gets drunk and writes obscenely large checks."

"My kind of party. Did you tell him what you were donating?"

"Not exactly. I mentioned it was something that would bring in a lot of money for the hospital, but he was leery without seeing the proof."

"I would be, too. Sounds like a pyramid scheme."

We inch closer to the bar, and Lacey tosses her hair over her shoulder. I spot a little red mark on her neck, a souvenir from earlier in her room, and I bite back a grin at the sight of it.

I want to leave a dozen more on her body.

"I know the hospital needs funding, but he's so money hungry. I'm willing to bet he gets a cut of the earnings brought in from tonight. How is that fair? He has his employees working fourteen and fifteen-hour days while he sits up in a nice office and doesn't get his hands dirty." She pauses to take a breath and shakes her head. "Shit. Sorry, that was so unprofessional of me. Especially at a work function."

"No, it wasn't. Your career is your livelihood, and you're allowed to not be happy with it from time to time. Hell, some days I really don't want to be out on the football field."

"Really? But you love football."

"I do. I don't always like it, though, and that's okay."

"Huh. That's a good way to look at it."

"There was this coach I had when I played in college—he only lasted a year before getting sacked—and I told myself I would *never* be like him if I decided to pursue a coaching role. He was lazy and mean. Didn't give a shit about his players and only looked out for himself. It was *him*, not *the team*. Your boss sounds a lot like that, and I'm sorry you have to put up with his shit."

"Nancy? Is that you?"

Lacey looks over her shoulder, and the smile she plasters on her face is the fakest display of emotion I've ever seen from her.

"Speak of the devil," she mumbles under her breath before rolling her shoulders back. "Director Hannaford, hi. Nice to see you this evening."

A seedy-looking man with a tweed jacket and an obvious toupee approaches us. "I didn't see your silent auction item on the table," he says, and I can hear his disappointment. "Did you decide not to donate this year?"

Lacey brightens and looks at me. Her lips tug into the same smile I saw in her bedroom before we got here. It's a little sly, a little mischievous, and it makes me want to kiss the red lipstick off her mouth.

"I wanted my donation to be a surprise," she says. "Director Hannaford, this is my boyfriend, Shawn Holmes. I'm not sure if you're familiar with D.C. sports, but he's the head coach of the Titans. They've had a great season so far, and they have their sights set on the Super Bowl. When he was playing in the league, he won five titles with the Philadelphia Lightning, and he holds the league record for most yards on receptions by a tight end in a single season. Almost fifteen hundred of them, plus one hundred career receiving touchdowns."

My mouth pops open, and I gape at Lacey. I've never heard her say a single football statistic in my life, and the fact that she knows *my* numbers makes me brim with pride.

She's been learning the game.

I'd *never* ask or expect her to be knowledgeable on the sport; it's not her thing. I know that, and I don't care if she can't tell me a single goddamn fact after tonight.

She's trying, though.

For me.

And, *fuck*, that's incredible.

Her director—Hannaford—looks me up and down. He blinks twice and pulls the wired-framed glasses off the end of his hooked nose. "Your boyfriend?" he asks, and Lacey nods like a bobblehead.

"Yeah." She rests her head on my shoulder and I loop my arm around her waist. There's something settling about having her in my hold, and when my hand moves to the curve of her ass, I don't miss how she inches closer to me. "We've been dating for a couple of months, and he was kind enough to accompany me this evening. He's also donating two private one-on-one coaching sessions for the silent auction."

"Nice to meet you," I say, and I stick out my hand.

Hannaford nearly drops his drink to reach for me, and he shakes my hand vigorously. "I didn't know we would have a celebrity in our midst tonight," he says, and I hate how he uses that word. It makes me feel like a prop for an agenda I'm not a part of. "How *wonderful*. Oh, this is going to bring in record-breaking contributions, I'm just sure of it. Well done, Nancy. Well done."

Irritation flickers through me, and I drop his hand from my hold. "Why do you keep calling her that?" I ask.

"Because that's her name," he says, and my palm flexes against Lacey's dress.

"No, it's not. Her name is Lacey. Lacey Daniels."

"Sorry, sorry. There are so many names to learn, and I'm bound to slip up," Hannaford says, and I can't hear a hint of remorse in his apology. "I'm sure you don't know everyone's name on your team."

"I do, actually. Down to the janitor who cleans the locker rooms after our home games." I glance at Lacey and smile. "His name is Todd. We drink coffee together on Tuesday mornings, and he likes to give me shit. You'd adore him."

Her smile matches mine. "I love him already."

I turn my attention to Hannaford. "Say her name back to me so I know you understand. I want to make sure you have it committed to memory, and there isn't any confusion."

"Uh." Hannaford looks between us, and he's almost blue in the face. "Lacey. Lacey Daniels."

"Fantastic. And do you know where she works?" I ask, and I tilt my head to the side. I'm not usually a guy who uses my size to my advantage, but I'm definitely trying to make myself bigger right now. "She's been there six years, so you should be pretty familiar with her contributions to your hospital."

He clears his throat and adjusts his tie. "She's a nurse, isn't she? Over in pathology."

"Jesus Christ," I mumble. "She's a pediatrician at the office attached to your hospital. Literally right next door. Her patients love her, and it's a shame someone in a management role hasn't learned who his employees are."

Hannaford almost breaks the glass in his hand. "I'll be better," he says, and I smile brightly.

"Great." I gesture toward the bar. "If you'll excuse us, we're going to grab a drink."

"Would you come up and say a few words?" he blurts out. "Just, you know, it would be good for the people attending tonight to see who's here. It'll make next year's event even more enticing."

It's hard to not roll my eyes at how desperate this asshole sounds, but I nod anyway. I'm here for Lacey. This whole fake dating thing started because of this moment right here, so I smile and nod.

"Of course," I say. "I'd be happy to."

Hannaford scurries away, and Lacey clutches my arm. Her fingers dig into my jacket, and she's grinning.

"Holy *shit* Shawn. Did you just tell off my boss?" she asks.

"I didn't tell him off." I play with my cufflinks, and my lips twitch. "I reminded him how a leader should act."

"That was—" Lacey takes a breath and pulls me into a tight hug. She's warm and soft in my arms, and I bury my face in her hair. "Thank you," she whispers. "That was so cool."

"I would do it again, too," I say, and I squeeze her hip. "Come on. We're next for drinks."

We grab two whiskeys and head back to the table. By the time we find our seats, our friends are slipping into their chairs. I want to laugh at the obvious hickey on Maggie's shoulder and the way Aiden's tie is crooked, but I keep the jokes to myself.

Almost two years together, and they still can't keep their hands off each other. I think they're more in love now than when they first got together.

I shouldn't make fun of that.

"Why are you smiling?" Maggie asks.

"Shawn told off Hannaford," Lacey says, and she giggles. I think her drink is already going to her head.

"*What*? Shawn, what did you say?"

"Nothing he doesn't already know." I shrug and pull out Lacey's chair for her. I wait for her to sit then scoot her forward with a single push. "He sucks, by the way."

"We know," Aiden says. He drapes his arm around the back of Maggie's chair, and I see lipstick on his cheek. "Literally anyone would be better at his job than him."

"One of you should apply," I suggest.

"With no experience?" Maggie bursts out laughing. "That's not how it works."

"Why not? Wouldn't kill you to try," I say, and Lacey pats my thigh.

"The first part of our scheme is working; we convinced Hannaford you're my boyfriend," she says. "The man practically thinks you're a god. Maybe this will fast-track me to the chief physician position."

"I hope it does. Next up are my parents. They're going to be a little harder to convince, but I think we'll be fine."

Lacey lifts her glass and knocks it against mine. "I'd pretend to be your date anytime."

"Flirting with me, Daniels?" I ask.

"In your dreams, Holmes," she says lowly, and she throws back her drink.

"Lace, what happened to your neck?" Maggie asks. She reaches over and touches the red mark I left on her skin. I've been looking at it all night, too. "Are you okay?"

"Oh, yeah. I'm fine. Curling iron." Lacey sets her napkin in her lap and smiles at her best friend. "Thirty-four years on this earth, and I still manage to burn myself."

I bite my lip to keep from laughing and look away. As I do, I swear I see Aiden glance between us and grin.

"THANK YOU ALL FOR COMING," Hannaford says into the microphone. "I have a feeling this is going to be a great year of raising funds for the Metro Hospital and all our entities. There's a special guest with us tonight, and we're honored he could be here. He's also graciously donated two highly coveted items to the silent auction. Please welcome Shawn Holmes, head coach of the D.C. Titans."

The room gives me a standing ovation as I make my way toward the stage, and I blush. I'm used to being on camera, but it's always where I'm comfortable. On the field. After a game. I've spoken at galas and events before, and I haven't loved the attention on me. But tonight is important; Lacey is involved, and I want to make sure things go right for her.

"Good evening, everyone." I raise the microphone then shove my hands in my pockets. "I'm Shawn, and I'm thrilled to be here tonight. When I heard there would be a silent auction to help raise money for hospital resources, I was more than happy to donate two one-on-one coaching sessions. They come with a tour of UPS Field, and I'll make sure you get to meet some of the players, too."

The crowd breaks into another round of applause and I pause to take a breath, scanning the room for Lacey.

I spot her right away, sitting on the edge of her seat with her hands clasped together and watching me.

Seventy thousand people in a stadium or four hundred people in a museum. It doesn't matter. I always find her, and I'm happier because of it.

"I hope when you look at the items you can bid on tonight, you see you're not just bidding on a nice dinner or a weekend at a cabin in Steamboat Springs. You're bidding to help enrich the lives of the employees at Metro Hospital. You're bidding on state-of-the-art technology, the first of its kind. You can help make Metro Hospital the number one patient facility in the country. In addition to the silent auction items, I'm personally donating two million dollars."

The applause grows louder, and everyone is back on their feet. Hannaford nearly falls off the stage, and, as much as I'd like to deck him in the face for being a self-righteous asshole, I give him a smile instead.

"Before you all start spending your money, I want to add one last thing," I say, and the noise quiets. "There are a lot of people in this room who have done incredible things. I want to take a minute to recognize my girlfriend, Lacey Daniels, who also happens to be my best friend. She's a pediatrician, and I see how hard she works. Some of her afternoons are so busy, she can't even stop for lunch. But she shows up every day with a smile on her face, ready to do good and help out the kids in our community. She's unbelievably smart, and she's damn near perfect at her job. Thank you for letting me be here tonight with you, sweetheart. I'm so proud of you, and I hope we get to spend every holiday together going forward. You're the best Christmas present I could ever ask for."

Lacey grins at me and her hands settle over her heart. Seeing her happy makes me want to do everything in my power to make sure she keeps smiling like that. Fake boyfriend, best friend, or some guy she forgets about in five years, I don't care. I'm going to make it happen.

I walk down the stairs and head for our table. Aiden whistles and Maggie presses a kiss to my cheek, then I turn my attention to Lacey. I cup her chin in my hand and tilt her head back.

"Hi," she says, and she wipes her eyes.

"Hi, Lace Face."

"That was some speech you gave up there."

"Someone mentioned wanting a yacht. I thought this might be better."

"You called me sweetheart."

"I did. Did you absolutely hate it?"

"No." She touches my cheek and runs her thumb down my jaw. "Not one bit."

"Look at us making progress."

"I think we definitely sold our relationship to everyone, and the line to bid on your coaching sessions is forty people long."

"People with money like to feel like heroes," I explain. "I

have no fucking clue what their donations are going toward, but if there's one thing I've learned from being in the sports world, it's that everyone loves a comeback story. Anything to help Metro Hospital be number one in the country."

"Hey." Her touch moves to my hand, and she threads our fingers together. "Two million dollars? Are you kidding me? That is so generous. Is that—can you—"

"Afford it?" I laugh and rest my forehead against hers. "I can afford it fifty times over, sweetheart, then I could still buy you whatever you want."

Lacey bites her bottom lip, and I want to kiss her there, right on her Cupid's bow.

I don't think I'm supposed to want to kiss my friends, even if it's allowed.

But, *fuck*, do I want to.

It's getting harder and harder to stay away from her. Harder and harder to keep my hands to myself and behave in front of our friends. Harder and harder to distinguish what's real and what's pretend between us.

"Will you come back to my place after?" Lacey asks, and I squeeze her palm.

"You know the answer to that question, sweetheart."

THIRTY-ONE

SHAWN

LACEY all but pulls me into her apartment, which is cute, because I would've walked in willingly.

My hands are in her hair and her fingers are unbuttoning my shirt before we even make it through the door.

"Did you stay up all night reading about my career?" I ask, spinning her and pressing her against the wall in her foyer. I'm not sure I'm going to make it much further. "Kind of seems like you're trying to flirt with me. Like you might like me, just a little."

"Don't flatter yourself," she answers, and her mouth dips to my neck. "I wanted to seem like a good girlfriend."

"Oh, you're certainly good, Lacey girl. I never knew hearing about how many touchdowns I scored in a season would turn me on." I pull the strap of her dress down and kiss her bare shoulder. "Fuck, I've wanted to touch you all night."

"You want to talk about flirting? You donated *millions* of dollars to the place where I work." She pushes my jacket off and nudges it out of the way with her shoes. "What's that about, Holmes?"

"Like seeing you happy," I say, and my breath catches when

her fingers skim down my shirt and settle on the front of my pants. She cups my length, and I'm having a difficult time remembering how to speak. "Doesn't matter how much it costs."

The heat of the moment dies.

Lacey stills, and she pulls back to look at me. Her eyes are bright, and her red lipstick is smudged in the left corner of her mouth.

"Thank you. It's a silly thing to say, because it doesn't seem nearly sufficient enough for what you did, but, really. Thank you, Shawn. It means so much to me. I know you might not notice that money leave your account, but the amount of *good* it's going to be able to do is truly life-changing. And you were a part of that."

She sniffs and turns her cheek, trying to keep her tears from me.

"Hey." I touch her chin. "Remember what I said in my bedroom? No hiding from me."

"I know. *I know*. It's just... I'm having very real emotions about your generosity, and it's all confusing."

"We might pretend to be in a relationship, Lacey, but I would've donated the money even if we weren't faking anything. It's important to you, which means it's important to me, too."

She kisses me again, and I lift her off the ground. I work the other strap of her dress down until I see her bra. It's dark green and made of lace, and it makes her tits look incredible. Combined with the red silk bunching at her waist, she looks like a Christmas present I want to unwrap.

"Bedroom," she says, and she unfastens the button on my pants. "Please."

"Don't have to tell me twice." I push away from the wall and keep her in my arms, heading down the hall. "I wish you hadn't worn underwear tonight. Then I could've slipped my fingers inside you while we were eating dinner. No one would've known, would they?"

"You can slip your fingers inside me now." Lacey lets out an irritated huff and moves my hand up her thigh.

"So demanding." I kick open the door to her bedroom and put her on her feet. "Take off your clothes."

"Now who's demanding?" She grins and works the zipper down her back, stepping out of the dress. "Anything else?"

"No." My eyes roam down her body, and *god*, she's a fucking vision. "I want to look at you."

Lacey sits on the edge of her mattress and spreads her legs. I'm watching her like my life depends on it, and I think it just might. If I don't get my head between her legs, I'm going to be a dead man.

"Do you like what you see?"

"I could stare at you all night." I undo my bow tie and let it fall to the floor. I kick off my shoes and walk toward her. "Take off your bra."

She smiles and unhooks the bra from behind her back. Her hands cup her tits, and she plays with her nipples. *Fuck*, I'm not sure I even need her to touch me; I could get off from just this.

"I love that you love my body," she says. Her hand slides down her chest to her stomach, and her fingers fan out over her smooth skin. "You make me feel sexy."

"Because you're sexy as hell," I say. I unbutton my shirt and toss it away, and my pants come down next. I'm itching to get my hands on her, and watching her tease herself is intoxicating. Better than any drink I've ever had. "Get naked. I want to see all of you."

Her fingers hook in the waistband of her underwear, and she lifts her hips to work the lace down her legs. She slingshots the fabric at my face, and I laugh.

"In case you want another souvenir," she says.

"I'm definitely taking those home." I bring the underwear to my nose and inhale. "Fuck, you're already wet, aren't you? Lie back and get comfortable."

Lacey adjusts her position on the bed, scooting onto the mattress and resting her back on the sheets. "Shawn," she says, and she pants my name. "You're too far away."

"I'm sorry." I pull my briefs off and add them to the collection of clothes sitting in a pile on the floor. "I don't mean to be."

She relaxes when I rest my hand on her knee, and she takes a deep breath. "I like when you're touching me."

"Scoot back and grab the headboard, Lacey girl. Be good for me and don't let go." She moves again, her fingers curling around the edge of the mahogany and her legs dropping open at her hips. I trace my hand up her thigh and low across her stomach to the other side of her body. "There you go. This is what you looked like when we had that video call. I was going out of my mind not being able to touch you."

"I kept pretending you were here. I was hoping you'd barge through the door," she says, and her eyes close. "You're the only one who knows how to take care of me so well."

"I have a lot of fantasies about you," I admit, and I slide two fingers inside her. I drop a kiss to her hip bone when she cries out, and I give her a minute to get adjusted to the stretch. "Wildly inappropriate ideas I'd like to try. But I have other ideas, too. Dreams I shouldn't be having. Like you in my bed every night, so I can make sure you're eating and getting enough sleep. I tell you how wonderful you are and how proud I am of you." I get flat on my stomach, and I push her legs open wider with my free hand. My tongue circles her clit, and I smile against her when she moans. "Those are my favorite things."

I find the rhythm and pattern she likes best with slow circles and adding a third finger. I get her close to the edge then pull back, waiting until she's really panting my name before I *feast*, my lips covered in her arousal and my fingers drenched.

"Shawn. I need to—I have to—*please*," Lacey begs, and her hands almost slide down the headboard.

"Please what?" I ask. I sit up on my knees and bend over her so I can kiss her. "I told you I'll give you whatever you want. You just have to ask."

"I need to come. Please let me come."

"You've been good, haven't you? Okay, Lacey girl. You can come. Then you're going to take my cock because I know you want more."

She whimpers and tightens around me, a few seconds of bliss before she lets out a long, loud moan. It's a sound I've come to love, because I love knowing I made her feel *good*.

"Fuck," she whispers, and I kiss her neck.

"One more, sweetheart. You can give me one more, right?" I ask as I circle her clit, and her breathing changes again. "There you go. *Fuck*, you're so pretty when you come, Lacey. You make me want to keep you in my bed all day."

Lacey pulls me down into a kiss, and I kiss her back. She bites my lower lip and reaches between my legs, her hands wrapping around my cock and stroking me up and down. I close my eyes when she squeezes me tight and adds a turn of her wrist.

"You're so big," she says. I feel her moving on the mattress, and the bed dips under her weight as she shifts around. "Biggest I've ever had."

"You're really boosting my ego tonight," I say, and she eases me onto my back.

"I want to ride you," she says, and I nod. "I want you to touch me while I do."

I open my eyes and find her straddling me. I sit up on an elbow and swirl my tongue around her nipple.

Lacey hovers above me and lowers herself an inch, the head of my cock pushing through her entrance. "*Shit.*"

"It's okay." I cup both her tits in my hands and squeeze. "Take your time, sweetheart. We'll make it fit."

"How is this so much better than last time?" she whispers, and she leans forward. Her body weight rests against mine, and she sinks another inch lower. "You're going to fill me up, aren't you, Shawn?"

My palms move to her waist, and I grip her hips as tight as I can. I lift off the bed, meeting her halfway until I'm fully seated inside her.

"Goddammit," I groan. "Feels so fucking good. You're still so tight."

"Tight for you," Lacey says in my ear. "Wet for you. All of it's for you, Shawn."

She works me up and down, her hands on my chest and her head thrown back. She looks like a goddess on top of me and I can't help but stare. I watch her chest bounce every time she slams down on me. I watch her fingers play with herself— pinching her nipples. Touching her clit. Dragging her hand down to her stomach and running it back up her body.

It's too much. It's never felt this good before, and pleasure crawls up my spine.

"Lacey," I rasp. "I'm not—if you want me to pull out, tell me."

"No," she whispers. "I want your cum in me. All of it, Shawn. You know I won't waste a drop."

"You won't," I say, and there are stars in my vision. "Because you're my good girl, aren't you?"

"Yours. Just yours."

Mine.

The orgasm hits me and I lift my hips, my release spilling inside of her. Her movements slow, and sweat rolls down my cheek as she pulls off of me.

"Fuck, Daniels. You sent me to outer space."

Lacey bursts out laughing and curls up by my side. "That far, huh?"

"Even farther, probably."

"Is it okay if we cuddle?" she asks and I open one eye.

"Of course it's okay." I loop my arm around her waist and pull her against my chest. My hand runs down her back then back up. "That was—I'm not sure I have words. I've entered a catatonic state."

Her palm settles over my heart, and I sigh. "We're good together, aren't we?" she asks, and I manage to nod my head.

"It's never been like this for me before," I admit.

"Me, either."

"Speaking of, I'm sorry we didn't talk about boundaries. I'd never say some of those things outside of the bedroom, and I hope I didn't—"

"You didn't." She pushes up on her elbow and looks down at me with a wide smile on her face. "I like all of it. I promise."

"Okay. Good. That's—glad to hear it."

"I like it when you blush, too." Lacey presses her fingers to my cheeks. "It's so cute."

"Just what every forty-something man wants to hear. That he's cute," I say, and she pokes my side.

"You know what I mean. I like that you have this assertive side, but I like the softer side, too," she says.

"I like being both with you," I admit, and she kisses me.

"So do I."

"Do you want me to go?"

"No." She shakes her head and curls back up against me. "I'd really like it if you stayed. For a little while. For the night. What-ever you want."

"Okay." I squeeze her shoulder and close my eyes. My body settles, and I feel myself starting to fall asleep. "I'm not going anywhere. Wake me up for my game on Sunday. Until then, I'm out of commission."

"I'm going to run to the bathroom and clean up. I'll be right back," Lacey says, and I nod.

"Okay," I say again, and I miss her the second she leaves my side.

THIRTY-TWO

LACEY

"I'M GOING to grab some popcorn," Aiden says. "Does anyone want anything?"

"Can you bring me a beer?" I ask. "This game is stressing me the hell out, and the Titans are up by fourteen."

"Sure. Anything for you, sweetheart?" he asks Maggie, and she shakes her head.

"Nope. I'm good, thank you." She kisses his cheek and pats his chest. "Hurry back."

"Have you two ever had a fight?" I ask as Aiden walks away. "I swear it's nothing but smooth sailing with you all."

I scoot closer to her as a burst of wind rips through the stadium. The temperature is unforgiving today, dipping well below freezing and making my hands turn red even inside my gloves. It hasn't deterred the crowd, though. The Titans fans are out in full force, their blue jerseys bright against the backdrop of the setting sun and their cheers ringing through the air.

"We definitely argue. We agree on most things, but sometimes tensions will get high and we have to take a step back. There's never any yelling, and after a few minutes, we realize how stupid we're being." Maggie smiles and rests her head on my shoulder. "I'll take a bad day with him over a good day with anyone else."

"Was it scary to let Aiden in like that?" I ask. "To be vulnerable with him?"

"Is this a hypothetical question, or is there something you need to tell me?"

"Totally hypothetical. Consider it investigative research."

She hums and loops her arms around mine. "Okay, I'll play along. Of course it was scary. It's fucking terrifying to let your guard down. We live in a world where everyone expects to see the best versions of you. And then you come out of the woodwork and say, *surprise! I'm divorced and infertile*, and they all kind of look at you like you have two heads because suddenly you're not perfect and put together. But the right person will still think you're perfect. Two broken halves are still a whole."

"That is incredibly wise coming from the woman who gave the guy she met at a strangers' photo shoot a few hours prior a list of things she wanted to try in bed," I say, and I laugh when she pinches my side. "I'm just kidding. I love your love story. When you know, you know, right?"

"Yes and no. I think some love is hot and heavy. It burns fast and bright, like the flash of lightning in a summer storm. Other love takes more time. It's more... raw. Real. Slow and steady. It's uncovering bits and pieces of someone and dusting away that coat of armor they've put around themselves. It's also relentless, because it keeps showing up. It's sneaky and it's annoying, because just when you think you've escaped, just when you think you've gotten away without being burned, you realize you're totally obsessed with someone and your world is on fire when they're around." She sighs. "Love is beautiful, isn't it?"

"Yeah." I stare at the field, and my eyes find Shawn. He's pacing on the sideline, his hands tucked under his arms and his shoulders curved forward. "I guess it is."

Could he love me like that?

The thought races through my mind, and before I allow it to manifest, before I allow it to take shape and form into something meaningful, I shove it away. *Far* away, in the compartment where I keep the other things I adore about him.

I'll open it up on a rainy day in March when the flowers start to bloom. I'll remember what it was like when he held me close, and I'll think maybe, *maybe* there's a chance someone could love me one day.

Like the way I deserve.

"You okay?" Maggie asks, and her question is thoughtful. Careful. I wonder if she can read my mind and see all the secrets I'm hiding.

"I'm fine." I smile and watch the Titans huddle up. "Is it just me, or does something seem off today?"

"What do you mean?"

"Shawn doesn't seem like himself. He's pacing more than normal, and his shoulders are up by his ears. The Titans are winning, too. Usually when they're up, he's laughing and having a good time. That's not the case today," I say, and my smile melts into a frown. "I hope he's okay."

"Been keeping an eye on him?" Maggie jokes, and my cheeks turn pink.

I *have* been keeping an eye on him, but I won't admit it to her. I always find him when he's on the field. It's like he's a beacon of light and I can't look away.

My frown deepens when he rubs his chest. It's the third time he's done it, and I know it's not because he's nervous. It's different. Something new and something I haven't seen before. I wish there was a way to ask him what's going on; I've tried to get his attention, but every time he moves down the sidelines, he keeps his gaze on the field, not the stands, and it's completely out of character.

I'm worried.

"Maybe he's cold," I say, even though it's a lie. The man is a tattooed human furnace. "He should put his jacket on."

"Men," Maggie mumbles under his breath. "He won't be having any fun if his fingers fall off."

Neither will I, I think, and I bite back a grin.

"You know they—"

I stop talking when Shawn walks behind the Titans' bench. He crouches down on the turf and pulls off his headset. His hands shake as he brings them to his forehead. I watch him rock back and forth, his shoulders curling in on themselves.

"What's going on?" Maggie asks. "What's wrong with Shawn?"

"I think—I think he might be having a panic attack," I say, and my voice cracks. "I need to get down there."

"*What*? I didn't know he—oh my god, Lacey, is he okay?"

"I don't know. I don't know if he's okay, Maggie, but I need to get down there. Right now," I say again, and I can hear my hysteria. "When Aiden gets here, will you—"

"Yes. *Yes.* How are you—the only way onto the field is through the tunnel."

I stare at the metal railing in front of me with a determined glare. "No, it's not." I swing my legs over the ledge of the concrete block. A security guard standing on the field glances up at me, and his eyes widen. "Tell Aiden what's going on."

"Lacey." Maggie reaches out and holds my shoulder. "He's going to be okay."

"I know." I nod, but my eyes fill with tears. "I just don't want him to be alone," I whisper, and she nods. I take a deep breath and heave myself out of the stands and onto the field.

I land on my feet, and three security guards charge toward me.

"Ma'am, you're not allowed down here," one says.

"You are trespassing, and you will be ejected from the game," another says, and I try to push past them.

"I have to see him. That's my—he's my—I need to make sure he's okay," I say. "Please, let me check on him."

"We can't do that. You don't have the credentials to be down here," the third says, and he pulls out a walkie talkie. "Step back. Now."

"Fuck the credentials," I yell as Jett leads Shawn to a tent on the sidelines. I can't see him anymore, and my panic rises. "That is the man I care about and he is *not alright*. Let me go, or I will get over there however I can."

"Hey." I hear a sharp voice, and I see Dallas running toward me. "She's fine. Let her on."

"We're not—"

"I don't give a fuck what you're allowed to do," he snaps. "That's her boyfriend, and he needs her. You can take it up with him after the game if you want, and I'll pay the fine. Let her through."

My eyes sting with fresh tears, and I want to scream at the top of my lungs. The security guards step back, and I take off toward Shawn. Dallas touches my arm as I pass, and my bottom lip trembles as I look at him.

"Thank you," I say.

"He's going to be okay," he says, and he gives me a quick hug. He smells like sweat, but I lean into his comforting embrace anyway. "Jett got him into the medical tent. There's no press in there."

"Got it." I sprint past the rest of the players and into the tent. I spot him immediately, and my heart lurches in my chest.

It's amazing how someone so big can look so small.

He's sitting on a leather table with his head in his hands. He's rocking back and forth again, and I hear soft whispers like he's talking to himself.

"Shawn." I drop to my knees in front of him and rest my hands on his thighs. "Hey, it's me. Lacey."

"Lacey?" He lifts his chin and his eyes find mine. "What are you doing here?"

"I thought you might want some company." I stand up and stroke his hair. It's damp with sweat around his forehead, and I brush a couple of rogue pieces out of his eyes. "Is it okay if I stay with you for a little while?"

"Yeah. Of course," he says, and I climb onto the table. "I can't believe you're here."

"I didn't have to travel very far." I sit behind him and I pull him toward me so his back is against my chest. I rub his shoulders and down his arms, trying to ease the tension he's carrying in the pressure points of his body; his hands. The slope of his neck. The valley between his shoulders. "I would've traveled farther if I had to. There's nowhere I'd rather be."

"I think I'm having a panic attack," he whispers.

"Oh, sweetheart, you're definitely having a panic attack. But it's okay. You're in the medical tent now. You're safe in here. I won't let anything bad happen to you, okay?"

"Okay."

I fumble with my phone and pull it out of my back pocket. I search for a song on the internet and hit play. The soft opening chords of Pachelbel's Canon fill the small space, and Shawn's shoulders instantly relax.

"You're okay," I murmur in his ear. "You're alright. I'm here."

We stay like that for a while. The game continues on without Shawn; I can still hear the whistle and the crowd and the players walking back and forth on the sidelines. But in here, we're in a tiny bubble. A fortress no one—not even one of his panic attacks—can break into.

The music loops, a one-hour version that plays on repeat. I hum along to the violins and hold Shawn's hand. His tattooed arm drapes down my thigh. When the third round of the canon comes around, Shawn perks up.

"I'm sorry," is the first thing he says, and I shake my head.

"We're not going to do that," I say softly. "Do you remember what I told you when you came to my apartment after your first loss of the season? I said you don't have to be perfectly put together around me."

"You're a safe space for me," he mumbles, so quietly I barely hear him. It hangs there in the air, weighty and heavy, before he continues. "Just like these other parts of my life I associate as somewhere I can be myself and make mistakes. I also feel it with you."

"That's how I feel about you, too." I rest my chin on his shoulder and sigh. "It's lovely to have a place that feels so nice, isn't it? A place that feels like home."

Shawn folds his hand over my knee. His fingers fan out around my thigh and his thumb rubs along the stitching of my fleece-lined leggings. "You feel more like home to me every day."

If there was a way to see inside my chest, I'm certain there'd be a picture of my heart stitching itself back together with those words. Every second this man is in my arms, the walls I've put up slowly start to come down.

There are so many times in my life where I feel like I'm alone. Watching my friends find love and settle down. Mediocre dates that never pan out to anything besides awkward conversation and a few drinks. The ask to change myself for someone else because how I am isn't *good enough*.

With Shawn by my side, I'm never alone.

"It's a nice house, isn't it?" I ask.

"Yeah. I really like what you've done with the place." He lets out a sigh and rolls his shoulders back. "I think I'm better now. That was the worst I've had in a while."

"What do you think triggered it?"

"I'm not sure. Maybe it's because we're leaving for my parents soon. Maybe it's because—" he stops himself short of saying anything else, and I frown at the secret he's holding on to. "It doesn't matter. It's over now. I'm sorry I worried you."

"You're not allowed to apologize to me. Not over something like this. Can I look at you and make sure you're alright?"

He nods, and I adjust our positions. I sneak out from behind him so we're sitting side by side, and I smile at him. There's color on his cheeks and a twinkle in his eye. His breathing is back to normal, and he looks *good*, like the man I had in bed with me until early this morning.

Before I know what I'm doing, I lean forward and kiss him. It's frantic and hurried, but I need to make sure he's okay, *really okay*.

I'll be a mess if he isn't.

Shawn groans against my mouth, and his hands find my hair. He pulls the beanie off my head and throws it to the side. His fingers thread through my braids and he tugs on the long strands.

"Lacey," he says, and he lifts me into his lap. "I love when you wear your hair like this."

"I'm not fucking you in the medical tent with thousands of people outside," I warn him, and his laugh is warm against my skin. "You're not in the right headspace for that."

"No, I'm not. I just want you close. Thank you for coming to check on me. It means a lot that you're here."

"I told you there's nowhere else I'd rather be." I kiss his forehead and run my hand down his cheek. Stubble prickles the pads of my fingers, and I like the scruff he has today. "Do you have to go back out there?"

"I should. I don't want anyone to worry about me. Or for them to start writing articles that I'm banging my girlfriend on the sidelines."

"Or in supply closets," I add, and he tilts his head back and laughs.

"Or supply closets. I wish I didn't have to go back to the game, though. I'd like to just escape."

"What if we did escape? We can make up an excuse and leave. Food poisoning is a good one."

"You'd do that for me?" he asks, and I understand there have been times in Shawn's life—too many times—where he's had to put on a brave face for people when all he wants to do is hide. "I don't want you to miss the rest of the game."

"Like it'd be any fun without you. Your ass looks great in your joggers. It's pretty much the only reason why I'm here."

"And to cheer on Dallas," Shawn says. "I remember you liking his jersey."

"I don't know what you're talking about." I sigh when his tongue traces across my collarbone. "You're my favorite guy on the squad."

"Good answer," he whispers, and he buries his face between my breasts. "I'm afraid to go back out there."

"You won't be alone. I'm right here," I say, and I rub his scalp with my fingernails. "Your place or mine?"

"Yours. I like yours."

"Then that's where we'll go."

THIRTY-THREE
SHAWN

WE SNEAK out of the stadium through a side door in the tunnel and climb into my Range Rover before anyone from the media can realize I'm gone.

I had a quick huddle with the guys before I left, and I let them know I'd see them on Tuesday. They pulled me into a group hug and murmured words of understanding. Support and encouragement. Affirmations I still feel in my chest.

I've always loved the camaraderie of a team, but this is different.

This is a support system, my brothers who stand with me when the going gets tough. I'm not letting them down; they're lifting me up. It's a collective effort—sometimes I'm going to carry them, and other times, like today, they're going to carry me.

A ball of emotion sits in my throat as we head toward Lacey's apartment, a spool of thread that slowly unravels the further we get from the stadium. It's hard to describe how much it means to me to know I have dozens of men who have my back and *love* me.

The woman holding my hand and drawing circles on the inside of my wrist doesn't hurt either.

We don't talk on the drive, settling into the notes of a

random classical music playlist I find on the internet instead of mindless conversation.

I like it, though.

Even the quiet with Lacey is nice.

Fifteen minutes later, she lets us into her apartment and locks the door. For the first time since the coin toss, I let out a breath and relax.

"Do you think there will be articles about you?" she asks, the one to break the silence. "The Titans ended up winning, so who cares why you left?"

"Everyone will care." I kick off my sneakers and nudge them against the foyer wall. I line them up next to the row of Lacey's shoes, and I like how our things look beside each other. "I'm sure it will be a top headline on ESPN tomorrow."

"That's bullshit."

She unzips her jacket and hangs it on the hook by the door. She puts her hands on her hips and glares at me. There's fire in her eyes, and I can't wait to hear what she says next.

"What's bullshit?" I ask.

"Why do people care? You dipped out early—big deal. What if there was a family emergency or something happened in your life you *didn't* want to share with America?"

"We don't have that luxury, unfortunately. I'm not saying it's fair, just that I'm used to it." I walk to her living room and get comfortable on her sofa. I almost melt into the plush leather, and it takes all of my energy to not close my eyes and fall asleep right away. "Sometimes I wish all the people in the comment sections on social media who tell me it must be so easy to be an athlete could be really rich for a day. They'd see money isn't everything. Even the greatest athletes can be unhappy."

"I know your bodies take a pounding and what you do is physically grueling, so please don't take this the wrong way," Lacey says, and she sits next to me. "I don't understand why people hold athletes to unobtainable high standards. You all get sick. You all get hurt. You all have bad brain days when the world feels like it's caving in, just like Joe Schmo who works in accounting or architecture does. Sure, it's broadcast to billions of people, but why does it mean you're failing when it happens to you?"

"I wish I had an answer for you." I stretch out my legs and rest my feet in her lap. Her hand wraps around my calf and she presses her thumb into my muscles. I groan as the tension I've been holding onto leaves my body. "The public knows I've had a panic attack before. Maybe I should come clean. I can tell the world on my terms so I can control the narrative."

"You should. You have a big following, Shawn. I'm not saying you don't use your platform for good, because you do. I know that. But maybe being more outspoken about these things you experience might encourage other athletes to talk about them too."

"I think you might be right," I say. I fold my hands over my stomach and close my eyes. "You're wise beyond your years, Daniels."

"It's because I have to keep up with your geriatric ass," she answers, and I burst out laughing.

I feel instantly lighter with her joke, like I'm levitating high above the shit swarming around in my brain. Lacey has that effect on me; she always knows exactly the right thing to say. Sometimes I think she's in my head and reading my thoughts, because there's no way someone can be so in tune with my emotions.

"I'm weak right now. You aren't allowed to make fun of me. Not in my vulnerable state."

"I'm sorry," she says, and I open one eye to find her watching me. "I hope you know I'd never make fun of you, and I'm sorry if it came across that way."

"Sweetheart, you making fun of me is what I look forward to every day. You know why? Because you treat me like you would anyone else. You give me shit. You hold me accountable. You make me laugh. For the first time in my life, I don't feel like I have to act a certain way around someone. I'm myself, and that's enough," I admit, and her lips pull up into a soft smile.

It's a beautiful thing when Lacey grins. If she were mine, I'd make sure she smiled every day. A hundred times a day, because the world is a better place when she's happy.

"You're allowed to rest when you're with me, Shawn," she says, and like everything else she tells me, I know it's true. "You're more than enough."

There's never a spot where I feel safer than with her two feet away from me. My body knows it, too, because my limbs go pliant. My heart stops racing, and the breath I take doesn't feel like a thousand knives are stabbing my lungs.

Progress.

"You can rest with me too, Lacey girl," I say, and her smile stretches wider. "You don't have to go so fast."

"I know I can. I have been for a while now. Since you first kissed me, I think," she says. "It's been nice to slow down."

We look at each other at the same time. It's like we're sneaking glances, stolen moments no one else can see. There's the urge to tell her she can rest with me forever, if she wants. Long after New Year's comes and goes, we could still do *this*.

Whatever the hell *this* is.

"Are you hungry?" she asks. "We could order pizza and watch a movie."

"Sounds like a plan to me."

I pull my wallet out of my pocket and toss it her way.

This woman saved me tonight, and I'm starting to wonder if she wasn't put in my life by accident but for a very specific reason.

To be mine until the end of time.

―――――

AN HOUR and a half and six slices of pizza later, we're sprawled across her couch. Her legs are over my thigh and my foot presses against her ribs. A movie is playing on the television in the corner, but I'm not paying attention to it.

I'm too busy listening to Lacey tell me about her childhood. Too busy watching her use her hands to gesture wildly about the dog she had growing up, the golden retriever her parents said went to a farm and never came home. Too busy smiling at her stories about her imaginary friend Kevin when she was six years old.

I could listen to her talk for hours.

"What?" she asks. She rests her head in her palm and looks at me from across the couch. It's almost pitch black in the room except for the lamp bathing her face in colors of yellow and gold. She looks like a pretty angel. "You're staring at me."

"Just..." I take a breath, and there's a pull in my gut. A twist in my chest the longer she looks at me. It's warm and pleasant. Dizzyingly so. I want her to keep looking at me and to never stop. "You," I say, and I gesture up and down her body. "You," I repeat, and it sounds more important the second time.

Lacey swallows, and I track the bob of her throat. Her eyes soften and she reaches out for me. Her fingertips graze my palm, a gentle touch that has me wanting to beg for more. "Can I hold you?" she whispers, and my soul nearly splits in two.

"Yeah," I say, and my voice dips with the single syllable. "Yes. Please. I'd like that."

The pizza box gets pushed to the side. I pull off my hoodie and she adjusts the pillows. We maneuver around the couch until she's stretched out longways and I'm settled between her thighs. My back rests against her chest, and her arms drape over my shoulders. I'm locked in place, but I'm not planning on running anywhere.

I hum, content and comfortable. I can feel Lacey's heartbeat, a staccato rhythm that starts to slow when I settle in her arms. Mine starts to slow too, like I reached the top of a mountain and I'm finally going down the other side.

That's exactly what Lacey does for me; she reminds me life isn't always an uphill climb. Eventually the hard things get easy, a steady descent I can take at my own pace.

"This is nice," she says, her voice low in my ear. She kisses my cheek, and I move my head so I can kiss her lips. "Kissing you is nice."

"It's not supposed to be nice," I say against her mouth. I reach up and hook my arm around her neck to bring her closer to me. "It's supposed to be better than nice."

"You just want me to compliment you."

"Flirting with me, Daniels?"

"In your dreams, Holmes," she says, but she kisses me again.

This feels an awful lot like heaven.

I don't need anything else.

Her tongue swipes across my mouth and my lips part to welcome her in. She sighs, a sound I want to hear her make again. I run my thumb down the curve of her jaw and over the slope of her cheek. She's warm under my touch, all soft skin and soft lines.

I haven't just made out with anyone in years, and I like doing it with her. My teeth sink into her bottom lip and I smile when she whimpers. When she pulls on the tufts of my hair to tell me she wants more.

I untangle our limbs and flip over so I'm hovering above her. My knees rest on either side of her hips, and she looks up at me with wonder painted on her face.

"You're beautiful," I whisper, and it's an admission—a fact—I won't be allowed to say soon. "You're the most beautiful woman in the world, Lacey."

Her fingers dance up my arms and to my neck. Tenderness glimmers in her eyes, and it seems like there's something on the tip of her tongue. Something hangs between us, a realization that this is different than the other times we've kissed.

Those moments were hurried and frenzied, a desperate need to touch and lick and taste. Slick slides of skin and my hands under her dress. My fingers buried deep inside her. Down her shirt.

But not right now.

She lifts off the couch and meets me halfway. Her hands cup my cheeks and her nose brushes against mine.

"Maybe I am flirting with you," she says, and it sounds like she's telling me a secret. "Just a little, because I've never felt more beautiful than I do when I'm with you."

I should ask her about the end date we set for ourselves. Maybe we can push it to Valentine's Day or stretch it out to Memorial Day. Fuck, maybe we can make it a year and celebrate Christmas together next year, too.

When she lifts her hips and pins them against mine, I want to ask her to marry me.

When she kisses me with fire behind her mouth, I want to tell her I'll give her anything she asks.

When she rubs the back of my neck and holds me close, whispering *I'm so glad you're here with me* into my ear, I realize that I was wrong.

I've massively fucked up, a mistake I can't undo.

I didn't make other men not good enough for her.

She made other women not good enough for me.

Lacey ruined me, all while I was trying not to ruin her.

THIRTY-FOUR
LACEY

I DON'T EXPECT the knock on the door.

I look up from the couch and put a bookmark between the pages of the romance novel I'm reading so I don't lose my spot. It's the first time I've had a chance to sit down and escape from reality in a couple of weeks, and it feels *good* to turn my mind off for a little while.

I check my phone to see if Maggie texted me, but I don't have any new messages.

"Huh," I say, and I shuffle across the living room.

When I peer through the peephole, I see Shawn's torso and the Titans logo proudly stretched across his chest.

"Special delivery," he says when I open the door, and I grin.

"What the heck are you doing here? I didn't think I'd see you until the day after tomorrow when we left for your parents'."

"I was in the neighborhood and thought I'd stop by." He holds up a crinkled paper bag and I spot the logo of my favorite bakery stamped on the front. "I come bearing gifts, too."

"You should've led off with that. We'd already be halfway to the kitchen." I open the door wide and tug him into my apartment. "What did you bring? Anything good?"

"I don't know." Shawn shrugs, and his lips pull into a knowing grin. "Just a couple of lemon scones and a slice of their chocolate and raspberry cheesecake. Interested?"

"Is saying *fuck yeah* too aggressive?" I hurry him into the kitchen and grab two plates. I nudge them his way so he can dole out the desserts. "Do you want something to drink? I just opened a bottle of wine."

"Sure, I'll have what you're having. I won't stay long, though. I don't want to interrupt your night."

"You're not interrupting anything." I fill a glass with a generous pour of the cabernet, and I slide it across the counter. "I'm grateful for the company. I was just doing some reading. My vacation started today, so I've been taking it easy."

"I'm officially off, too," he says, and he sits on a barstool at my island. He looks so big in the seat, and I think he might break the tiny piece of furniture in two. "I'm giving the guys the next week off. We're either going to come back rejuvenated, or we're going to get our asses handed to us at the game on New Year's Day."

"I saw the press conference you did after your panic attack the other day," I say gently, and I sit next to him. "How are you doing?"

"I feel great. I had an appointment with my therapist, and I told the reporters the truth. It went better than I thought." Shawn picks up a scone and takes a big bite. His moan is low and loud, and half the pastry disappears. My thighs clench together at the sound, and I try not to stare at his tongue as it darts out of his mouth to lick away a dusting of crumbs. "Fuck, that's good. I would commit serious crimes for a basket of these things."

"I'll drive the getaway car," I say, and I eat a sliver of the pastry. "I'm proud of you for opening up to people you don't know. I'm sure that wasn't easy."

"It definitely wasn't, but I'm glad I did it. I've already had dozens of messages from other athletes—some in the NFL and some at the collegiate level—telling me how much they appreciate me speaking out. We all agree that we want to normalize being not okay sometimes." He pops the last bite of dessert in his mouth and dusts off his hands. "I guess that's life, isn't it? We're all just trying to figure it out."

"I'll drink to that." I lift my glass, and we knock our drinks together. "Are you excited to go home? When was the last time you saw your parents?"

"For my mom's birthday back in August. It's not a long drive to Philly. Hell, the flight is only an hour, but organizing things during the season and with my sisters' schedule can be chaotic. They've got kids. I've got the team. We have to plan family events a year in advance," he says, and he scoots the cheesecake my way. "Ladies first."

"Such a gentleman." I cut a bite of the decadent dessert and bring it to my mouth. "Holy *shit*. Unreal."

"Seriously, I would do anything to have more of this." Shawn takes a bite, and another groan sneaks out of him. "I sound like I'm in a porno, don't I?"

"You do make similar sounds in the bedroom," I joke, and he kicks my shin. "I'm kind of offended the cheesecake gets more enthusiasm than me."

"Until you cover yourself in raspberries and chocolate, you're always going to be second best, Lace. Sorry, this is a competition you cannot win."

"Well, don't tempt me with a good time. I have chocolate syrup in the fridge."

Shawn laughs, and I like that sound.

I like him in the quiet moments, too, like when he was in my arms the other night after we left the game early, but there's something about knowing *I'm* the one who gets him to smile that spears me right through my chest.

"I should go," he says. "I don't want to overstay my welcome."

"No." I reach out and grab his arm faster than I can blink. "Stay," I say, and I stick out my bottom lip. Heat flares behind his eyes, a burning gaze I feel deep in my belly. "Please. I like you being here more than I like being alone."

"Okay." He hitches his thumb and fingers around my chin and tilts my head back. "I'll stay."

"Want to go into the living room? It's more comfortable out there."

"I do love your couch." He scoops the glass of wine off the counter and gestures out of the kitchen. "Lead the way."

"Are you going to look at my ass again? You're becoming predictable, Holmes."

"And you're still just as hot as you were the last time I wanted to look at your ass, Daniels," Shawn answers, and I grin.

I walk toward the living room, but a tug on my arm stops me halfway there. There's a flurry of movement and limbs, and suddenly I'm pressed against the wall. I look up, and Shawn is staring down at me.

"What's wrong?" I ask through an exhale. My chest rises and falls as he takes over my space, and you'd think I've been sprinting for miles. I can feel the heat of his body against mine, and one of his palms rests next to my ear. "Are you okay?"

"You're wearing the shirt you took from my house," he says, and it sounds strangled. Strained. Like it takes all of his effort to speak. "You wear my shirt around your house?"

My cheeks flame bright red, and I dip my chin to hide the blush crawling up my neck. "I wasn't expecting company."

"That doesn't answer my question, Lacey. Do you wear my shirt around your house?" he asks again, and this time, there's a fierceness in his tone.

I swallow and close my eyes. I let out a breath before giving him a single nod. "Yes," I whisper. "I do."

"*Fuck*," he croaks. He pulls me into the living room and sets his wine glass down. He runs his hands over the front of the cotton, cupping my breasts and squeezing my nipples. "That's so hot."

"I sleep in it, too," I say, my tongue loose and my inhibitions lowered. "It's my favorite thing to wear."

"We're still friends who fuck, right?" he asks in my ear, and it sounds like sin. His teeth nip at my skin, and I tilt my head to the side to give him better access to my neck. I want to feel him everywhere. "Can I have you?"

"Yes," I manage to get out. I hitch my knee up to his hip, and he runs his hand up my leg. His fingers dance across my stomach, dipping lower and lower until his knuckles brush against the inside of my thigh and my eyes roll to the back of my head. "Yes, we are, and yes, you can."

"I want to see how much you love wearing my things when you touch yourself. I want to see how much you want me," Shawn says, and his palm falls away from my body.

I let out a frustrated moan, a ravaged sound that has my hands grabbing his shirt and pulling him toward me. He kisses me rough and hard, scorching presses of his lips against mine.

"Shawn," I say. "I want you."

"You can't stay away. I can't stay away either. Go bend over the couch."

My foot falls to the floor, and I'm shaky as I walk across the room. I hear Shawn behind me, the stomp of his boots and his ragged breathing. He's just as affected as I am.

"How do you want me?"

"Over the arm," he says, and I barely recognize his voice. "Get your ass in the air."

The leather is cool against my skin and my shirt bunches

above my ribs. I glance over my shoulder, and Shawn is watching me with molten eyes and his hand down the front of his jeans. He strokes himself, a twist of his wrist, and red splashes up his neck.

"Do you like what you see, Shawn?" I ask. I raise up on my tiptoes, and I wiggle my hips. "Do you want to touch me? Or am I going to have to do it myself?"

His throat bobs, and he closes the distance between us. He bends over, folding his body into mine. "We can keep pretending we're just fuck buddies, Lacey, but you're wearing my shirt with nothing underneath it. What about this feels *fake* to you?"

Nothing, I want to yell.

There's no warning before he slams into me, a thrust so forceful, I tip forward and almost fall face-first onto the couch. My blood runs hot and electricity cackles at the tips of my fingers. I grip the cushions to stay upright, and Shawn reaches his hand around to pull the shirt up to my neck.

"Fucking love your tits. Want to cover you in my cum."

"You can." I gasp as he gets an inch deeper, the roll of his hips deliriously satisfying. "I'd like that."

He grunts out his appreciation as his mouth settles on my left shoulder, sucking the skin there like it's his key to survival. His hand doesn't know where it wants to be; pinching my nipple or circling my clit, an alternating pattern that's too much stimulation but not enough at the same time.

Shawn trades out his thumb with the heel of his palm, and I grind into him, unabashedly chasing a high. I've never been self-conscious about what I like in the bedroom, but for the first time in my life, I feel myself just *letting go.*

Enjoying the moment.

Savoring him and the way he makes me feel so *goddamn* good.

"You take me so well, Lacey girl," he says, and fire licks up my spine. It's a heady rush of heat I'm desperately clawing for. "I like watching you like this. I like having you like this. I love when you come on my cock, sweetheart. It's our secret, right?"

That's all I need.

My orgasm rushes over me and sweeps me out to sea.

Shawn doesn't stop, one hand still between my legs and the other clasped around my throat, taking every burst of pleasure from me he can get.

He's greedy for it, and I give him everything I have until the pulse of delight dulls to a quiet hum. Until my legs quiver and my hips slam back against his, meeting him thrust for thrust.

I'm exhausted.

Bone-achingly tired and perfectly sated, but I want to get him there, too.

I want to be the one to push him over the edge.

I reach behind me and put my hand on his stomach. My fingers fan out across the hard lines of his muscles, and he stops immediately. I slide him out of me and sit on the arm of the couch.

"I want to be good for you." I tug his shirt over my head and throw it to the floor. When I push my breasts together, his eyes go wide. "Use me, Shawn."

"Fuck," he curses, his thighs bumping into my chest and his hand weaving through my hair. His jeans sit around his ankles, and I love that he never bothered to take them all the way off, too caught up in the moment. "Careful, Lacey. You keep saying things like that, and I'm never going to let you go."

Good, I think.

Don't.

I sit up a little straighter. I lean forward from my hips and take his cock between my breasts. I rub him up and down, and he pulls my hair tight.

"You like to be the one to take care of me, don't you, Shawn?" I ask, and his pupils are as dark as the night sky. "I want you to come. I'd like that a lot."

His hand wraps around his shaft, and he gives himself three rough tugs.

"Lacey," he whispers, a warning before his release covers my chest. Sticky and salty, it clings to the top of my breasts. A little gets on my shoulder, too, and I like that it's hard for him to control himself around me.

I run my hand through the mess. Shawn pants as I bring my fingers to my mouth, and I swear he's already half-hard again. My tongue licks up the length of my finger, and I hum.

"Good," I whisper. I put my clean hand on his thigh and swirl my tongue over the tip of his cock. "So good for me, Shawn. I like watching you come undone."

He blows out a shaky breath, and he rests his weight against the couch. For a minute, I think he's going to fall over before he rights himself and hooks his fingers around my chin.

"You're incredible," he says, and he bends down to press his mouth against mine.

Kissing him is addicting, a vice I never want to recover from.

"Right back at you," I say, and I brush a few pieces of sweaty hair away from his forehead. "Want to stay and eat the rest of that cheesecake? We could put on a movie."

"Course I do. We can't just not eat it, right?" he asks, and he pulls his jeans up his thighs.

"Now that you've had both in the same night, which is better? Me, or the dessert?"

"Ah, Lacey girl." Shawn rubs his thumb down the curve of my cheek. The lights from my Christmas tree twinkle in his eyes, and he's wearing the biggest smile. "You win every time. It's not even close. Even with a billion choices, it would still be you."

THIRTY-FIVE

SHAWN

LACEY IS in the lobby of my apartment five minutes before eight.

She's sitting on a leather bench tucked away in the corner and staring at her phone. A suitcase is next to her, a bright orange monstrosity that makes my eyes hurt. Her fingers type away on her screen, and there's a small smile on her lips.

My phone buzzes in my pocket, and I pull it out.

LACE FACE

I'm really disappointed your building doesn't have an ambiguous sculpture.

What do visitors talk about? Kind of awkward.

A laugh rumbles out of me and I walk toward her.

"They don't talk about anything," I say, and Lacey lifts her head at the sound of my voice. "Everyone sits in silence and stares at each other."

"Hey." She jumps to her feet and grins when she spots me. "Good morning."

"Morning." I bend down to give her a hug, and I run my hand over the small of her back. "I could've picked you up, you know. You didn't have to trudge all the way over here with your bags."

"It was nice to get some steps in. We're going to be sitting for a while, and I wanted to work out some of my nervous energy."

"Don't be nervous. Everything's going to be fine. We're going to go in, spend a couple of days with my family, make them think we're head over heels in love with each other, then leave. Super simple," I say, and she nods.

"You're right. It's no big deal. We know each other and we're comfortable around each other. We kicked *ass* at the game Aiden made us play. There aren't going to be any issues."

I nod toward her bags. "Want me to take that for you?"

"That's okay. I can handle it. Thanks, though."

Lacey follows me into the elevator, and we take it down two floors to the parking garage. I lift her luggage and put it in the trunk, and I add my bags beside it.

"You're bringing a lot of stuff," she says. "It's making me feel like I'm wildly unprepared."

"Most of it is presents. Don't worry; I wrapped them and put both our names on them."

"Oh, thank you. I have a bottle of wine for your parents, but I didn't know what to get anyone else. Speaking of presents, I have a couple for you. Can I give them to you when we get home?"

"I'd like that. I have some for you, too." I shut the trunk and open the passenger door for her. "I already got the seat warmers turned on for you. It's nice out today, so I'm not sure how much use they'll be."

"Like the balmy days of late July," she says, and I offer her my hand so she can climb inside. "Looks like snow on Christmas, though. Just in time for me to kick your ass in a snowball fight."

"Dream on, Daniels." I shut the door and hustle to the other side of the car. I slide into my seat and shift the car to drive. "Pretty sure my right arm is stronger than yours."

"Are you sure about that?" She kicks off her shoes and crosses her legs in the seat. The black tights she's wearing stretch over her muscles, and they're the same distracting pair she wore on Thanksgiving. I remember those little frills at the top like the back of my hand. "Is there anything else I need to know about your family?"

"What, like if we do any sacrifices in the basement? A little late to be asking about that, don't you think?"

Lacey rolls her eyes and reaches over to poke my ribs. I dodge out of the way and grab her hand, threading it through mine. "Tell me about your nieces. What does your parents' kitchen look like? Is there a tire swing in the backyard?"

I rub my thumb over her knuckles and smile as we head north. "I have five nieces. The oldest is eleven and the youngest turned two last month. Parker, Madeline, Eliza, Megan and Perry—which is short for Persephone. My parents' kitchen got remodeled four summers ago. There's no tire swing in the back-yard, but there is an old wooden bench under this big oak tree. All of our initials are carved into it."

"So many girls." Lacey brings her knees to her chest and turns her body to face me. "You'd be a good girl dad."

"Oh yeah?" My eyes flick over to her, and she's watching me with her chin cradled in her free hand. A smile pulls at her lips, and I wonder what she's thinking about. "What makes you say that?"

"Because I know how you treat me, Maggie, and Maven. You're not grossed out by period stuff. You think women can truly do anything. You're patient and kind and... I don't know. You'd be a great boy dad, too. All those football helmets and tackling and stuff. But you're soft, Shawn. Your heart is gentle, and sometimes you like to be quiet. Perfect for girls."

I swallow, and images of Lacey and me being parents run through my mind.

A line of girls, and I'm trying to tie ribbons in their hair.

Pink shoes.

Pink soccer cleats.

A breakfast table full of high-pitched laughter and squeals.

Fuck.

Fuck.

What the *hell* is going on? I've never imagined myself as a parent before, and definitely not with someone I've slept with a handful of times.

But it's there, clear as day, like a bruise you can't get rid of.

A thread in me pulls tight at the vision, and I blink it away.

"Thanks. Being a girl dad would be pretty fucking cool." I squeeze her hand and let go. Maybe touching her is making me think these things, a whole life of happily ever after stretching out in front of me every time her palm connects with mine. "Want to put on some music?"

"Sure. What are you in the mood for? How about some songs from the sixties? That's close to your generation."

"Jesus, Daniels. It's too early for that kind of attack," I say, but I laugh anyway. "Nothing from the sixties, thanks. Or country. I hate it."

"How can you hate country?" she asks, and she sounds appalled. "An entire genre is on your shit list?"

"Yup. I don't see why anyone would find a tractor sexy, but that's just me."

"So I shouldn't sign you up for Farmers Only?"

"God, no. Can you imagine what people's bios must say? *Must love chickens.* I'm all set."

"Missed opportunity for it to say *must love cocks* and for it to not mean you're talking about organizing an orgy," she answers, and then she bursts out laughing.

It's uncontrollable, and I almost have to pull the car over because I'm cackling too hard. Tears fill my eyes, and my sides ache. Lacey howls beside me, her face buried in her hands and her shoulders shaking.

God, she's fun.

I could listen to her stupid jokes for hours and they'd never get old.

"You know, if the whole badass-pediatrician-who-helps-the-community thing never pans out, you might have a career in standup," I say when the giggles subside.

It dulls to quiet, and all I can hear is her gentle breathing. The sound of the road beneath the car. The beat of my heart when she practically climbs across the center console to loop her arm around mine and rest her head on my shoulder. I should tell her to stop being reckless, to sit back down and not get too close, but I can't.

She makes me want to be reckless, too.

"Glad to know I have a backup option," she says. "Though, to be honest, I think you can only talk about cocks one or two times before someone starts to think you really *might* be trying to organize an orgy."

"Three times a charm. Hey, I want to talk to you about tomorrow."

"Okay. What's tomorrow?"

"There's this thing my family and I do every year. It started back when my dad was a mail carrier—he delivered letters for thirty-five years. Christmas was always his favorite time of year. He would read the letters kids wrote to Santa, and he'd partner with local companies to surprise them with a gift off their wish list."

"Wow. That's incredible. That's a great way to get in the holiday spirit."

"It is. It kind of grew over the years. I remember the first time we went around we had fifteen families to drop off gifts for. It wasn't a lot, but it was enough to make them smile. When I signed my rookie contract, I wanted to make what he was doing an official organization, so I did."

"Oh, Shawn. What a thoughtful gesture." She nestles her cheek onto my arm and squeezes me tight. "Please keep talking. I want to hear more."

"It's called Operation Give Back, and we've kept that gift giving tradition in place. It's grown a lot, and so many people benefit from it. It's a good reminder of what the year is about, you know?"

"I definitely know. Whenever I walk through the hospital to visit Maggie in November and December, you see these folks who are sick or hurting but they're still smiling because they're surrounded by the people they love. They don't have a million presents under the Christmas tree, but what they *do* have, they're so grateful for."

"Exactly. Tomorrow is the day we designated to deliver gifts. I'm sorry I didn't tell you—I feel like I've been running around the last couple of weeks, and I forgot you don't know what my family does for the holidays. It's going to be cold and we'll be spending a lot of hours on our feet, so please don't feel obligated to join. I just wanted to give you a heads up for where I'll be tomorrow when I disappear."

"Are you kidding? I'd love to join you all, if that's okay."

"It's more than okay." I turn my cheek and give her a quick kiss on her forehead. "I want you there, and I'm glad I'll have you by my side."

THE DRIVE IS SHORT, and traffic is light for a holiday weekend. We zip up I-95, and soon we're turning onto my parents' street. The sun inches higher in the sky, and I'm hit with a wave of nostalgia from being back in a place I know so well.

"That's their house on the corner," I say. I park the car on the road and turn off the ignition. The driveway is full of rental cars and my parents' Subaru—matching white Outbacks they've had since 2015 and refuse to trade in. "Ready to get this party started?"

"Let's do it." She reaches over and high fives me, and I chuckle when she jumps out of the car. "I didn't even ask, but I'm assuming we're sharing a room?"

"Yeah. Shit, I'm sorry I didn't run that by you. I can sleep on the floor or something."

"Shawn. You've seen me naked. You've bent me over my couch and jerked off with a pair of my underwear. We can survive sleeping in the same bed."

"If you feel uncomfortable in the middle of the night, you can kick me out," I say.

"It's really sweet of you to think I'll be able to move your two-hundred-pound body," Lacey says, and she grins. "I'm sure I could push you with all of my might and you wouldn't go anywhere."

We head up the driveway, and I nod toward a bush on the left. "My sister Katelin shoved me into that shrub once when she found out I hid all of her Paramore CDs in the backyard."

"I'd shove you in it, too," she says, and I pinch her hip. She squeals and runs toward the door, raising her fist to knock. "Wait, do we just walk in? You don't technically live here anymore."

"Sweetheart, my blood is literally on these front steps from the time I stumbled home drunk on my eighteenth birthday. We're not knocking."

"The audacity of them to put stairs here, honestly."

"Can't believe they didn't ask me about my drinking habits when they bought the place a year before I was born."

"Okay, so we're just—"

The door flies open before Lacey can finish asking her question. Three small bodies barrel into me and wrap their arms around my waist.

"Uncle Shawn," Parker, my oldest niece, says. "You're here."

"Hey, princess." I set my bags down and pick her up. She's halfway through her first year in middle school and getting taller every time I see her, but she still lets out a giggle as I spin her around like a helicopter. I've been doing it since she was a toddler, and I hope she never asks me to stop.

"Me next," Eliza demands, her eight-year-old personality shining through. I switch girls, spinning her around too, and she squeals with delight.

"Last but not least. The tiniest princess," I say, and I pick up Perry. I toss her high in the air and catch her. "Merry Christmas, gang."

"Who's that?" Eliza asks, and she points to Lacey.

She's standing off to the side, letting me have a minute with the girls, and I smile. I've never introduced a woman to my family; there have been the occasional run-ins at games where the person I'm sleeping with meets my sister, and it's unbelievably awkward.

They always try to insert themselves into the moment, like they're establishing themselves as an important fixture in my life when I don't even know how they take their coffee in the morning.

Not Lacey, though. She's biting her bottom lip and watching the madness unfold, a twinkle in her eye as her gaze drags to mine. I motion her forward and she shuffles toward me, shyness in her soft smile.

"This is Lacey," I say. "She's my girlfriend, and I like spending time with her."

"Pretty," Perry says. She touches Lacey's hair then her nose. "Princess."

I chuckle and kiss Perry's cheek. "She is kind of a princess, isn't she?"

"Do you love her, Uncle Shawn?" Eliza asks. "Mommy says Christmas is about being with people you love. You must, if she's here with you."

Our eyes meet, and the color on Lacey's cheeks deepens from pink to a deep shade of red.

"I like her very, very much," I say. "She's my favorite person in the entire world."

"The entire world?" Eliza wrinkles her nose. "But there are a lot of people. You haven't met them all."

"Doesn't matter. She's still my favorite," I say, and Lacey wraps her fingers around my wrist. Brings my hand to her mouth and kisses my palm, right in the center.

"Hi. I'm Lacey. I'm very excited to meet you. Your Uncle Shawn has told me a lot about you all," she says.

"Do you like Barbies?" Eliza asks. "Would you play dress up with us?"

"Of course, I would," Lacey says. "That sounds so fun."

"I like her, Uncle Shawn," Parker says, and I chuckle.

"I do, too. Let's get you kids back in the house before your moms yell at me for letting you stand out here without a coat on. I can't get in trouble before we open presents," I say, and I corral the girls inside.

I set Perry down, and they all take off toward the kitchen. I spy the Christmas tree in the living room, its lights turned on and ornaments dangling from the branches. The smell of apple pie wafts through the air, and I inhale, happy to be home.

"You love it here," Lacey says softly. "It's one of your safe spaces."

"Yeah." I nod, and my shoulders relax. "There's no place like home, right?"

"Right," she agrees, and I tug her toward me. I cup her cheek with my palm, and I smile as she glances up at me.

"This is going to be the best year yet, though. All my favorite people are in one place. What could be better?"

"An orgy," she says, and I tuck my laughter into the crook of her neck. I wrap my arms around her and hug her tight.

We stay like that for a minute, the wreath on the door our only witness, and I kiss her forehead. She's warm under my mouth, and I want to kiss her everywhere.

"Ready?" I ask, and I take her hand in mine.

"Let's do it." Lacey smiles at me, a grin as bright as the twinkling lights draped over the fireplace and the stockings hanging from the mantle. "Best Christmas ever. I can already feel it."

THIRTY-SIX
LACEY

I WANT Shawn's family to adopt me every Christmas.

They're loud and they're funny and there's so much *love* in their house.

The kitchen isn't a big space—it can barely hold all eight adults—but it's brimming with joy and cheer.

Wine glasses get passed around. There's laughter and stories from holidays past. Kids dart between people's legs, and I think I spot a cat, too.

Shawn keeps me close to him, his arm around my shoulder and his side pressed against mine. He's my buoy. When the conversation turns a little too personal, a little too inquisitive about our relationship timeline and what our plans are for the future, he pulls me back in, a sturdy sureness keeping me afloat.

"Want another drink?" he asks as he taps the inside of my wrist, and I shake my head.

"No, thank you. One more before dinner, and I won't make it through the meal," I say. "And I'm going to destroy the lasagna your mom made."

"I'd take care of you, you know," he says soft in my ear. "I'd make sure you were alright."

"I know." I twist the fabric of his sweater in my hand and nod. "You'd probably wash my hair and put me to bed, too."

"I would. I'd also tuck you in and leave you a glass of water. You're safe with me, Lacey girl," he says, and he presses his lips to my cheek in a kiss that ignites a flame of desire before walking away.

It almost sounds like a dream, but I know Shawn would take care of me. He'd keep an eye on me until morning, and that makes my heart sing.

I haven't been able to stop thinking about him since he came over to my apartment two nights ago and bent me over the couch. Since he asked me what about our arrangement felt fake and held my hand for half the drive here.

Nothing about it feels fake.

It hasn't for a while now.

"Hey." Katelin and Amanda, Shawn's sisters, slide up next to me, and I blink out of my trance.

"Hi." I set my glass down and smile. "Is it time for the sister interrogation?"

"God, no," Katelin says.

"The fewer details we know about our brother's personal life, the better," Amanda adds. "We just wanted to say hi."

"Oh. Well, hi. I'm so glad I get to be here with you all. It's only been a few hours, but I already feel so welcomed by your family. I'm so happy."

"Us, too," Katelin agrees. "When the video of you two kissing at the game went viral, we were worried. We didn't know if it was staged or something Shawn got dragged into doing. But it's so obvious you two care a lot about each other. God, the way he looks at you is how my husband looked at me the first year of our relationship. Now I have to snap my fingers to get him to pay attention to me."

I laugh. "Shawn is..."

Great isn't sufficient.

Neither is *wonderful.*

I'm not sure there's a word out there that's big and vast enough to describe how *perfect* he is.

"I'm lucky," is what I settle on, because I am.

It's getting harder and harder to understand I'm going to have to walk away from him. There are only nine days left until the New Year, and I intend to spend every single one of them with him.

When the clock strikes midnight, I'll look back and be happy about what we shared. I won't let myself be sad but grateful to have learned so much more about my best friend. For all the little moments and the big ones, too.

"Brought you a snack," Shawn says, reappearing by my side. He sets a napkin in my hand and rubs my shoulders. "That should hold you over until dinner."

I smile at the bunch of grapes and pull one off the stem, popping it in my mouth. "Thank you."

"You're welcome, doll face."

"Oh, my god." I scrunch my nose and shake my head. "Absolutely not. That's going on the avoid list forever."

"I think we're missing something," Amanda says to Katelin, and I laugh.

"Sorry. He keeps coming up with these horrendous pet names," I explain. "They're getting worse and worse."

"There's only one she likes," Shawn says, and he loops his arm around my waist. His fingers fan out across my hip, and his thumb draws a torturous pattern on the hem of my shirt. "All the others have been vetoed."

"Two, actually. I really, really like two of them," I say softly, and his eyes twinkle.

"I remember when I was stupid in love," Katelin says. "The beginning part of a relationship is always the most fun."

"Maybe. But I'm going to make sure we're still stupid in love in ten years," he says, and he looks down at me. "I'm going to make sure we're still having fun, too. Would that be alright with you, Lacey girl?"

It's an act.

I *know* it's an act, but that doesn't stop my stomach from swooping low. From my heart racing in my chest. From a warm and fuzzy sensation rolling down my shoulders and settling behind my ribs. From envisioning Shawn ten years down the road, his hair a little gray but his smile just as wide.

"Yes," I say, a hysterical sound that bubbles up my throat and falls out into the world.

I don't know if I'm saying yes to the pretend version of us or something that could be real, but I let it slip out anyway because I don't care. With him, I always want to say yes.

Maybe I don't have to have it all figured out right now. Maybe Shawn and I can just *exist*, soaked in gratitude and warmth and the spirit of the best time of the year. Maybe the rest will work itself out, what's meant to be finding a way to be. Maybe we don't have to rush it; it's something we can ease into, like a bath or fresh cup of coffee.

If I blinked, I would've missed the way Shawn's eyes widened. The dip of his chin and the touch of pink on the tips of his ears.

But I don't miss it.

I see it as clear as day, just like I see him.

THE REST of the evening passes in loud laughter and hearty conversations. In seconds and thirds of lasagna, and a bottle of scotch replacing the bottle of wine. In Shawn's hand on my thigh, the press of his fingers into my stockings a distracting thing.

We wind down by the fireplace, the logs crackling from heat and smoke rising to the chimney. I sit tucked into his side, my chin on his shoulder and my breath warm on his skin.

The two youngest girls have been put down for the night, and the adults are talking about the plans for tomorrow.

"We have a lot of houses to get to," Shawn says. "This is the most donations Operation Give Back has ever seen."

"People are in a giving mood," his mom, Kelly, says. "Sometimes when the world is shit, you try to latch on to the good things happening around you. For a lot of people, that's helping the community."

"How many families are on your list?" I ask. "What's a normal year look like?"

"Normally we have two hundred houses. This year we'll be able to get to over three hundred," he says.

I almost fall off the couch. "Oh, my gosh. Shawn, that's wonderful. How does the day work? Do you drop the gifts on the porch? Do you stay and talk for a while?"

"Most of the families don't know we're coming. A couple do, because the kids asked for specific things we needed to get approval for; a dog from the rescue shelter. A wheelchair ramp for their grandmother to get in and out of the house. We didn't want to show up and have the big gifts be a total surprise. I try to hang around for a few minutes, but I do want to make sure we get to everyone. We're going to be hustling tomorrow."

"That makes sense." I take a sip of my drink and look around the room. "Do all of you participate?"

"We try to," Katelin says. "It's gotten harder with kids, especially the little ones. They get fidgety, and with the temperature dropping tonight, we don't want them to get too cold."

"I'd be happy to watch them," I offer. "This is your family's tradition, and I don't want to take any time away from what you could be spending together."

"You're not, sweetheart," Shawn says, soft enough for only me to hear. "I told you I want you there, and I do. We have a schedule so everyone can rotate and help out. Dad and I are the only ones who stay the whole time."

"Okay. If you're sure."

"I'm sure." He brushes his lips against my forehead and I smell the scotch on his tongue. I want to taste it on mine. "I'm sure about everything with you."

I smile and nestle into his embrace, a deep cocoon of warmth I never want to leave. Kelly watches us from across the room, and there's a knowing gleam in her eyes. I feel a gentle twist in my gut as I remember I won't be here with them next year. There might be someone else in my place, and Kelly could be looking at her like that, too.

I hate it.

I want it to be me.

"We're going to head to bed," Amanda says. She picks up a sleeping Eliza and cradles her in her arms. "We'll see everyone in the morning."

"Do you need help with her?" Shawn asks, nodding to the eight-year-old spitfire who's quiet for the first time all evening.

"We're good." Amanda hands her off to her husband and bends down to kiss her father's cheek. "Night."

Everyone else begins to say their goodnights. Glasses are collected, and the fire is put out. The tree lights are turned off, and the house starts to grow quiet.

"Ready?" Shawn asks. He stands up and offers me his hand.

"Yeah," I say, and he pulls me to my feet. "Good night, Kelly and Michael. Thank you for a lovely first night."

"Of course, sweetie." Kelly squeezes my elbow as we pass. "We're so glad you're here."

I smile as we climb the stairs to Shawn's bedroom. His old space is in the back of the house, where it's cool and quiet.

"How many girls have you had in here?" I ask when he opens the door and locks it behind us. "A thousand?"

"You're severely overestimating my teenage capabilities. I played football six days a week. The hours I wasn't playing, I was studying or spending time with my friends and family. I've never —" he pauses, the briefest flash of anguish on his face. "You're the first."

"I am?"

"Yeah." His head bobs, and he busies himself with a jar of pencils on his desk. The old kind you have to sharpen, and my lips twitch in amusement. "Couldn't ask for a better person to lose my virginity to."

The laugh wooshes out of me, and before I know what I'm doing, I'm jumping in his arms. I tickle under his ribs and he launches me onto his bed, a plush mattress that bounces me twice before I settle against the sheets.

My laughter dies in my throat when I see Shawn staring at me.

"What?" I ask, a ghost of a question.

"You," he says, and I reach for him the same time he reaches for me.

His lips crash against mine, a bruising display of affection after hours of pent-up tension. Small touches and subtle grazes of his fingers up my thigh. My chest against his back and the swish of my hips as I walked away from the dinner table.

"There's not anyone here," I whisper against his mouth before he drags his lips down my neck. Presses a kiss to the spot behind my ear. "We don't have to pretend."

Shawn pulls back. He looks down at me, and there's a divot of wrinkles between his eyebrows. I try to rub them away with my thumb, but they don't disappear. "What are you talking about?"

"Just... you know. In here we can be ourselves. We don't have to act like we're..."

"Do you—I still want to kiss you," he says. "I always want to kiss you, even if we're the only ones in the room. Is that... would that be okay with you?"

"Yeah." I wrap my arms around his neck and bring him close to me. He tumbles onto the mattress, knees knocking against mine. "That would definitely be okay, because I always want to kiss you, too."

It's the first time I've really seriously thought about us having something long and lasting after the holidays have passed. Something we won't let end but keep tending, keep building and growing.

A relationship.

A *real* relationship full of love and laughs and so much fun.

It wouldn't be much different from what we have now.

He's always been my safe space, my favorite person in the world from the moment I first met him.

Maybe he could be that for me forever.

When Shawn sets me on his lap and pulls my shirt over my head, I see it in his eyes.

He's thinking it, too.

THIRTY-SEVEN

SHAWN

I WAKE up to Lacey mumbling about penguins.

I'm barely on the edge of consciousness, still somewhere stuck in a dream, but I can hear her loud and clear.

I blink into the half-dark room and find her, arms looped around my stomach and her head on my chest. When I see her, I smile.

We clung to each other all night long. I didn't mean to, but subconsciously, I drifted toward her. It looks like she drifted toward me, too, because her legs are tangled with mine and her hand is on my ass.

I didn't know I was into my ass being touched, but I guess I am.

Maybe it's because Lacey is the one doing it.

She stirs beside me and stretches her arms above her head. The white sheet slips down her chest and pools around her waist as she burrows into the pillows, and I see the pink marks I left on her stomach last night when my hands were between her legs.

I left one on the inside of her thigh, too, just above her knee.

I'm really, *really* glad we're kissing each other.

"Hey," she croaks, and her eyes flutter open. When she smiles at me, I feel it behind my ribs. It fills the empty places in my chest and the spots that are slowly becoming hers. "Good morning."

"Morning." I bend down to kiss her forehead, and she smiles even wider. "How'd you sleep?"

"Really well. You're a human furnace. Thank you for keeping me warm." She sits up and brushes a strand of knotted hair out of her face. "What time is it?"

"Early. Too early. I'm going to get up and get started on a few things, but you should go back to sleep. I'll come wake you up when you need to get ready."

"That's okay." She yawns and rubs her eyes. There's a line on her cheek from the pillows, and I trace over the crease with the tips of my fingers. "I'm up. How did you sleep?"

"Great. You're like a fluffy pillow, Daniels. I've never slept so hard in my life."

"Is that supposed to be a compliment?" She lifts an eyebrow and flicks me off. "Seems like you could come up with something a little better."

"Alright." I climb over her, one leg on either side of her naked waist. "Your hips drive me wild. I like that you were the first thing I saw this morning, even if you were talking about sea creatures."

"I was not," she says, aghast. "I don't talk in my sleep."

"You definitely do. What else? Even when you have drool on your face—" I use my thumb to wipe away the dried mark on the corner of her mouth. "You're the most beautiful person in the world."

"Oh." She dips her chin and blinks a dozen times. She reaches out and outlines the tattoos across my chest. Sharp nails dig into my skin, just over the vine of an inked plant, and I huff out a strangled breath. "That was way better than what I was expecting."

"Good." I kiss the end of her nose and climb off of her. "I'll make us some breakfast. Today is usually a grab and go morning since we're all going eight different directions. Tomorrow you'll get to try some of Mom's frittata. Fuck, it's so good, Lace. You're going to love it. I've tried to make it myself, but it's shit compared to hers. And I—what?" My train of thought derails because she's staring at me with a brightness in her heavy-lidded eyes, and now I'm distracted. "What's wrong?"

"Nothing. I just like seeing you so..." she trails off and gestures up and down. Lets out a breath and bites her bottom lip. I want to bite her bottom lip, too. "So you," she finishes.

"Is that a good thing?" I ask, and I didn't realize how badly I want her answer to be yes.

"It's a very good thing. I've known you as Shawn, the football coach. Shawn, my friend in D.C. And I like that I'm seeing you as Shawn, the son, uncle and brother. I like that you get excited about the little things. Like frittatas and those little cannulas we had after dinner last night."

"Once you try my mom's breakfast, you'll understand why I'm excited."

"I have no doubt. If it's anything like her lasagna, I'll be in an extreme food coma."

I move off the bed and rifle through my suitcase. I slip on a pair of jeans and tug my shirt over my head. Lacey is moving behind me, and I hear the zip of her bag and the rustle of her clothes.

"We're going to be running around today, but it's supposed to be cold. Make sure to bundle up," I say over my shoulder. I find my favorite blue pullover and tuck it under my arm. "You can leave a jacket in the car, too. You'll ride with me and Dad."

I'm about to turn around and ask her if she wants to use the bathroom first, but her arms wrap around me from behind. They slide around my waist and pull me flush against her chest. Her cheek rests on my back, in the spot between my shoulder blades, and I fold my hands over hers.

"I know today is going to be busy," she says into my shirt. Her words sneak through the threadbare cotton and are warm on my skin. "Before we get going, I wanted to take a second to tell you how proud I am of you. You're one of my favorite people in the world, Shawn, and getting to be here with you while you—we—do something so important means more to me than any gift ever will."

"Hey." I tug on her arms, a gentle pull to bring her in front of me. Her back rests against the wall and her smile is soft around the edges. "Today has always been my favorite day of the year, but now that you're here, it's even better. Before you and I started this—this thing between us, there was a ghost that felt like it was following me. I could feel it in my back. Over my shoulder, when I watched Maggie and Aiden together. The closer we got to December, the more dim everything felt. It wasn't like how it's always been."

I pause for a breath to carefully choose my next words. I'm done talking about what's happening between us like it's pretend. Like it's fake. Like she and I both can't feel the immense pull we have toward each other, a thread unraveling as we get closer and closer.

I can tell it's happening when our gazes lock from across the room. When she looks up at me from my childhood bed late at night, her chin on my chest and a constellation of freckles on her bare shoulders, and asks me to tell her about how I fell in love with football like it's the most important story in the world.

"And then?" she asks, coaxing me forward.

"Then I kissed you during the middle of a football game. What I thought was the stupidest thing I could have ever done, the biggest mistake that would have ruined our friendship and everything I cared about, ended up being the greatest decision of my life. That ghost is gone, and now it's just you. And, yeah, you like to talk in your sleep about marine birds—I'm partial to puffins, if we're keeping track—but I guess I didn't realize how fucking *lonely* I was until I kissed you. Until I met you, I guess. I was, and now I'm not. You here with me, willing and eager to join in and do something I love, well." I shake my head and drop my chin to my chest. I don't know where this whole fucking monologue of emotions is coming from, but I can't stop. "It's the dream, really."

Lacey's breath stutters. She squeezes me impossibly tight, almost hard enough to knock the wind out of me. I run my hands up her arms then back down. "There's nowhere else I'd rather be. If you gave me a million options, I'd choose here with you every single time."

"Funny. I'd pick you a million times, too."

"I'm so happy," she says, but it's soft. Like she's not sure she's allowed to admit it and she's been holding onto a secret for years. "This has been the best holiday season ever, and it's not even Christmas yet. This sounds so cheesy, but there's all this joy in my life, and I want to keep spreading that joy. I'm healthy. I have a good job and great friends. I love my parents, and even though I'm not spending Christmas with them, I know I'll see them soon. And then there's you."

"Yeah?" I tip her chin back and stare at her. She looks delicate in the early morning light, like someone I need to—*want to*—take care of not just for a few more days, but for years and years. "What about me?"

"You're my best friend. The person I have the most fun with and the person I laugh the loudest with. I didn't expect you to kiss me at your game, but I'm so glad you did. You're my favorite present this year, Shawn. Totally unexpected and exactly what I wanted."

"Flirting with me, Daniels?" I ask, and she rolls her eyes.

"See if I'm ever nice to you again," she says. She tries to wiggle out of my hold, but I don't let her.

"Hey. You're my favorite present too, Lacey girl. I hope you know that. Nothing under my tree will be as wonderful as you."

She blinks and lifts up on her toes. She's closer to me now, and her eyes sparkle like stars. Her lips brush against mine in the faintest of kisses, but it's heaven.

She's warm and soft and perfect. A place I want to curl up and stay awhile. It's too quick, barely long enough for me to indulge in how good she tastes, how sweet the sound of her sigh is, how nice it is to have her hands around my neck before she's pulling away.

"I know." She nods against my shirt and unwinds her arms from my body. "I'm going to freshen up."

"Okay. Come downstairs when you're ready. I'll get the food going."

I peek at her over my shoulder as she heads to the bathroom, and when I do, I find her looking at me, too.

THE KITCHEN IS EMPTY.

I click on the stove and pull a pan out from under the oven. Even with the remodel, everything is in the exact same place it was twenty-five years ago, down to the spatula in the drawer to my right and the spice rack in the cabinet to my left. I move around, grabbing everything I need for scrambled eggs and toast, and I get to work.

The stairs creak and groan, and then there are soft footsteps on the hardwood floor. Lacey appears around the corner, already bundled up with a puffy white jacket that makes her look like a marshmallow, and I smile at the bright pink beanie on her head.

"I love that hat," I say.

"You do?" She touches the big pom pom on top. "It's not over the top?"

"Nope. It fits you just right."

She laughs and takes a seat at the table. "Can I help with anything?"

"Not a thing. Do you want coffee? I'm making eggs for you; scrambled with a little cheese on top, right?"

Her neck jerks up and she stares at me. "You know how I eat my eggs?"

"You know how I eat *my* eggs," I remind her. "I couldn't be the friend who doesn't know your egg order. Besides, you had that whole argument with me the night we did breakfast for dinner at Maggie and Aiden's a couple months ago. You gave me a lecture on the egg to cheese ratio, and I swear to God I've never seen someone talk about something so passionately. You had more enthusiasm than the people who preach about world peace."

"Because I take it very seriously. Maybe the secret to world peace is a perfectly scrambled plate of eggs."

"Fuck, now I'm nervous. I hope I get this right, otherwise, I think I'm going to be in deep shit."

I slide the plate her way and hand her a fork. I lift an eyebrow as she takes a bite, closing her eyes and slowly chewing so she can give me her honest opinion.

"Well?" I say.

"Damn you, Holmes. These are better than when I make them." She shovels another bite in her mouth, and I pump my fist in the air. "What's your secret?"

"A chef never tells."

"Oh, come on. This isn't some family recipe of yours that's been handed down for millennia."

"A splash of milk and a hint of cream. Makes them nice and fluffy."

"I'll have to try that when we get home."

We eat our breakfast and I start a pot of coffee. I know the smell of caffeine is going to wake up the masses.

"We're going to head out in about an hour." I pull out the sheet of paper from my back pocket and smooth it out on the counter. "This is the house here," I say, tapping the small square.

"What's that?" she asks, and her finger lands on the blob to the left.

"It's supposed to be a Christmas tree."

"It looks like a dying fish. Maybe you should stick to sports."

"Oh, fuck you. I'm a great artist. My houses are almost three dimensional. Look. There's a goddamn roof."

"Okay." Lacey pats my hand and smirks. "Whatever you say, honey bunches of oats."

"Veto. Jesus, Daniels. I'm not a box of cereal. Have some class."

Her laugh is light and loud, and I smile at the sound. "I'm sorry," she says. "Please continue, Picasso."

"The nerve of some people," I mumble under my breath, and her fingers dig into my side. "We'll loop around the perimeter of town, then zig-zag back in. A quick stop for lunch should have us wrapping up around four, which is just in time for dinner tonight. Having you here is going to help us go much faster."

"This is incredibly thought out." She traces the lines of the road and the markings on the crumpled sheet. "What do the symbols by each house mean?"

"If it's their first time receiving gifts, or if they've been on the list before. It doesn't really mean anything. They can be on the list for five years, and I don't care. I just like to check in with folks. Make sure they're doing okay. It's impossible to expect someone to get back on their feet in a year. I like to keep track of the people who might need a little extra help."

Lacey's lips quiver. I press my finger against her mouth, and she kisses my knuckles. "I'm going to cry so much today, and I am *not* a crier. It's usually only when I see those sad dog videos where the pet is reunited with their owner after three weeks apart. God, I turn into a blubbering mess. But this—" she gestures at the paper and taps the drawing— "this is going to ruin me."

"I'm not curing cancer. Thousands of people do this every year, and I'm not any better than them. Hell, I'm giving away toys, not cars."

"Maybe it's because you're immune to the reach you have, Shawn, but this is pretty freaking spectacular. The kids are going to be more appreciative of a Nerf ball than a Ferrari. Imagine waking up and thinking you're not going to get anything for Christmas, then this tall, hot, tattooed—"

"You think I'm hot, Lacey girl?" I ask.

"You know you're hot. My mom knows you're hot. Everyone knows you're hot."

I lean my elbows on the kitchen table and crowd her space. "I don't care about everyone. I care about you. And you think I'm hot."

Lacey rolls her eyes, but her cheeks turn pink. "Yes, you're hot. Now tell me your secret for being such a nice guy."

"I don't know." I sit back in my chair and move the eggs around my plate. "It's not a secret. I just think we should treat everyone the right way and do a little good if we can. I'm still figuring out my own shit, but I can at least be nice to people along the way."

"You're going to be husband of the year when you settle

down. Dad of the year. Human of the year. Can you teach a seminar on how to not be a dick to the rest of the male population? Because you're way, way, *way* above the standard."

"Doing the bare minimum shouldn't be the standard, Lace. You gotta stop settling for dudes who have a vendetta against stadium camera people. There are better things out there. A whole world of men who are just *waiting* to hold a door open for you."

"I know that now. You hold the door open for me."

"I do."

"Would you—" her throat bobs as she swallows. She looks away and focuses her attention on the salt and pepper shakers instead of my face. "Do you think you could keep holding the door open for me?"

It's ambiguous. Open-ended and with a thousand different meanings. I know what she's asking, though, and I know what my answer is.

"Yeah," I say. "I'll hold it open for you as long as you'd like. Would that be okay with you?"

Her fingers rip up the napkin in her hands. She opens her mouth, but before she can answer, I hear my dad's booming voice as he rounds the corner into the kitchen.

"Is that coffee I smell?" he asks. "Morning, you two. How'd you sleep? Was it warm enough up there for you?"

"Morning." I stand up and collect our plates. "We slept great. I think we're both tired from a long couple of weeks at work. It was nice to wake up and not have to think about anything."

It was also nice to wake up with Lacey naked in my arms.

"Let me eat some food and grab a cup of coffee, and we can get going," my dad says.

"Where are all the presents?" Lacey asks. "I haven't seen any besides the ones under the tree in your living room, and that's not nearly enough for three hundred families."

"In a storage unit," I explain. "Dad starts collecting them in early October, and we keep them locked up until today. We change places every year so people don't pick up on what we're doing and try to steal the gifts."

"Are they wrapped?"

"Wrapped and labeled and organized. I wish I was able to get up here and help more, but this season has been extra busy."

"We can handle it just fine," my dad says. "It gives your mother and I something to look forward to now that we're not working anymore. I can only do so many crossword puzzles."

"You're awfully sharp for a man approaching seventy," I answer. "Lace, we use my dad's truck for the gifts. There's a trailer we attach and we load it up. It takes about an hour to get everything ready, so if you want to stay here, we can swing back by and—"

"No," she interrupts me. She shakes her head and sits up in her chair. "No. I want to do every step with you. I don't care about manual labor. I can do some heavy lifting."

My dad's eyes meet mine over the rim of his mug, and he gives me a thumbs up.

Yeah, Dad. I think she's pretty fucking great, too.

THIRTY-EIGHT

LACEY

SHAWN ISN'T REAL.

He's something made of dreams and wishes, because I cannot believe this man is just walking around the world and existing in this frustratingly nice and obscenely hot way.

I always thought he was generous; a good tipper (sixty-five percent, always). A door holder (even when someone is twenty paces away and he has to wait). A *please* and *thank you* user (every time, all the time).

But today he's catapulted himself to an elusive category of men that are increasingly impossible to find: the all-around good guy who's not just trying to get into your pants.

I really think he might be the only one on that pedestal, a category made up of only him, because no one else I've ever met in life comes as close to perfection as he does.

Perfect.

It's the only way to describe him.

We've been outside in the cold for hours, but he's unfazed. He hasn't lost the spring in his step or his megawatt grin. It's still in place as we go house to house, bearing presents and holiday cheer.

There's no press or cameras. There's no one to put on an act for; it's just me, him, his dad, a rotation of family members joining us throughout the day and Christmas music blaring from the speakers of the truck. I've never heard someone sing "Jingle Bells" so loudly in my life.

I'm not sure he even brought his cell phone with him. I saw him leave it on the foyer table before we left, and I don't think he ever picked it back up.

He's thorough with his time and considerate to every family we meet. He stops to take photos and sign jerseys, the hometown guy who made it big showing up on their porches with a sack full of gifts. One kid made Shawn wait while he dug out his rookie season trading card, and Shawn was speechless.

He dipped his chin and wiped his eyes after.

I'm in the stadium with him for every home game, but I've spent almost two seasons only knowing him as a coach. The guy who makes the play calls but isn't actually out on the field. I forget he's had this whole other life with his career, years in the league and giving his heart and soul to his team.

Today is the first time I've truly been immersed in how well-known and well-liked he is. *Millions* of people look up to him, and it blows my mind he never acts like he's better than anyone else just because his name is printed on the back of a jersey and he has a hand full of Super Bowl rings.

"Ready?" Shawn asks from behind the wheel. He gives my knee a squeeze and taps the denim of my jeans. "There are only ten houses to go."

My feet are sore from the miles of walking. My muscles ache from the stairs we've climbed. My arms hurt from carrying the boxes of gifts as carefully as I can, not wanting to drop a single one. My cheeks are pink from the wind and the cold, and I stopped feeling my toes an hour ago.

Still, there's a hum in my chest. The quiet swell of a wave in the cavity behind my heart. The urge to want to keep doing more, as if the first two hundred and ninety houses we visited weren't enough. A smile on my lips that bleeds into an ear-splitting grin as he puts the car in park and turns off the ignition.

Shawn's dad hops out of the backseat, the spot he valiantly claimed when we started our day seven and a half hours ago, refusing to switch places with me when I pleaded with him to take the front.

I see where Shawn gets it from.

Maddening, delightful Holmes' men.

"I'm ready." I unbuckle my seatbelt and adjust the annoyingly festive necklace I'm wearing. It's made up of two dozen bulbs, big Christmas lights that twinkle and flicker and change colors when you click a hidden button on the back. "This is the best day of my life."

"Mine, too." He tugs on the strand around my neck and I lean forward, right up in his space. I can see the flicker of the lights in his eyes, a rotating rainbow that repeats itself again and again. "Can I kiss you, Lacey girl?"

I blow out a breath, and the cold from outside begins to seep into the car. "You've never asked to kiss me before."

"I know. But before my dad and half the city weren't watching."

"I'm yours, right?" I ask, and his throat bobs.

"Right," he says, and his voice is hard around the edges but soft in the middle with the single word. "You are."

"Then you should know you can kiss me whenever you want. Audience, no audience. The answer will always be yes," I whisper, and the air leaves my lungs when he captures my mouth with his.

It's sweet and tender, both palms on my cheeks and his body

heat mixing with mine. I tilt my head to deepen the kiss, to bring him closer, because every time Shawn kisses me, I lose a little part of myself.

That small, insecure voice in my head that tells me I'll never find anyone good enough begins to fade. It begins to take the shape of the man beside me, down to the tattoo of a cactus on his right hand—a drunken night in Vegas when he was twenty-six, he told me last night—an image that's startlingly sharp and clear.

My heart knows he's become more than a friend. More than a fuck buddy. More than someone I can sleep with once—or six times—to fill a need and then walk away from. He's worked his way into my life, and I don't ever want him to leave.

He's taken the spot I've left vacant for years, the tiny crater I'm not sure I'd ever fill, and made it his own. It's different than how I imagined; it's a little flawed. A little messy. A little loud and chaotic and uncertain, but I'm learning I like messy.

I like messy with *him*.

How did we go from casual and light to *here?* My heart in my throat as I think about tomorrow, and the next day after and the next day after. A thousand more days, and I could have them all with him.

Maybe our souls were fused together months ago. Back on the night when we first met and he shook my hand, smiled my way, and told me he was excited to finally meet me.

Back on the night he first kissed me, a leap of faith off a high ledge. The little moments in between; scrambled eggs done just the way I like and talking on the phone until the early morning, neither one of us wanting to be the first to hang up.

"You're smiling," he says against my lips, and I can feel him smiling, too. "What are you thinking about?"

"You," I say. "Me. Us."

"Us, huh?" Shawn fixes my hat, making sure it's snug on my head and covering my ears. He straightens my jacket, his hands fumbling with the zipper as he pulls it up toward my chin. I think he's trying to find any excuse to touch me. "That sounds promising."

"I think it could be."

There's a tap on the glass. Shawn's dad waves through the window, a kind reminder that we're on a tight schedule.

"We should go," Shawn says. "Lots more presents to deliver."

"We'll come back to this?" I ask.

"Yeah." He nods, a promise in the bob of his head. "We will."

I unbuckle my seatbelt, climbing out of the car and into the bitter cold. The wind has started to die down as sunset approaches, but it's still hard to breathe. I hurry to the trunk and we grab the row of presents for the Whitaker family, double checking to make sure we have all the boxes and bags.

Shawn leads us up the stairs toward the door and knocks. He rests his hand on the small of my back, and the same nervous energy rolls through him like it did for all the other houses. I look up at him with the Santa hat on his head, and I can't help but grin.

God, I'm head over heels for this man.

The door opens, and a little girl with red curly hair pokes her head out. Shawn steps away from me and crouches down, his jeans rubbing against the wood as he gets on her level.

"Hi, Clara. My name is Mr. Shawn. Is your dad home?" he asks, his voice gentle and kind.

He's greeted everyone—every kid, every adult, every second cousin who lives in the basement—by their first name, a feat I'm still trying to figure out. It took me fifty houses to realize there's a laminated spreadsheet in the truck, a list of all the people he'd encounter today, so he knows how to approach them.

So goddamn perfect.

"Yes," the little girl says, and I see the war in her eyes. A strange man is standing on her porch with gifts, and she doesn't know what to do. Hell, I would've slammed the door in his face ten seconds ago. "I'll get him."

There's the pitter patter of little feet disappearing, and I rub Shawn's back with my free hand. He clasps his palm in mine and squeezes tight while we wait. Soon there are voices, growing louder as they approach the door.

"Can I help you?" a man asks. He uses a cane to walk, and it takes him a minute to fully open the front door. "We don't want to buy anything."

"Hi, Derek. My name is Shawn. This is my girlfriend, Lacey, and my dad, Michael," he starts, and my heart turns to goo when he calls me his girlfriend. "We're with Operation Give Back, an organization that partners with businesses in the community to provide gifts for local families." His eyes flick to Clara, the little girl wrapped around her dad's leg and hiding behind his thigh. He smiles at her, and she smiles back. "Your daughter wrote a letter to Santa asking for a new Barbie dream house. Santa is a little busy getting everything ready for Christmas, but he sent us to deliver some presents."

"Santa sent you?" Clara whispers. "All the way from the North Pole?"

"Mhm. He told us you've been doing very well in school, and you like to share your toys with your little sister. Is that true?" Shawn asks, and she nods.

"Some kids at recess have two toys, but Lily and I only have one. I don't want her to not have anything to play with, so we share," Clara explains, and she steps out from her hiding spot. "I don't mind that we play together. It's more fun than playing alone."

"I agree. Giving up your toys so someone else can have them

is a very nice thing to do," Shawn says. "Santa wants to give you some more toys to share."

We bend down and set the stack of wrapped boxes and bags on the porch. They're taller than her, almost three feet high. She tugs on her dad's pant leg and points at the gifts.

"Look, Daddy," she whispers. "Christmas magic."

"I'm sorry, but we can't—there's no way for me to pay for these," Derek says. "I'm out of work after an injury and her mom —" he pauses to take a breath, and his eyes fill with tears. "Thank you, though."

"They're free, Derek," Shawn says. "We want you to have them."

"What's the catch?" he asks slowly, and Shawn chuckles.

"No catch. Just Christmas magic." He winks at Clara, and she giggles. "Oh, and one more thing." He pulls out an envelope from his back pocket and passes it across the porch. "Something for you, too."

Derek's hands tremble as he opens the letter, and he lets out a sob when he finds out what's inside.

The remaining balance of his mortgage—seventy-five thousand dollars—paid off.

Tears sting my eyes and I bury my face in Shawn's shoulder, overwhelmed by the generosity of this man.

He really isn't real.

"Where—why—how did you know?" Derek asks.

"Santa has elves everywhere," Shawn says, and he winks at Clara again. "Merry Christmas, you all."

"Merry Christmas," I say, and I wave to the family. Shawn takes my hand in his, and leads me down the stairs.

"Hey," Derek calls out, and we look over our shoulders. "You look a lot like that guy who ran back a touchdown in Super Bowl 40."

"I do?" Shawn smiles and dips his chin. "Huh. Never heard

of him. I'm more of a baseball fan. Sounds like a great athlete, though. Wish I had those legs."

Derek stares at him, understanding clouding his features just as we slip back into the truck and "All I Want for Christmas is You" begins to play.

THIRTY-NINE

LACEY

I'VE ALWAYS WANTED a Christmas Eve like this, with too many bodies squished together in one room.

Festive music is in the air, playing just loud enough to be heard over the laughter and conversations.

Cookie dough is spread out on the kitchen island and all the counters.

My hands are covered in flour and there is sugar on my cheeks.

Still, though, I can't stop smiling.

There's merriment. Tears. Horrible, off-key singing of some of my favorite Christmas songs. Stories from then and now. One of Shawn's nieces is sitting on the counter in front of me, and she helps me with the rolling pin.

My heart is full, in a way it hasn't been for a very long time.

"Lacey," Eliza says, and she stops helping to eat a handful of chocolate chips. "Do you love Uncle Shawn?"

My eyes find him across the room.

He's leaning against the wall, in deep conversation with his brother-in-law. There's a beer in one of his hands, his fingers curled around the glass bottle, while the other sits tucked in the pocket of his jeans.

He must sense me looking at him, because he turns his head. He scans the room and when his gaze settles on me, he grins.

Flirting with me, Daniels? he mouths, and I roll my eyes.

My heart also skips a beat.

"Do you remember what Uncle Shawn told you? That he liked me very much? That's how I feel about him, too," I explain.

"Good. I hope you like him forever, because I like you. I want to see you again," Eliza says, and she sneaks a piece of cookie dough into her mouth. "I like that you play dress up with us."

"We'll find a way to see each other again." I smile and wipe a clump of sugar away from her forehead. "People who like each other always find a way to stay around."

"Good." Eliza points to the ground. "Can I go down? I want to play with Parker."

"Sure." I lift her off the counter and sit her safely on the floor. "Have fun, kiddo."

"Mind if I join you?" Kelly asks as Eliza runs away, and I motion to the empty spot on the other side of the island.

"I'd love if you did. Just watch your hands. It's kind of a disaster over here."

"Looks a lot like the kitchen did when I had three kids living in the house." She laughs and grabs a cookie cutter. "What shape? Reindeer or snowflake?"

"Snowflake," I say. "Perfect for the snowball fight tomorrow."

"Oh, I'm so sorry you got dragged into that, sweetie." Kelly presses the dough and wiggles the cookie cutter around. "I thought they'd outgrow that dangerous game when they had kids, but nope. It's still a tradition."

"All this talk is making me wish I brought a helmet," I admit.

"Maybe I'll hide out behind a tree and hope for the best. They can carry on without me."

"You can try." Kelly sets the snowflake on the sheet pan and glances up at me. "I have a feeling Shawn would find you pretty quickly. He seems to know exactly where you are, all the time."

A prickly sense of awareness starts at the back of my neck. It's the sensation of being watched, of being the object of someone's attention. I lift my head and find Shawn staring at me from across the room. His eyes dart between his mom and me, and he gives me a thumbs up then a thumbs down.

Okay? he mouths, and I dip my chin in a subtle nod.

Perfect, I mouth back.

"Thank you so much for letting me spend the holidays with you all," I say to Kelly. "Shawn told me how much you enjoy being together this time of year, and I'm glad I get to be a small part of it." I grab a metal tree and cut a piece of dough. "You have beautiful traditions. Getting to go around town yesterday and hand out gifts was..." I blow out a breath, because I'm trying really hard to not cry in front of his mom. It's difficult to hold it together, though, when I feel a swell of pride and admiration in my chest when I think about *him*. "I'm very grateful."

"It's a good thing they do, isn't it? I know there's always this pressure on people who are in the spotlight to help the community. Oftentimes I worry the good deeds are done not for the people who need the help, but for the recognition that comes with being the one to do it. When Shawn used his contract money to form an official organization with his father, he made it very clear it's not about him. I've loved to see how much it's grown."

"It must be beautiful to watch something you love turn into something bigger than you," I say, and Kelly nods.

"Having you join him yesterday meant a lot to him," she says, and her voice turns softer. "He's been very careful with his heart,

Lacey, and I can't tell you how happy I am to see him let someone in and break down those walls."

"We haven't had a ton of conversations about our pasts, but I know he's selective about the people who get close to him. And, the more I get to know him, the more I understand how difficult it must be for him. His heart is gentle and he loves the things in his life fiercely. He doesn't want to put up walls, but he also wants to be sure about the company he keeps."

I find Shawn across the room again as I say it because I can't stop looking at him, and he's switched out his drink for his littlest niece. Her head rests on his chest and he rubs her back as he rocks her side to side.

It looks like they're in their own little world. The snow falls in the window behind them and the kitchen lights paint them in soft hues of yellow. I think he's dancing with her, whispering words in her ear that make her smile and giggle.

"When he started in the league, I told him to be cautious but open. It's really difficult to watch things get said about the kid you love, but Shawn bounces back. Every time. I knew the year he brought someone around for the holidays meant he found the one." Kelly's eyes flick to mine, and there's love behind them. "I've given him grief about being single and not putting himself out there. I stopped over the last couple of years because I could tell it was wearing on him, and I'd never want him to feel pressured or to settle for something that doesn't bring him complete joy. All I want is for him to be happy, whether that's alone, with someone else, or any other version of happily ever after that's out there. I was afraid at first when he mentioned bringing you. I thought it was just to appease me, but I see the way he looks at you. He's never looked so bright."

I listen to her words, and my fingers dig into the cookie dough.

I haven't let myself believe it, because it's easier to ignore this intensity between us than to give it a name. To understand that, deep down, this might have started as something for other people. A ruse to benefit from the attention neither one of us wanted.

I really did just want one night with him. Something without merit where I could lose myself, if only for a little while.

I lost myself in him instead.

The pockets of time turned from *I have to* to *I get to* and *I want to.*

My desire to be independent and self-sufficient fizzled to the achingly strong desire and need to be with *him*. To be cared for, to be heard, to be treated as someone worthy of love without having to change any part of myself.

Shawn does take care of me. It was hard to give over that power when I've been doing just fine for so long, but he's been careful with my heart, too. He carries it around in a steel box so nothing can ever touch it.

There might be an imaginary deadline waiting for us in a few days' time, an out to give us a clean and clear transition back to how we were before: friends.

Best friends.

I know in my heart I'm not going to be able to walk away from Shawn, though. Not as just a friend. Given the option, I'm going to pick him every time.

And I'm ready to work my ass off to prove it to him.

"Hey."

The deep voice I could recognize in the dead of night without eyesight caresses down my cheek. Glides down my back and spreads over my shoulders. It settles against my heart, a cat curled up for a nap in the indulgent summer sun.

Shawn slides his arm around my waist and kisses my cheek. His lips are warm, and I melt under his touch. The air is lighter. The music is brighter. Everything is better with him by my side.

"Hi." I glance up at him and find him smiling at me. "Did you come to help make cookies?"

"No." Kelly laughs and shakes her head. "He doesn't want to help; he just wants to eat the dough. He does this every year."

"Sorry, buddy. Only people who help can have a taste," I say, and I bump my hip against his. "You're going to have to find someone else to give you a snack."

"Fine. I won't eat the dough." His gaze softens, and he pushes his thumb into the point of my chin. "Can I still stick around? I missed you."

"Oh." I wipe my arm across my forehead, needing something to do besides look at him with hearts in my eyes. "Of course. I'd like it if you were here."

"Good. Mom, do you need any help getting things ready for dinner tonight?" Shawn asks. "You know I love making the stuffing."

"I already have you down for that." Kelly smiles and wipes her hands. "I'm going to run and check on my husband. He's supposed to be in here supervising the kids, and I'm willing to bet he's fast asleep in his recliner by the fire. Lacey, can you finish these cookies?"

"Absolutely. Go easy on him when you find him, though. I sat in that recliner last night after delivering gifts, and I almost didn't get out of it," I say, and she laughs.

"I got it for him so he'd stay out of my way in the kitchen, but now I need him *in* the kitchen." She slips off her apron and squeezes my arm. "Thank you for talking with me, sweetie. I'm so glad you're here."

"Me, too," I say, and I watch her head for the living room.

"Look at you getting the mom stamp of approval." Shawn leans against the counter and smiles at me. "What did you all talk about?"

"You."

"How'd that go?" he asks, and it makes my heart ache to hear the hesitancy in his voice. Like I'd learn something about him that would make me want to leave when all I want to do is stay.

"Really well." I rest my palm on his cheek, and he doesn't seem to mind the dough and flour all over my fingers. He leans into my touch, and his eyes flutter closed. "We were talking about how great you are."

"Flirting with me in front of the children? You're unbelievable, Daniels."

"Ass." I nudge his hip with mine again and gesture to the counter. "Will you make yourself useful? We have four dozen cookies to bake, a neighborhood to serenade with caroling, and a delicious meal to eat. The longer these take, the less time you have for the other things."

"Fine." He takes the apron his mother abandoned and pulls it over his head. He looks ridiculously out of place when he rolls up his sleeves and shows off his inked arms. "Anything for you," he says, and he grabs a rolling pin. "Anything at all, Lacey girl."

FORTY

SHAWN

"ARE YOU TIRED?" I ask Lacey.

She is curled up beside me on the bed, a book in her hand and her feet tucked under my thighs. There's a steaming mug of hot chocolate sitting on the table next to her, and I lean over to grab it by the handle. I pop one of the marshmallows in my mouth and take a long sip.

It's nearing midnight, and every minute of our Christmas Eve has been busy. We spent hours making cookies, then followed up the cooking with caroling and helping my parents wrap gifts for my nieces.

The living room looked like a war zone covered in wrapping paper and ribbons when we finished for the night, and I'm going to make sure I'm up extra early in the morning to help clean up.

"No," she admits, and she drags her thumb across my upper lip. "You have a whipped cream mustache."

"Is it a good look?"

Lacey tilts her head to the side. Her eyebrows wrinkle like she's deep in thought, then they smooth back out. "I don't hate it."

"That's significantly better than no." I set the drink down

and drum my fingers against her shoulder. I'm buzzing with energy, and I can't sit still. "Want to go on an adventure?"

"An adventure?" Lacey taps her phone screen to check the time and frowns. "It's midnight."

"It's not far. Just a few steps away."

"Oh, God. This is the part where you kill me, isn't it?" she sighs, an exasperated sound that fills the room around us. "I knew watching all those true crime shows would come back and bite me in the ass. You were too good to be true."

I laugh and pluck the book from her hands. I make sure to put her bookmark in place so she doesn't lose her spot. "I'd be too lonely if I killed you. Who would make me pumpkin pies? Who would I bring magnets to? I have a whole box of them at home. I can't just be the magnet guy."

"Wait." She sits up and tugs on my shirt. Her fingers curl around the sleeve and she pulls me toward her. "You have a box of magnets?"

"I do," I say.

"Why?"

I open my mouth, but there's a moment of hesitation.

I want to start being honest with this woman. About my feelings. About where I see things going with her when we get back home.

I've never really been scared in my life; you can't be when you're an athlete. You have to anticipate. React. There's not a lot of time to be afraid when you're sprinting down a football field.

Having feelings for your best friend is different. It's a lot of flailing. Thinking you're up a creek without a paddle all because she fucking *smiled* at you, and you feel like you're flying.

It's being worried she might run—not because she doesn't want you, too, because it's so obvious she does—but because she's also scared.

I'm going to go slow with Lacey. Not give it all away at once but ease her into the idea of us. A version of this story that doesn't have an ending but a new beginning instead.

I have no fucking clue *how*, but I'll figure it out.

"I buy four or five magnets every time I travel somewhere," I explain. "I give you one, but I keep the others in case you don't like what I picked. In case yours breaks or gets lost. In case I stop coaching tomorrow and I can never go back to these places, I want to be able to keep giving you something. I have this plan to give you a new one every year until you're the magnet girl."

"There's a shoebox in your closet of magnets with California burritos on them?" she asks.

She reaches for my hand, and her fingers press into the pulse point of my wrist. I hum, distracted by the drag of her nails and the way her skin is fair and smooth.

"Yes," I say around an exhale, a whoosh of wind leaving my lungs. "Yes, there is. Beavers, too. And apples for New York. There are about eighty of them in there."

"And you want to give them all to me?"

I curl my fingers around her chin and tilt her head back. Her eyes are as wide as saucers and as green as the grass in the summertime.

"When the timing is right, they're yours. If you want them."

Her lips form an O, and I can tell a dozen questions linger on the tip of her tongue. "I would," she finally says, and my heart jolts in my chest. "I would like them."

"Good." I rub my thumb down the curve of her cheek. "Will you go on an adventure with me?"

"Yeah." Lacey nods, and I'm going to pretend she's agreeing to every adventure with me, not just this one. "I will."

I climb off the bed and point to her jacket. "Bundle up. We're going outside."

"It's twenty degrees."

"That's why you're going to wear a coat." I grab my own

layers and pull on a beanie and gloves, making sure to take the heavy blanket off the bed, too. "We won't stay there long."

"Okay." She hurries to her suitcase, shrugging on her coat and shoving her feet into her boots. "I'm excited."

"Maybe I shouldn't have been so enthusiastic. It's not that great."

"I doubt that. Everything with you is wonderful."

That makes my heart jolt, too.

I hold out my hand, and she laces her fingers through mine. I turn off the bedroom light and unlock the window. The glass creaks and groans in the cold as I open it.

"Ready?" I ask.

"Ready," she repeats, and I duck outside.

I came out here earlier when Lacey was playing with my nieces. She let them put every color of eyeshadow on her face and pounds of blush on her cheeks. I shoveled the roof off to make sure we'd be able to walk without slipping. I've done this a thousand times, but never with someone I care about so much.

My foot gets a strong hold on the shingles, and I lift under her arms to help her through the window.

"Come on." I move us slowly down the slope of the roof, and Lacey grips my arm tight.

"Is now a good time to tell you I have an aversion to heights?" she says, and her laugh is a nervous sound. She stays stationary, and I move back to her side. "I'm not sure about this."

"It's a few steps to our left. I'm going to walk in front of you so if you fall, you land on me. I've done this a ton of times and you can trust me, Lacey girl. I'm never going to let anything hurt you. But if you want to stay right here, we can do that, too. Whatever you're most comfortable with."

Lacey takes a deep breath. She wraps her arms around my bicep and gives me a feeble nod. "We can move. Just go slow. Please."

"I promise." I kiss the ridge of her knuckles and start toward the other side of the roof. "You let me know if I'm going too fast, okay?"

"Okay. This is—this is good so far."

"Good. You're doing great. We're almost there, then we can sit down."

Her grip on me eases up and her stride becomes surer, a confidence in her step. When we reach the other side of the roof, she lets out an exhale that could move mountains.

"I did it," she says, and her teeth chatter. "Fuck, it's cold."

"I'm so proud of you." I pull her into a sitting position and drape my arm over her shoulder. I wrap a blanket around us to create a cocoon, and she nestles into my side. "Better?"

"Much. What are we looking at? Your secret lair where you chop up bodies?"

I chuckle and point to the lake behind the house. The water is frozen and the moon reflects off the ice, making everything white and gray. I point to the stars next, the dozens of constellations in the night sky.

"This."

"Wow," she whispers, and I look down at her. "It's beautiful."

"Yeah," I agree, but I'm busy studying every inch of her face. Her button nose. The slope of her jaw. The stars twinkling in her eyes. "It is."

Lacey tips her chin up and brushes her lips against mine. It's a soft kiss, tentative, but it's enough to warm my insides. I cup her cheek and my thumb settles in the hollow of her throat. I can feel her heart beating under my touch, and it's racing, just like mine.

"Shawn?"

"Hm?"

"I'm so glad I'm here with you."

"Shucks, Lacey girl. I'm glad you're here with me, too."

My tongue sits heavy in my mouth, and I want to tell her more. Like how I want her here every Christmas for the rest of our lives. A tradition we'll do until we're old and gray and can't use our legs.

She blinks up at me, and it hits me like a bolt of lightning.

It strikes my chest and zips through me like a live wire.

I've been electrocuted.

A single word echoes in my head like a drum, a beat I can't ignore.

Love.

I'm falling in love with this woman.

I have been for some time, I think.

God, I'm a fucking idiot.

How could I be so stupid?

No wonder I can't stay away from her.

No wonder I want to touch her every chance I get.

No wonder I'm happier when she's around, like none of my problems exist.

No wonder there's a sour taste in my mouth when I think about letting her go.

I'm fucking obsessed with her.

Laughter slips out of me, and my shoulders shake as I try to hold it together.

"What's so funny?" she asks.

"Nothing. I'm fine."

"You're laughing like a hyena."

"Is that what you think I sound like?"

"Well, you do. Your voice got all high and squeaky." She side-eyes me, but she scoots closer, too. "Are you sure you're okay?"

I clutch her hand like it's my lifeline. I trace over her knuckles. The space between her fingers and the back of her palm.

Mine, I think.

All mine.

Of all the people in the world, this is the one that stormed into my life.

I wouldn't have it any other way.

I'm the luckiest fucking guy in the universe.

"I'm okay." I drop a kiss to the top of her head. "I'm better than okay. I'm happy."

"Me, too." She's quiet for a minute, and I wonder if she fell asleep. "Can I ask you a question?"

"Of course you can."

"Could we—maybe next year, could we come back?" she asks, so soft I'm afraid it's going to be snatched out of the air. "I'd like to be here with you again. This place is starting to feel like a safe space for me, too."

"Yeah?"

"Yeah." She pauses then adds, "but maybe that's because I'm with you."

I grin like an idiot.

My cheeks hurt from how hard I'm smiling. I pull her into my lap and bury my face in her hair. Even on top of me, she's still too far away.

"We'll come back, sweetheart. I promise."

She tucks her chin into my chest and speaks right to my heart when she says, "I'd like that a lot."

A cold and bitter wind rips through the air, but I don't care. I'm in no rush to go inside. I could stay out here with her forever, nothing but the trees around us and the woman of dreams in my arms.

FORTY-ONE
LACEY

"HOW AGGRESSIVE IS THE SNOWBALL FIGHT?" I ask Shawn on Christmas morning. I jump into my ski pants, the only clothing I brought that will keep me warm while we roll around in the freshly fallen snow. Flakes started to come down when we climbed off the roof last night, and it was the perfect ending to a perfect day. "Like, *Fight Club* level? Or something you'd let Maven participate in?"

"Fuck, no. There's a reason none of my nieces are allowed to join," he says, and he grabs his beanie from his suitcase. "Last year, someone needed three stitches on their forehead because they ran into a tree."

"For heaven's sake." I zip up my jacket and sigh. "If something happens to me, tell my parents I love them. Tell Maggie, too. She can have all my books."

"Normally I'd offer to keep you safe, but not today. Today you're on your own, sweetheart." Shawn rubs a smudge of black paint under each of his eyes. "And I'm going to kick your ass."

"Wow. I'm finally seeing that athlete mentality from you." I grin and wiggle my fingers into my gloves. "Is there a trophy?"

"Of course there's a trophy. What kind of athletic event would it be if there wasn't a trophy?"

"I don't know. Still a made up one, probably. And one that doesn't land someone in the hospital." I put my hands on my hips and level him with a look. "I'm very competitive, Shawn. There's a reason Maggie and I can't be partners when we play charades; I yell at her too much. Just know that whatever I say out there doesn't represent how I really feel about you."

"You're cute when you think you're being a badass." Shawn taps my nose, and I narrow my eyes. "Let's see if you can back it up out there, Daniels. I'm not sure you can."

"Oh, I'll back it up. I'll make you wish I was on your team, Holmes, because I'm going to mop the floor with you," I say, and I press my finger into the center of his chest. "You better watch over your shoulder."

He grabs my hand and presses a kiss to the middle of my palm. "I really wish the guys in the league shit talked like you do. Would've kept my temper in check when I was playing."

"I can't imagine you getting into any fights. You're always calm on the sidelines."

"It was different when I was a player. I had all this pressure on me to perform to a certain standard. There were milestones I was expected to hit. Once I passed one, I was given another, then another and another. It was fucking exhausting. I was never mean, but I had a short fuse when it came to certain things. When people questioned if I worked hard. When people said something and I interpreted it as a personal attack when really, they were just talking shit to rile anyone up. The older I got, the more I cooled off. The more I understand that if I lost a game, it wasn't the end of the world." Shawn shrugs. "There was always going to be another chance to play. Just don't say anything about my mom, and I won't have to totally knock you over."

I laugh and clutch my heart. "I would *never* talk poorly about

Kelly. She's a ray of sunshine, and she raised a fantastic man. Even if his taste in backyard games is questionable and border-line violent."

"She likes you, too. She told me she hasn't seen me this happy in years." He pauses, and his eyes meet mine. I see shyness behind the gray, like he's not a man who whispered filthy things in my ear last night. "I told her she was right."

"She said the same thing to me." I reach up and touch his cheek. Run my fingers down the sharp lines of his jaw and commit every one of his beautiful angles to memory. "Moms know best, don't they?"

"Yeah." He brushes his lips against mine, and I lean into the kiss. "They certainly do."

I wonder if I can convince him to stay up here all morning.

It's our last day before we head home, and I'm afraid I'm going to spend it concussed when there is still so much I want to do with him.

I could drag him back to bed and strip off his clothes. I could get him to lead another singalong of "The Twelve Days of Christmas," laughing as he acts out each gift with theatrical flair for his delighted nieces. I could sit with him by the fire, stuffing toys and candy into stockings and just *being*.

"Shawn," Amanda bellows up the stairs. "Quit hiding and get your ass down here. It's time to go."

"Looks like we've been summoned." He pulls on my hair and tilts back my head so he can kiss me again. "Good luck out there, Daniels. Don't get hurt. I'd miss you too much if something happened to you."

"Watch yourself, Holmes. Don't think I won't do everything in my power to throw you off your game."

"Sweetheart, I've been to the Super Bowl six times. I've won five of those times. I don't get distracted."

I stand up on my tiptoes and nip his ear with my teeth.

"Famous last words," I whisper, and I run my hand down his chest. My fingers trail down the front of his jeans, and his hips jerk forward under my touch. "I'm going to make this very, very difficult for you."

I drop to my knees and undo his zipper with my teeth. His breathing stutters and hitches, and his hands weave through my hair. "Lacey," he murmurs, and I like how my name sounds. It almost makes me feel bad for what I'm about to do.

"Yeah?" I blink up at him as I shimmy his jeans down to his knees and reach into his briefs. "Is this okay?" I ask as I wrap my hand around his shaft.

"*Fuck*. Of course it's okay. God, that feels good. I like you on your knees."

I move my hand up and down his length, leaning forward and taking his cock in my mouth. I swirl my tongue around the tip, and he moans. When I hollow out my cheeks and let him thrust down my throat, he yanks on my hair so tight, my eyes flood with tears.

I give him two more tugs, my hand following the path of my mouth, before I slip him back in his underwear and stand up.

"Better get going," I say, and I pat his shoulder.

His eyes fly open and he stares at me with his jaw unhitched and his mouth wide.

"You are such a deviant shit," he says, and his hand squeezes into a fist at his side. "A little menace. I think you're going to kill me."

"All's fair in love and war, right?" I ask. I kiss his neck, and he groans as I give him one more stroke over his briefs. "I'll see you out there, hot shot."

Point, me.

WHEN SHAWN TOLD me there would be a snowball fight, I was expecting a small game in the backyard, not a man hunt through the forest next to his house.

My lungs burn as I run to duck behind a tree and the snow crunches under my feet. I clutch my chest and curse myself for not doing any physical exercise *ever*. I'm getting my ass handed to me.

I've been hit twice, once by Katelin's husband and the other by Amanda's spouse. I've barely seen Shawn the whole time we've been out here, and I've spent two hours frantically looking over my shoulder, waiting for him to pop out from behind a bush and throw a snowball in my face.

He doesn't though.

I hear the snap of a stick and I crouch to the ground. I gather a ball of snow in my hand and jump out from my hiding spot, expecting to find someone right in front of me. There's no one there, and when large arms wrap around my middle, I almost scream.

"It's just me," Shawn says softly. He's lost the gloves he had on earlier, and his hands are as cold as ice as they slide under my sweater and rest on my stomach. "You're way out of bounds right now."

"I am?" I glance around, and I don't recognize my surroundings. I can't even see the smoke coming from the chimney back at his house. "Shit. No wonder I couldn't find you."

"Looking for me, Daniels?" he asks. He sets me down and spins me to face him.

"Don't flatter yourself," I say, and I fan my face. It's freezing out here, but the sudden rush of adrenaline makes me warm. Sweat prickles my back, and I take a deep breath. "Aren't you going to throw a snowball at me and end the game?"

"That's not fair. Technically we're not playing the game right now since we're outside the boundaries."

"Oh." I let out a sigh of relief. "Good. Should we head back, then?"

"In a minute." Shawn kisses me, and I hum against his mouth. "I've missed you."

"I've been too quick. How did you even know where I was?"

"I followed your footsteps in the snow. Figured you probably went off the path a little bit, and I was right. You aren't too cold, are you?" he asks, and he rests his hand against my throat, at the top of my chest.

"No," I say, and I swallow. "I'm just right."

"Good. That's good."

I slide my hands up to his neck, and his skin is warm under the collar of his sweater. "I'm sorry about earlier. That wasn't fair of me to touch you then leave."

"That's okay, Lacey girl. You were in the moment. Ready to kick my ass and charge into battle." Shawn unzips my jacket. "Can I touch you now?"

"Won't someone see?" I ask, but my thighs clench together.

"Come here." He leads me to a thicket of small trees, a circle that's protected from the rest of the woods. I haven't seen anyone else out here in twenty minutes, and I doubt someone is going to pass by now. "Better?"

"Yeah." I shrug my jacket off and it falls to the snow. "Touch me, Shawn."

"Buy me dinner first, Daniels," he says, laughing as he pulls me flush against his chest and eases us onto the ground. He sits on my jacket and spins me so I'm between his parted legs.

"If you won't, I will."

"That's not the taunt you think it is. Unzip your jeans and spread your legs. I want to watch you finger yourself."

Fuck.

The people I've been with before have been *boys,* because

this man knows exactly what he's doing. He knows exactly what to say to make my blood sing and my body heat. He makes me want to do everything he says and not give a damn about the repercussions.

I fumble with the button at the top of my jeans, unfastening it and working the zipper down. Shawn helps me ease the pants off my waist, and the denim slides halfway down my hips. I lean back against his chest, my knees opening and my hand low on my stomach.

I drag my fingers down and slip them inside my underwear. Behind me, Shawn goes as still as a statue, but I can feel his breath on my skin. He reaches out and covers my hand with his larger one, guiding me, and I close my eyes when I slide the first finger inside.

"Yes," I whisper. I drop my head against his shoulder and wiggle my hips, too constrained by my jeans. "That feels good."

His free hand yanks down my pants until they're sitting around my ankles, and I hiss at the cold bite of air against my bare legs.

"Pull your underwear to the side," Shawn rasps, and my free hand moves the lace out of the way. "God, that's hot."

"You like watching me, don't you?" I arch my back as I add a second finger. "I think you might have been watching me for years, Shawn."

"You're a gorgeous woman, Lacey," he says, and he sucks on my earlobe. "I'd be out of my mind to not look at you. Wanting to run my hand up your leg and taste your pussy are recent fascinations, but now that I've had a bite, I don't ever want to stop. Open your legs wider. You can add a third, sweetheart. Let's get you ready for later tonight when I fuck you nice and hard. You'll have to be quiet, though. We can't have my family knowing what a slut you are, can we?"

I squeeze my eyes tight and moan. The third finger takes a second to get adjusted to, and I heave out a ragged breath as I start to relax enough for it to feel *so fucking good*. "Shawn," I whisper. "Can you—will you—"

"Anything, sweetheart. Anything. What do you need?" he asks, and his touch dances up my thigh. He circles my clit to the same pattern as the slick slide of my fingers, and I see bursts of color behind my eyes. "Is that good?"

"So good. You're the best I've ever had," I admit in a moment of weakness. "I don't want anyone else."

"Because you're mine, aren't you? I'm going to keep taking care of you, Lacey." He pulls my fingers out and exchanges them with his own. I choke out a sob as he turns his wrist half a degree to the left, hitting a spot I've never found myself. "I'm going to take care of your heart. I'm going to take care of your brilliant fucking mind. Lift up your shirt. I want to see your tits bounce when you come."

My hand scrambles with the hem of my sweater, and I'm on fire. Burning from the inside out. I pull it up to my neck, and he yanks down the cups of my bra. I'm nearly naked in the middle of a forest, and I've never been more turned on in my life.

"I'm close, Shawn," I say, and I squeeze his forearm. I dig my fingers into his skin, and he hisses at the contact. "Don't stop. Please."

"I'm never going to stop," he whispers in my ear. "You're going to be mine until the end of time, Lacey girl. Now come on my fingers, beautiful, so I can taste you."

I freefall from a cliff with his command. I tremble and shake and cry out as he coaxes me through wave after wave of pleasure. It doesn't seem to stop, a second round hitting me until tears fall down my cheeks and I can't remember my own name.

"*Fuck*," I groan. I gulp down a lungful of frigid air, and the cold awakens me. It forces me to sit up and adjust my underwear. To pull my shirt down and rub my legs, my muscles utterly exhausted.

"Hey." Shawn kisses my forehead, and he brushes loose pieces of hair out of my face. "Come here. Let me hold you."

I nod, and he lifts me into a sitting position on top of his legs. Wordlessly, I bury my face in his shirt and try to get my breathing under control. When I finally remember how to speak, I giggle.

"I really, *really* hate how good you are in bed," I say. "You had to go and be the whole package, didn't you?"

"Would you like to file a complaint?" he asks, and my giggles turn into full-fledged laughter.

"No. *No.* Please never stop using your fingers like that. They could end world wars."

"Now *that's* going to be my platform if I run for president. Forget healthcare; I have miracle hands."

"You really do." I sigh and stare at my jeans. "I guess we should head back."

"Probably. My mom might think someone got seriously hurt," Shawn says, and he drags my pants up my legs. He buttons them and gives my hip a tap. "This was fun."

"We should definitely do it again sometime."

"I can be persuaded." He kisses me, and I melt into his chest. "But I'm afraid you're going to be mad at me."

"What?" I pull back and stare at him. "Why?"

Before I can blink, a snowball crashes on my head, and Shawn grins.

"Because you're out, Lacey girl."

"But you said we were out of bounds," I exclaim, and I scramble off his lap.

He stands too and brings his fingers to his mouth. His

tongue sneaks out and licks up the mess I left on his hand. I've never been so angry and turned on at the same time.

"Sorry, sweetheart," he murmurs, and he brushes his mouth against mine. I can taste myself, and I hate that I grab him by his sweater and pull him closer. "All's fair in love and war. And payback is a bitch."

FORTY-TWO

SHAWN

"CAN I OPEN THAT ONE?" Eliza asks, and she points to a box under the tree with a red bow in the right corner. "It's so big."

"Sorry, princess. That one is for Parker," I say. "But I have this one for you."

I reach behind my back and slide a bag her way. Her eyes light up and she grabs for the present, gleeful giggles spilling out of her.

"What do you say?" Amanda says, and Eliza leans forward to kiss my nose.

"Thank you, Uncle Shawn," she whispers, and I give her a tight hug.

"You're welcome, kid."

"Good planning," Lacey says from beside me, soft enough so only I can hear. "I imagine you have to really think out everything ahead of time when it comes to kids and presents."

"Everyone has to have the same number of gifts," I explain, and I rest my hand on her knee. "You know how kids operate. They see things in quantities, not qualities. Eight smaller gifts are better than two nicer gifts. If they have less than the others, it's a tantrum waiting to happen."

"You've done a good job. Definitely solidified yourself as the coolest uncle."

"I'm the only uncle."

"Doesn't mean there isn't a competition," she says. "The scooters were a big hit."

"I thought they might be. Those kids are always on the go. I'm sure my sisters are going to be pissed about the mayhem they're going to cause, but it's not my problem. After this, we get to go home and sleep in silence."

We watch the kids open the rest of their presents. Piles of toys start to stack up around the room, and you can barely see the floor. We take a break for cookies, a plate of sugar and chocolate chip treats making its way around the room.

When my mom hands me a small box, I look up in surprise.

"You already gave me something," I say, and she smiles.

"I know I did, but this is for you and Lacey. It's nothing big," she explains. "But I've gotten one for everyone else. Now it's your turn."

I hand the box to the woman beside me. "You open it."

"No way. I've seen how you open gifts. You'll scream if you learn I just rip the paper in two, and I really don't want us to have our first fight while I'm eating a delicious cookie."

"Monster." I peel the tape away from the paper and unfold it carefully. I wiggle the top off the box and stare at the glass ornament sitting on a small stack of tissue paper. "Mom. This is very nice of you."

"What is it?" Lacey asks, and she rests her chin on my shoulder.

"It's an ornament for us. Our First Christmas, it says, with the year underneath it." I turn it around, and I see our names engraved on it, too. "It's perfect. We'll hang it on the tree next year."

"Just a little something to commemorate your first holiday together," my mom says.

"This is so thoughtful, Kelly."

Lacey pushes off the couch and walks to my mom.

A rush of love hits me as I watch them. I know our relationship started as something artificial and fake, but I also know she'll be here with me next year. On this same couch, with these same people. We'll have a second Christmas and a third Christmas together, amassing them until we've collected fifty ornaments, and we'll have a tree decorated in mementos documenting our love story.

There might be an end date for this arrangement between us, but I'm not letting Lacey Daniels walk away from me. Not when my mom hugs her tight and plays with the ends of her hair. Not when my nieces—all five of them—barrel into her and ask her to play dress up and house and pirates with them. Not when I can't wipe the stupid smile off my face when she glances at me from across the room later that night at dinner, the brightest twinkle in her eyes.

We're going to have to adjust the terms.

I love her so much it hurts.

It hurts to think about saying goodbye. It hurts to think about a life where I don't wake up next to her. It hurts to imagine her making someone else happy when she makes me feel on top of the fucking world.

I'll take one more day with her over a thousand with anyone else.

"THANKS FOR THE PRESENT, MOM," I say as I drop the last dirty plate in the kitchen sink and take a seat at the small table next to her. "You didn't have to do that."

"I know I didn't, but I wanted to." Her eyebrow lifts and she rests her chin in her hand. "I'm onto you, you know."

"What do you mean?"

"Sweetie, I've been your mother for forty-six years. I know you better than you know yourself. Do you honestly think you'd find a girlfriend and bring her to Christmas, and I wouldn't know it was fake?"

My cheeks burn and I rub my temples. "How did—why—" I sigh and shake my head, not even bothering to come up with an excuse. "Shit. I'm sorry."

"Tell me the story."

And I do. About the kiss cam and how I wanted to take away Lacey's embarrassment. About the decision to pretend to date each other through the holidays.

I leave out telling her about the supply closet. Lacey's couch. Upstairs in my bed last night—twice—because I don't think she needs to hear *all* the details.

When I finish, I take a deep breath and reluctantly bring my gaze to meet hers.

"I'm a shitty son, aren't I?" I ask.

"What are you talking about? Do you know how horrible it is to know you thought you had to *lie* because it would make *me* happy? Darling, all I want is for *you* to be happy. I don't care if that's by yourself or with someone else. I'm so sorry I ever made you feel like you had to have a partner."

"It's not your fault." I sigh and lean back in the chair, kicking my legs straight out in front of me. I cross my ankles over each other and look at the ceiling. "I think I've just been so desperate to be... not alone. And this was an excuse to not be alone, again, for another holiday season."

"Tell me about Lacey."

My lips twitch, and I glance over at the brunette leaning over the sink, soap up her arms and a sponge in her hands. "She's a breath of fresh air. She's the first woman who hasn't been impressed with my name or how much money I make. If I lost everything tomorrow, she'd still be right there. And that's scary, because she sees me. I can have a panic attack, and she'll hold me after. My team can lose a game and she'll order pizza with me and sit on the couch like it's no big deal. I feel like I've been drowning for years, and she's pulled me to the surface. With her I can laugh. With her I can just... just *live*. I can finally breathe."

My mom takes my hand in hers and holds me tight. "I want you to listen to me, Shawn. What you have with her is special. I don't care if it's friendship or if it's something deeper and more complex. You've taken care of your heart for so long, and it's okay to let someone else in who will help take care of it, too. You don't have to do it alone."

"I know." I squeeze my eyes shut and take a deep breath. "She's the most important person in the world to me, Mom. I'm desperate for her attention and greedy for her time. She smiles at me, and I go weak in the knees." I laugh and shake my head. "I sound obsessed, don't I?"

"No." My mom kisses my cheek and rests her cheek on my shoulder. "You sound like you're in love."

I POP my head into the bathroom and find Lacey in the tub. Bubbles cover her body, and her head rests against the porcelain. Her eyes are closed and her hair sits on the top of her head, and I smile at how relaxed she is.

I knock my knuckles against the door softly, not wanting to disturb her. One of her eyes opens, and she sits up when she sees me.

"Hey. There you are."

"Hi. I was reading bedtime stories," I say. "How's your bath?"

"Incredible. I'm not leaving here tomorrow. This is my home now."

"Might get a little cold, don't you think?" I walk over to the tub and sit on the edge. I dip my fingers in the water and swirl the bubbles around. "Can I get you anything?"

"No." She sighs and lifts her arm to me. Her hand touches my cheek, and I turn to kiss her palm. "It's so peaceful in here. I need to wash my hair, but I'm too tired to move. The snowball fight today taught me I'm wildly out of shape, and you can't be trusted when a trophy is involved."

"I'm sorry." I bend over and kiss her forehead. "You're never going to forgive me for that, are you?"

"I will. Only because you gave me the best orgasm of my life minutes before."

"The best of both worlds. Get comfortable. I'll wash your hair for you."

"What?" Water trails down her neck and catches in the hollow of her throat. "Have you ever washed someone's hair before?"

"First time. Can't be too hard, can it?"

"I'm sure you want to spend the last few hours of our time here with your family."

"No." I shake my head and pull down on her bottom lip with my thumb. "I want to spend it with you."

Lacey lets out a breath, and I see her guard come down. She swallows and dips her chin, the smallest indication that she's giving me control. I smile and kiss her softly before grabbing the shampoo bottle and the showerhead.

She adjusts her position, scooting down the slant of the tub and pulling her hair free from the scrunchie keeping it in place. Brown waves spill over her shoulders, and I turn the water on, checking the temperature before I bring it to her head.

We don't speak as I wet her hair and squeeze shampoo into

my hands. I rub my palms together and massage the strands until her scalp is covered in suds.

"That feels nice," Lacey whispers. "Much better than when I do it."

"Good." I kiss her shoulder and press my thumb into her neck, working out the tension in her muscles. She melts into my touch, her eyes fluttering closed and her breathing slowing down.

Her throat bobs and she stays still while I rinse out the shampoo, making sure I lift the hair off her shoulders to get those pieces, too.

It's the most intimate I've ever been with a woman. It feels more monumental than fucking her into a mattress for the first time, like there's weight in the way I use the conditioner next and rinse that out, too.

Her arm loops around my neck and she brings me to her lips, kissing me as my shirt gets soaked and her wet hair tickles my ear. It's tender and it's sweet, and I realize she's too far away and I have to be with her right this very second.

I break our contact and stand, pulling off my jeans and underwear. My shirt follows, and her eyes roam down my naked body, taking in every tattoo, every muscle and every line.

"Come here," she says, reaching for me and practically pulling me into the tub.

I climb in and water sloshes over the sides. We barely fit, the basin just large enough for us to not be completely on top of each other, but I don't care. I lean back and pull her toward me, her back against my chest as I hold her.

"What are you thinking about?" I ask, because I've never heard Lacey this quiet.

"That I like being here with you." She traces my knee, her fingers drawing designs on my skin. "That this moment is perfect."

"It is, isn't it?"

"Ten out of ten. No complaints."

I chuckle and rub her shoulder, resting my chin in the crook of her neck. "My mom knows we're not dating."

"What?" Lacey spins around and gapes at me. "Are you serious?"

"Dead serious. She told me in the kitchen when you were washing the dishes."

"Oh, no." She buries her face in her hands, and I have to pry her palms away. "I can never see her again."

"She doesn't care. She's just happy I'm happy. And fuck, Lacey girl, I'm really happy."

"You are?" she whispers, and I nod as a grin stretches across my lips.

"I am. I haven't been this happy in a very, very long time. Not ever, I don't think."

"I'm happy, too," she says, and I kiss her again.

It's more frantic this time, like we're both well aware we're leaving tomorrow and heading back to reality. This is hurried and desperate, teeth and tongue and hands everywhere they can reach.

I bend my neck and kiss her chest and the spot between her breasts. I wrap her hair around my wrist and give a gentle tug, just hard enough for a moan to slip out of her mouth.

She tastes like the whipped cream on the top of the pie we had for dessert, sweet and sugary and a delicious slice of heaven. Lacey climbs into my lap and hovers over me, her thighs on either side of my hips and a question in her eyes.

"Yes," I say, and my hand curls around her throat. "The answer is always yes. Tonight. Tomorrow. Six months from now. Everything I have is yours, Lacey girl."

Her eyes soften as she sinks onto me, and we hiss in unison.

I'll never get over how *good* she feels, tight and warm and absolutely perfect for me.

"Shawn," she whispers, and her fingers dig into my shoulders. Her hips move in a small circle, and I bite on my bottom lip to keep from yelling her name.

"You take me so well," I whisper back, and my free hand dips into the water, finding her clit and rubbing her in slow circles. "Every inch is yours."

"I feel you everywhere." Her palm folds over the one wrapped around her neck, and she drags my hand to her chest. "Here," she says, and my hand squeezes her tit. She moves our hands to between her legs, her fingers brushing against mine. "Here." She guides my hand to her heart, and I feel it race under my touch. "And here."

I close my eyes and lift my hips to meet her, getting another inch deeper as more water splashes over the edges of the tub.

I love her. I love her. I love her.

"Open your eyes, Shawn. I want to watch you while you come undone."

My eyes fly open and I stare at her as she lifts her arms above her head, a goddess in her skin and an angel on Earth.

"I'm not—you feel too good, sweetheart," I say, and my breaths come out ragged. "You make things very difficult."

"I could stop, if you want," she says, and her smile hitches up when I kiss her chin and the slope of her jaw.

"No," I say roughly. I rub my cheek against her chest and take her nipple in my mouth. "Never, ever stop."

"Use your thumb," she whispers, her words stuttered and strained as she tightens around me. "I like when you use your thumb."

I switch out my fingers for my thumb, listening to her guidance because I'm never one to deny her. Her moan comes out like a laugh, sweet music to my ears when she tumbles over the edge, her orgasm causing her to rock forward and almost fall in my arms.

"I've got you," I say in her ear, and my hands scoop under her thighs as I thrust into her. I feel her teeth sink into my neck and bite the skin, and I let out a grunt.

"I want you to come in me," says, her tongue running over the marks her teeth just left behind. "Fill me up, Shawn. Let everyone know I'm yours. Because I am, you know. I am yours."

I groan as pleasure barrels into me. I lift my hips again, my release spilling inside her until my legs go numb and my lungs stop hurting. I think I've died and ascended to heaven because all I see are whites and yellows behind my eyes.

"Hell." I drop my head back and pant. "You are incredible."

Lacey nestles into me and runs her hand over my chest. "That was good."

"Better than good."

"Eh. I'd give it a seven out of ten," she says, and I lift an eyebrow.

"A seven out of ten? Guess I need to try again." My fingers run up her thigh, and she shivers against me. "I can't stop until I get it completely right."

I love her. I love her. I love her, I think as I lift her out of the water and carry her to my bed, her laughter something I want to get tattooed across my skin to keep forever.

FORTY-THREE

LACEY

THE SUN DIPS low in the sky and covers the dashboard in yellows and reds. We were stuck in traffic for an hour, I-95 backing up for miles in a gridlock because of an accident outside Baltimore.

I didn't want to leave Shawn's parents' house, and it was hard to drive away. We spent forty-five minutes saying goodbye, and it still wasn't long enough. I want to be back there already, an ache in my chest the further away we drive.

"How do you want to do presents?" Shawn asks as we approach the city. "I have your gifts at my place."

"And I have yours at my place. We really should have thought this through," I laugh. The bracelets his nieces made for me jangle on my wrist, and I touch the beads. "Poor planning on our part."

"I can drop you off, head to my apartment, then come back to your place? I can pick up dinner on the way, too, then we can dive into some dessert and presents."

"Sounds like a great plan to me. What are you in the mood for?"

"Italian? You like spaghetti, right?"

"Shawn, you saw me eat two plates of your mother's lasagna. Of course I like spaghetti, and it scares me that there are people out there who *don't*."

He laughs and taps his fingers against the steering wheel. "Italian it is. Should I grab some garlic bread?"

"The answer to that question should always be yes. I have a pie in the freezer, and I'll take it out when I go up. I'm not sure it will thaw in time, but we'll give it a shot."

"Is it one you made?" Shawn asks, and his excitement bleeds through the question. He wiggles in his seat a little, and I smile. "I've been craving your baking."

"It's apple. Is that okay?"

"Lacey, you could feed me a pie made of dirt and I'd eat it. Forget food and presents. I'm coming straight up."

"No way. I have things I need to get ready for you."

"Things? I thought we were only doing one or two gifts."

"To be fair, we didn't specify numbers. They all reminded me of you, and I couldn't resist." I gnaw on my bottom lip and twist my hands together. "I hope I didn't go overboard."

"There's no way you did." He grins at me from across the car, and the last rays of sunlight sneak in through the window behind him. It almost looks like he's glowing, and he seems so happy. "Besides, I have a stack for you, too."

"I'm beginning to think gift giving is your love language."

"It's definitely my love language, especially for people like you."

"What do you mean?"

His eyes flick over to me in the quickest of glances, and his grin settles into something softer around the edges. Quieter in his heart. "People I care about very much."

"Oh." I gulp down a breath and scoop up his words. I commit them to memory so I can still have them close by in case they ever try to sneak away. "I care about you too," I blurt out. "You know that, right?"

I'm desperate for him to know it.

Shawn keeps his attention on the road but reaches for me across the center console. His hand finds mine, his palm smooth and warm, and intertwines our fingers. "I do. It's one of my favorite things about you."

There's a pressure in my chest. It's not quite an ache but something more pleasant. Something warm and delightful that begins to sprout and grow like a flower in the spring the longer his hand is in mine.

Suddenly I feel it everywhere; on the back of my knees. In my belly. Between my breasts and at the base of my spine.

It envelops me, *engulfs* me, a welcomed hug I haven't felt in years. Maybe I've never felt it all.

Not like this, and not until this moment right here, because it's never been this nice.

Love.

Every second I'm with him, I fall a little deeper. Soon I'll be twenty feet underground without a way out.

I don't think I ever want to climb out.

I love him so much, with every corner of my soul and every beat of my heart.

You love him, it says.

You've loved him for a long time.

"You okay?" he asks. He squeezes my hand and gives my arm a little shake. I feel the sensation there, too, in the valley between my fingers where his grip locks into mine. "Where did you go, Lacey girl?"

"Nowhere," I say, and I realize I'm staring at him the exact same way he stared at me on his parents' roof. Maybe he loves me, too. "I'm right here."

We pull up to my apartment ten minutes later and find a lucky spot out front. Shawn grabs my bags from the trunk and wheels my suitcase to the sidewalk. My fingers curl around the handle, and we stare at each other.

"I'll be right back," he says, but his feet don't move. "Thirty minutes, tops."

"Take your time. You know where I'll be. Just buzz when you get here, and I'll let you up."

"Okay." He steps toward me, and the toes of his sneakers bump mine. His hand rests on my cheek, in the spot he always finds. "Text me if you need me, alright?"

"I will." I reach up and kiss him in the middle of the crowded sidewalk because I want to, and I really don't care who sees. "I can't wait to see you again."

His lips curve up. "Flirting with me, Daniels?"

"In your dreams, Holmes. I just really want some presents."

"At least you're honest." Shawn taps my hip, his fingers fanning out over my waist. "Let me move my car before I get a ticket. That would be a mood killer."

"Okay." I pat his chest. "Go. I'll see you soon."

He takes my hand in his and kisses each finger. "Soon."

I watch him drive off, and I didn't know it was possible to miss someone when they just left, but I do.

I SPEED CLEAN MY APARTMENT.

I take out the trash. I make my bed and arrange the pillows in a neat little line. I wipe down the kitchen counters and light a candle.

It feels like I'm getting ready for a date, and a nervous buzz of energy zips through me.

Shawn knocks on the door twenty-nine minutes later, gifts tucked under one arm and a bag of food tucked under the other.

"Talk about punctual," I say. "I'm impressed."

"I'm a man of my word. I would've been here sooner if I didn't have to circle around the block six times trying to find parking. And don't even get me started on that garage across the street. I'd lose my mind if I had to spend half my life in that damn building of hell."

"It's shitty, isn't it? That garage is the sole reason I take the Metro. The only cars that can fit in those spots are Mini Coopers. You're screwed if you have something bigger than a sedan." I gesture to his arms. "Can I help with anything?"

"Nah, I got it."

He heads for the living room and puts the gifts under the Christmas tree next to the presents I have for him. He's careful as he sets them down on the tree skirt, and he makes sure you can see all the boxes and bags. It looks like a family lives here, and my heart stutters in my chest.

I've never had presents under the tree from someone else before.

"Food first," I say, and I pull down two plates. "We need to have full stomachs for gift giving."

"I was a little overwhelmed with menu options," Shawn admits. The paper bag he slides across the counter is ripping at the seams. Cutlery sticks out from the top, and one handle is broken. "I didn't know if you wanted regular spaghetti. Spaghetti carbonara. With or without meatballs. Cacio e Pepe. So, I ordered all of them."

"Holy shit." I unload the four boxes and burst out laughing. It looks like a buffet line spread out in my kitchen, complete with an entire loaf of garlic bread. "The chef probably thought you were ordering for six people."

"Or sixteen. Wrong; I'm just one indecisive asshole." He sits on the barstool and motions for me to join him. "Have you talked to your parents the last couple of days?"

"I called them yesterday when you were in the shower after the snowball fight. They sound good; my mom is learning how to crochet, and she said she's making me a hat. My dad complained about the Orlando basketball team after another loss. Pretty typical conversation for us."

"I'm glad they're doing well." Shawn serves a helping of all four dishes onto my plate. "Dig in, Daniels."

I start with the carbonara, and I hum my approval. "What would you eat as your last meal on Earth? If there was an asteroid approaching the planet and you only had twenty-four hours to live, tell me what you'd pick to snack on in your dying minutes."

"I love when things get morbid at the dinner table. Let's see. I'd do a combo meal. Chips and salsa, for sure. That was my go-to snack after practice back when I was in the league. I feel like you can't go wrong with a nice, juicy burger. Throw some pickles and mustard on there with a single tomato? Fuck, I would murder that thing. For dessert I'd either pick you or one of your pumpkin pies."

"I would be dessert?" I laugh and take another bite of my pasta. "Of everything you could have, you'd pick me?"

"Have you tasted yourself?" Shawn asks, and he lifts an eyebrow. "You're delicious. Now I'm imagining eating pumpkin pie off of you, and I'm getting hard."

"That's all it takes? You sure are easy to please. Hell, we could do that after dinner and presents."

"I think I've died and gone to heaven." He taps my foot and nods. "What would you pick?"

"I agree with you on the chips and salsa. Some good queso would be nice too." I rip off a piece of garlic bread and toss it in my mouth. "I have to pick sushi, obviously. I'd commit a murder for a good spicy salmon roll. Dessert I'd go with chocolate brownies. Fudgy, gooey, delicious things."

"Kind of pissed you didn't choose my dick, but I'll let it slide," Shawn says, and he twirls his noodles around his fork. "It's too bad I can't build an asteroid-proof bunker in twenty-four hours so I can survive and keep eating this spaghetti. This might be my new favorite place."

"How'd you find out about it?" I ask. "You don't strike me as someone who eats out a lot."

His mouth curls into a grin. "I did a lot of eating out on the bathroom counter a couple of nights ago," he says, and I throw a napkin at his head. "Nah, I prefer to cook. I like being in the kitchen. Dallas recommended it to me, and it gets my stamp of approval."

"Mine, too." I slurp down a noodle. "Back to practice for you all tomorrow, right?"

"Yup. We'll see who got off the couch in the last week, and who spent their time drinking eggnog. Don't forget we're hanging out with Maggie and Aiden at the end of this week, too, when they get back from their trip." Shawn wipes his hands and nudges his empty plate away. "Can you eat faster, please?" he asks, and a demand has never sounded so polite. "We have lots to get to."

"Like presents and pie?"

"Exactly, Lacey girl. The most important things in life."

"I'll come back and finish. Let's do some unwrapping."

FORTY-FOUR

LACEY

SHAWN ALMOST SPRINTS to the tree, and I'm amazed he doesn't fall and hurt himself on the rug.

He grabs a bag and hands it my way. I laugh at his enthusiasm and sit on the couch, getting comfortable as I drape a blanket over my legs.

"Lacey," he says in warning, and my laugh grows deeper.

"*Okay*. Hang on." I pull the tissue paper out and watch it fall to the floor. "It feels heavy."

"Stop shaking it, Daniels. You might break it," he says, and he wraps his arms around my waist. His chin settles on my shoulder and he watches me wrestle with the bag.

"Okay, it's a box in a bag—a stethoscope?"

"I know men in the past have made you feel like you can't celebrate all these incredible successes in your life, including your job. It's a reminder that the person who loves you—" he pauses for a second, and I swear his fingers tighten around my waist—"the person who cares about you will think you have the coolest career in the world. You change lives, Lacey, and not a single goddamn person should ever diminish that."

"This is—Shawn. This is not a cheap gift." I bring the metal to the inside of his wrist and slip the ear pieces into my ears. "I can hear your heart."

"Thank god. Means I'm alive and the gift works. Two birds, one stone."

"It's beating fast." I pull off the headset and look at him. "Are you feeling okay?"

"Yeah." He nods and clears his throat. "Guess it just beats faster around you."

I've heard the joke a million times and it's always been so corny, but I like it when he says it. It doesn't sound like he's trying to be funny.

It sounds completely true.

"Thank you. I've been wanting a new stethoscope. This is perfect."

"Did I pick the right one? I asked Maggie and Aiden for help, and they—"

"I love it," I say, interrupting him. "It's my favorite brand. The best of the best."

"Good." Shawn breathes a sigh of relief, and I kiss his forehead. "I had no idea there was such a market for medical equipment."

"You could stock your own hospital with the stuff you find online." I rifle through the stack of gifts and pull a large box from the back. "Here."

"This is big." Shawn starts to unwrap it carefully, and I remember he's someone who likes to take his time with presents. He doesn't rip the wrapping paper like I do, not a care in the world. He's meticulous and careful, and even folds it in neat little halves after he's finished admiring his gift. "Wait. What is it?"

"It's silly. You told me about your grandmother's old stereo in her condo kitchen, so I hunted down something that might be close to what she might have had. I doubt it even works."

He stares at the box and turns it over. He checks it from every angle, his mouth hitching open wider and wider with every turn. "Lacey. This is—" he closes his eyes. "This is the exact stereo she used to have. Down to the color."

"Oh," I whisper. "I hope I'm not devaluing something you loved as a kid. I just thought with the music and—"

"It's perfect. It's fucking perfect, and you are fucking perfect. Thank you, so much," he says, and he pulls me into his lap. He buries his face in my hair, and his breath is warm on my skin. It tickles the back of my neck and slips down my shirt, heating me as it moves away. "I can't wait to show my mom. She's going to remember it, too."

"I know it's not as fancy as some of the nicer things out there, but maybe you can put it somewhere in your apartment."

"Oh, it's going front and center in the kitchen, sweetheart. I'm going to show it off."

I smile and rub up his arm. "I'm so glad you like it."

"I don't just like it. I love it." Shawn kisses my cheek, and I can feel him smiling. "Your turn. Grab the one on the end there."

I reach for a rectangle box and turn it side to side. It's lighter than the last gift, and I rest it in my lap. "I wonder what it could be." I rip the paper down the middle and pull the top off the box. "Oh my god."

I hold up the blue and white jersey and gape at it. It has the Titans logo on the front, but when I flip it over, it's Shawn's last name and number.

"You said you didn't have a Titans jersey. Now you do," he tells me. "And I'm absolutely not letting you wear anyone else's name."

"This is so nice." I rub my thumb over the stitching, the 44 big and bold in the center. I trace the outline of the letters, and each one feels special under my finger. "When did you get it done?"

"Immediately after the game where we kissed. I had to explain to the guy three times that I *know* Shawn Holmes doesn't play for the Titans. Couldn't break it to him that I was the one ordering it." Shawn laughs and folds the wrapping paper into squares. "Anyway. Now you have something to wear to the games that will actually fit you. And I'll still get to see my name on your back, but this time, with the right team."

"I like wearing the jerseys you played in, but this is so special. One of a kind, I bet. Will you sign it so it has the full effect?" I ask.

"Of course I will. Right across your chest. Maybe I'll write *Shawn was here* on the left boob."

"You will do no such thing," I say, and I fold the jersey back into its box. "This is the best present ever."

"I'll get you a couple more so you can rotate them. You look good in blue, so I figured I'd buy you that one first."

"Pretty soon, my whole closet is going to be full of things with your name on the back," I joke, and heat flares behind his eyes. I grab a smaller present and hand it to him. "Here."

"What is this? A wallet?" He peels back the tape on the rectangle shape, and I wait patiently for him to finish.

This is the gift I'm most nervous about. It took the most time, and it's the only homemade item in the bunch. The idea came to me when I remembered what he said to me the first time he visited my apartment; his words stuck with me, and now I want to give them back to him.

"Be careful," I say. "It's kind of fragile."

"I'm intrigued." He wiggles open the small box and sucks in a sharp breath. "Are these—is this—"

"Photos of us," I whisper. "And me."

"Is this why you kept asking to take photos together this month?" Shawn asks, and he flips through the stack of photographs.

367

There are fifteen in all, and they're all from different moments over the last month we've spent together. The one I snapped of us on Thanksgiving in his car after his game. In Maggie and Aiden's kitchen. The one from his apartment, me in his lap and his eyes on me. A dozen more, each showing the same thing.

Two people who care a lot about each other.

Two people in love.

When I was putting them together, I could see myself falling for him in real time.

My smiles got bigger. My face got brighter. Every moment is the happiest moment of my life, and he is there in all of them.

"I wanted you to have something you could carry with you, if you wanted. I have one in my purse of us, too."

He touches the edges of the photos, careful to not smudge the matching grins we're wearing. "This is the greatest thing anyone could have ever given to me. I'm going to rotate them every month. Every time I open my wallet, you'll be the first thing I'll see. And that makes me so fucking happy."

"I'm glad you like it."

"Like it? I love it. God, you're amazing, Lacey. Nothing could ever top this."

He tips my chin and kisses me. I adjust my legs around his waist, straddling him so I can face him and run my hands up his chest. Across his neck and into his hair. He hums, and I feel the sound down to my toes.

I love him.

I love him, I love him, I love him.

I try to tell him with hot presses of my mouth. Rolling my hips and unbuttoning the top button of his shirt. Biting his earlobe and smiling into his skin when he moans. When his hands rub up my thighs, I sigh, totally content.

Waves of emotion I've never experienced before hit me like a ton of bricks as I sit in his arms. Gratitude. Joy. Immense, over-whelming love.

Love for this man.

Love for the way he loves me.

Love for every maker of fate who led us together.

I want to tell him.

It sits on my tongue, so close to coming out, and I know one day soon, it will.

"I'm so grateful for you," I whisper into his neck.

Shawn lifts me up and walks me toward the bedroom. The rest of the gifts sit forgotten as the lights twinkle on the tree. I don't care about them—not when the man I adore is kissing me like his life depends on it. Setting me on my bed and pulling off my clothes like I'm the most precious thing he's ever seen. Sinking into me, his hand over my heart and my name on his lips.

Mine, I think as he pushes me to the brink of ecstasy and sends me tumbling over the edge.

Mine forever, I think as he holds me in his arms until the sun comes up, neither one of us wanting to leave.

FORTY-FIVE
SHAWN

"YOU'RE DEEP IN THOUGHT," Aiden says as we stand in his kitchen the day before New Year's Eve. "Everything okay?"

"Yeah." I tip my beer back and swallow the last sip of alcohol before wiping my mouth clean. "Kind of. Everything *is* okay, but I'm... confused."

"Oh?" He turns to face me, his back resting against the edge of the marble countertop and his arms folded across his chest. He studies me, a divot between his eyebrows and his head tilted to the side. "Want to talk about it?"

I don't know what I want.

That's not true.

I know I want Lacey.

I just need to stop dicking around and fucking tell her.

We've had the *almost* conversations, where we get just close enough to talking about what's been going on between us before we skirt away and find something else to say.

It's like we both know what the other is thinking, but when you put it out in the world, when you give it a name and a voice and a permanent fucking spot in your heart, there's room for rejection. For it to blow up in your face and ruin everything.

"The day you met Maggie," I start. I blow out a breath and reach for another beer. "Can you tell me about it?"

"You've heard this story a dozen times," Aiden says. "We met. We slept together. I was an idiot who let her walk out of my apartment, then we found each other again. What else do you want to know?"

"What was going through your head when she left? You two had instant chemistry; why didn't you tell her how you felt?"

"Why does anyone keep their feelings inside? Because talking about them fucking sucks." Aiden laughs and rolls his shoulders back. He plays with his cuffed sleeve, the plaid shirt rolled up to his elbows. I see the two Ms he has tattooed right in the center of his bicep for Maggie and Maven, and my lips twitch. It pairs with the A and M Maggie has on her arm, and these two are so fucking in love, it makes my stomach sick. "Putting yourself out there for a maybe isn't easy. I knew we were attracted to each other. I knew I could see a future with her, even after twenty-four hours together. But actually saying the words and asking her to stay? That was hard."

"You were miserable after she left," I say, and I remember the night he showed up at my apartment, dark circles under his eyes and his clothes wrinkled as if he had been walking through the city for days. I'd never seen him so lost. "But you reached out to her."

"I did. I was willing to take anything she had to give me, even if it meant yelling at me to leave her alone." His laughter turns softer, more restrained. "Just tell her, man."

"What?" My eyes cut to him with a sharp glance. "What are you talking about?"

"Come on, Shawn. Don't pull that shit with me. I've known you for forty years. You've never looked at anyone the way you look at Lacey." He dips his chin and runs his hand over his jaw.

"No one's looked at *you* the way she looks at you, either," he adds, and I think I'm knocked off balance.

I huff and pop off the beer cap. I spot Lacey across the apartment, sitting on the couch with Maggie and Maven. She's showing them pictures from my parents' house; the one of me on the couch with my five nieces, all of us fast asleep.

Christmas afternoon, when she stuck a bow on my forehead and I drew a red dot on her nose.

She quickly scrolls past the one of us in bed, the sun rising behind us and my lips on her cheek, her smile blindingly bright.

"I like her, Aiden. I like her a whole fucking lot," I admit.

It's the first time I've said it out loud, and it's like a weight leaving my body. I'm lighter after it's out in the open, a breath I've been holding for weeks.

"Good." He clasps my shoulder, and I hear a soft *whoop*. "What's your plan?"

"Tell her, I guess. Which is the hard part. What the fuck do I say? 'Hey, thanks for being my friend for almost two years. Want to go steady with me?'"

"Okay, you're showing your age, old man. Maybe something else."

"Our agreement is supposed to end tomorrow," I say. I peel the label back on the beer and rub my thumb over the neck of the bottle. "I'm also supposed to be on a plane tomorrow."

"So tell her you don't want the agreement to end. Problem solved. It's not rocket science."

I laugh at his optimism. "I think I'm going to wait until I get back. What if she says no and then I'm the idiot on New Year's Eve who just told a girl he—"

Fuck.

"Going to finish that sentence?" Aiden asks with a lifted eyebrow. "Here, you can practice on me." He clears his throat and straightens his back. "Hi, Shawn," he says with a high-pitched voice. "Is there something you want to tell me?"

"Oh, fuck you." I shove his shoulder, and he grins. I wait a beat and set my drink down. "I love her."

"I know you do."

"I think she loves me too."

"She definitely does."

"I just... I want to be good enough for her. That woman over there deserves the entire world. Fuck, she deserves the entire galaxy. I'm not sure even I can give that to her, no matter how big my feelings are."

"Shawn." Aiden nudges my side and lifts his chin. "That woman spent Christmas with your family. She comes to your football games and she cheers for you every week. When you had a panic attack, she almost got arrested so she could be by your side. And look how much you do for her. You donated two million dollars to the hospital because of her. You let her talk without interrupting, and you listen to what she has to say. You kissed her in front of seventy thousand people because you'd rather be ridiculed than see her hurting. You know Lacey—do you think for a goddamn second she'd stick around if she didn't think you'd treat her the way she wants?"

"No, but—"

"And guess what? Some days you won't be able to give her the entire world. That's fucking life, man. You're going to mess up, and so is she. You're going to be scared. But no one is ever going to love her like you do." He hums, a low sound that tells me he's about to bring this home. A bullseye on a dartboard, and the cherry on top. "I think to her, you're everything. And that's enough."

I stare at him. Nothing has ever made more sense than what Aiden just said.

I don't know where I'll be five or ten years down the road.

Still coaching the sport I love, hopefully, with a healthy body and a healthy mind. I don't know if I'll be in D.C. or somewhere in the Midwest. There's no crystal ball I can look in that will tell me the future and how things will turn out, but there is one thing I am sure about.

Lacey.

She's always felt right.

From the moment I first met her, everything's always been a little bit better when she's by my side.

"You're good at this deep shit," I say. I chug my beer and drop it in the recycling bin. "You make me want to just shout it at her from across the room like it's a walk in the park and not the scariest thing I've ever done. A plus for you in the relationship department."

"Not my first time around the block with the whole being in love thing." He pats my back and nudges me forward. "What are you waiting for? Go get your girl."

"I'm going to wait until I'm back from the game. I'm going to get her a magnet. Something stupid. *Colorado is for lovers*. Then I'll tell her I love her, too. It'll be cute and shit," I say.

"Jesus." Aiden rubs his forehead. "You have got to stop watching those romcoms with Maven. Normal people don't go around doing these grand gestures for people they care about. I think just telling her would be fine."

"Ah. That's where you're wrong." I clasp his shoulder and give him a grin. "I donated two million dollars for her. Normal isn't going to cut it."

"Going forward, can you let me know before you rent a yacht or a spaceship and whisk her away on a fancy date? Those of us with average salaries need time to prepare so we can have an excuse for why *we* aren't chartering a rocket to Mars for our women."

"Asshole." I laugh. "Thanks for dinner. It was good to see you all."

"Hey. Good luck at the game." Aiden shakes my hand then pulls me into a hug. "You all should be a lock for the Super Bowl."

"We'll see. Don't want to get our hopes up too much." My eyes flick over to Lacey. She's listening to Maven talk, her legs pulled up to her chest and her chin on her knees. "Ready to go, Lacey girl?" I ask.

"Yeah," she says with a smile. "I am."

"THANKS FOR WALKING ME HOME," Lacey says. She shoves her hands in the pockets of her jacket and shivers. "We probably should've taken the car."

"What? Twenty degrees isn't invigorating to you?" I ask. I drape my arm over her shoulder and pull her against my side. "Makes me feel alive."

"You're also two hundred and twenty pounds of muscle and hot all the time. You're not allowed to comment on not being cold."

I laugh and guide her around a patch of ice on the sidewalk. "Fair. What do you have going on this week? Anything exciting?"

"No. I go back to work on the fifth. You know I love my job, but it's been nice to take a step back. To have a minute to breathe. I've been trying to take care of myself, and I want to make sure I do that when I get back in my routine, too."

"I'm proud of you. Have you heard anything about the chief physician position?" I ask. "Has Hannaford said anything?"

She snorts and shakes her head. "Please. He's skiing in the Alps right now; his out of office email is on until halfway through January. On the plus side, your silent auction items brought in a million dollars. I guess I'm going to have to bring you back next year. See if we can make it a million and a half."

"Yeah?" I tug on her hand and stop her in front of her apartment building. It's quiet out here, everyone already in for the evening and out of the cold. "I'll go back with you, even if I don't donate anything. I like being by your side."

Lacey lifts her chin, and her eyes meet mine. "Do you want to come up?"

I do.

More than I want anything in this world.

I want to lay her on her bed and whisper in her ear how much I love her. I want to put my head between her legs and tell her I'm going to take care of her for the next fifty years. I want to hold her through the night and give her whatever she asks.

But I don't want her to think how I'm feeling is a heat of the moment thing. Said for the first time because I'm buried inside her after a couple of beers late at night. I'm going to get this right, because Lacey deserves it.

"I do, but I think I'm going to head home," I say, and she bites her bottom lip. Disappointment flashes across her face, and I rest my palms on her cheeks. "Do not think for a second I'm rejecting you, Lacey girl. I'm tired, and I have a little bit of work I need to catch up on."

"Okay." She nods and glances over my shoulder. "When do you leave? Tomorrow?"

"Yeah. Tomorrow night. We'll be back on the second." I take a breath and swallow away the lump in my throat. "Can I see you when I get back?"

"Oh." Her eyes light up and twinkle under the street lamps. "Yeah. I would—that would be nice."

"What did I tell you about nice?" My hand moves to her chin, and I tilt her head back. "You deserve so much better than nice."

"I do. I know that now. Thanks to you."

"Good. Let me know when you make it upstairs."

"It's ten floors, Shawn, not ten miles," she says.

"Don't care."

"Worried about me, Holmes?"

I bend down and kiss her. I loop my arm around her waist and dip her toward the ground, never letting my lips leave hers. "Always, Daniels," I whisper against her mouth, and she grabs me by the collar of my coat.

"You can't kiss a girl like that then leave," she says, her tone ripe with irritation. "That's cruel."

"Is it?" I kiss her again, more heat behind the press of my lips and the hand that roams under her sweater. My fingers fan out across her stomach, and she squirms in my hold. "I don't want to be cruel."

"I hate you," Lacey grumbles, and I chuckle.

"No, you don't."

"No, I don't." Her gaze locks on mine, and I see it in the outline of her smile. In the pink staining her cheeks. In the way she won't let me go, not even when she's shivering from the cold. "Will you let me know when you get home?"

"Of course."

We're delaying the inevitable. A goodbye neither of us wants to have.

I know there's going to be an us after the clock strikes midnight tomorrow night. I'm not walking away from her. But out here on the sidewalk, it still feels like a monumental moment is close to happening; the end of our agreement that made us fall for each other in the first place. The scheme that kicked our asses into gear and showed us the feelings we didn't know we had.

Fuck, I'm glad I kissed her that first time.

"What are you thinking about?" she asks. She reaches up

and runs her fingers down my cheek. Settles her palm on my chest, right over my heart.

"You," I say. I squeeze her hip and put her back on two feet. "Seriously, Daniels. Let me know when you're in your apartment."

"I will, I will. Good luck at the game. I'll be cheering for you."

"I'm sure I'll hear you all the way in Denver."

"Come home quick, okay? I'll miss you."

"Shucks, Lacey girl. I'll miss you, too." I drop one more kiss on her forehead and give her backside a tap. "Go on up."

"Going to watch me walk away?" she asks, and her smirk is wicked and knowing.

"You know I can't resist your ass."

"Why do you think I wore this skirt and decided to freeze my legs off? Gotta keep the people happy." Lacey pulls away and sways her hips from side to side as she walks to the lobby door. She looks at me one more time, her chin on her shoulder and a gleam in her eyes. "Night, Shawn Yawn."

"See ya, Lace Face," I answer.

When she blows me a kiss through the window, I know the next forty-eight hours are going to be the longest of my life.

I already can't wait to be home with my girl.

FORTY-SIX

LACEY

THE LIQUOR I added to my hot chocolate helps me feel less lonely as I watch the couples on the television kiss in anticipation of the new year.

They jump up and down, waving at the camera before grabbing for each other and standing close. A make out session begins, and I chug half the contents in my mug.

My heart drops to my stomach when I spot the timer in the bottom right corner of the screen. Another minute closer to midnight, and another minute without Shawn.

I miss him so much, and I hate that he has an away game tomorrow.

I can't stop thinking about the feel of his lips. How he sucked on my skin, just below my ear, and left a little mark I had to hide with a turtleneck on Christmas night.

I can't stop replaying the noises he makes; the soft groans of approval when I take him in my hands and twist my wrist.

His heavy exhales when he's asleep and holding me in his arms.

When he whispers my name and makes it sound like a prayer.

I can't wait until he's home.

My phone rings, and I grab it off the coffee table. I smile when I see Shawn's name on the screen, and I set down my mug.

"Hey," I answer, and I rest my chin in my hand. "Happy almost New Year. Where are you?"

"I'm heading somewhere that feels like home. The place where I feel the safest," Shawn says, out of breath, and I wonder if he's running through the airport. "What are you doing?"

"Sitting on the couch and getting ready to watch the ball drop. Pretty uneventful night over here," I say.

"Are you alone?"

"Jealous, Holmes?"

"Curious, Daniels."

"Yeah. It's just me and my favorite blanket. Oh, and a spiked mug of hot chocolate."

"Sounds like the perfect night," he says.

"It's not half bad," I say. There's a knock on my apartment door, and I sit up. "Hang on. Someone's here. That's weird; Maggie told me she and Aiden are spending the night celebrating with a nice dinner out."

"Maybe they're stopping by to say hi."

"And interrupt time they could be home alone doing God knows what? Doubtful. You know those two can't keep their hands to themselves."

"Ah. Young love," he says.

I walk across the living room and turn the lock. I open the door and freeze when I find Shawn standing on my welcome mat, right over the words that say *go away*. "What are you doing here?"

He ends the call and slides his phone into the pocket of his jeans. The tips of his ears are red, and his nose is, too. His cheeks are flushed, and it looks like he's spent the last twenty minutes outside in the freezing cold.

"Hi, Lacey girl," he says.

"Hi," I whisper. My voice cracks around the edges, and I suck in a sharp breath. I reach out to touch him—his cheeks, his chest, the scruff of the beard he decided to grow—to check if he's real. "You're supposed to be on a plane to... to somewhere. But you're here?"

He lifts an eyebrow and leans against the door frame. "Keeping track of me?"

"No. Yes. Maybe." I squeeze my eyes shut then open them, and he's still *right there*. Six inches away from me. "Aren't you— are you allowed to not fly with the team? Won't you get in trouble?"

"That's the best thing about being the head coach." Shawn takes a step forward and crowds my space. Heat radiates from his body, and I want to wrap myself in one of his hugs. "I get to make the rules. Can I come in?"

"Yeah." I nod and gesture for him to join me inside. "Of course."

He walks into my apartment, and I hold the fleece blanket tight around my shoulders. It's my shield in case I need it.

"You still have your tree up?" he asks. "Decorated, too."

"Yeah. I didn't want to take it down yet. I'm not ready to let the holiday season go," I say.

Shawn glances at me over his shoulder. "I'm not either," he says. He pulls off his beanie and runs his hand through his hair. Snowflakes fall from the dark brown waves and litter my floor like confetti. "Come here."

I walk to him on instinct. If he told me to jump, I'd ask how high. I've become reliant on him, the other half to my whole.

My feet glide across the floor and my shoulders shake. "You still haven't told me what you're doing here," I say.

"There was going to be a whole thing with magnets and a

planned speech, but I couldn't wait. I had to be here with you. It's almost New Year's."

He looks at the television and the countdown plastered on the screen. There are only four minutes until midnight, and the camera pans to the ball high up in Times Square. It glitters and sparkles, the sequins catching in the spotlights. Another second passes, then another and another.

Three minutes and thirty seconds to go.

I stop in front of him and tilt my head back so I can look him in the eye. The blanket falls into a heap at my feet, and I shiver at the change in temperature. "The end of our arrangement. You wanted to tell me in person," I whisper, and my chest aches.

I'm not ready to say goodbye to him yet.

Shawn's eyes roam down my body and his smile melts into a grin, a bright and beautiful thing that makes his eyes sparkle and his hand twitch by his side. I think he wants to reach out and pull me to him.

"You're wearing my shirt again," he says.

"Oh." I glance down. The threadbare material has seen better days, torn on the left sleeve and a hole forming under my right breast, but it smells like him and it feels like him. I never want to take it off. "Yeah. I am."

"What if we don't end it?" he asks.

I stare at him. "Not end what?"

"Our arrangement."

"What do you mean?"

"What if we were in a relationship? A *real* relationship?"

"For real? For real how?"

"Well." He runs his knuckles down my jaw and hums. "For starters, I could sleep over. I could spend every night with you, then wake up next to you in the morning. I'd cook you breakfast; scrambled eggs, just the way you like them."

"You want to cook me breakfast?" I whisper, incapable of any other words except for his own mirrored back to him.

"I do. I could give you a key to my apartment and let you have free rein. I could stop by when I got back in town from games and not have to go home alone. Bring you with me on the team plane and sneak you into the bathroom so I could kiss you senseless without anyone teasing us. And I would tell you I love you. Very much and very often, because I do. I do love you, Lacey. I don't want to let you go just yet. Can I keep you a little while longer?"

My bottom lip wobbles. My hands tremble, and I sniff. "How much longer?" I ask.

"How does forever sound?" Shawn asks. His lips pull up higher in the corners and his nose scrunches. Little wrinkles form around his eyes, and there's so much *joy* on his face.

"You want to be with me?"

"More than I want anything else in this world, Lacey girl," he says, and my heart nearly bursts out of my chest.

I grab the lapels of his fancy coat and pull him toward me. He chuckles when I stand on his boots to make myself taller, but I need to be as close as I can to him.

"Forever is a long time," I say.

"And it still wouldn't be long enough. I love you so very much. I think maybe I've always loved you," he whispers. His voice is hoarse, but he's sincere, resolute, a sure thing he knows with absolute certainty.

"I love you too," I whisper back.

I choke out a sob as I say it, the four words barreling into me with a wave of emotion. My fingers dig into the wool of his jacket, and I clutch onto him for dear life. I'm afraid that if I let go, my feet will come off the ground.

"Sometimes I think you're this perfect person I dreamed up."

He takes a deep breath, and energy builds between us. "And it scares me you might not be real. That what we have might not be real."

"I'm real," I say, and my eyes prickle with tears. "And this is real. What I feel for you is as real as the sky is blue."

"I think about you when I'm away. I miss you when I'm gone. I count down the seconds until I can see you again," Shawn says. He wipes a tear from my cheek then kisses his thumb, as if he's collecting the drops to save for later. "I can't—I don't *want* to go through life without you by my side."

"You won't have to. I'm here with you, Shawn. I'm yours. I've always been yours, and I'm always going to be yours."

I loop my arms around his neck and pull him close. I stand on my toes and kiss him so hard I think I might explode. His nose brushes against mine, and a giggle lodges its way into my throat.

"You make all of this tolerable," he says. "The traveling, the long days, the sleepless nights. But I'd give up football tomorrow if it meant keeping you. If you want to do this without cameras and without games on the road and without stretches of time where we don't see each other except for once or twice a week, say the word, baby, and I'll walk away from the sport right now."

"No." I shake my head. "Football is who you are. There's room in your heart for me and the other part of you that you love. I know there is. It'll take some getting used to, but we'll make it work. We're going to make it work. You're my best friend, Shawn."

"Fuck." He scoops me into his arms and walks toward my bedroom. His shoulder knocks a picture off the wall, but he ignores it and keeps going. "I missed you so much. I saw you yesterday, and I still missed you. There's a hole in my heart when you aren't around, Lacey. Do you know I hear you in the crowd? I hear you scream my name and I hear your laugh. I listen for you. I don't care about the other seventy thousand people. I only care about you."

"I love you." I bury my face in his neck and revel in the smell of his cologne and the heat of his skin. "You're the only one I'm ever going to cheer for."

Shawn kicks the door to my room open. He sets me down on the mattress and takes off his coat. "Let me touch you," he says. He runs his hand down my bare leg and tugs on my sock. "Let me take care of you."

"You always take care of me," I say.

My breathing hitches when he moves his hand up my thigh and under my shirt. His warm palm travels over my stomach and up to my breast. His thumb brushes over my nipple, and my back arches off the mattress.

"Because you're mine." His hoodie and T-shirt come off next, and a heap of clothes forms on the floor near my bed. He presses a kiss to my knee, and I let out a soft moan. "I know what you want. What you like. I know what makes you happy. I know that this..." he runs his fingers down the front of my underwear and shoves the fabric aside. "This turns you on. Look how wet you are for me."

"Fuck me, Shawn," I whisper. I hook my fingers in the waistband of my underwear and pull them down my legs. I toss the cotton away and take off my shirt. "This time, I'm really yours."

"You've always been mine. You were mine from the first time I saw you. The first time I kissed you. The first time I sank inside you," he says, low and rough in my ear.

He kicks off his boots and slides his pants down to his ankles. He steps out of his jeans and nudges them away. His briefs come next, and soon he's naked, too.

It feels different from before; slower. More tender as he kisses every inch of my body.

My neck. My chest. The spot on my stomach just below my

belly button. My hip bone and the small scar on my right knee. He claims all of me, leaving no spot untouched until I'm twisting on the sheets and panting his name.

"Shawn," I say. "I need you."

His laugh is sweet like honey, and he slips two fingers inside me. I can't even get a groan out before his mouth is on mine, his tongue silky and smooth as he swallows down whatever noise I try to make. "Are you going to come for me, Lacey girl?" he asks, and fireworks explode in my blood.

He bites my bottom lip, his teeth sinking into the skin. His question ricochets down my body, and I wrap my arms tightly around his neck.

When he presses his thumb against me and starts a slow and cruel circle, I tip over the edge, stars in my vision and my limbs heavy against the mattress. It's explosive. It's electric. It's the best it's ever felt. A cry slips out of my mouth and he takes that, too, again and again until I push him flat on his back and straddle his legs.

I curl my hand around his length, and he's hard and warm in my hand. I stroke up and down, his skin slick and my name tumbling from his mouth. His large palm folds over mine, and he guides himself to my entrance.

We gasp in unison when he pushes into me, and I rock forward, needing him deeper. I want to feel him everywhere.

"You were made for me," he says into the valley of my chest, his hand cupping my breast and his tongue circling my nipple. His hips lift, and there's no more space between us.

I look to where we're joined, and my breath catches in the back of my throat. "I love you," I say. "I love you so much."

"I love you too, Lacey girl," he says. He drags his gaze up to meet mine, and he stares at me with adoration in his eyes.

"Show me," I whisper, and he does.

Over and over again until the moon turns into the sun and the starry night gives way to morning.

FORTY-SEVEN

SHAWN

I WAKE up to Lacey's arm around my waist and her hair in my face.

It's exactly how we spent the nights at my parents' house, our bodies wrapped around each other, and it feels like we never left.

Fuck, she's pretty in the morning with her swollen lips and the hickeys on her chest. I kiss her forehead and cheek, not wanting to wake her up, but I have to get on a plane and I'm not leaving her without saying goodbye.

Her eyes flutter open, heavy-lidded and still half-asleep, and I smile down at her.

"Good morning," she says, her voice thick with exhaustion.

"Morning, sweetheart," I say.

I hook my fingers around her chin and bring her mouth to mine. She sighs against my lips, and I roll myself on top of her.

"I could get used to waking up like this." She drapes her arms around my neck and loops her legs around my waist. "A tattooed man looking at me like he wants to devour me? Who could complain?"

"I love you." I dip my chin and kiss the top of her chest, the space directly above her heart. I want my words to sit there so she'll never doubt them. "I love you, Lacey."

"I didn't dream it?" she asks, and a smile pokes through the question.

"No. All real." I take her nipple in my mouth and suck on the peak. Her back arches off the mattress and she reaches between my legs. "We're going to wake up like this for a very, very long time."

"You won't get any complaints from me." Her fingers wrap around my length, and she gives me a gentle squeeze. "We're going to tell our friends, right?"

"I think we should," I say around a ragged breath. I move my mouth to her other nipple, and I bite and suck until little pink marks form on her skin. Until she's panting and squirming on the sheets. "It's going to be obvious."

"Because you can't keep your hands off of me?" She tugs on my cock, and I rock forward. "You haven't been able to keep your hands off of me for a month."

"I'm weak when it comes to you," I admit. "I'm kind of obsessed, if you haven't been able to tell." I kiss down her body to her stomach. My tongue traces across her belly button to her hip bone. "Out of my mind." I smile into her knee as I position myself between her legs. I part her with my fingers, and she's wet already. "A total goner."

"I love it," Lacey says. She runs her hand through my hair and pulls on the longer strands near the base of my neck. "I love how much you want me."

"More than I want anything else in this world. You're my dream girl." My thumb circles her in the pattern she likes, and I run my tongue up her entrance. "God, I love you."

"You love my pussy." She laughs, and I give her clit a light slap. "Am I wrong?" she asks, and her voice breaks on the last word.

"Of course I love having my head down here—I'm so fucking attracted to you. But I love your heart, too. Your smart mind and your ability to make everyone feel welcomed and loved. How selfless you are and your determination. Do you know what else I love?" I slide two fingers inside her, and I bite the soft flesh of her thigh. "How you act like my family is your family. How you love Maven like she's yours. Your thoughtfulness and your generosity. If someone asked me to show them my perfect girl, all I'd have to do is show them you."

"Flirting with me, Holmes?"

"I've got my fingers buried in your cunt, and I'm stretching you out so you're ready for my cock. Of course I'm flirting with you Daniels."

"I love you, too," Lacey whispers, and her touch dances down the side of my face.

"Now who's flirting with who?" I ask. I turn my cheek and kiss her palm as she huffs out a laugh. "Does that feel good, pretty girl? Do you like my fingers inside you?"

"Yes," she breathes out. "I love when you touch me, Shawn."

"What do you need to come? Tell me, and I'll give it to you."

"You. More," she gasps, and I'm a man of my word.

I sit up on my knees and add a third finger. I kiss her gently as her hips open and she begs me to get deeper. "There you go. You take me so well, Lacey."

Her nails dig into my skin. Drag down my shoulders and across my back, claw marks I'll have under my shirt today at the game, and no one will know. She draws me closer to her, touching everywhere she can reach.

I touch her, too. Her neck. Her tits. The hollow spot on her throat that gets her to say my name like a prayer. I map out her body until she's grinding against my hand. Until she whimpers and moans, the two sounds that tell me she's close.

"I love you," I whisper into her skin as she tightens around my fingers. As she falls over the edge with a gasp and a cry. I hold her steady, easing my movements until she's motionless on the mattress and a smile curves on her lips.

"Forget the praise," she pants. She wipes a drop of sweat from her forehead and pushes up on her elbows. "Just tell me you love me. That will get me there every time."

"Noted." I grin and bring my hand to her mouth. "Open up," I say, and she does. I press all three fingers on her tongue, and she licks them clean.

Lacey reaches between us and wraps her hand around my length. I'm hard, half from watching her come undone and half from the love declarations. Possessiveness rolls through me knowing she's *mine*—mine for real.

It's not going to take much to get me to finish. When she pushes me on my back and drags her tongue up my length, my eyes roll to the back of my head. When she takes me all the way to the back of her throat, I'm cursing. When she blinks up at me, her mouth full and her eyes brimming with love, I lose it.

It's the yank of a rope. The blaze of a fire. Mind-numbing pleasure rips through me, and I say her name until my mouth goes dry. Until my legs stop shaking, she swallows, crawls up the mattress and curls into my side.

"Jesus," I mumble.

"Lacey," she says, and I press my fingers into her ribs. She squeals and tries to roll away, but I keep her close. I don't let her get too far. "When do you have to go?"

"I should've already left. My flight is in two hours, and my stuff is in my apartment. I'm flying straight to Denver."

"I'm going to miss you."

"I'm going to miss you, too. Do you want to come with me?"

"To Denver?" she asks. "You want me to go with you?"

"I always want you to come with me—as long as it's not interfering with your work schedule. You don't have to. I know it's last minute and—"

Lacey cuts me off with a kiss. "Of course I'll go with you. I need to shower. And pack. But—wait. I don't have a ticket."

"Oh." I rub the back of my neck, and my cheeks turn pink. "I might have already bought you one when I bought mine on the way here last night. Just in case you said yes to the whole forever thing."

A laugh rolls out of her. Soon she's clutching her side, tears tracking down her cheeks and snot coming out of her nose. I wait for her to finish, my arms crossed over my chest as I level her with a look.

"Buys a last minute plane ticket in case the woman he's dating decides to come to the game with him. NFL coaches: they're just like us," she says through a fresh wave of giggles. "I'm never going to get used to it."

"You're officially a WAG now, sweetheart. You better get used to it."

"Am I allowed to be called a WAG if the guy I'm with is on the sidelines and not on the field?"

"Semantics." I wave her off. "I know you can take care of yourself, Lacey girl. I know you're financially stable, and you have a great job. But you're going to have to get used to me spoiling you, because I'm going to. Frequently and often. I promise it won't be shit you won't ever use, but if you want to fly out to my game, I'm going to buy you a ticket. I do it because I love you, not because I want to show off my money. Not because I don't think you're capable of purchasing things yourself. Let me do these things for you, yeah?"

"Okay." She whispers and folds her hand over my heart. "Yeah. Yes. I won't make any jokes. I promise."

"I never said anything about not making jokes." I grin. "You can make all the jokes you want from our first class seats."

"Ten minutes. That's all I need then; I'll be ready. I'll pack light."

Her phone buzzes on the bedside table, and I reach over to hand it to her. "It's Mags. She's FaceTiming you."

"Shit." Lacey covers her bare chest as if Maggie can already see her. "What do we do?"

"No time like the present." I shrug. "We might as well tell them now. How else would you explain your sudden departure on New Year's Day?"

"Okay. Yes." She pulls the sheets up under her arms and tries to brush some of her hair with her fingers. "Don't say anything at first."

"Yes ma'am." I lean back against the pillows and wait to see what her plan is.

"Hey, Mags," she says, and she waves at the screen. "Happy New Year."

"Happy New Year," Maggie says. "I just wanted to call and check on you. How are you doing?"

"Oh." Lacey smiles. "I'm good."

"You are? I thought maybe you'd be feeling a little sad because you and Shawn—"

"I was for a little bit, but I'm over it now. Do you mind if I call you back in a few? I'm kind of busy with something," Lacey says.

"Uh, sure. Are you—did you hook up with someone?" Maggie hisses. "Is he there with you right now?"

"Hang on." Lacey sets the phone down on the mattress and scoots it my way.

I smile as I pick it up, and Lacey moves back into the frame. "Morning, Mags. Happy New Year," I say.

Maggie blinks at us. She stares for three seconds before she lets out a scream so loud, I have to cover my ears.

"Fucking *finally*," she says. "Please tell me this isn't just a one night thing. I can't take you two looking at each other like sad little puppies anymore."

"It's definitely not a one night thing," I say, and Lacey rests her head on my shoulder. She tips her chin and looks up at me. I bend down to kiss her and she melts against me. "It's a forever and always thing."

"Thank god." Maggie disappears from the screen, and soon Aiden pops up. "Tell him."

"Tell me what?" Aiden asks. "Hey, Shawn. Hey, Lace. Happy New—what the fuck?"

Lacey buries her face in the crook of my neck, and I wrap an arm around her. "Yes, we're together. Yes, we're stupidly in love. Yes, we've been sneaking around and hooking up. I promise we'll give you all the details after we get home from Denver. Our plane leaves soon, and neither one of us is ready."

"I wonder why that is," Aiden says, and he arches an eyebrow. "It's about damn time. You two have fun. Come by when you get home. We want to hear all about it."

"If we don't hang up, you'll see for yourselves," I say.

Lacey snatches the phone out of my hand and tosses it away. I laugh and pull her into my lap.

"That's enough of that," she says, and I grin.

"Fine. If you say so." I drum my fingers against her hip. "Ready to get going?"

"Yeah. But before we go, I want to tell you I love you. I love you, Shawn. You're going to get sick of me saying it so much."

I rest my chin on her shoulder and drape my arms around her waist, rocking her back and forth. "I love you too, Lacey girl. You can tell me as many times as you like. It's never going to get old."

"Are you going to be okay sitting on a plane with regular humans?" she asks. "People who aren't superstar athletes who might be playing in a Super Bowl in a month's time?"

"I have you." My fingers curl over her knee, and I draw a heart on her skin. "I'll be just fine."

FORTY-EIGHT
LACEY

"DO WE HAVE TO GO INSIDE?"

"Why wouldn't we? We've been here a thousand times."

"I'm nervous," I admit. Shawn's hand settles on the small of my back, and he guides me forward with a gentle push. "I mean, this changes everything, right? If one of the couples breaks up, sides will have to be taken. It'll get messy."

"Are you planning on breaking up with me, Daniels?" he asks, and my elbow lands in his ribs. "It's them, and it's us. Just like it's always been. People would have had to take a side when the two of us were just friends. It's not any different now."

"It's totally different." I huff and stop in front of Maggie and Aiden's apartment door. I reach out and adjust the wreath, making sure it's straight. "I really love everyone. And I'm kind of scared, too."

"Hey." Shawn rests his hand on my cheek. "I know you're scared because you have a big heart and you care about those around you. I know this is a big change, but it's still you and me, sweetheart. You're going to keep giving me shit. I'm going to keep trying to make you laugh, and we're going to be okay. I promise I'll always communicate with you, and there's never going to be a time where you don't know exactly where my mind is. And, it's safe to assume, for the foreseeable future, it'll be thinking about you."

I blow out a breath and bury my face in his shirt. It smells like his cologne and the cinnamon toast we had for breakfast when we finally dragged ourselves out of bed around noon. "Thank you. You always keep me steady."

"Friendship means a lot to you, and I wouldn't have told you how I felt if I didn't think this was something that would truly last forever."

"I'm being silly. Thank you for talking me down."

"You're not being silly. I promise I'm going to take care of your heart, Lacey. You're going to be stuck with me for a very long time."

I stand on my toes and kiss him. The brush of his lips is soft and sweet, and I lean into the feel of his mouth against mine.

I love this man.

I love him so much, and I already dread the day I can't be with him anymore.

I made a promise to myself three mornings ago. We were on the plane to Denver, and Shawn fell asleep with his head on my shoulder and his hand threaded through mine. I couldn't stop looking at him and smiling at all the parts I know about him and all the parts I've yet to learn.

I was—I am—so abundantly happy, and nothing in life has ever been this good.

I'm going to appreciate every moment with him. The loud ones at the football stadiums where I'm screaming his name and he's pacing up and down the sidelines. The softer ones on the couch with our arms around each other, just the two of us and all the time in the world.

I don't want to rush a single second with him.

The door to Maggie and Aiden's apartment swings open, and

our heads turn to the side. Maven stands in the doorway, her mouth open and an apple in her hand.

"What the *hell*?" she asks. "Is this—are you—when—oh my god. Are you two together?"

Guess the cat is out of the bag.

"Hey, Mae," Shawn says. He looks down at me and runs his thumb across my bottom lip. "Yeah. We're together."

"*Finally*," she squeals, and I've never heard her so excited about something. "Do Dad and Maggie know? Please don't swear me to secrecy—this is too good not to share."

"They know," I say. "This is the first time we're seeing them since we spilled the beans, though, so prepare your eardrums. You know Mags is going to flip out."

I take Shawn's hand in mine, and we walk into the apartment. It feels exactly like it did four days ago when we were here last, with the heat set at sixty-eight and the scent of a candle lingering in the air. My shoulders relax at the familiarity, at the feeling of *home*.

My best friend pops her head up from behind a cabinet and stomps toward the foyer like she's been summoned. She puts her hands on her hips and looks between me and Shawn. "You assholes have a *lot* of explaining to do. But, hell, I'm so happy for you," she says, before pulling us into a tight embrace.

"Hey, Mags." Shawn hugs her back and kisses her cheek. "We're ready for the interrogation."

"Thank god, because the anticipation has been killing me." Maggie leads us to the living room. "Get comfortable. I'm not letting you leave until I know every detail."

We take a spot on the couch, side by side, and Maven sits in a chair across from us. She won't stop grinning, and it makes me laugh.

"I kind of feel like an animal at the zoo," I whisper to Shawn. "Everyone's going to point at us."

"Which animal would you be? I kind of want to be a gorilla. Maybe a lion," he whispers back.

"I'd want to be a sloth. There's no need to hurry; people expect you to take eight hours to do a single task. Sloths seem so unbothered, too, which I love."

"It's been fun to slow down, hasn't it?"

"Yeah." I grin and touch the jut of his chin. "It has been."

"There are the lovebirds," Aiden says as he walks into the living room and tugs a sweatshirt over his head. "I could hear Maggie yell at you from down the hall."

"Any bets on how many times they call us that tonight?" Shawn asks me out of the corner of his mouth, and I burst out laughing. "I think at least fifteen, but no more than twenty."

"I'm going with twenty-one. They've been waiting for this moment since the day you and I met."

"You're on, Daniels."

Maggie and Aiden sit on the couch to our right. She leans forward and drops her elbows to her knees. "Please start talking."

"We all know about the kiss cam kiss. That's where all of this started. I went over to Shawn's the day the video got out and proposed the idea of continuing to pretend to date through the holidays. We made a list of rules, and one of those rules was to not be physically affectionate with each other unless it was necessary," I say.

"Which I was doing *really* well with, until Lacey came to my game wearing Dallas' jersey," Shawn says. He rolls his eyes but puts his arm around my shoulders, tugging me closer to him. "I pulled her into a supply closet at the arena, we kissed, and I thought it was a one-off, spur-of-the-moment thing."

"Hang on. The game where you made her meet you in the tunnel?" Maggie asks, and she turns to me, grinning from ear to ear. "No wonder you looked so happy when you came back to our seats, Lace. Must've been a hell of a kiss."

I touch my lips as if I'm there in the closet with him again, the moment that started everything for us. I can feel his hands on my skin and I can see the look in his eyes when he said *fuck it.*

I'm so glad I wore that jersey to get a rise out of him.

"It was a very, very *not* nice kiss," I say.

"I didn't think anything else would happen," Shawn says. "We agreed we would still be our normal selves, and I thought that was that. We had the rules we were going to stick to, and it was a heated moment. Then Lacey came to my apartment again with a different proposition."

"One night together," I say, taking over. "We had chemistry when we kissed, and I thought if we had a quick hookup, we could get whatever tension and attraction was happening between us out of our systems and go our separate ways."

"Way to go Aunt Lacey," Maven says, and Aiden shoots her a sharp look.

"Don't get any ideas, kid," he says.

"The plan would've worked, but it wasn't just one night. It was more kissing. More hooking up. Everything started to feel less fake and more real. There was a night at my parents' house when we were sitting out on the roof. I looked at her, and I knew," Shawn says, and his voice turns soft. A story only for me. "I knew I was in love with her. Getting to have her as *mine*—even if it was just pretend—showed me I never wanted to give her up."

"So you're telling me you two have been sleeping together for a *month*, and we had no idea?" Maggie asks. "How did— when—I can't believe we missed the signs."

"Looking back, we were so obvious. Remember the night of the gala when you asked me about the mark on my neck, Mags?" My cheeks turn pink and I bury my face in Shawn's shoulder so my words come out muffled. "It was a hickey. He helped me get dressed, and one thing led to another."

"Had to do it, Lace. We were going to an event where you looked hot as sin. I needed the other men there to know you were spoken for," Shawn says. He lifts me up and settles me in his lap as his arms fold around me. "I'm very protective over what's mine, and even then, I wanted you for myself."

"We weren't hiding our relationship," I explain. "To us there wasn't a relationship to hide. We both truly thought this was physical. The first time we slept together wasn't because we were emotionally invested in each other. We both had a goal, and we figured we could have a little fun along the way. Over time, it turned real. I look at Shawn and—" I stop to take a breath. To control my heart that's racing a mile a minute in my chest. "I feel this immense joy, deep in my soul, when I see him. I've never experienced that with anyone else."

"When did you know?" Shawn asks. "What was the moment for you?"

"The first night we were at your parents' house, I thought about being with you when you had gray hair. It was the first time I actively realized I didn't want this to have an end date. I saw a future, and I saw it with you. I held onto that pull I experienced toward you because I was afraid. You're safe. You've always been safe. Taking the leap and letting you in as someone more than the guy who stops by my office and brings me coffee... it was scary. But I'm so glad I jumped."

"I am, too. You know I'll always be there to catch you when you fall, Lacey girl," he says.

I do know that.

He'd go to the ends of the world for me, and I'd do the same for him.

Shawn bends down and kisses me, and I smile against his

lips while our friends cheer. I forgot they were in the room for a minute, too pulled into his orbit to remember anyone else.

"I'm happy for you two," Aiden says, and I look his way.

He wipes his eyes, and I frown. "Aiden, why are you crying? This is a good thing."

"I know it is. I just love love so much, and you two are fucking happy. Fucking finally," he adds, and Shawn shimmies me out of his lap so he can stand and give his best friend a hug.

"I am happy," I hear Shawn say. "I've never been happier."

I haven't either.

"THAT WENT WELL." I watch Shawn in the bathroom mirror as he moves around his bedroom. "I'm glad everyone's okay with us being together."

"I also feel really dumb for not realizing everyone else clearly noticed that we liked each other before we did." He pulls his sleep shirt over his head and runs his fingers through his hair. "Guess you really have been flirting with me for almost two years, Daniels."

"Maybe you were the one flirting with me." I put my toothbrush in the holder next to his on the vanity. He handed it to me the night we got back from Denver, just before he showed me the space he made in his closet and dressers for my things. "Maven *did* say you were always looking at me."

"That's funny, because every time I was looking at you, I saw you looking at me, too," he tosses back, and I think he might have a point.

I shut off the bathroom light and shuffle toward the bed. Shawn pats the spot next to him, and I smile as I crawl under the sheets. I turn on my side and reach for his hand. "Back to work for me tomorrow. I've kind of forgotten that the rest of the world exists."

"I'll bring you lunch. Or coffee. Anything, really, so I can find an excuse to stop by and see you." His phone buzzes on the nightstand, and he frowns as he checks his text messages. "Huh."

"What?" I rest my chin on his shoulder and read the screen. "Why is your publicist reaching out to you so late at night?"

"We're playing the Cincinnati Renegades this weekend. Theo Asher, their quarterback, is the guy dating Ella Wright, that big pop star everyone loves. Haley said Ella's agent reached out to her and asked if you'd be interested in sharing a suite with her."

"I'm sorry—*what*?" I sit up and gape at him. "You're telling me the woman who sells out every stadium in the country wants to sit with *me* and watch a football game?"

Shawn chuckles and rubs little circles on my back. "I guess so. Haley says Ella loves our love story and wants to meet you."

"What if she writes a song about us? She could call it... hang on." I push up onto my knees and stretch my arms out to my sides. "Love through a lens. Come on. How good is that?"

"I love it. You're a creative genius," he says, and I know he's giving me shit. "What do you want me to tell her?"

"You tell her yes, Shawn Holmes. A hundred percent hell fucking yes. Oh, my god. Wait. Her boyfriend plays for the other team. Isn't that like, a conflict of interest?"

"It's a football game, baby. You're not trying to represent a family member in court. You're allowed to sit with whoever you want."

"If I'm going to be caught on camera at another football game, being next to Ella Wright is a hell of a lot cooler than having some guy not kiss me," I say, and I flop back against the pillows. "This is amazing. I'm so glad you're rich and famous."

"I'm going to buy you a dictionary so you can learn what the definition of famous is, because it is *not* me." Shawn tosses his phone to the side and leans into my space. "But I'm glad you're happy."

"You could have nothing to your name and I'd be happy with you, Shawn." I touch his cheek, and he turns his head to kiss my palm. "You're the greatest gift I've ever been given."

"You and me, Lacey girl. I'm going to be pulling you into supply closets until the end of time. Bringing you home for Christmas and spending late January with your parents. I'm going to keep loving you, when I'm on the field and when I'm off. And, most importantly, we're going to have a big family together. We'll have matching pajama sets and create our own traditions," he whispers in my ear. "I love you so much."

"I love you too, Shawn," I whisper back. "But if you think for a *second* I'm going to let you win another snowball fight, you've got another thing coming."

"You're cute when you're delusional," he says, and he presses himself above me. "If you want to touch me, you could just ask."

I roll my eyes and grab a pillow from behind my head. I smack him in the face with it, and his laughter rings in my ears until the early morning when he holds me close and I know I'm home.

EPILOGUE

Lacey
One year later

"I'M SO NERVOUS!" I yell. I wring my hands together and stare at the field. There's only two minutes to go, and the Titans are down six points.

"Shawn knows what he's doing," Maggie yells back, leaning in close and trying to talk over the deafening roar of the crowd. It's nearly impossible to hear her with a hundred thousand fans who descended on Las Vegas to cheer on the Titans at the Super Bowl. "He doesn't even look nervous," she adds.

I'm glad she's been keeping tabs on him, because I've been too afraid to look at him the whole game. I chance a glance at him now during a timeout, and I see him laughing. Elbowing one of his players on the sideline and patting their back. Twisting his hat backwards on his head and adjusting his microphone closer to his mouth.

He puts his hands on his hips, and his spine straightens. It's like he can sense me staring at him. He turns around and looks at me over his shoulder, and he's grinning from ear to ear.

Shawn holds up a finger to an assistant coach and jogs my way, waving off the security personnel who try to stop him from getting too close to the stands.

"Watching me, Lacey girl?" he shouts from eight feet below me. "I was starting to think you might be crushing on someone from the other team."

"I'm worried," I answer.

I didn't think it was possible for his grin to stretch wider, but it does. I see his teeth and the wrinkles around his eyes—those laugh lines I love so much. He reaches up to the top of the concrete wall and pulls himself onto the ledge so we're inches apart.

"Hi," he says.

It's reminiscent of our first kiss over a year ago, down to the camera showing us on the big screen.

A lot has changed since then, though.

I took over the chief physician position at my pediatrician's office, and Hannaford was fired. My work-life balance has never been better.

Shawn led the Titans to last year's Super Bowl, but they lost. A string of injuries derailed their hopes of a championship.

They bounced back stronger than ever. That loss made them hungrier. More determined. They started this season with a three-game losing streak, but they've gone on to have the best record in the league. Shawn won Coach of the Year, an accolade that came with a shiny trophy. He keeps it in his office at the stadium because he says he wouldn't have won anything without his team.

He's the most humble guy I know.

And now they're close—*so close*—to finally winning it all. What he's been working on for five years is almost here.

The Titans just need to score one more touchdown, but the clock isn't on their side.

They have yards to go, and the seconds are slipping by like sand in an hourglass.

Still, Shawn is here with me, and there's not an ounce of strain on his face.

"Hey," I answer. "Is this allowed?"

"Fuck if I care. I dare them to fine me. Why are you worried?" he asks, and he pulls on my pigtail.

His voice is softer now, the same reverent tone it takes when it's early in the morning and I'm in his arms, half-awake under the rising sun.

Late at night when he's above me, his hands on my body and whispering words against my skin.

In the afternoon when we're in the kitchen and he kisses me without a reason, devotion behind the press of his lips and the way he tells me he loves me every single day.

I step toward him and run my palms up his chest, letting them settle around his neck. "Because you might win a Super Bowl," I say. "And that makes me so happy for you."

Shawn leans close, and his eyes are as bright as a clear summer's day. "I don't care about the win," he says, and it sounds like a secret he's not supposed to tell me. He touches my cheek and dances his fingers down my jaw. "I already won by having you here with me."

I roll my eyes, but my heart cinches tight in my chest. It always does when he tells me how much I mean to him. "It's a bummer they don't hand out extra points for the cheesiest lines. You'd certainly win, and this game would be long over."

"It's true. You know why? In fifteen years, I might not be coaching anymore, but I'll have you. I get to have you for the rest of my life," he says, and he rests his forehead against mine.

"Are you sure about that? Dallas tried to ask me out to dinner in the tunnel and—"

Shawn pinches my hip, and a laugh tumbles out of me. "Whose jersey are you wearing today?" he asks.

"Yours."

"Whose jersey are you going to wear thirty years from now?"

"Yours," I say. "It's always going to be yours. I love you, Shawn, and I'm so damn proud of you. Win or lose, you're incredible."

"I love you too, Lacey girl," he murmurs.

He kisses me soft and slow, just like he does every night before bed. Just like he does when he brings me coffee and tells me he's the luckiest guy in the world. Just like he does after we argue over silly things, after we fuck, after we split a piece of toast while we wait for our eggs to cook.

I kiss him back, my palms moving to his cheeks and my heart in his hands. My feet come off the ground, and I think I might be flying. It's the only explanation for why I still get butterflies when he's near, a thousand wings taking flight right behind my ribs.

I don't think I'll ever tire of that feeling.

I hear applause. There's a whistle and catcalls. The wedding march plays over the loud speaker and I pull away from him.

"What is it with you and kissing me in front of a bunch of football fans?" I ask. "Is this going to be a tradition of ours?"

"I'm obsessed with you," he says. "Can't keep my hands to myself."

"You should try, because the guys are already back on the line of scrimmage. You have a game to close out."

"Look at you knowing your football." He grins and pulls down on my bottom lip with his thumb. "Want to get married in Vegas tonight?" he asks, and I almost fall onto the field.

"What?"

"Want to get married in Vegas tonight?" he asks again, and I stare at him.

"You—me—us—*here*?"

Shawn shrugs, and a grin tugs up the left corner of his mouth. "Why not?"

"Because you haven't proposed to me?" I say, half a question, half a statement, and he slaps his forehead.

"Oh, I haven't? Shit." He glances at the field, then back to me. "Hold on to that thought." He kisses my cheek and jumps down onto the turf. He waves and jogs back to his team with long legs and tattooed arms, and I watch him go.

"What did he say?" Maggie asks, and my shoulders shake.

I'm not sure if I'm laughing or crying. Whatever it is, love balloons in my chest. It inflates as I watch him duck his head and talk to Dallas and Jett. It gets even bigger when he checks the scoreboard. It comes dangerously close to popping when he turns around, meets my gaze, and taps his heart, the spot where I know I'll always be.

"Everything," I answer. "He said everything."

She takes my hand in her left and Aiden's in her right, and we watch the next two minutes unfold. My throat burns from screaming. My fingers throb from squeezing Maggie so tight. My legs hurt from jumping up and down.

The Titans miraculously charge down the field, ten yards away from a touchdown with twelve seconds on the clock.

"Here we go," Maggie says.

"I can't watch." I squeeze my eyes shut. "I'm too scared."

"Lacey." She elbows my side. "You have to watch. Shawn is about to win a Super Bowl."

"You have so much confidence," I say. I open my eyes and watch the players get in position. They crouch down, ready to take off, and I've stopped breathing. "Can you see the future?"

"I wish." Maggie laughs and steps closer to me. She tugs

Aiden with her, and we're in a small cluster. "Only one down to go. Come on, Jett," she screams.

I glance at Aiden over Maggie's shoulder. "Who knew she was such a sports enthusiast?"

"I'm not complaining," he says, stars in his eyes as he looks at his other half with awe. "Can she get any more perfect?"

"Okay, knock it off, lovebirds," I say. I grin and focus my attention on the game. "We have a Super Bowl to win."

The whistle sounds, and the ball is snapped. Jett takes three steps back, and his eyes scan the field. A defender breaks free from the line of scrimmage and charges toward him. Jett moves left then right, faking out his foe as he takes off for the end zone.

"He's running it," Maggie screams again. "Holy shit."

"Go, Jett, go," I yell until my voice cracks.

Jett spins out of a defender's hold and narrowly avoids being taken down. Quick footwork saves him, and he's only eight yards away from a victory.

Seven.

Six.

He hits the five-yard mark, and his stride gets longer. He looks over his shoulder, the ball clutched tight to his chest. Finding no one but his own teammates, he crosses the goal line just as time expires.

The stadium erupts. The Titans swarm their quarterback, and a pile of players forms in the end zone. Tears blur my vision, and I see Shawn running down the sidelines and jumping in the air. He pulls off his headset and throws it, his hands raised in celebration.

"It's not over," Aiden bellows, and he points at the scoreboard. "We're tied. We didn't take the lead."

"What?" Dread ices my blood, and I grip the railing in front of me. "What does that mean? Do we go to overtime? There's no time on the clock."

"No. The NFL permits an extra point kick to determine the game's outcome, even if there's no time left in regulation," Aiden explains, and my knuckles turn white.

"So Dallas has to kick," I whisper. "And he has to make it."

"Yeah." Aiden nods. "If he misses, *then* we go to overtime."

My eyes find Shawn again. He has his head against Dallas' helmet and his hands on his kicker's shoulders. They're leaning in close, exchanging whispered words no one else can hear.

I think I'm going to be sick.

The special teams jog onto the field. Jett and the offensive line are still celebrating, but they're quiet now. A hush falls over the crowd as everyone waits with bated breath for Dallas' kick.

"How many of these do you think he's kicked in his life-time?" Maggie whispers.

"A million, probably," Aiden says. "He can do it with his eyes closed."

"What about when a Super Bowl victory is on the line?" I ask. "Makes it a little more complicated, right?"

"Nah." Aiden smiles. "Not to him. This is just another Sunday night on the field where he grew up learning how to kick. In his mind, he's alone. There's no crowd. There's no press. There's not a hundred million people watching him on their couches, calling him every name under the sun. It's him and that nasty right foot of his. That's it."

The guys line up, and I hold my breath. The ball is snapped, and Justin Rodgers, the holder, catches it perfectly. Dallas takes three steps forward, his head down and his eyes on the ball. His right leg winds back and his cleat connects with the leather so loudly, I can hear the sound from here.

We watch as the ball lifts off the ground and soars toward the goalposts. It passes over the yellow crossbar with feet to spare and sails perfectly through the air. The referees lift their arms and signal the extra point is good, and the players storm the field.

Dallas gets put on someone's shoulders. Confetti falls from the rafters. "We Are the Champions" starts to play from the speakers, and I stare at the field, flabbergasted.

A security guard runs toward me. He's talking on a walkie-talkie, and gestures for me to lean over the railing.

"Coach Holmes wants you out there," the man says.

"What? No. He's with his team."

"He requested all three of you." He nods toward Maggie and Aiden. "We can't have people storming the field, but family members are allowed."

"Are you sure? How do we get down?"

"Jump." He holds out his arms, and I burst out laughing.

"What? Are you out of your mind?"

"Lacey." Maggie gives me a gentle nudge. "You've jumped off a ledge this high before. Go. Go get your guy."

I scramble over the railing before I can think twice. I sit on the edge of the concrete wall and look down. Adrenaline courses through my blood, exactly like it did the night I ran to Shawn when he was having a panic attack, and I push myself off the ledge and into the arms of the security guard.

I'm glad no one is threatening trespassing charges this time.

He catches me with ease and sets me on the ground before motioning for Maggie and Aiden to follow. I sprint across the field and make a beeline for Shawn. I run straight into his back, my arms slipping around his waist and my cheek pressing against his shirt.

He tugs my hands so I'm in front of him, and his smile is wide and bright. "I'm so glad you're here."

"Congratulations." I choke out a sob and throw my arms around his neck. He lifts me off the ground and holds me tight as he spins me around, a dizzying circle of happiness. "I'm so proud of you."

"Why are you crying?" he asks. He wipes away a tear and cups my cheek. "There's no crying in football."

"They are happy tears," I explain. "You've worked so hard. The guys have worked so hard. You deserve this so much."

"Ah, shucks, baby. You're too good to me. I couldn't have done this without you."

"I didn't do anything. This was all you."

"No." He pulls back and stares at me. His eyes are glistening with tears, too, and I've never seen him so happy. "You encourage me. You believe in me. You stay up late with me and listen to me talk about lineups and plays even though you don't understand half of what I'm saying. You taught me it's okay to not be okay, not all the time, and you're my safe space to go to after every win and every loss." He pauses to kiss me soft and slow, and it electrifies every one of my nerve endings. "You're my home, Lacey girl, and I love you so much."

"I love you too. I love you to the stars. To the depths of this universe and every one beyond."

"Sounds like you're obsessed with me, Daniels. I like it. I like it a lot."

"Don't flatter yourself, Holmes. I just want to be in the parade next week. That's all," I whisper, and he laughs. I hold that sound close to my heart, in the space I know he'll always be. "About what you said earlier."

"What did I say earlier?" Shawn asks. Mischief laces his question, and there's a glimmer of glee in his smile. "Can you remind me?"

"Getting married in Vegas. Is that—were you serious?"

"Do you want me to be serious?"

I swallow and nod, a chaotic bob of my head that makes

more laughter burst out of me. "Yes. Yes, I do," I say. "I want to keep you forever and ever. I want to have your name on every jersey I wear, but I want it to be my last name, too. I want to adopt eight kids with you and take obnoxious photos on Christmas with our matching pajamas."

"All of that?" he asks.

"All of that. And lots more."

"Is that so?" He sets me down and reaches into his pocket. He pulls out a velvet box and drops to his knee. "Guess I have a question to ask you, then."

I gape at him. "Shawn."

"Lacey. I know our relationship didn't start out on the most truthful of terms," he says. He reaches for my hand and threads his fingers through mine. "We couldn't admit we were attracted to each other. It was fake. Purely physical. Something we joked about but never believed in until that night on the roof at my parents' house. You looked at me, and I thought I was struck by fucking lightning. I wanted to learn everything about you. I wanted to meet your family and give you whatever resources I had to help you accomplish your goals and dreams. That was the moment I realized you would never be just a friend to me ever again. That was the moment I knew I was falling in love with you. But it wasn't falling. It was jumping in head first, because loving you has been the easiest thing of my life. It's been the most fun I've ever had, and God only knows how much fun we've yet to have."

I drop to my knees and rest my forehead against his. I ignore the sweat on his arms and the pieces of blue and white confetti clinging to his shirt. I hold on to him by his collar, and I smile.

"I love you and your gentle heart," I say softly. A crowd forms around us, but I want this moment to be just for us. Words only Shawn can hear. "I love how kind you are and how well you treat others. I love your love for your team, and I love your love for me. You make me feel like the most special girl in the world, every single day. I look at you, and my soul is happy. With you, my soul knows it's safe. There are a lot of things I'd do over in life, but I'd choose you again and again."

"What do you say, Lacey girl? Will you keep doing life with me? Will you stand by my side and come cheer at every game? Will you be the one I look for in the crowd, because you're the only one I ever want to see?" Shawn asks.

He opens the box and I gasp at the ring inside. The diamond sparkles under the stadium lights and the night sky, and I hold out a shaky hand for him to slide the piece of jewelry on my finger. It fits perfectly, and I wonder how much help he had from Maggie in getting the sizing right.

"Yes. Yes, of course I will." I lunge for him and wrap him in a tight embrace. I'm never going to let him go. "I'm so lucky to be loved by you," I whisper as he presses his mouth against mine.

I can feel his smile in my heart. I can hear his quiet laughter and his soft sigh as I knock off his hat and pull on the ends of his hair. His thumb traces down my cheek and his palm settles against my neck. I wonder what his touch will feel like when he has a ring on his finger, too.

He kisses me again—harder this time—for all the cameras to see. There's a flash of light in my peripheral vision and I smile as reality crashes into me, a wave that knocks me off balance.

Football game.

National television.

Super Bowl.

My fiancé kissing me in front of thousands—no, *millions*—of people, and there's no place I'd rather be.

"That's an awful lot of declarations. Flirting with me, Daniels?"

I huff out a laugh and poke his ribs. He grabs my hand and kisses the inside of my palm, his eyes a little wild but so full of love.

"In your dreams, Holmes."

COMING SOON

Stay tuned for Dallas' story coming in early 2024!

ACKNOWLEDGMENTS

As always, thank you, dear reader, for taking a chance on something I created. I hope you loved Shawn and Lacey's story as much as I loved writing them. If you did, I would be grateful if you left a review on Goodreads or Amazon. Positive reviews do wonders for indie authors like myself.

Writing a book isn't easy, and this wouldn't be in your hands if I worked alone. I wanted to thank a couple of people who helped make this the novel it is.

To my beta readers Katelin, Haley, Amanda, Amanda, Megan, Lindsey, Sammie, Linna, Addy, Kelly, Shay, Kae, Kristen and Katie: thank you for your immensely valuable feedback, constructive criticism and joy you had for this book. Every comment and every suggestion made this better, and I can't thank you enough for help.

To Kristen: Thank you for working with my chaotic brain and chaotic timelines. I appreciate you and your flexibility.

To Sam: Thank you for creating the cover of my dreams—again. I'm glad we get to work together, and I can't wait to see what other magic you create.

To Ellie at LoveNotesPR: Thank you for handling my TikTok and distributing ARCs. You are such a gem, and I'm glad I get to work with you!

To Mike and Riley: I'm so glad we're in a house where I can have an office to write books and a space for us to grow old together. I love y'all.

To the book community: Thank you for your constant support of authors. It's difficult to put yourself out there with something you created, and you all keep lifting us up. There's nothing I love more than getting messages from readers telling me their favorite parts of my books.

And lastly, to anyone who's out there wondering if they should take a leap of faith and do something outside their comfort zone: do it. You won't regret it.

ABOUT THE AUTHOR

Chelsea Curto is a flight attendant who lives in the Northeast with her partner and their adorable dog. When she's not busy writing, she loves to read, travel, go to theme parks, run, eat tacos and hang out with friends.

Come say hi on social media!

instagram.com/authorchelseacurto

tiktok.com/@chelseareadsandwrites

amazon.com/author/chelseacurto

ALSO BY CHELSEA CURTO

Boston series

An Unexpected Paradise

The Companion Project

Road Trip to Forever

Love Through a Lens series

Camera Chemistry

Park Cove series

Booked for the Holidays

Made in the USA
Columbia, SC
08 December 2023

28111224R00241